"**D**id you bring the Marines along?" Owen asked once he'd released her inside his cell. "Or is this a social call?"

Emma, Owen thought as he watched her gaze rise to a thin band of silver across the top of his door, did not look amused. Her dark eyes were flecked with red, reflecting back firelight.

"Put these on," she said, and thrust a bundle into his hands. Fatigues, beard, and wig. "You're going to escape from this place and, like it or not, you're going to do it my way."

Owen started to pull the fatigues on. "It's all right with me," he said. "What about the rest of the hostages?"

"They're not going anywhere tonight. DIA has the option on them, on orders from the President, and the Pentagon's making a flap over risks and casualties."

The sound of the wind howled in Owen's ears. The people of Uxmal were thirsty for blood. . . .

Fawcett Crest Books
by Marilyn Sharp:

SUNFLOWER

FALSE-FACE

A novel by
Marilyn Sharp

FAWCETT CREST • NEW YORK

A Fawcett Crest Book
Published by Ballantine Books
Copyright © 1984 by Marilyn Sharp

Library of Congress Catalog Card Number: 84-13241

ISBN 0-449-20796-X

This edition published by arrangement with St. Martin's/Marek

Printed in Canada

First Ballantine Books Edition: September 1985

For Jeremy,
a small blond boy more interested in Martians than Maya

January. A bleak day with clouds threatening snow over the flat Indiana farmland where the Pendleton State Reformatory sat like a great square block of brick and stone, exposed to the wind and the open sky, impenetrable and foreboding. A man was standing at the window of his cell, looking out over the prison walls, past the searchlights mounted between guard turrets to the stubble of cornfields lying dormant through winter. Drab gray earth, frozen, void of life, stretching to the edge of the sky and the trees that ran along the horizon. All of it waiting for spring. Waiting, like the man, for rebirth.

The trees were one of the first things he noticed about Indiana. No matter which way you were going or how far ahead you could see, there were always trees along the horizon. Skeleton trees, black and barren. A full growing season had passed in the time he'd been here, and it might have been more if it weren't for the fact that the man had no criminal record, or if he hadn't agreed to cooperate and plead guilty. He smiled now, remembering his day in court. Of the crimes he had thought society might one day hold against him, one was not stealing a car. That was what made being here so perfect.

He was in his forties, of medium height and trim, like a runner. His hair was black and cropped short, his eyes blue and quietly thoughtful. His face was pale, but lean and strong, and his manner was purposely inoffensive. And of course they wouldn't have captured him if

1

he hadn't wanted them to. He had no use for a stolen car beyond his own plans for capture. He had wanted to come here, to plan and to wait, because no one would think to look for him in Pendleton, Indiana, least of all in a prison. These walls, designed to keep him inside, were actually his protection.

A gust of wind rattled the window in its casing, and the man pulled his jacket closer. The temperature outside had dropped below freezing, so one of the guards had told him. It was hard to tell from here. The town lay on the northeast side of the prison, out of sight from the window. He could see only the stubbled fields and one small cluster of buildings—a white farmhouse with a gray barn and silo, a wooden shed where the farmer stored his tractor and the combine whose lights had flickered across the fields into the night through autumn. The man had been watching. Now the harvest was in and the farmer, too, was left waiting.

But the man's waiting was over. He turned at the sound of a voice.

"Time to go, Miller."

Parole, granted last month. Early release based on his own good behavior. The time had come to leave his protection behind, to face what he had to, to put his revenge into action.

The iron-barred door of the cell slid open at the touch of a switch by an unseen hand, and the man called Miller stepped through it. He had already changed from his prison grays and was wearing the clothes he'd had on the day he arrived here. Tweed jacket, dark pants, light blue turtleneck sweater—all bought off the rack at a secondhand shop, undistinguished and untraceable.

The prison food wasn't quite what he'd been used to. There was no steak au poivre here, no saddle of lamb, no cold baby lobster. He had lost some weight, but he'd kept himself in good shape with isometrics. His muscles were tight, his reflexes as sharp as ever. A few weeks at Cap Ferrat or the Côte d'Azur and he would have his weight back. The prison pallor would fade away, like the memory of the iron bars and the view from his cell

2

window. A vanished chapter out of his life, of the past. Forgotten.

But not yet.

He followed the guard down a corridor with cells like his own on both sides. Voices called out to him. . . .

"So long, Miller."

"Good luck."

"Take care . . ."

Not sad farewells; they were used to this around here. Freedom for one meant hope for the rest. And anyway, statistically, he would be back before most of his fellow inmates had time to apply for parole or live out their sentences. Recidivism was as common here as escape was difficult.

But the man called Miller had no intention of coming back to Pendleton. He had one more job, self-imposed, his toughest. And even if he survived, this would be his last one.

"So long, pal."

"Take care . . ."

The voices faded behind him as he followed the guard downstairs and through the labyrinth of the prison complex, through the administrative section to a room where gray light streamed in through tall windows. A clerk with thinning hair and tiny, pinched features was standing behind a counter that ran waist-high the length of the room. In the opposite wall was a door to the outside— the escape hatch, as it was known to the inmates. The man took a deep breath. Final processing, like a checkpoint in the Berlin Wall. Freedom reduced to printed forms and rubber stamp approval.

The clerk took his fingerprints, matched them against the prints made when he arrived, and gave a small grunt of satisfaction, as if there were some achievement in the fact of the two sets matching. Then he took Miller's picture, a parting shot, and laid it aside to develop. "I'll need your signature on these," he said and pushed forward several sheets of paper.

Miller didn't bother to read them, merely picked up the pen and signed. A false name. False documents,

3

false papers. A sense of excitement stirred in his stomach. The old sense of danger, running close to the edge. Too close. Real photographs. Real fingerprints. *Real* danger. But survival was almost irrelevant now. His last job was that important.

The clerk dropped the forms into Miller's file and looked up again. "You understand the terms of your release?" he began.

"I've been through it all with my lawyer."

"Then you know you'll report to your parole officer once a month, first Mondays. And you're not allowed to leave the state without his written permission."

Miller worked to hide his impatience. There was little chance he could have avoided knowing these rules, even less that he would oblige them.

"Will you need transportation?" the clerk asked.

"A friend is picking me up."

"I see. Well, you're entitled to financial assistance if you—"

"No, thanks," Miller said. "I don't need it."

"I beg your pardon?"

"I said I don't need it."

The clerk stared at him briefly, his thin lips drawn up in a tight little bow. Independence, it seemed, was distasteful to him—a sign, perhaps, of his own lack of options. "Suit yourself," he said finally. He picked up the rubber stamp, hit the ink pad and Miller's file. Release became official. Then his eyes shifted past Miller, and his mouth tightened into a smile. "Ah, here's the assistant superintendent."

Miller turned around. The walls of the room were a faded green—a suitable backdrop, he thought, for the faded, pudgy-faced man coming toward him. A picture flashed through his memory . . . of the commandant's office in Budapest, and the commandant himself, with a face so fat his eyes were like slits in a pumpkin. One face blended into another, pound for pound, slit for slit.

But this was only the assistant superintendent, here to give Miller the Car Thief a second chance. A noble

4

gesture. An ironic last touch. Miller suppressed an urge to laugh and tried to look grateful.

"Good-bye and good luck," said the pudgy-faced man. "If we can ever be of assistance to you—"

"Thanks," Miller said, cutting him off. The kind of help he needed wasn't likely to come from a prison official. In fact, there was only one man who could help him now, and that man might be anywhere from Majorca to Addis Ababa. He might be in London or Tokyo, in Moscow, or possibly even making a pass through Langley, as he was known to do when it suited him.

Still, the assistant superintendent was not without his value. "There is something," Miller said, and produced a white envelope from his jacket. "I've been expecting a visitor, a man I know who can help me with a job on the outside. I've written him a letter, and I still think he'll show up. . . ."

"And if he does, you want us to give him the letter." The pudgy-faced man took the envelope, smiling, slits growing more narrow. "Certainly. This is his name? Mr. Conrad?"

Miller nodded.

"I'll see that it's taken care of."

"Thanks," Miller said again. Then he shook the man's hand and walked out the door, straight ahead, through the prison gates to the outside, where cold air closed around him. He paused there a moment—stretching, growing, coming alive—enjoying this moment of freedom.

For how long? he wondered. He was free now, as free as he ever had been. No one knew he was here. But sooner or later, it would have to become known that he had surfaced.

And then?

Gray clouds massed overhead, and the wind rose again, stinging his face, causing his eyes to water. But the man smiled. It would have to become known. He only wished he could be there, in the Oval Office, when it happened.

He pulled up his collar against the wind, shoved his bare hands into his pockets, and moved ahead, toward the highway and the railroad tracks running parallel to it. Just before he reached the tracks, the road forked to the left and wound its way to the country club adjacent to the prison. He didn't stop to question the planning that resulted in such an unlikely pairing of neighbors. He followed the fork to the parking lot reserved for country club members.

And Billie was there, as he had known she would be.

She was sitting behind the wheel of her daddy's blue Cadillac, bundled up to the ears in white rabbit fur, her face in profile to him, and she looked as young as she did the day he kissed her good-bye in Athens. But then that was only three years ago. She was young, not yet twenty-five, still unmarried, still living at home in Muncie with her parents. These were things Miller researched before his arrest, and part of the reason he'd chosen Indiana. Because Billie was close by with a car; he didn't care to use the official transportation. Because of her youth and her innocence. Billie was yet another form of protection.

And a little more than that.

She turned as he approached the car, and a smile spread slowly across her face. Her dark hair was knotted carelessly at the back of her head, with strands falling loose around her ears and forehead. Her eyes were green and seductively framed by softly arching dark eyebrows and thick brown lashes. Her features were flawless, her face pink from the cold. He'd forgotten how really lovely she was. A woodland nymph. More than lovely. Exquisite.

She rolled down the window. "Hello, Grant."

He returned the smile.

"Well?" she asked softly. "Are you going to stand there or get in the car?"

He walked around and got into the front seat beside her. For a moment he said nothing. Old feelings stirred, and the years faded sharply . . . to Athens and the Acropolis, to a sidewalk cafe in a tree-lined square, to warm summer nights in the Plaka . . . to Billie, fresh out of college and on her first trip to Europe. The grand tour, a gift from Mother and Daddy. Only Mom and Dad never knew that Billie had canceled Venice and Rome to stay on in Athens with the man she knew as Grant Martin.

The rabbit fur jacket was cut short, giving way to long legs in jeans and leather knee boots, and was soft to his touch as he pulled her to him and kissed her. A moment later Billie drew away, not too far, just enough to gaze into his eyes with a look he remembered and still thought she was too young to handle. "I got your postcard," she said.

He laughed. "So I see." He had mailed the card a week ago, omitting any mention of the prison, suggesting only a rendezvous at the country club in Pendleton. "I'm glad you came," he added and meant it. "I wanted to see you."

"So much that it took you three years?"

There was no bitterness in her voice, only teasing, and Miller knew he'd done the right thing, asking Billie to come here. She was smart enough to help him and reckless enough not to ask too many questions. Of course, she thought he was one of Uncle Sam's spies; he'd encouraged her to think so. It was partly that—the mystery of him—that made him attractive to her. And the falsehood wasn't entirely false. He had been once. An easy role to recapture.

But Billie was a mystery to him as well. He didn't know if she was what she seemed to be—a free spirit, unhindered by the propriety of her background—or if she were simply rebelling from a way of life that had her imprisoned. He wondered why she'd never left home, or moved into a place of her own. Maybe she was too attached to the easy life that came with her father's money.

His hand brushed her cheek. "I told you I wouldn't be able to write very often."

"You're a man of your word," she said and smiled. "But what are you doing *here*? Never mind, I know. Making the world safe for democracy. I wouldn't have thought Pendleton was in danger."

Miller chuckled. "I've got some time off," he said. "Let's get out of here."

"Where do you want to go?"

"To Indianapolis. I need to find a good bookstore. And after that, a toy shop. I want to buy you a present."

"One bookstore, one toy shop, coming up." Billie leaned forward to turn on the ignition.

Wet snowflakes began to spatter the windshield as she pulled out of the parking lot by way of the prison grounds—a few at first, but then more and more, the start of a sudden blizzard. The man beside her turned to the window for a last look at the prison, which was dimly visible now through the snow, shrunk by perspective to less awesome proportions. Soon of the past. Like Miller the Car Thief, paroled and forgotten. And he smiled. For the man called Miller had ceased to exist with the sound of the prison gates behind him. In his place was the man he had been before.

Michelangelo. The assassin.

One last job to do. Uncle Sam himself. The President. And the son of a bitch would know soon enough. Then he, too, would be stuck waiting.

But first things first. A bookstore. The assassin smiled. First he had to make contact with an old friend, still the best the CIA had. First he had to locate Richard Owen.

2

There was nothing gentle about the Yucatan peninsula, even here in the southwestern Puuc region where flat plains gave way to a hilly terrain. The land was still more rock than earth, the jungle a bramble of trees and scrub, the heat intense, like the glare of the fire-eyed Istin, lord of the sun. Richard Owen pulled off his hat and wiped the sweat from his face with the back of his hand. The climate here was as bad as it could be anywhere in Mexico; it was humid enough to breed mosquitoes and fill the jungle with snakes, but not enough to bring more than a sprinkling of rain except during the summer. Now, in February, the wind raised dust to sting the eyes. The land was dry and ungiving.

Owen shielded his eyes with his hand as his gaze swept the ruins—Uxmal, one of the great white cities of the ancient Maya—and the jungle that closed in around them. There was no towering rain forest here, as there was in the Mayan highlands of Guatemala and Honduras, little tropical vegetation, no lush growth. No, Uxmal rose out of the Yucatan bush, which was wild and scrappy, like a briar patch spreading thickly across the peninsula, so dense that its trees never grew above thirty feet, so tenacious that highway workers had to burn it back to keep it from smothering the paved road to Merida. The bush was deceptively rugged, and not wisely breached by visitors without a guide, a gun, and a machete.

Owen brought his own guide with him—his old friend

9

Francisco Luc-Can, who grew up in Muna, eleven miles north of Uxmal. These ruins had been Frank's childhood haunt, his playground, and he knew the surrounding countryside as Owen knew the secret corners of Cairo and Rome, Beirut, Istanbul, and New Delhi. But Owen had no intention of hacking his way through the jungle. His interest was here, in the pyramids and temples where high priests and princes once studied the stars and passed down their wisdom. Enormous structures built of stone, stripped bare now of their whitewash, burnished by the heat of the sun, reduced to enduring silence.

Yes, here. Somewhere. Michelangelo's secret.

It would help, Owen thought, if he knew what he was looking for. A message carved in stone? A weapon buried in the dry earth? A document stowed in a crevice of rock? Any of those, or something else. A photograph. A piece of film. A clue to the identity of a killer.

Uxmal was nothing if not vast. Countless ancient structures still lay buried in the jungle. Ten had been cleared in a rectangle that was roughly a mile long and a half-mile wide. Hard dirt paths wandered among them, breaking through the fast-growing scrub, which was knee-high, or chest-high, even over the head in places; green, parched to brown, and broken here and there by leggy sprays of tough yellow wildflowers. Rocks were strewn the length of the site, alone or in piles. Plain building blocks rubbed smooth by the years. Broken door lintels. Pieces of sculptured temple frieze. Carved effigies to the god of rain: Chac masks by the hundreds.

Uxmal had been abandoned for nearly a millenium, and if Michelangelo hid something here, it would probably take that much time again for Owen to stumble across it.

Owen's eyes scanned the ruins and failed to find Frank, whom he'd last seen poking around the Dove Cote at the far end of the site, taking Owen's explanation, such as it was, on faith, trying to help without prying. A good friend by Owen's own definition. He would do as much if Frank needed help. And anyway, if he'd been inclined to give Frank answers, he didn't have them. Michelangelo offered only one clue to narrow the scope of Owen's work—*Go to the ruins and look beneath the moving islands of the sea*—but the clue meant nothing to Frank, who should know if it had Mayan origin, nor to Owen. Uxmal was located inland, a hundred miles from the Gulf Coast, at least twice as far from the Caribbean. There was no sea here; there was no natural source of water at all, not even a puddle. The ancients survived for as long as they did by storing summer rain, until it dried up, and then on futile prayers to Chac, who was stingy with his rain at best and more often not listening.

No sea. No water at all. Nothing remotely resembling moving islands.

Owen ran a hand through his sun-streaked brown hair. He was forty years old—tall, lean, and gracefully built, with even features that defied classification. By appearance reserved—cool-eyed, pragmatic, invulnerable. He had taught himself not to speak and rarely to think about caring.

But he did care about Michelangelo. Enough to kill, he cared. There was between them an old score to be settled.

Owen had worked to erase the traces of his own origin, and to acquire others, a storehouse to draw on, a limitless range of identity and appearance. Such was his usefulness to the CIA. Given the proper back up from Technical Services and Documentation, and his own bent for disguise and diversion, he could drop in almost anywhere and pass himself off as a native—drop in, do his job, and vanish.

At the moment he was traveling as an American— David Stuart, archaeologist—a cover designed for a job in Jakarta, where he was scheduled to go last month before Michelangelo's message changed his mind and his plans. He had canceled Jakarta with a cryptic note to Nichols: *Pursuing something more urgent. Will let you know when I know what it is.* Meantime, relax, he might have added, but didn't, because Nichols would sputter with or without Owen's advice. He would sputter and

11

swear, probably curse Owen's name, and no doubt order his contract terminated. But he would also get over it and send someone else to Jakarta. Firing Owen was out of the question. At the moment, Nichols wouldn't know where to send the pink slip.

Owen put on his hat, which was woven of pale straw and broad-brimmed, a gift from Frank for a *gringo* friend who might be inclined to underestimate Lord Istin's sunshine. Owen hadn't needed the gift—he did not underestimate as a point of principle—but he liked the hat. It was perfectly plain, like the straw hats worn by the guides who ushered tourist groups around Uxmal, and it had a nice added feature: a long, slender chain of hand wrought Mexican silver wound several times around the crown, like a scarf or a layered hatband.

He adjusted the brim to shade his eyes and made his way into the quadrangle known as the Nunnery—four huge buildings, single-storied save one, facing an open courtyard, with access through openings at each corner and through a formal, corbeled arch that divided the south building into two sections.

The Nunnery. Owen smiled. A misnomer supplied by the Spanish. The Maya worshipped the sun and the stars. Their priests were mathematicians and astronomers, and so were their priestesses. There were no nuns at Uxmal and never had been, unless the conquistadors brought them.

Still, Owen acknowledged a certain appropriateness in the name. The buildings were done on roughly the same horizontal plan, classically Mayan. They were massive rectangles built of stone, with frieze sculpture carved across their upper halves and open doorways lined up at even intervals across the bottom. Behind each door lay a room, and behind that a separate, inner chamber—smaller rectangles in a double row, each longer than it was deep, running the length of all four buildings.

Owen counted the doors; there were at least eighty-eight separate rooms in the Nunnery alone. No one today knew their purpose. But this was, indeed, the sort of place where a person might want to hole up after taking the vows of chastity.

Eighty-eight rooms. They would need a full day for thorough searching, but maybe it wouldn't come to that. Owen crossed the courtyard to the north building, which was set higher than the others on a huge stone terrace, dominating the quadrangle. Pillared temples were built into the lower level at each end. Between them, a wide stone staircase rose to the edge of the terrace and the upper part of the building. Owen glanced over his shoulder. There were few tourists in the courtyard now. Most of them, wisely at this time of day, were in their hotel rooms observing the siesta, or sitting it out with a cool drink in an air-conditioned hotel bar. Just a handful of students with backpacks. A couple of gray-haired ladies. A man and woman with a small blond boy, who was clearly more interested in Martians than Maya; he had climbed a pile of ancient debris and was activating his rockets. For the moment, Owen had the north building to himself, but he noticed a large new tour group moving up toward the Nunnery from the ancient Ball Court at the center of the ruins. He turned back to the steps, took them two at a time, decided to start at the left end of the building.

A dank, musty smell filled his nostrils as he stepped past the patch of sunlight that lay like a mat on the stone floor in the doorway. Beyond the door the sun faded sharply; the air was damp and cool, and the room cast into shadow. Owen produced a flashlight and probed its beam into corners where light probably hadn't shone since Uxmal was abandoned. Piles of loose rock and dirt, cigarette butts, discarded cellophane wrappers. Nothing else. Nothing of interest to him.

Turning slowly where he stood, he moved the light back and forth across the walls of the room, blackened stone blocks built row upon row, and then up into the ceiling, which was corbeled like the main arch—made with inverted stairsteps rising on each side to meet at the center and then plastered over. Corbeling was clearly a favored technique of the old Mayan architects, or maybe it was the only way they knew how to achieve the height they wanted. Owen lowered the light and stepped into the inner chamber, into near-total darkness. And there he discovered that Uxmal was not, after all, uninhabited.

Bats, hundreds of them, he guessed, attached up there in the darkness of the arched ceiling. The stench alone was enough to turn a strong stomach queasy, and the clatter of their wings against stone added nothing to the ambience of the chamber. A few of them cried out eerily, unhappy with Owen for disturbing their slumber. He decided not to incite them further with the flashlight; he kept its beam low, checked the walls, the floor, and the corners. More rocks and dirt, but less litter. The tourists, it seemed, didn't hang around here.

Nor did Owen. He turned to go. The upper reaches of the ceiling would have to wait for a nighttime search, when the bats were out marauding, and with any luck he would find what he was looking for before that.

But Owen didn't believe in luck, though he took it when it came his way, and he certainly never counted on it.

He stepped back through the outside door, into the heat and glare of the sun, and was moving toward the next pair of rooms when something across the courtyard caught his attention. The tour group he'd seen moving up from the old Ball Court was assembled now in front of the east building. A guide in straw hat and bright red bandana was running through his spiel for a dozen men in casual, hot-weather clothing. Young men and older, Americans from the look of them. But this was no ordinary group of tourists. With the Americans came five more men in Mexican army khaki; they had automatic rifles slung over their shoulders and eyes that gazed not at but over and around the ruins.

Armed *guards*? Owen stopped where he was, squinting into the sunlight, wondering who these Americans were that they would need such protection. Then one of them turned to study the building where Owen was standing and answered his question.

The man was instantly recognizable to anyone who followed power in Washington or a given week's worth of political news. He was Reuben Shackford, the flamboyant congressman from Maine, whose face was as familiar as the President's. Congressman Pious, as Ed Nichols called him. He was in his mid-sixties but looked younger, mostly because of his height and trim physique. Owen had never seen him in the flesh before and hadn't realized he was so tall, six foot three anyway, maybe taller. Congressman Reuben Shackford towered above the rest of the delegation.

For a delegation it was. Now that he had a context, Owen recognized yet another member of Congress—Jack Renaud of Chicago, who was prominent in the news even before the voters sent him to Washington. Shackford, Renaud, and two others Owen couldn't put a name to—the American delegation to the Cozumel conference between the U.S. and Mexico—taking a day off from fishing rights, oil, and illegal aliens to view the ancient history of the host country. Owen produced his cigarettes and lit one from a slim gold pocket lighter. No wonder the armed guards! American officials in Mexico these days could not make assumptions about their safety.

Nor, he knew, were fishing rights, oil, and illegal aliens the real issues of the Cozumel meeting. Legitimate problems, to be sure, but a cover for talks about something else: increasingly savage anti-American terrorism too close to a U.S. border, spawned by years of Big Brotherism. Ill-timed, so Washington thought, to put it mildly, since most of Central America was in revolt at one stage or another. Big Brother intended to come to grips with the problem, and the Mexican government was glad to sit down and talk, though not publicly. Terrorists, after all, weren't known for their bent toward compromise and might just as easily turn on the powers that be in Mexico City. Interference was one thing, but ultimately one didn't want to stray too far from Big Brother.

Now Owen understood the armed guards. Two American businessmen had been kidnapped and murdered by Mexican terrorists in the last six months, and the U.S. ambassador to Mexico had been threatened, which explained what would normally be an excessive amount of security for the visiting congressmen. But the congressmen and their security were not his responsibility. He drew on his cigarette, turned away, getting back to his own business.

The second pair of rooms was like the first in size, layout, and aroma, and so was the third. In the fourth he found something different. Plastic chairs—haphazardly stacked, cheaply made, and, he decided, not Mayan. Rocks, litter, and plastic chairs. No sign of Michelangelo's mysterious moving islands. Owen stepped out into the sunshine again.

The congressmen and their entourage were now climbing the steps toward him. He stopped where he was, standing back—not for them, but because of a distant sound that was vaguely alarming. He turned an ear to the north, the direction it was coming from. An engine, perhaps more than one, growing louder. The guide paid no attention. He took off his hat and used it as a pointer as he described the details of the building's facade. But the guards, Owen noticed, were alert to the sound, as he was. Engine noise. And, yes, the whooping beat of rotary blades.

Helicopters? Here?

Why?

Owen looked up, scanning the sky, seeing nothing but high white cirrus. The sky was entirely peaceful, but the sound continued to grow persistently louder. And then, suddenly, there was noise all around him. A helicopter appeared over the top of the building, machine guns protruding from it—one helicopter and then two more. Hot wind swirled across the courtyard dimming the sun, raising wind and confusion. Owen produced a handkerchief to shield his nose and mouth. Squinting, he saw the guards pull their rifles from their shoulders. Too late. Other gunmen erupted onto the rooftops of the

Nunnery, through the ceremonial arch and the spaces between the buildings. A hundred of them, it looked like. They were brown-skinned, most of them . . . black-haired, some bearded, some merely unshaven . . . dressed in combat fatigues or torn T-shirts and jeans, overalls, suspenders. A motley bunch, but well trained and highly motivated. Their eyes were ablaze with a fierce fighting spirit, their shoulders crouched over automatic rifles, like the guards, whom they greatly outnumbered. And then, Owen noticed, even that didn't matter.

He caught a glimpse of Shackford's face, blanched white, eyes tearing from the dust, expression more startled than frightened. And Renaud, dark eyes wide and staring, caught in the shock of attack unexpected, not yet quite comprehending. Around them their colleagues stood rigid with fear, or doubled over and coughing. But not the Mexican army guards. They were calm as they raised their rifles and aimed them—not at the attackers, but at the men they were supposed to protect.

No wonder they were alert to the sound of approaching engines. They were in on the attack! *Waiting* for it.

A gunshot rang out on the other side of the courtyard, like the sharp rap of a gavel, and someone cried out in English. "No one move!" Owen, standing apart, waited no longer. He seized the advantage of dust, shock, and confusion, spun around and ran, head down, shoulders in; he ran with the force of hot swirling wind behind him. The corner of the building loomed ahead, the edge of the stone terrace. He leaped off the end, a twenty-foot drop, his knees bent to take the impact and deflect it. He landed, pulled up, and was poised to run on, but a blow from behind caught him short of his stride. A rifle butt came down savagely across the back of his neck and shoulders.

Owen rolled with the blow and swung around toward his assailant, brought his fist up hard. He caught the bastard square in the jaw with a sharp crack of sound, sent him reeling into the wall of stone terrace. Two more men appeared on his right. He stiffened an arm, struck one down with a blow to the chest, cracked an elbow

17

into the stomach of the companion. Then, all at once, the terrorists had him surrounded—eight men, ten, a miniature batallion. Two grabbed his arms and twisted; two more seized his legs. He struggled to resist as they pushed him down, but resistance proved futile.

A boot crashed into his ribs and pain spread coldly across his chest, but he didn't flinch, wouldn't give them the satisfaction. Then the barrel of a rifle was pressed to his skull, and four others took aim from a distance of six inches. Someone tied his hands behind his back. Owen, pragmatic, raised no objection.

They picked him up by the shoulders, dragged him into the courtyard once more, and pulled him to his feet at the bottom of the steps that rose to the north building. The terrorists had taken full control; some stood guard with their rifles while the rest collected wallets, identifying the hostages. One man, tall and thin, stepped forward from the others.

No, he didn't step; he *edged* forward, with a rippling of muscles under smooth skin, with a show of understated strength that was menacing and impressive. He reached into Owen's pocket, drew out his wallet, and glanced through the David Stuart passport. Then he cast it aside for someone to retrieve and rose up on the balls of his feet, swaying back and forth across Owen's line of vision.

"Mr. Stuart," he hissed, making the name an accusation.

Owen's ribs ached and his knees felt weak, but he stood his ground and regarded the terrorist coolly.

"My name is Ramon. For the next few days, or weeks—perhaps *less* if your behavior requires too much patience—I will be your host here."

Owen watched him, saw tension coiled in the man's eyes, anger waiting to strike. "Very gracious, I'm sure. It's kind of you to have me."

Ramon replied with the back of his hand, with a stinging blow Owen felt in his jaw, in his neck and chest, and all the way to the soles of his feet. Owen, hands tied, wiped a trickle of blood from his mouth against his shoulder, then looked up and said, "No need to get testy."

Ramon made a sound, a mixture of growl and laughter, a rattling rasp in the back of his throat. He alone among the terrorists was clean-shaven, face and head, even eyebrows. His head was small, set on a long neck, and the bones that stood out where his eyebrows had been protruded over little round eyes that were all black, all pupil. Snake eyes. When he smiled his lips all but vanished, and the smile spread around his jaw, almost to his ears, which were so flat against his head that from the front they seemed to be nonexistent.

"Wit will do you no good here, Mr. Stuart," he said. "For the moment, I'll let your impertinence pass, because I have other things to attend to. Next time, I won't."

Owen didn't comment, and Ramon crept away, muscles rippling as if propelling him inch by inch. Except for the drone of the helicopters, there was silence across the courtyard. Shackford, Renaud, and the rest stood where they were—faces stunned, bodies drained—watching and waiting.

Owen felt the barrel of a gun in his back, a hard shove at his shoulder. Several thoughts raced through his mind all at once: Michelangelo. Moving islands. His search of the ruins disrupted. Michelangelo's secret was not to be found for the moment. Or was this all a part of it?

In some way, of course—for if Owen didn't believe in luck, he believed even less in coincidence, or in the good intentions of his old partner.

The terrorist pushed him again, and Owen moved forward. His mind focused. Uxmal had been seized and secured by extraordinary manpower. A group of American congressmen and their aides had been captured. For what purpose, he didn't know. But he joined the group. The terrorists thought he belonged there, that their fate would be his. There was only one problem. Nichols, who was Owen's control as well as head of the CIA, had no reason to guess where he was, to know he was a hostage.

Unless Frank told him.

Owen smiled to himself. There was hope, if not much. His old friend, an amateur. He wondered if Frank, too, had been captured.

Francisco Luc-Can was inside the temple room at the top of the smaller pyramid when he heard the same sound that caught Owen's attention. He looked out through the door, saw the three helicopters flying in a kind of reverse V-formation and approaching the ruins from the north. He frowned, for the moment merely puzzled, but then the scene broke loose before him.

An army of terrorists burst out of the trees, brandishing rifles, swarming across the terrain. Tourists screamed and fled for the exit, but more terrorists were waiting there to round them up and hold them in a group at gunpoint. Frank stared, disbelieving, his thoughts confused, but one thing came through to him clearly. The main thrust of the attack was at the Nunnery, where the helicopters were hovering now, which the terrorists had surrounded.

Then a gunshot rang out in the distance.

Owen!

Frank's eyes swept the north end of the ruins, the steep steps on both sides of the giant Pyramid of the Magician, hoping Owen was there. But he wasn't. Frank's gaze shifted. He had known where Owen was going to start, had seen him enter the quadrangle. And he knew where Owen was now. *Inside* the Nunnery!

He moved fast, out the door and around the top shelf of the pyramid, down the back side, which had been allowed to grow over with scrub, giving him hand and footholds. He scaled down fast, half running, half falling, and hit the ground with a jolt. He took a moment to catch his breath. Then he pulled himself up and ran on, not looking back, away from the ruins toward the dense green wall all around them.

His playground. His old haunt. Frank disappeared into the jungle.

3

The President sat back, drink in hand, shoulders and lap draped in a barber's cape, watching Max Kuperman's dexterous fingers in the mirror. Max hummed while he worked and occasionally threw in a line or two of lyrics. The President liked having him around, because Max cheered him up. And because Max was entirely comfortable with the trappings of the White House, which was more than Henry Brendan could say for himself.

But then Max was a professional. He'd been cutting the President's hair for twenty-five years, since Henry arrived new in Washington, a handsome young congressman from Massachusetts. Max had his own shop on Capitol Hill and trimmed a good many of Washington's most famous heads there, but he also spent two days a week at the White House. It was one of the prerogatives of the President, naming the White House barber, along with the Secretary of State and the Chairman of the Federal Reserve, and installing him part-time in the basement of the West Wing. Max charged his usual rates here. For his extra trouble, he was paid in prestige. A bit like being shoemaker to the queen.

In fact, very much like being shoemaker to the queen. Max was a good barber, but he had other qualities the President valued more—a sympathetic ear, a selective memory, and a tightly zippered mouth. More than one Washington journalist had tried to set him up as an inside source, but Max would have none of it, which is how he kept long-term clients like Henry Brendan, and

Congressman Reuben Shackford, and Conklin Pierce, the Speaker of the House of Representatives, the most powerful man in Congress. The queen's shoemaker would never divulge the size of Her Majesty's feet, nor would the President's barber reveal the formula for the shade of the President's hair.

And yet, typically, Henry hadn't appointed Max, but kept him on. If Ben Riker, Henry's predecessor, had preferred a different barber, then Henry probably would have kept him on instead, in spite of his twenty-five years with Max. But Riker was also one of Max's regulars, and so Henry was spared the decision. Max stayed, like so many of the old staff. It was Henry who was the interloper.

An interloper, but still President. Whatever they said.

Henry rarely made an appearance in the West Wing barber shop; he preferred to have Max come here, to his dressing room on the second floor, where he could relax with a drink, escape from advisors, and forget, if only briefly, that he had to go back to the Oval Office. Today more than most days he would like to forget.

Morning began with an Israeli jet shot down over the Sinai Desert; Henry went back to sleep deeply troubled. Then Congress passed a trade embargo Henry had vowed to veto in hopes it would never get that far; now he supposed he would have to. His sister called (Mother sick again) to remind him that being President was no excuse for neglecting his family. And at last the director of NASA dropped by with a piece of news so bad it simply had to be delivered in person: a problem with the space shuttle that could result not only in the scrub of the launch next week but in an indefinite grounding of the whole space shuttle program. Billions of tax dollars down the drain. The Russians laughing up their sleeves. Henry's trip to Florida canceled.

Well, that much at least was a blessing, since he dreaded the trip as he dreaded them all—and the space shuttle program, if the truth were known, had paid for itself a hundred times over again—but by noon, Henry had a headache. He switched from Bloody Mary's to

Scotch. The day wasn't over yet. His problems had only started.

Now, Scotch in hand, he wondered if Max would ever write his memoirs. Not that he cared. By the time that could happen, Henry would be a long time out of office—beyond the reach of advisors, congressmen, voters; powerless to solve crises or to botch them; free to thumb his nose at the pressures, to get what he wanted out of life.

Hell, when had he *known* what he wanted from life? He was guided into politics by his father, like the lesser, second son who did not inherit; went to Congress, never really knew if he wanted to be there. He was chosen to run for Vice President by his party, precisely because the job suited him so nicely, the highest form of political brush-off. And then he became President by accident, because Benjamin Riker died on a ski slope a good many years before his time. Without warning he died, catching the country unprepared. Exit Roosevelt, enter the haberdasher.

As a matter of style Henry had almost nothing in common with Harry Truman, but perhaps he, too, would fool them.

Perhaps . . .

He tasted his Scotch, accidentally caught his own eyes in the mirror, and turned away. Physically, with no little help from Max, Henry was the perfect politician. He was tall enough to appear to have stature and slim enough to look good in expensive pinstripes, his hand-tailored shirts, and designer ties. His hair was dark with the "first" faint traces of silver, his features even, his face still handsome at fifty-nine. All of that spoke well for his breeding; he was born with good bones, blue blood, all the rest. But when he looked into his own eyes he saw something quite different: sometimes weakness, sometimes arrogance, always doubt.

Now here he was, almost a year in the White House and still not sure if he liked it, a President intimidated by himself. There was an old saying in politics—that you got in to get something done and stayed in to get even. Henry raised his glass to the mirror, chuckling out loud.

Liking wasn't always the issue. In an odd way, he felt right at home here.

"Something funny, Mr. President?" Max asked.

"I was thinking about my job."

"Thinking what, if you don't mind my asking."

"That it's too damn tough."

Max shrugged. "I don't know. I think work keeps you young. Look at me. I'm seventy-six, worked pretty near every day of my life, and except for a few minor aches I never felt better."

Henry didn't doubt it. Max kept himself in good shape. He radiated athletic good health, and he had a wonderful face, deeply lined, full of wisdom. "That's your work, not mine," he said. "Around here they serve me disaster with breakfast, lunch, and dinner."

"Oh, yeah?" Max laughed. "Listen, not long ago I cut a senator too short just before he was going on 'Meet the Press.' You think that's not a disaster? He'd have had me on the next troop ship to somewhere if he hadn't needed me to bail him out."

"How'd you do that—glue the hair back on?"

"Nope, I fixed him up with a hairpiece."

Henry nearly choked on his drink. "You're kidding! Just for 'Meet the Press'?"

"I don't know, it might have been 'Issues and Answers.' Thank God there aren't many like him! Of course you find more in the Senate than in the House—"

"Like who?" Henry asked. "Which senator was it?"

"Sorry, Mr. President, you know I can't say."

"Come on, Max, tell me. I need all the help I can get with my tax bill in the Senate."

Max put down his scissors and picked up a brush, and began to sweep loose hair from the President's shoulders. "I know you," he said. "That's not your kind of tactic."

"If it's not, it should be."

"Maybe so, but I can't tell you." He handed Henry a mirror and turned the chair around for him. "How does it look?"

Henry gave up reluctantly, knowing it was futile to

24

press Max on what the barber considered a matter of professional privilege. He wouldn't reveal the name of the shorn senator any more than he would repeat Henry's own private remarks. Anyway, Max was probably right. If Henry knew the man's name, he still wouldn't use it. He wouldn't have the nerve to.

"Looks fine," he said.

"Thanks. By the way, we'll have to do a touch-up next week. You're getting some gray where you don't want it."

"Don't tell me about it, just do it," Henry replied sharply. He was still embarrassed about having his hair dyed, but he worried more about aging. He looked up as the connecting door from the bedroom opened and the First Lady stepped through it.

Lucy was one thing Henry knew he wanted. She was his rock. He cared not a whit what the press said about her. She did not make his policy decisions, and she only kept people away from him when he was drinking. His rock. The rest of this was all very fragile, but he knew Lucy was devoted to him, and that she would still be at his side when the political hangers-on had transferred their allegiance to a successor.

Lucy Brendan was small and blond, an elegant woman, more beautiful in middle age than she was when Henry met her. But now her neatly rouged lips drew themselves into a thin, hard line. Her clear blue eyes looked worried.

"What's wrong?" he asked.

Lucy glanced at the glass in his hand, then at Max, whose eyes met hers briefly. "I was just leaving," he said.

Henry caught the look and felt angry. "No, Max, don't hurry. Mrs. Brendan and I have the run of the house. In our bedroom we're even allowed a modicum of privacy. I'll see you next week."

He pulled off the cape, got out of the chair, and led the way into the bedroom, taking his drink with him. The First Lady followed, closing the door.

"Please, darling—"

Henry spun around. "No, Lucy, *you* please. I don't want to hear any lectures today. I've got enough on my mind."

She stared at him for a moment in silence, which annoyed Henry, though he wasn't sure why. Then she sighed. "Whatever you say."

"Thank you for that. Now, what is it?"

Lucy's face changed, and her voice became briskly efficient. "Some startling news. We've lost the Jefferson portrait."

"*My* Jefferson portrait?"

"I'm afraid so."

Henry frowned, not understanding. The portrait, nearly two hundred years old, done by Rembrandt Peale from life in 1800, was no small thing to lose, though the canvas itself wasn't large. Of course it didn't really belong to Henry—it was part of the White House collection—but he'd chosen it to hang in his West Wing office when he was Vice President, and he'd developed a kind of proprietary feeling for it. So much so, in fact, that he planned to have it moved to the Oval Office when he moved there himself, but changed his mind when Lucy suggested he might enjoy it more in the privacy of the residence. And so it was hung in the West Sitting Room, where Henry and Lucy spent their leisure hours.

"Lost?" he asked. "How could it be? I just saw it this morning."

"No, dear, what you saw was a copy. A very good copy. The original is gone. Worse, probably stolen."

"*Stolen!*" Henry stared at her, astonished. "That's impossible!"

"You'd think so."

"*When?*"

"No one knows."

Lucy crossed the room and sat down on the bed she shared with her husband, gracefully balancing one knee on the other. She found cigarettes in the drawer of the bedside table, where she kept them for private moments, since she never smoked in public or any place

26

where a photographer might be lurking. She lit one, inhaled, and began to tell him what she knew.

"Mr. Bingham discovered the forgery this morning, and he just called me back to confirm it. The painting we've had in the sitting room is a copy. The original can't be accounted for. It's not in the house, nor in storage—nor anywhere else that we know of. There's no record of its having been moved, no record at all. And I'm afraid there's only one conclusion: Sometime in the last year or so, someone substituted the copy to cover a theft. Mr. Bingham has been in touch with the Secret Service."

Mr. Bingham was the White House curator and not likely to be mistaken.

"Someone?" Henry said. "Good *God*!"

Lucy studied his face with steady blue eyes. "Yes. Precisely."

Henry looked down at his drink, swirling it absently in his hand, listening to the sound of ice against glass as if he were listening to silence. Things were stolen sometimes from the White House, occasionally an ashtray or a small souvenir, even by the most distinguished of guests. As Vice President once, so ticklish had been the diplomacy of the matter, Henry himself had been dispatched to retrieve a silver spoon from an aging Supreme Court justice, who claimed he'd dropped it into his pocket while fetching a drink for the wife of the ambassador from Chile. The woman, as Henry remembered her, might well have been a distraction, and he found the judge's disclaimer entirely plausible. Now that he thought of it, maybe diplomacy hadn't been so ticklish. Perhaps the errand only demonstrated Benjamin Riker's high regard for his Vice President.

Still, an antique painting—the Jefferson portrait—was no small souvenir. He glanced up at Lucy, who was going on about servants, and how she had *thought* she could trust them. An upstairs maid, in cahoots perhaps with the third assistant chief butler, would be for her the least painful solution. Henry preferred to think of servants as staff, or at least employees, but Lucy had a point just the same. Aside from the domestic staff, damn few people had access alone to the private rooms of the White House.

"Maybe the original gift was a forgery," he suggested.

Lucy shook her head. "That occurred to me too, and I asked Mr. Bingham about it. All gifts are authenticated when they're received and examined from time to time thereafter. The Jefferson portrait was last looked at by an expert when it was sent down for cleaning a year ago last November."

Henry nodded. "I remember. I was still Vice President. It was hanging in my office—"

"And it might have been stolen then," Lucy said, "while it was out. Or possibly when it was moved upstairs last March. Otherwise, it had to be taken from your office sometime during the last few months you were there. Either that, or from the family quarters."

"That's great! An art thief in the White House!" Henry lifted his glass, took a stiff drink of Scotch. "Well, it certainly won't come as a shock to the public. They think we're all scoundrels anyway, and maybe they're right." The phone buzzed once on the table next to Lucy, and he glanced at his watch with a small show of irritation. "I'll get it," he told her. "At least a stolen painting isn't a problem I have to handle."

But he didn't feel as casual as he sounded. The headache was coming back now, throbbing at the base of his skull. He looked at the phone as his hand paused above the receiver. Then, quickly, he picked it up.

"Yes?"

Daniel Callahan, the Secretary of State, was calling from the State Department's Operations Center. Calmly, professionally, he broke the news about Uxmal.

Henry's eyes closed and his jaw tightened. A wave of nausea passed through him. He knew what was coming, knew and dreaded to hear. "Who are they?" he asked.

Callahan named the congressmen who were hostages.

Henry looked at Lucy, then averted his eyes. "Oh, God! Oh, no . . . !" Nausea. Head throbbing. He suddenly felt himself sinking, overwhelmed by doubt and by the enormity of the role he had undertaken. Then Lucy was there beside him. She didn't know, but she understood. His rock, his strength. Her eyes said it all: You must never forget—*you're* the President now!

Henry swallowed hard, but his voice was calm as he spoke into the phone. "All right, Dan, I want you to call an emergency meeting of the National Security Council. Have them all in my office as fast as they can get here. And under the circumstances, we'd better include the Speaker. He'll want to know how we handle this." He paused, then added, "In fact, call Connie first. I want to see him before the rest of you get here."

Lucy listened, smiling, proud of him. Henry knew the smile would be short-lived. He hung up the phone and told her. "Terrorists have seized a place called Uxmal in Mexico. Four congressmen have been captured."

A flicker of fear passed through Lucy's eyes, but she was strong. Damn it, *so* strong!

"Yes," Henry said harshly. "Reuben, Jack, and Tom are among them." His closest friends. Or the closest thing he had to friends after twenty-five years in Washington.

Lucy's face went rigid as she took in the shock and absorbed it. Fear rose again briefly in her eyes, then gave way to doubt, but she pulled herself together.

"Henry," she said, "this is your *chance.* . . ."

"My chance! My God!" He felt sick inside, a Judas goat, faced by the consequences of his own weakness.

"I'm sorry, I didn't mean it that way. I just want you to know I *believe* in you. But you're the one who has to believe." Lucy's eyes, clear blue, deeply earnest, beseeched him to listen.

Henry drew himself up, as if the act of standing tall might make a difference. He looked at his drink, at himself cold and hard. If ever he needed a clear head, it was now and in the days to come. If ever he needed a delicate hand, a good sense of balance . . .

He turned and put his drink down on the table. "I'll call you," he said. Then he left the room without looking back, without giving Lucy a chance to make him smaller.

Ed Nichols was a big man who had never acquired, nor sought to acquire, the social panache one learned to expect from someone who had been long years in Washington. He was tall and big-boned, with a fresh open face, a quick smile, and bright eyes behind old wire-framed spectacles. On the surface he seemed likable, easygoing, even simple, but there was nothing simple about him. On the contrary, he had taken over the CIA as an outsider and made it his own; he'd survived the shifts of political wind and outlasted Presidents. There had been no one like him in Washington since the FBI changed hands—and before that, Nichols hoped, since he had little more than grudging respect for the memory of J. Edgar Hoover.

4

Ed Nichols was a big man who had never acquired, nor sought to acquire, the social panache one learned to expect from someone who had been long years in Washington. He was tall and big-boned, with a fresh open face, a quick smile, and bright eyes behind old wire-framed spectacles. On the surface he seemed likable, easygoing, even simple, but there was nothing simple about him. On the contrary, he had taken over the CIA as an outsider and made it his own; he'd survived the shifts of political wind and outlasted Presidents. There had been no one like him in Washington since the FBI changed hands—and before that, Nichols hoped, since he had little more than grudging respect for the memory of J. Edgar Hoover.

There never was enough room for Nichols's long legs and large body, even in the deep wing chairs that flanked the fireplace facing the President's desk in the Oval Office. He shifted awkwardly, like a small boy forced to sit through a sermon. But the man speaking now was a long way from being a preacher. He was Colonel Alfred Hayfield, director of the Defense Intelligence Agency, and a smooth talker if Washington ever had one.

Hayfield was as slick and polished as Nichols was brusk. He was faultlessly dressed—bold of face, smug of heart—and wore a scar sharply drawn across the cheek like an extra battle ribbon. Nichols always wondered, in fact, if one of the ribbons that marched in six rows across Hayfield's heart had been earned for valor in a duel at dawn. Such was his concept of honor, it seemed, a grudge match with pistols drawn.

But none of that explained why Nichols—unsmiling now, eyes merely thoughtful behind the glint of light against his glasses—was in a rage on the inside, wondering how deep the hatchet should fall on the CIA field forces controlled from Mexico City. Hayfield's boys in the DIA certainly did get a leg up on this one. His agents had picked up the first rumblings out of this place called Oosh-mal. They had been the first to report the news and had their surveillance planes in the sky almost before the takeover was finished; the proof was here in detailed reconnaissance photos. And where was the CIA all this time? Probably surveying the reef off the shore at Acapulco, or paddling around in the pink jeeps from Las Brisas.

In Washington, being first was all that mattered. People who finished second rarely got here.

But Nichols said nothing for now, not among these Galahads of the Riker–Brendan administration. No, not here. He would set his own house in order—drop the hatchet—in the privacy of his office on the top floor of the CIA headquarters building at Langley, Virginia.

"Uxmal," Hayfield was saying, his finger pausing briefly over a circled area on the map he had propped against an easel where everyone could see it, "is perfectly situated for strategic defensive purposes. Here, near the Yucatan–Campeche border, surrounded by jungle, which is largely impenetrable; at best there would be extremely slow movement through it. There's only one paved road"—his finger traced a thin line running down from Merida—"and it would suffice for heavy troop movement, but not where surprise is required. Even a well-trained commando unit would be spotted miles away from the target area."

"How so?" asked Bert Engel, the President's National Security Advisor, a man of forty-odd years who was blunt, strong-willed, controversial, and brilliant. "Wouldn't the jungle act as cover for the road and anyone on it?"

31

"Not in Yucatan," Hayfield relied. "This is bush jungle, essentially flat. The road stands out like a white ribbon running through it. And the terrorists have the advantage of position." He produced a large photograph and propped it against the map. "This pyramid, called the Pyramid of the Magician, rises above the jungle. It stands nearly one hundred feet above the surrounding treetops. The figure you see at the top is a man, a lookout, posted there precisely because he has an unobstructed view in all directions. Beyond that, we know they're using the helicopters for regular aerial surveillance."

"I see." Engel pursed his lips, frowning—looking, Nichols thought, vaguely bothered by some point in Hayfield's presentation. But if he were, he chose not to raise it now. Beside him, Conklin Pierce leaned forward.

And every eye in the room was drawn to him. Pierce was the Speaker of the House and a great deal more. He was, in a sense, the patriarch of the government. Now past eighty, he had been in Congress for almost fifty years and had served under eight different Presidents. He was a small man, so small that he seemed dwarfed between Engel on one side and Secretary of Defense George Dent on the other, though they were not men of exceptional size. His eyes were soft in a deeply lined face; there were no hard edges showing. He was rarely known to raise his voice or use political threats to rally his forces, but he ruled Congress as few men had, with intelligence and a firm hand. In his presence it was comforting to remember that he was second in line to succeed the President. Nichols knew he would feel more confident if Pierce were in the White House now instead of Henry Brendan.

"And the hostages?" Pierce asked. "Where are they? Do we know?"

Hayfield produced another large photograph, an aerial view of the ruins, and propped it against the first. "They're being held in two locations. The American delegation—including, we think, the congressmen—is inside the ruins, in a building called the Governor's Palace. This one." He glanced at Pierce uncomfortably.

"We think?"

"We don't know. We've not been able to identify the congressmen among the hostages in any of the pictures, but we have identified some staff members, all in this area. We think the terrorists have divided our delegation from the rest of the hostages—tourists, guides, whomever—who are being held here, in the hotel across from the ruins. It's a small place, one of the Club Med's Villas Arqueologicas, but we assume there were guests there, and hotel staff. We don't know how many."

"Or if any of them are U.S. citizens," Daniel Callahan interjected. The Secretary of State was gray-haired, craggy-faced, and composed, as always. He was about sixty, a skilled professional diplomat. A traditionalist. "We're trying to find out who they are," he said, "but Colonel Hayfield is right. We simply don't have a clear hostage count, and we don't know if anyone has been injured."

"Or killed," the President said.

"There's no evidence of that," Hayfield broke in. "No sign of bodies in any of the pictures."

"That's something, I guess." Henry didn't look relieved. His face was a mask. Nichols couldn't tell what was going on behind it. "I keep thinking about those two American businessmen who were murdered, and the threats to our ambassador. Do we know who the terrorists are?"

"Not yet," Hayfield said. "No one's claiming credit."

General Marks, the chairman of the Joint Chiefs of Staff, whose iron gray hair matched his iron gray face, leaned forward to explain. "There are several different terrorist groups operating in Mexico, and any of them, with the proper backing, could be responsible for this. They're not well organized among themselves, like the Red Brigades for example. They operate independently from each other."

"And as you know," Callahan added, his eyes still on the President, "our initial attempts to make contact with

33

them have failed. We don't know their purpose yet, but that's not unusual at this stage. They may be willing to negotiate."

"But are *we* willing to negotiate?" Henry Brendan asked.

Callahan raised his hands. "That's always the question. Do we dignify a terrorist act by talking to the people who've committed it? Or do we ignore them as a point against this sort of behavior in the future? My opinion is that we have little choice. If any of the hostages are killed, the pressure on you, Mr. President, would be enormous. I don't believe they'll kill anyone as long as we're willing to talk, but we have to be careful. We must find a peaceful way out of this."

The traditionalist. Callahan was utterly predictable.

Henry nodded silently, neither agreeing nor disagreeing with the secretary's comments, but everyone in the room, including Ed Nichols, knew what he had to be thinking. Most of the official hostages were congressional staff, and that was bad enough. Four were members of Congress—Reuben Shackford of Maine, Thomas MacGregor of Minnesota, Jack Renaud of Illinois, and Andrew Cass of Ohio. Symbolically, that was worse. But among the four, three were the President's best friends, and given Henry Brendan's reluctance to make tough decisions, that could be a disaster.

Best friends, in fact, Nichols knew, didn't really describe the relationship. Shackford, Renaud, MacGregor, and Brendan had formed a clique twenty-five years ago when, as freshman members of the House, they perceived the importance of coalitions in the legislative process. On certain key issues they agreed to vote as a bloc, in spite of their individual philosophical differences—no, partly because of them—and to deliver any other votes they could influence. In the beginning they didn't have a lot of clout, but over the years they acquired power, alone and collectively. Three were now committee chairmen in the House—among them they headed Foreign Affairs, Intelligence, and Armed Services—and Henry, the least likely among them, was President. They had been through a lot together.

Nichols didn't know much about what's his name—Cass—but he saw the chief hostages lined up in his mind like the partners in a venerable Washington law firm. Pious, Pompous, and Gooch, plus What's His Name, with Henry in charge of bringing them home. It was not a picture that stirred his heart to gladness.

And now, as he studied Henry's face, he worried. It wouldn't be easy for anyone to put personal feelings aside under the circumstances, to put the needs of the nation first, or even to be objective enough to know which was which. Some Presidents, Nichols knew, could stand up to that kind of pressure—he had served under one who did—but probably not Henry Brendan. Henry's hands were trembling, he noticed. It was only by accident that Henry was even running this show, and that made Nichols extremely nervous.

"I don't agree," Bert Engel said, his eyes on the Secretary of State, with whom he rarely agreed. "Negotiating with terrorists is the same thing as giving them sanction. I know there are lives at stake here—people we know, and that makes it worse—but there are times when national honor is more important. I think we have to hit back and hit hard. If we don't do it now, our elected officials won't be safe in their own bedrooms!"

Callahan cleared his throat. "Hit back with what? We can't sever diplomatic relations with terrorists. We can't cut off aid or trade. We can't impose sanctions."

"I'm talking about a military operation. Rescue, if possible. Otherwise a limited offensive strike, with a threat of more—*much* more—unless they release the hostages."

"And if they don't?"

"Then we make good our threat."

Callahan shook his head slowly. "If we go in there with a heavy hand, without even waiting to find out what they want, we'll only make martyrs out of the terrorists. Remember, the Mexican people—and a good many others—consider those ruins a treasure. If we damage or destroy them, we'll have more trouble than we've got now. We have to *try* to negotiate. We have to wait."

Engel glared back at him. "Waiting will make us look weak."

"No, patience takes *strength*."

"You know that, and I know that, but the terrorists of the world will see it as a sign that we lack resolve, or muscle, or both. We can't let this thing get out of hand."

"Gentlemen!" The President leaned forward on his desk, putting himself figuratively between them. "Let's not let this meeting get out of hand."

Nichols smiled to himself. Sometimes Henry surprised him, and this time, he was starting to think, might be one of them.

Henry picked up his coffee cup, using both hands to steady it. He took a drink, put the cup down, and looked at Hayfield. "Well?" he asked. "*Can* we rescue the hostages?"

Hayfield, Nichols thought with some satisfaction, looked a little deflated. His dueling scar puckered rebelliously as he tried hard to keep his face as well pressed as his uniform. "Not at this time, Mr. President."

"Why not?"

"Because, as I've tried to demonstrate here, the terrorists are in an optimum defensible position. They chose well when they chose Uxmal. They're extremely well armed. They have helicopters, automatic rifles, and at least six submachine guns. They have a pair of flame throwers, and Yucatan is dry at this time of year; they could start a firestorm with even one of them. They also have a small missile launcher with which they could shoot down approaching aircraft—"

The President slammed his desk with his fist, rattling the china coffee cup in its saucer. "What the hell!" he exploded. "We're fighting a goddamned army!"

General Marks spoke up. "That's what I meant, sir, when I mentioned proper backing. Money, supplies—"

"*Whose* backing?"

"We don't know."

Hayfield produced more photographs, large blowups,

grainy, but good enough to make clear the work they depicted. "Beyond the protection of the jungle," he said, "we think the terrorists have planted minefields all around the ruins, in two circles—one close in, the other between two and three miles out. In other words, they've effectively cordoned off the area. Surprise attack from the ground or the air is out of the question, and we think any kind of rescue attempt would be an extremely high-risk operation."

The President studied Hayfield's display coldly and then leaned back in his chair. "It's a son of a bitch," he said.

"Yes, sir, that pretty well says it."

"All right, what about you?" Henry asked, turning back to General Marks and George Dent, the Secretary of Defense, who was sitting beside him. "Do you agree with Colonel Hayfield?"

Marks, glancing at Dent for confirmation, gave a sharp nod. "Yes, sir, we do. We strongly recommend against a military rescue at this time."

"At this time?"

"Until we have a better picture of what's going on down there, and possibly time for specialized training of our own forces. If we tried to go in there now, we think our casualties might well be total. And that wouldn't do much for our national honor."

Nichols, listening, could not find a weak spot in the Pentagon argument, but he believed nothing was impossible. One only needed to think and rethink, to shift point of view, to seek the creative solution. But based on the evidence offered by DIA, this one seemed pretty damned airtight. At the moment, he had to agree with Hayfield's conclusions.

So did Henry Brendan, he thought, but the President, whose eyes shifted to Engel, lingered briefly, and then moved to the Secretary of State, didn't say so.

"What do the Mexicans say?" he asked.

Callahan produced a pair of reading glasses and balanced them on his nose, then a file folder from the attaché case beside his chair. He removed and scanned a two-page cable. "Well," he said finally, "the foreign minister has pledged his fullest cooperation and that of his president. They've already investigated the army guards who turned against the hostages; as we might have guessed, they were imposters. The terrorists apparently got their hands on an advance duty roster. The real guards were found, bound and gagged, in an empty house at Cozumel."

"I'm glad they assigned us their best," Henry muttered.

Callahan glanced over the top of his glasses. "It could have happened here too."

"That's not comforting. What else?"

"They're willing to act as third-party negotiators, if the terrorists are willing, and we are. They'll commit troops for a rescue attempt, for us or with us, or let us act on our own pending full notice and approval of a specific plan. Needless to say, they're rather embarrassed by what's happened."

"I should think they would be," the President said, and pulled himself up in the chair. "Well, Dan, I want you to notify the foreign minister that we accept their offer of cooperation. They may succeed where we haven't. I want them to try to make contact with the terrorists as soon as possible, with the goal of negotiating a peaceful settlement."

Engel sat forward abruptly. "But Mr. President—"

"I'm not rejecting your arguments, Bert. A dramatic military rescue would be politically popular, after all, and next year is an election year. And I'm sure you're right about the deterrent effect of tough action. But I'm taking Dan's advice for now. I believe our national honor requires one thing from us—that we weigh what we do responsibly and wisely. We're a nation that values human life, and if it's within my power I intend to bring these hostages home alive, whatever it takes. More than anything else, I suspect it may take patience. We could be in for a long siege."

A small smile appeared on Nichols's face. He wasn't sure he agreed with the President's position, but in a perverse way he was pleased to see Henry Brendan taking charge of the situation. Or had Henry merely found that perfect level of alcoholic consumption, enough to loosen up inhibitions without producing obvious drunken behavior? Was Henry's new confidence real, or was it bravado? A stalling tactic. A front for indecision.

"Mr. President," Nichols said when Henry had finished, "do I take it this means you've ruled out a military option?"

"For the time being, yes."

"Then perhaps we should be working up a contingency plan, a *nonmilitary option."

"A CIA operation?"

"Yes, sir."

"That's the *last* thing I want!"

"I beg your pardon?"

"Rightly or wrongly," the President said, "the CIA has come to represent the worst of American power in Third World nations. There's no point in further inflaming the terrorists, or in undercutting whatever support we might get from the bulk of Mexican citizens. Obviously, the CIA should report all related intelligence. You'll be kept fully informed, and your people should stand by in case they're needed for action. Otherwise, I want the CIA to keep its hands off Uxmal."

Nichols was stunned. Hands off? An unthinkable order! "But we have to have an emergency plan," he sputtered. "What if they start killing the hostages?"

"I expect the Pentagon to be ready for any emergency. DIA already has agents in the area, and they'll continue, even step up, their surveillance. I don't want any jurisdictional squabbling. If you have suggestions regarding a contingency plan or anything else, I expect you to take them up with Colonel Hayfield."

Nichols felt his face getting warm. "And if the colonel and I have a disagreement?"

"Then you come to me, and I'll resolve it."

It was small consolation—at least he still had access to the President—but Nichols knew this wasn't the time to argue. Whatever Henry was, he was not indecisive! He had made himself absolutely clear. DIA got there first and staked out its turf, while the CIA did nothing. That had to change.

Nichols no longer wanted to fire his agents in Mexico. Now, he wanted to *lynch* them!

A line of limousines was drawn up on the snow-covered drive as Nichols stepped through the West Wing door; the ladies and gentlemen of the press, wrapped in coats and stomping their feet to keep warm, were waiting there with them. Reporters, photographers, and the headless figures behind the shoulder-held minicams were all vying for the latest word on a fast-breaking story—or, barring that, the pictures and video footage of the decision makers as they left the White House, grim-faced, to back up quotes from unnamed sources. Rumors and guesswork. Coverage of a crisis in progress never had been easy work, but journalists weren't assigned to this beat if they liked their hours short and their jobs simple.

Nichols, who avoided publicity as a matter of policy and had probably stayed in power longer for it, and who knew the President was partly right about the CIA's image—that it wouldn't do for his face to be featured in the evening news, beamed by satellite to the world and possibly even to Uxmal—signaled his driver to wait at a distance and stepped back inside the doorway. Let them get Hayfield's picture! Nichols wanted a private word with the Speaker.

Pierce's friends called him Connie, but only his friends. "Mr. Speaker," Nichols said as the old man approached him from the carpeted corridor, moving slowly and silently on a gold-headed walking stick.

Pierce looked up, his eyes soft, his face gentle. "Yes?"

Nichols drew him aside, away from the guards and receptionist, people waiting, others leaving. "I know this is a personal crisis for you, and I wanted to tell you I'm sorry."

The Speaker looked at him for a moment. Then he nodded and waited for Nichols to say what he really wanted.

A wise old bird, not easily fooled.

"I'm worried about the President," Nichols said, dropping his voice almost to a whisper.

"In what way?"

"Is he drinking again?"

The Speaker paused before he answered, but then he answered truthfully. "He was, but he's stopped."

"Is that enough?"

Pierce smiled gently. "I believe you're questioning Henry's competence."

Nichols didn't try to deny it. "That's putting it too strongly," he said. "God knows, I understand—having to fill Ben Riker's shoes would drive a lot of men to drink—and I hope you aren't offended. But I am worried."

"I don't offend easily," Pierce replied, "not after all these years. And I understand why you're worried. I was worried myself until I saw Henry today. I know him better than anyone, except his wife, and I believe the change we've seen in him is authentic. I think this crisis has shocked him into being the kind of leader he could have been all along if he'd only known it. Henry has always been a good man, and I think he's about to prove it."

"I hope you're right," Nichols said.

"I do too, for more reasons than one. I happen to be very fond of Henry." The Speaker started to move away, but then he turned back to Nichols. "No President is competent to handle this kind of crisis alone," he added. "For what it's worth, I intend to be there helping."

Helping or watching? Nichols wondered.

But the Speaker had gone. Through the glass-paned doors, Nichols could see him talking to a familiar TV anchorwoman, who was listening to him earnestly. Then Pierce walked on to his car, moving carefully down steps that had been cleared of snow but were still wet, not too proud to accept the arm of his chauffeur. The car drove off, but not before Nichols observed a bumper sticker on the back and smiled to himself. END THE ARMS RACE, NOT THE HUMAN RACE. Someone must have put it there as a joke, on the back of the Speaker's own limou-

41

sine, since Conklin Pierce wasn't exactly dovish on such issues. For all his gentility, Pierce was a hard-liner. He had seldom been outdone in Cold War rhetoric over the years, though the Cold War had been through several phases of freezing and thawing. Yet the bumper sticker remained. Nichols wondered if Pierce knew it was there and shared the perpetrator's amusement.

They were all gone now, except Nichols, and the press was starting to disperse, hurrying off to meet evening deadlines. As soon as they were gone too, Nichols pushed the door open, nodded to the guards outside, and made his way down the driveway.

His own assigned car was a long black Lincoln, nearly as old as the Speaker himself, part of a government fleet that had been retired because of gas consumption. Nichols managed to hang onto this one because in it he could stretch his legs their full length and be comfortable. He told his driver to take him to the office. Then he settled into the back seat, thinking.

He felt better after his brief talk with Pierce—it was good to know that someone close to the President would be keeping an eye on him—but he had no intention of playing flunkie to Hayfield and the Pentagon in the matter of the Uxmal crisis. A plan had begun to form in his mind even before he left the Oval Office. The military might not be able to sneak up on the terrorists, but one man might. One man, the *right* man. Richard Owen.

Nichols glanced through the window as the limousine slid through the White House gates and out onto Pennsylvania Avenue. Tourists along the iron fence with their pocket cameras turned to stare at the car, through its tinted glass, wondering who was inside. Nichols stared back, scowling.

Now all he had to do was *find* Owen.

5

The terrorists had given Owen a deluxe two-room suite in the Governor's Palace at Uxmal, a cell consisting of inner and outer chambers, like the ones he explored earlier at the Nunnery. This one faced west, away from the ruins, toward the jungle, and even now, in the afternoon, light was reduced to a patch of sun filtered through the iron mesh screen that covered his outside doorway.

The Governor's Palace was clearly the gemstone of Uxmal, and more than that. Some critics thought it was the most magnificent building anywhere in the Americas; others claimed it was one of the great man-made wonders of the world. It was horizontal, like the Nunnery buildings, but larger still—more than three hundred feet across the front—and set on a massive, three-tiered terrace that was artificial, built stone upon stone, and not part of the natural terrain. It was done in pure Mayan Puuc style, with a perfectly plain lower face and a carved frieze ten feet high above it. No, not just carved. The frieze was composed of thousands of cut pieces of stone—there were hieroglyphics and geometric patterns, figures in plumed headdresses, Chac masks, and thatched huts—and together, set into the cornice of the building, they formed a solid mass of sculptured mosaic. An enormously intricate design. The building was huge. It was grand in both scale and concept.

But it wasn't quite up to the Michelin standards. Owen's rooms were small, dark and dank, and like the others foul smelling, but they came complete with a cot, two blankets, and something that was supposed to pass for a pillow. A plastic basin, soap, and a towel. A toothbrush. Two bottles of purified water. Basic provisions for which Owen, if he followed the normal patterns of hostage behavior, would learn to be grateful. Fear and dependency were a powerful combination.

The provisions were meant to last a while. It seemed the terrorists were not concerned that Owen and the others might outstay their welcome. It also looked as if they intended to keep the hostages alive, reasonably clean, and healthy. Returnable. At least for the time being. They had even chased out the bats, and for that Owen *was* grateful. As company went, he preferred solitary confinement.

And so now he stood alone, near the outer door, through which he could see a broad flight of steps descending from the upper terrace to a flat overgrown area that had once been a paved plaza. In the middle of the plaza a stone platform rose to a height of about four feet, with steps on each side leading to a carved jaguar, a piece of original Mayan art remarkable for its endurance and its anatomy; it had one head on each end of its body. On the other side of the plaza, away from the Governor's Palace, the ground dropped off sharply. How far, Owen couldn't tell—the space below had grown in with jungle—but treetops were visible from where he stood. Twenty feet or more. That was all he could tell at this distance.

Beyond that the jungle rose up like a wall, unbroken except for an unclaimed pyramid—all green, entirely grown over—that sat at the edge, straight ahead, as if it were placed there for Owen to contemplate during his confinement. Through the trees to his left he could barely see the rooftops of the buildings where visitors paid their pesos for tickets, for souvenirs and refreshments. Near those he could see the huge, elliptical Pyramid of the Magician, but it was little more than a splash of stone against trees and sky in his peripheral vision.

And then there were the terrorist guards patrolling the building. They looked hot and bored, but not inattentive. This wasn't the time, Owen thought, to make a run for it. Anyway, it was cooler inside. And his nose was just getting used to the smell that lingered after the bats departed.

But he did want to keep his options open.

The iron mesh screen through which he viewed the world outside wasn't there for esthetic reasons, nor had it been placed there by the Maya. It was heavy and black, attached somewhere on the roof to roll down over his doorway, slightly wider than the door and loose at the sides and bottom; its weight held it flush against the building. Alone, it wasn't enough to keep a child from escaping, but it wasn't alone. Electric wires were attached to each side and then to a thicker cable, which ran down the steps, across the plaza of the two-headed jaguar, and into the first edge of low growing bush, where, Owen assumed, it was patched into Uxmal's lighting system. There was current running through the screen, or there would be. Owen smiled. It was one way to make sure your guests didn't get themselves lost in the jungle.

Then his smile faded. The terrorists were still installing the system, hanging iron mesh and electric wires over other doors all along the face of the building, and that gave Owen some time to study the setup. He took off his hat with the silver chain, moved up close to the screen, and reached out a hand to touch it.

Later, when the sun was gone, the sky violet over the jungle, and after a dinner of beans and rice delivered on a tray by room service, Owen set up his cot and stretched out. They had given him wood for building a fire, because the nights were cool here, and now patterns of flame flickered across the walls of his cell and up into the darkness of the corbeled ceiling. Outside, spotlights shone on the ruins, and with them had come a soft hum of sound. It came and was gone, a signal that current had charged the door screens. To touch them now would be foolish.

But inside his cell it was almost cozy. Owen lay on his cot, his eyes closed, listening—to sounds that came through the twilight from the jungle, and to the terrorist guards, more relaxed now with their prisoners subdued, conversing in Spanish out beyond his doorway. After a while the shifts changed, and Owen continued to listen. Different voices, same Spanish. They were cautious. Well trained. Nothing they said revealed their intent or their purpose. Owen wasn't surprised, nor was he disappointed. He was listening for speech patterns.

If there was anything Owen was sure of, it was his own ear for language. He spoke eight languages effortlessly, more when he put his mind to it, and had mastered dialect as well. He spoke English as an Englishman or an American—in Scots, Irish, Australian—and had an unerring ear for regional variations. For Parisian French versus Bordeaux French. For German as it was spoken in Munich and Bonn. For Bronx English, if English it was, and the nuance of difference he heard over in Brooklyn. For that matter, he could still read Homer in ancient Greek and Julius Caesar in Latin, and he did from time to time. But tonight he was content to listen.

And when, finally, he had heard enough, he let sleep overtake him. His last thoughts were notes of a kind, things he had to tell Nichols whenever he got the chance to. One thing above the rest. These terrorists weren't Mexican.

They were Cuban.

⚏ 6 ⚏

It was dark outside when Nichols arrived back at the CIA. He went straight to the seventh floor, where he found his chief deputy, Sam Ardry, waiting for him by the elevator, alerted no doubt by a call from the gate or security clearance. Ardry was a slight man in shirt sleeves and suspenders, and he looked as calm as Nichols had ever seen him. That wasn't a good sign. Ardry was always calm under pressure. With trouble, he turned stoic. In a crisis, he sometimes seemed to be almost sleeping.

Nichols raised a hand to fend him off and turned left down the corridor. "Whatever it is, I don't want to hear it," he said. "I've got more than enough to worry us both for the present."

Ardry fell into step beside him. "I'm sorry, Ed, but you have to hear this."

"Now?" Nichols glared at him.

But Ardry didn't flinch. "Yes, now." He lowered his voice. "We've had contact from Owen."

"You're kidding! That's wonderful news!" Nichols's impatience vanished, and he looked absolutely jubilant. "God may be with us, after all," he said, chuckling. "The hell with Hayfield!"

"Don't get excited yet," Ardry warned. "You haven't heard where he is yet."

"I don't care where he is. I want him back here on the double."

Ardry's expression turned a shade calmer. "We'd better talk."

47

Nichols was too busy gloating to notice his deputy's face or the tone of his voice. If anyone knew how to defuse the crisis at Uxmal, it was Owen. Hayfield may have got there first, but Nichols was about to come in with the best. He led the way into his office, a large room with a wall of windows overlooking the snow-covered hills of Fairfax County. City lights brightened the night sky, from Washington on the other side of the Potomac and from the sprawling Virginia suburbs that ran, one into another, along this side of the river. Nichols touched a button to close the curtains and sat down at his desk, where a single lamp gave off a soft glow. He leaned back in his chair, smiling broadly.

"So," he said, "Owen has decided to let us know where he is and what he's doing."

Ardry closed the door and sat down. "Well, yes, in a manner of speaking."

"What does that mean?"

"You're not going to like it."

"Quit stalling, Sam. I'm used to Owen's tricks. Nothing he's done could surprise me."

"Oh, yes? Try this one. Owen is one of the hostages at Uxmal."

Nichols froze in his chair. Doubt flickered through his eyes, a brief moment of hope, then vanished. The expression drained out of his face, along with the color, and for a moment he stopped breathing. He sat there, staring, stunned beyond any measure.

"Surprise," Ardry observed dryly.

Surprise was hardly adequate! Nichols couldn't have been more astonished if Ardry had told him Owen turned up at the South Pole in an ice cube! It took him a moment to find his voice, but when he did he exploded with questions. "Christ Almighty! Are you sure he's there? How do you know? I thought you said we'd *heard* from him!"

"Not directly." Ardry looked calmly at Nichols across the top of the desk. "Our relay station in Mexico City had a call this afternoon from a friend of Owen's—a Mayan doctor by the name of Francisco Luc-Can. Apparently he was at Uxmal with Owen when the attack occurred. The Mayan escaped. Owen didn't. But Owen had told him how to make contact with us in an emergency, and he did it."

"What the devil were they doing there?"

"The Mayan only said Owen was looking for something."

"*What*, for Pete's sake?"

Ardry hesitated, then blurted it out. "Moving islands."

Nichols scowled. "What kind of nonsense is that?"

"I don't know. The Mayan doesn't know, or says he doesn't. I'm afraid you're going to have to ask Owen."

"Oh, swell. Hand me the phone. I'll call him." Nichols turned away and closed his eyes. He took a deep breath, pulling air in through his nose, letting it out slowly—an attempt to relax, or at least minimize the tension that was building in the base of his skull, in his neck and broad shoulders. Owen always did have a perfect sense of timing! Then he looked back at Ardry. "Is there any chance the Mayan is wrong? Or lying?"

Ardry shook his head. "We've verified his story. We know when and where Owen entered the country. He's using the documents we issued him for Jakarta, and he flew into Merida yesterday afternoon. He rented a car there and drove south. His signature on the car rental form matches the samples we have on file. The name is false—David Stuart—but the handwriting is Owen's. And south, unless he's heading for Belize or Guatemala, there is only Uxmal."

"And the Mayan himself, this Francisco Luc-Can? Can we trust him?"

"As far as it goes, yes. He is who he says he is, and he is Owen's friend. They met years ago at Harvard."

Nichols sighed. "Then Owen *is* there."

"I'm afraid so. And if the terrorists find out who he is—"

"That's the first thing I thought of. *Damn!*" Nichols picked up a pencil and began to beat it absently against the edge of his desk. The color in his face was coming back, but his eyes were a little glazed and vaguely thoughtful. "I don't know if this is a problem or an opportunity," he said finally. "Five minutes ago, hell, I was ready to *send* him there—to pull this thing out of the fire for us. The DIA has done an end run around us, and they've got it all locked up. The President gave me strict orders. Hayfield's in charge. We work through him, like it or not."

A reaction actually passed across Ardry's face, however briefly—a hint of horror, more eloquent than language.

"And I have some questions I'm going to want answered before this thing is finished," Nichols went on harshly. "Hayfield did pick this up first. I want to know why our people had their heads in the sand."

"Of course he did," Ardry replied. "The Pentagon has a unit down there somewhere. Army Corps of Engineers. They're working with the Mexican government on an irrigation project."

"Johnny-on-the-spot. Is that it? Heard the news and called home? Well, I still want to know."

"I'll look into it."

"And that still doesn't change Owen's situation. I was going to send him there, and now I find out he's already there, a hostage! That's not quite what I had in mind. In a way it's a godsend—we've got a man on the inside—but if the terrorists find out he's one of ours, he probably won't last the evening." Nichols dropped the pencil and leaned forward against his desk, stroking his chin thoughtfully. "Let me ask you something," he said. "If you had an outrageous assignment, a really outrageous assignment, and Owen weren't available for it, who would you give it to?"

Ardry didn't pause for a moment. "Thatcher."

Nichols nodded. "Where is Thatcher?"

"In Marseille."

Nichols remembered the gist of it. An important job. Thatcher was after a man who was worse than a killer. But Uxmal was more important.

"Call Andrews," he said. "Tell them to have a plane fueled and cleared for takeoff in an hour."

Ardry reached for the phone. "Do you want me to go?" he asked as he punched out the number.

Nichols smiled. "Not this time, Sam. I want to see Thatcher myself. After Andrews, though, you can call my wife and tell her I won't be home for dinner."

It was a cold wet night in Marseille, with mist rolling in off the harbor. A man alone, walking purposefully along the quay, felt the chill of the air even through his thick fisherman's sweater and black peacoat. But he was not a fisherman. His face was hard, his eyes dry and bright, more evil for their lack of expression.

He stopped, turning to listen for the echo of footsteps behind him, but all he heard was the rise and fall of water against wooden pilings, the cry of a seagull—otherwise deep silence. The sailor who had been behind him all the way from the rue Catalans had vanished into mist, or maybe into his own drunken stupor . . . if he was what he appeared to be—a young seaman on shore leave and too much into the bottle. The man had many enemies. He never risked confrontation when he could avoid it.

He pulled up his collar and turned into a narrow street that led up away from the harbor, past brick walls eroded by time and salt air, past darkened doorways and sight-less, staring windows. Past faded women and hard-living men: thieves, prostitutes, smugglers. Opium dealers. Illegal arms merchants. And the old beggar who had worked the waterfront district for more years than anyone could remember. Familiar faces, most of them—with eyes, like the windows, unseeing. No one spoke to the man. No one acknowledged his presence. It was safer to deny that he existed.

Because, even here, the man was a pariah. His business was the slave trade. Free enterprise. He kidnapped children and sold them for profit—hundreds of them over the years, to whorehouses and sweatshops, to por-nographers, to snuff filmmakers, who considered violent death a form of entertainment. A pariah, but a man to be respected. Or feared.

And now his nose had picked up the scent of danger. A drunken sailor? He thought not. He let one arm fall loose at his side and turned it slightly to release the dagger strapped to his arm. The handle of the dagger slipped into his palm. His hand closed around it.

The man moved on, heading for one of the darkened doorways, a café where a cellar door gave access to the old waterfront sewer system. He sized up the distance between himself and the café entrance, just past the old beggar. About forty yards. Then harsh laughter erupted close by, and his eyes shifted back. A pair of swinging doors burst open across the street, and three more drunken sailors poured through them. The man glanced quickly over his shoulder. The first sailor had reappeared from the mist and had picked up a friend in his absence; two men were moving up the street from the harbor. The other three were closing in. The man was surrounded. He didn't know who, only what they were. Professionals. Instinct told him. But something was wrong. Professionals were rarely so easy to detect.

There was no time now for the man to consider his options. The dagger blade flashed as he started to run toward the café. Behind him, the sailors threw off pretense and took off after him, running. Ahead, the old beggar looked up. His face was confused, his mind clearly addled, his distorted body slow moving. He tried to get out of the way, too late. He could not avoid a collision.

But the man didn't swerve. He stuck out an arm to shove the beggar out of his path. The heel of his palm struck bone and flesh, but the beggar stood firm against it. His old arm shot up; gnarled fingers grabbed the man's wrist and twisted. A foot wrapped in rags struck the man's other hand, and the dagger went flying.

A sharp cry escaped from the man's throat as his feet left the ground; his body rose in an arc and was thrown back against the pavement. The pain he felt was bad enough, but the shock was worse. He'd walked into a trap! The drunken sailors were *meant* to be obvious. Whoever they were, they had set him up. They drove him straight *to* the beggar!

He was on his back, pinned flat by a knee, staring up into the beggar's face, into eyes as dark and hate-filled as his own. Not beggar eyes. The face was old, but the eyes were young. And they were the eyes of a woman.

The man smiled in shock before consciousness left him. He knew those eyes, as he knew his own fate. Not beggar eyes!

The woman was Emma Thatcher.

7

Emma started to shed her beggar's rags as soon as she was around the corner, leaving questions to be cleared up by the French intelligence officers who had provided her back up. They had more clout with the local *gendarmes* than she did, and Le Sûreté was welcome to the credit. A good night's work. The beast had been beheaded.

Erect now without the hunchback padding, Emma was tall and as slim as a ballerina. Under the rags she was dressed all in black. She pulled off the wig and let her own hair fall loose around her shoulders. It, too, was black, nature's contribution to camouflage in the nighttime. The gnarled hands were actually gloves; she slipped them off and tossed them into a trash bin. Then she began to peel away the years she'd added to her face—thin layers of rubber, folds of sagging flesh, lined and wrinkled.

And all the time she kept moving.

Emma was in her mid-thirties, but she never spoke of her age as she never spoke of her past, because these things were irrelevant. Her skin was fair in contrast to black hair and eyes, and smooth across well-defined cheekbones, a high forehead, a finely shaped chin and jawline. Grace was self-evident in the ease of her movements and only enhanced by self-assurance. But she felt drained now that the job was done. It had been impossible to keep her emotions out of this one. Children, for God's sake! Maybe she should have let the beast run to the sewer. He belonged there! But not as much as he belonged in a prison.

She was drained. Tired. More than tired, bone weary, and looking forward to nothing as much as a hot bath, a brandy, and bedtime. She had left her car near the quai des Belges and was almost there now. A short drive back to the hotel. She crossed the last street and stepped into an alley.

The car, small and dark, set close to the ground, was parked where she left it, at the rear of a building with windows that were painted black or shuttered. Mist swirled around the car and diffused the light from a fixture above the building's rear entrance. But something else drew Emma's attention: a man standing beside the car, clearly waiting. Emma stopped where she was. A big man in a dark overcoat, hands in pockets, bareheaded. The mist cleared briefly, and she recognized Ed Nichols.

"If it isn't the old mandarin," she said as she stepped out of the shadows to meet him.

"Mandarin?" Nichols looked puzzled.

"Keeping an eye on things without getting your own hands dirty."

Nichols snorted. "My hands aren't paid for that sort of thing. I trust yours have been successful."

"I got him, if that's what you mean."

"Good. I'm glad that's over."

From Nichols, it was high praise. Emma unlocked the car and climbed in behind the wheel, then started the ignition while Nichols got in beside her. So much for a hot bath, she thought. Obviously the night's work wasn't over. She glanced across at Nichols and smiled gently. He was squeezed into the small seat, his knees nearly touching his chin, the top of his head barely missing the roof. Like Alice in Wonderland, he seemed to be growing larger.

"I guess you ate the wrong side of the mushroom," she said. "If I'd known you were coming, I'd have chosen a larger model."

"I did mean to mention the car. Obviously you've not

been in touch with your friends on Capitol Hill. We're supposed to be *cutting* expenses."

Emma shrugged. "I needed transportation."

'A *Ferrari*?''

"Wait till you get the bill for my friend the beggar. Remarkable! Do you know he'd never *been* to Monte Carlo?" Nichols groaned as Emma put the car in gear and pulled out of the alley. "I don't suppose you came here," she said, "to chastise me for expenses."

"No." Nichols shifted awkwardly in the seat. "We've got a problem. It's Richard Owen."

Emma raised an eyebrow, interested. "Has he done something naughty?"

"He's got himself captured, that's what he's done! He's being held hostage by a bunch of Mexican terrorists at some place called—"

"Uxmal?" Emma turned to face him, eyes disbelieving, lips smiling. "You mean Owen is at *Uxmal*?"

Nichols nodded, and Emma burst out laughing.

It was funny, *very* funny, the last thing in the world she might have expected. Then she asked what Owen was doing there, and Nichols had to admit he had no idea. That was even funnier.

"Frankly," Nichols said, "I don't think it's amusing."

"No, you wouldn't." Nichols never had been known for his sense of humor. "But don't tell me you're *worried* about him."

"You bet I'm worried! Third World terrorists aren't generally fond of CIA field agents."

"Well, he's not likely to tell them who he is now, is he? Come on, Ed, you know he'll be fine. He could make them believe he's a monkey if he had to. And just because they have him doesn't mean they can keep him. He'll be out of there in two days' time, and he'll probably bring the congressmen out with him."

"It's not a question of confidence. How much do you know about what happened there?"

"Just the headlines. I haven't had time to read the papers today."

"Then let me tell you. These aren't small-time terrorists. They're well trained, well armed. Terrorists, hell—they're an army!"

Emma turned into the Canebière, driving absently, with no particular destination in mind. She was listening, thinking, and when Nichols was finished she was no longer laughing. The fact was, she *cared* what happened to Owen.

Still, it was hard to believe he was really in danger.

But Nichols clearly thought he was, and he'd come all the way to Marseille just to tell her about it. To tell her, and then . . .

"What do you want me to do?" she asked.

"I want you to go get him," he said. "I want you to rescue Owen."

8

Among his own people, who rarely measured more than five and a half feet, Francisco Luc-Can was a giant. He was five foot ten, a good two inches taller than Emma, and leanly built, with narrow hips and broad shoulders. Emma was a little surprised by his appearance. All she'd seen of him before she arrived at Merida was an old passport photo, which served its purpose—it helped her pick him out of the crowd at the airport—but it didn't really do justice to Frank, no more than a snapshot could capture the grace of the Parthenon or the Sphinx or the great white pyramids of the Maya.

Frank was a throwback to the past, to his own ancient ancestors, a figure from the murals at Bonampak, a piece of sculpture breathing. His hair was black, his eyes so dark they seemed black too, his skin the color of amber. And his features were pure Mayan—the sloping forehead, the aquiline nose, the slanting eyes and strong cheekbones—all were there in Frank's face, like stone rubbed to life, as if he had cast off his jaguar skin and plumed headdress and sprung full-blown into the twentieth century.

But not from the head of Zeus, Emma thought, nor even Itzamna. Frank belonged to two worlds. He was clearly as Mayan as the princes and priests who spawned him. On the other hand, to his credit, he had spent eight years at Harvard, which benefited, where Emma was concerned, from its proximity to Boston.

Frank met her at the airport, where she stepped off

the plane to heat so intense, especially after the chill of
Marseille, that she thought she'd stumbled into the devil's inferno. And maybe she had. On the surface Merida
was not an attractive city—a victim, like the people, of a
relentless climate, marked mainly by peeling paint, de-
caying sidewalks, and swarms of giant locusts, which
were, thankfully, dead in the streets and thus no longer
swarming. And dust. Dust everywhere—on the ground,
in the air, in the nose and mouth. A fine limestone ash,
the "soil" of the Yucatan, lacking water. It was a miracle anything grew or survived here.

They headed south, toward Muna and Frank's sister's
house, where he promised they could talk without being
overheard or interrupted. Twice they encountered roadblocks—at the edge of Merida and again at Uman—put
up not so much to contain the terrorists, who had shown
no inclination to leave, as they were to keep curious
visitors off the road to Uxmal. But Frank was well
known in this part of the country, the Harvard-trained
doctor who had passed up the chance for a lucrative
practice in the United States, in Mexico City, or Acapulco, and set up a clinic in his own rural Yucatan
village. He made the run to Merida often, for medical
supplies, always driving the white van that doubled as
his ambulance. No explanation was required of him. He
passed through the roadblocks with a wave and a nod.

And that was important because Emma, officially, had
gone to Paris and stayed there. Except for a handful of
people at the highest levels of the CIA, no one in
Washington—and certainly no one in Mexico City, should
anyone there care to ask—was to know she'd left one
country and entered another.

Frank had proved himself useful—and he would again,
Emma thought as she studied the passing countryside
beyond the van's wide windows. They were making
their way along the deserted highway, two lanes of concrete bleached by the sun, with the bramble of jungle
rising up on both sides, falling back where the edges
were blackened by fire or where an outcrop of limestone
broke through the growth, then encroaching again on the

59

road, even creeping up over the edges of the pavement. From the air the jungle looked harmless, and so flat Emma wondered if the Mayan skylords might have taken their hedge clippers to it, but here there was only a deep sense of isolation. The harshness of nature uncontrolled, uncontrollable. And Emma was not especially fond of nature. She preferred urban assignments—smog to fresh air, skyscrapers to trees, neon to starlight, and traffic noise most certainly to crickets. She preferred to work in the solitude that came with crowds, on city streets. But they'd seen no one since Uman. No one driving. No one, God forbid, walking. No one at all, just a lizard darting through waves of heat that rose off the highway, and now and then a buzzard circling above them. Frank slowed the van whenever one of the great ugly birds came into view, explaining that they had been known to mistake moving cars for legitimate prey and that windshields were little defense against them. Emma appreciated his care, since a lapful of broken vulture didn't much strike her fancy. At the moment, in fact, as she studied the view—scrub and bramble and glaring sky— she wanted to *curse* Richard Owen.

But she smiled to herself, remembering, as she had smiled when Nichols told her what he had in mind. She was here on a mission of mercy, and it served Owen right—for he thought he had saved her life once. In fact, he had, half a second before she was planning to save it her own way. He had never let her forget, and she had never properly thanked him for it. Nichols, bless his heart, had giftwrapped this opportunity, though he didn't see it that way.

Nor would Owen.

And yet she was relieved when Frank confirmed that Owen had been seen alive as recently as this morning. By Frank himself. He had been back to the ruins and witnessed the terrorists exercising the hostages. Owen was among them, alive and apparently in good condition.

"Then we've got some time," Emma said. "That's good, but I want to move as quickly as possible."

"I'm here to help any way I can."

"And you certainly can." Emma cast an appraising eye on Frank, who was wearing jeans and the native shirt, a white *guayabera,* with the collar open and the sleeves rolled to the elbows, revealing strong arms. He had known Owen for years, since his undergraduate days at Harvard, where Owen once spent some time studying pre-Columbian art and the Mayan language. Once she got over the feeling that Frank was himself a pre-Columbian relic, an *objet d'art* more appropriate on someone's mantel, she began to understand why he and Owen were friends. There was strength in Frank. Detachment. Cool thinking. These were qualities Owen lived by himself, qualities he admired in others. "You can start," she said, "by telling me what happened. Did Owen tell you why he came here?"

"No more than I've already reported."

"Yes, I know. Moving islands. That doesn't help much."

"I doubt if it was meant to. Owen never was very forthcoming."

"Then tell me everything," Emma said. "When did he make contact with you, or did he?"

"Oh, yes." Frank smiled and leaned back in his seat, his arms straight, his hands relaxed on the wheel of the van. He drove easily over familiar terrain. "I got a wire the day before he arrived here. 'Coming down to see your old playground,' he said. That's all. It was signed with an *O* and couldn't have come from anyone else. I don't get many telegrams to start with, and Owen's the only person I know who can drop out of your life, then send a wire a day ahead and expect you to know who it comes from."

Emma smiled. They knew the same Owen.

"Of course I assumed there was something more to it," Frank went on. "But he seemed perfectly natural when he arrived the next day—relaxed, cautious as always, but not unduly worried. Except he showed up in my waiting room between patients, a couple of kids with chicken pox, and *that* made him nervous." Frank chuckled. "It seems he's never had them."

"Chicken pox?" Emma laughed. So, Owen had an Achilles heel. Wait till the KGB found out about that one!

"In any case, I finished up and we drove out to the ruins. On the way he asked me about moving islands— *moving islands of the sea*, to be precise. He wanted to know if the line meant anything to me, in relation to Mayan history or myth, in relation to Uxmal. It didn't. It doesn't, as far as I know. So I asked him why, and he only told me he'd been sent here to look for something."

"For what, did he say?"

Frank shook his head.

Then, suddenly, Emma frowned. "You say he was *sent* here?"

"That's what he said."

"By whom?"

"He didn't tell me. I assumed—" Frank turned to her sharply. "You mean you don't know?"

"I haven't the slightest idea."

It wasn't Nichols, and Nichols himself controlled Owen. But if not Nichols, then who? And why? Had someone *wanted* Owen to be captured?

Emma turned to the hot air rushing through the window, felt it harsh on her face, loud in her mind. In an odd way it was bracing, isolating thoughts from fears. Had she been too quick to assume that Owen was only an accidental hostage? *Did* the terrorists know who he was? Had someone actually maneuvered him here on purpose? Then she caught herself doubting, like Nichols, and shook it off. Owen wasn't that easily maneuvered, unless he did know who and why and didn't mind. She turned back to Frank and said, "Go on. Tell me everything."

There was little more for Frank to tell, except it was clear that Owen thought someone might try to stop him. He had given Frank a phone number to call if there was trouble. At the ruins they split up, Owen taking the north end, Frank the south, and then trouble erupted with a fury.

Frank described what he'd seen the day of the seizure, from the first distant sound of helicopters to the gunshot, the silence that followed, his own escape. "I've been back four times since then," he said, "and I think I've got a pretty good picture of the way they're set up. I can show you better than I can tell you, as soon as we get to Muna."

"Are the ruins fenced?" Emma asked.

Frank smiled at her benignly. "All around. By the jungle."

She might have known, and preferred chain link. "How do you get there without being seen? The Pentagon seems to think it's out of the question."

"For the Pentagon, it probably would be. This isn't the place for anything heavy-handed."

"Do you know, for instance, that the terrorists have planted land mines all around the ruins?"

"I know and can show you where they are." Frank smiled again, enjoying himself at Emma's expense, or at the expense of the Pentagon. Then he went on gently. "My people have lived here for more years than anyone knows. We depend on the land for our existence. No change goes unnoticed. There's not a child in my village who couldn't spot a patch of hard earth, dug up and replaced, no matter how carefully, and then simply walk around it."

Emma smiled back. Yes, Frank would be useful—Frank or any kid on his block. The Pentagon, it seemed, had forgotten a very old lesson. *And a child shall lead them* . . .

"Do you know where they're holding Owen?" she asked.

"In the Governor's Palace, fourth room from the left. I can show you where it is, but I can't even guess how you're going to get to him. The Governor's Palace is set up high, as you'll see. It's extremely visible and heavily guarded. They've had at least thirty men patrolling it every time I've been there, and plenty of others standing by to assist them."

Emma had expected as much. "There's a way," she said.

"Maybe so, but it won't be easy. Even if you can get past the guards, they've got some kind of heavy screening over the doors. The screens are wired—"

"Electrified?"

"That's what it looks like."

Emma frowned. There were plenty of ways of dealing with electricity—shutting it off at its source, clipping the wires, even going into the nearest generating station and causing a blackout of the entire area. But she had to be careful not to provoke the terrorists or frighten them into rash action. Owen's rescue had to look like escape, unassisted, to discourage the terrorists from retaliating against Pious, Pompous, and Gooch and their friends, to keep the President and the Pentagon from asking difficult questions.

Frank slowed down for a curve in the road and held his speed on the other side. "Here we are," he said.

Emma turned to the window as they entered the village of Muna, where stone walls rose out of the dust on both sides of the road. They were crudely built and about waist high, like the stone walls that swept across the moors of Yorkshire and Scotland. But there was no feeling of space here. Muna was small and tightly packed, and the hard earth seemed to sprout chickens and children, dogs and geese, a few turkeys, and grown women who were little larger than children.

The women were walking beside the road in their embroidered *huipils,* carrying huge bowls of corn and meal or baskets of washing. At this time of day, the siesta just past, the men had returned to the fields, Frank explained. They farmed the way their ancestors farmed, with machetes and fire, by slashing and burning space out of the jungle.

And they lived the way their ancestors lived. Behind the stone walls sat clusters of small thatched houses—*chozas,* oval huts built of mud and sticks, some plastered and whitewashed under sharply peaked roofs, each with an open center door, some with windows. Most of the houses had electricity and running water, Frank said, but their design—the oval shape and peaked thatching—was as old as Uxmal. *Chozas* like these once surrounded the great white cities.

Emma nodded, saying nothing. Muna was colorful. Full of indigenous charm. Quaint poverty. And something else. Looking at the women by the road, she was once again startled by the pure lines of the faces. The Maya lived on here for better or worse, small and dark, enigmatic. Like the jungle itself, they took what they could from the land, made peace with the gods of sun and rain, replenished themselves, and continued. They survived this harsh life as they survived the Toltecs and the conquistadors—the foreigners come to castrate their sun—as their cities survived, with dignity and patience.

The women turned to wave as Frank's familiar van passed by them, and then, Emma noticed, they turned to each other, whispering and giggling. "I believe we're being gossiped about," she told him.

"I daresay!" Frank laughed lightly. "They worry because I'm not married—with some cause, I'll admit. There's not a lot for a bachelor to do in Muna on a night off."

No, not even a neighborhood cinema, though there was a Spanish cathedral. In this part of the world there was a cathedral for every city square, every village, and every hamlet, and most of them were built from the stones of demolished ancient temples. Beyond the cathedral lay two small concrete-block buildings, the schoolhouse, and Frank's clinic, home and office to him. No more public buildings. Muna was a far cry from Cambridge or Boston. Frank might belong to both worlds, but there couldn't be many women of either one who'd be willing or able to accept the other.

"Not an easy life for you," Emma said.

"No." Frank didn't argue. "But you needn't worry, the news of your presence won't spread far. We like to keep our gossip among ourselves here."

Emma wasn't worried. Frank was useful in more ways than one. Gossip made for good cover. They turned off the main road onto one that was unpaved and narrow, hardly more than a wide path through the trees, which met overhead and brushed the top of the van as it passed beneath them. The stone walls extended back off the highway and thatched huts still showed through the trees, though they came at wider intervals now. Muna's suburbs. Frank drove on a half-mile or more, then pulled over and switched off the ignition.

The house on the other side of the wall was like the ones along the main road, only larger. Actually it was two huts, a double *choza*, a squat figure eight, two rooms, one directly behind the other. A lop-eared black dog stretched out in the shade near the front door, and from inside came the sound of children laughing. All it lacked was a station wagon.

Emma climbed down from the van and followed Frank through an opening in the wall as a small, dark-eyed woman came to the door to meet them. Frank introduced his sister Nicte, who was wearing the traditional *huipil*, a long overblouse with a white petticoat and bright-colored flowers embroidered around the hem and curved neckline. Her hair was black, center parted, and pulled back from her face, and her features were like her brother's, only finer. On her face was the same demure smile of the women along the roadside, the same shy smiling eyes. No, Emma thought, not shy, merely gentle. Nicte was small—Emma towered above her—but her handshake was firm, her gaze steady.

"Please come in," she said softly. She turned, clapped her hands, issued orders in Yucatec, a regional version of the old Mayan language, and half a dozen children scampered out through the back door. The old dog, who had followed them into the house, loped off after the children. Then Nicte turned back to Emma and Frank, speaking English again. "I'll leave you alone while I start dinner," she said. "Could I get you something to drink first?"

It was cooler in the house by several degrees, but Emma's throat was dry from the heat and dust. She nodded. Nicte, she noticed as she watched her go, wasn't even perspiring. Her face was unlined, but her manner assured. She might have been eighteen or forty.

"Sit down," Frank said. "I'll get my maps and be right with you." He disappeared into the back after Nicte.

Emma stayed where she was, letting her eyes scan the front room, which was sparsely furnished with a table and chairs, a tall dish cupboard, and an old, treadle-model Singer sewing machine where Nicte had left some sort of work in progress. Whitewash covered the curving walls, a handwoven rug the concrete floor, and sleeping hammocks were pulled up into the ceiling. Emma sat down at the table, where fresh flowers were arranged in a pottery bowl. A crucifix hung on the wall above her, by a picture of Frank in his cap and gown—more important in this house, Emma guessed, than a portrait of the Holy Father.

A moment later Frank returned alone and put two glasses down on the table. Emma lifted hers—it was tea, strong and tart, lukewarm yet refreshing—while Frank spread his maps out before her. They were hand-drawn, his own work, done from observation and memory to show her the arrangement of the ruins and the countryside around them. She watched as his finger moved quickly from one location to another, listened as he described the pyramids and the temples, the position of the latest invaders.

When he was finished, she looked up. "How soon can I see it?" she asked.

"As soon as you like. The sooner, the better. It'll take a while to get there."

"How do we go?" She thought of the van. Too bulky.

"In comfortable shoes. On silent feet."

Emma knew what he was going to say.

Frank smiled. "We walk," he said. "Through the jungle."

▨ 9 ▨

No, Emma wasn't fond of nature, but if Owen had chosen to get himself captured here, in this scrappy jungle infested with a wide assortment of God's least attractive creatures, then here she would persevere, remembering as darkness drew near that reptiles were not nocturnal prowlers. Or maybe she had it backward, since night fell quickly deep in the bush, and the rattling she heard probably didn't emanate from crickets. All things considered, she was glad she'd thought to bring a guide who learned how to treat snakebite at Harvard.

Frank moved ahead of her, true to his word on silent feet, finding paths where Emma saw nothing but scrub and bramble. In one hand he carried a flashlight, its beam tightly focused, a thin laser ray which he kept to the ground, ever mindful of the terrorists' buried treasure. With his other hand he wielded a machete that could have been used on Marie Antoinette, so sharp was its bite, so heavy its blade. At his hip he wore an old service revolver. Emma had drawn her own automatic pistol, which was small but lethal at close range. There was more than one way to deal with a rattler.

Or a terrorist, though none appeared between Nicte's house and the ruins. Uxmal had been secured from within. The invaders kept vigil on the sky and for troop movements through the jungle. They had no fear of a lone man and woman, of native farmers, of anyone foolish enough to walk here.

Frank switched off the flashlight once they were past

the minefields, but he moved ahead with the unerring sense of a blind man in his own garden. Emma could hardly see him now; his clothes were as black as his hair, like her own, his face a vague blur in the darkness. She, too, moved by instinct. Heat had faded with the sun, and the air had turned cool and clammy. Clouds gave them cover, blotting out stars and moon, but ahead of them light glowed against the night sky, brighter for the surrounding isolation.

They reached the foot of a hill that rose at a sharp angle, a triangular mound of earth and stone thickly covered by vegetation. Frank touched Emma's arm, a signal for special caution. Then he started to climb the hill. Emma followed close behind him.

And suddenly, as they reached the top, Uxmal lay before them. Emma dropped to her knees and stretched out on her stomach. She pushed her automatic into her belt and produced a pair of binoculars. As she leaned against her elbows, her field of vision barely cleared the brush. She could see without being seen. Frank chose this spot well. It was the perfect position.

The great Mayan buildings were bathed in white light— and red light, and blue light, and green light—a *son et lumière* missing only the sound and voluntary viewers to see it. In between there were large patches of darkness, though a fire glowed from the center of the ruins, where terrorists on K.P. duty were busy cooking dinner. The rest of the terrorists, so it seemed, at least enough to portend serious problems, were in position at the Governor's Palace, which was ideally placed, stretched across Emma's view, straight ahead, about a quarter of a mile from them. Her binoculars, special order from the agency, brought faces into sharp focus, as if they were no more than inches away. Alert faces, yet relaxed. The terrorists weren't expecting trouble.

Emma studied Frank's maps in her mind and located their position. This overgrown hill was the Pyramid of the Old Woman, cleared once and then reclaimed by the jungle, which surrounded it on three sides. Without lowering her eyes she leaned closer to Frank, who was lying in the brush a few inches below. "Who was the old woman?" she whispered.

Frank looked up in the darkness. "You want to know *now*?"

"If there's a short version."

Frank's voice came back as low-pitched as her own. "By legend a witch, the mother of the magician. She hatched him from an egg full-grown, and then helped him become king of Uxmal."

Emma turned her binoculars to the right, to the huge elliptical Pyramid of the Magician, where grand staircases rose on two sides to a lofty house at the top, uninhabited now except for the guard standing watch on the roof, at the highest point of the ruins. "Ancient legend?" she asked.

Frank looked pained. "The people of Uxmal were wiser than that. Witches had no more place here than colored spotlights."

Emma swung her binoculars back across the ruins. Time had a way of improving ancient handiwork. Good lighting did too, etching carved facades deeper and clearer to the eye, but white light would have been sufficient. The colored spotlights were an attempt to add drama where drama already existed in abundance, to make tourist show. And yet Emma thought they might well serve a purpose.

She focused again on the Governor's Palace, where more fires burned behind door screens that were, in fact, wired into a central cable. Electrified. She counted off four doors from the left and studied the connections, one on each side, as well as she could in limited light. Then she focused in even tighter, and there he was— Owen, stretched out on a cot, a pillow doubled under his head. He had a cigarette in one hand, a paperback book in the other. Emma almost laughed. He was *reading*!

The ancient books of *The Chilam Balam*, if she had to guess, since Owen always liked to know his setting. Or maybe a guerilla manual lifted off one of his captors. Or perhaps he had chosen a light book tonight—*Bleak House*, or *Jude the Obscure*, or maybe the collected stories of

Nicolai Gogol. Emma preferred Euripides for her own light bedtime reading, but it wasn't the first time she'd disagreed with Owen.

At least he was alive and keeping occupied.

Emma watched him for several minutes with a mixture of exasperation, concern, and affection. Then she pulled back her binoculars to study the wide space between them. The Governor's Palace was, as Frank warned, set high on massive terraces. The uppermost tier followed the outlines of the building, forming a walkway around it, but the second one extended forward, a broad grassy plaza, in the middle of which a stone platform supported a piece of sculpture. Some sort of two-headed beast, an animal god perhaps, nothing Emma thought she would like to meet coming or going. Then the second tier dropped off sharply, creating a deep river of trees in a solid mass. It would probably be easier crossing the Nile or the Amazon.

"Are there paths down there?" she asked.

Frank's eyes followed the direction of hers; he shook his head. "There used to be, but they've all grown over. You can't go in that way without a machete, and machetes make noise."

"Then how do I go in?"

"The same way I came out. Underground."

"A tunnel?"

"A cave."

Frank explained: Geologically, the Yucatan peninsula was a huge limestone shelf, full of caves. To the south, dozens were visible from the road. At Chichen-Itza, one was open to tourists. But many, like this one, had never been charted or even explored. "I don't know if the archaeologists even know about it," he said, "but I think you can count on the fact that terrorists wouldn't."

Emma smiled at him in the darkness. "Don't tell me. You found it when you were seven years old and held your Scout meetings in it."

"More like nine," he replied. "No Scouts, just friends. It's a huge cave. The mouth is a couple of miles back, and there's an exit of sorts near that end of the ruins."

Emma didn't like the sound of that. "Of sorts?"

"If you don't mind climbing. It's really just a hole in the ground, but if I can get through it, you can."

"I see." The question was did she want to, and the answer affirmative against her better judgment—if for no other reason than to bring Owen back through it, making sure he knew what she'd sacrificed to get to him.

"Of course, that doesn't solve everything," Frank continued. "Where you come up out of the cave you'll still be in the jungle, and there's scrub for cover all the way to the end of the Governor's Palace. But from that point you'll be in the open. You'll be all right as long as no one is looking, but if someone does there's no place to hide."

Emma turned her binoculars to that end of the building, but what might have been seen from this angle was lost in darkness. She looked back at Frank. "Well," she said, "we'll just have to make sure no one does look."

"You have an idea?"

"Maybe. I'll need help."

"What about the electricity?"

"Same idea. Same help. What I need is a band of Mayan warriors."

"Warriors!" Frank looked at her as if he thought the heat of the day had affected her mind. "They aren't so easy to come by these days."

"I think you're wrong." Emma looked at her watch; nearly ten o'clock. "Come on, let's go. I think I know where to find them."

At midnight, a CIA agent in Merida broke into the Yucatan Power & Light Company and went through the office files. He didn't know exactly what was in the works, beyond the fact that it must be related to Uxmal. He only knew that orders had come from the seventh floor at Langley, and that if he ever mentioned what he'd done, even to a co-worker, he would get himself posted to Anaheim forever.

He found what he was looking for and left by way of a window.

72

* * *

At the same time in Elizabeth, New Jersey, another CIA agent was rifling through desks in the darkened headquarters of Computron, Inc. He was after diagrams. Someone high up at Langley wanted to see the inner workings of the company's model XR450 computer. He hadn't asked why. If he had, no one would have told him.

At 3:00 A.M. the Caribbean tide reversed itself and began moving toward the remote outer shore of Cozumel, carrying with it lobster, conch and shark, a fierce undertow, and a fleet of forty rubber rafts put to sea from a submarine that had surfaced briefly before diving again to hide beyond the island's famous clear blue waters.

This portion of Cozumel's seaward shore was unmarred by civilization. There were no hotels here, no houses— only long stretches of desolate beach, some set into hidden jungle coves where Blackbeard and Jean Laffite once lay in wait for passing Spanish galleons. Little had changed in a century or more. The men in the rubber rafts were also pirates.

They cleared the Palancár Reef, slipped ashore unseen under cover of overcast darkness, picked up what they came for, and sailed again, rowing harder now against their own weight, against time and tide and current. By prearranged schedule, the submarine broke through the surface of the sea as the first light of day spread across the horizon. Rafts vanished in the mist of dawn, along with their men and their cargo. Then the submarine dove and set course for deep water. By nightfall it would be replaced by another.

Colonel Boris Kreuzer's footsteps echoed the length of the empty corridor, where human sentries had been made obsolete by electronic scanners, the computerized eyes and ears of the command center, which was located on a fishing trawler in the bay. Any person or object not programmed into the system would set off a silent alarm and fill the corridor with numbing gas, against which those who worked here had been immunized, Colonel Boris Kreuzer among them.

Kreuzer was in charge and satisfied with the progress of the operation. The corridor and the rooms opening from it were made of prefabricated wallboard, painted a sterile white and sealed with spray-on foam that blocked sound and light absolutely when it hardened. The complex had its own generator, its own air-conditioning system. There was no hint of moisture in the air, no sign of stalactites or stalagmites, no evidence that the complex existed within a series of caverns.

He removed a plastic card from his pocket as he reached the end of the corridor and pushed it into a narrow opening in what appeared to be a solid wall. A moment later the wall slid open before him, revealing a chamber with a red light glowing down from the ceiling. He slipped the card into a second slot in the wall of the chamber. Ten seconds passed. The corridor closed behind him. Another ten seconds and the red light went out, throwing the tiny space into darkness. Kreuzer, who suffered from claustrophobia, took a deep breath as he counted off the last seconds.

Finally, a second security wall opened and he stepped into one last room, where light filtered past an ordinary door that opened with a key in a double cylinder. Kreuzer waited for the soft click of the wall sliding shut behind him, then fit his key into the lock and emerged into the fresh, cold air of the outside.

Abraham Lincoln towered above him. White marble columns. Wide steps descending to a shallow pool filled with snow now instead of water. An unsuspecting U.S. Parks Service guard in winter coat and hat with ear flaps. And all around, official police barriers.

Cars were beginning to move along Independence Avenue, getting an early start on rush-hour traffic. A few serious runners were already out on the paths that lined the Mall. In the distance, beyond the Washington Monument, the dome of the Capitol washed pale against the bright winter sun, ahead of the day's rush of tourists and legislative action. But the Lincoln Memorial had been closed for two weeks, and so were the caverns beneath it.

Colonel Boris Kreuzer, dressed in workingman's clothes, nodded to the guard and hurried down the steps to his car, an American-made compact model. It had been a simple matter to arrange a slipping of rock that undermined the safety of the structure, an easy thing to come in with the low repair bid. That was all done beforehand. Now the underground complex was finished, on time. Kreuzer smiled. All that remained to be done today was to signal the trawler in the Chesapeake. The real work would get underway tomorrow.

By the middle of the morning, Emma had accomplished her initial objectives. She had contacted Nichols with several requests, including supplies, which would be delivered by courier on the four o'clock plane at Merida. She had learned what she needed to know about the lighting system at Uxmal. She had located a store that sold Glenfiddich and rewired a computer. She had taught Frank how to pick a lock. And she had found her Mayan warriors.

Or maybe they were priests; it didn't matter. Either would provide what she needed.

When, finally, she went to bed, she was tired enough not to mind that "bed" was one of Nicte's sleeping hammocks. She needed rest more than anything now. Her main objective would be accomplished before the sun rose tomorrow. Her plan was set. She would rescue Owen this evening.

⚒ 10 ⚒

"Mrs. Brendan will agree, I think," said Judd Sims, and Lucy could feel his eyes turning to her. She could feel the weight of his gaze, his appeal to her, his unspoken dismissal of Henry. "Won't you, Mrs. Brendan."

She was sitting with her back to the room, to Judd Sims, and to Henry, leaning against the sofa cushions, one hand lightly tracing patterns of frost on the Palladian window panes rising above her in an elegant fan of glass. It was a few minutes past noon, and the sun was just starting to strike this west window, to melt the frost and reveal the snow-covered White House grounds through a blur of moisture. Cold air seeped past the edges of glass, but Lucy's face was flushed with irritation. It bothered her when she couldn't see things clearly.

Now, though she had heard every word, she turned and said, "I beg your pardon, Judd?"

Sims, the President's chief of staff, a small man of thirty-five with a thatch of blond hair and flat eyes set into a flat face, was sitting in a chair at the end of the couch, closer to Lucy than to Henry. "I think the President should call a press conference on Uxmal without delay," he said. "I'm talking about prime-time TV. I want him to show himself willing to face the press on a tough issue and, at the same time, explain his position to the people before the opposition can seize momentum and start to make him look ineffective. I think he's got to do it, not only as a matter of maintaining control, or the appearance of control, but also with an eye on next year's election. I thought I could count on you to help me convince him."

Henry, of course, would prefer to deliver a formal prewritten address. Lucy knew he hated press conferences, as he hated all forms of confrontation. She lifted her chin defensively, confused by the inner sources of her own irritation. She had made Sims repeat himself because what he'd said once was even worse the second time, and she wanted to make sure Henry noticed. She resented Sims for his lack of respect for Henry, though it showed in subtler ways than it had when Henry was only Vice-President. She resented herself for thinking of him, yet another Riker holdover, as the *President's* chief of staff and not Henry's. She resented Benjamin Riker himself for casting a shadow so large that it lay over the White House even now, nearly a year after he died, making Henry's own shadow fade all the more by comparison. But she also believed that Sims was right and enjoyed the look that showed on his face as he waited for her approval. She liked the influence that was hers by default, liked and hated it at the same time. She did not want to be a puppeteer to her own husband, but for too many years she had been bored by the role assigned to her in Washington.

Her eyes shifted to Henry, who looked tired, she thought, a little more gray, a little less groomed, and then back to Sims. "Does he need convincing?"

The answer was clear in a slight lifting of eyebrows on the part of the President's chief of staff, clear but fleeting. Sims brought his face quickly under control, which was somehow more disrespectful than if he hadn't.

"The President," Lucy said, against her own feelings, "will make these decisions for himself."

Across the room, Henry's mouth tightened, and he glared at Sims over the rim of his coffee cup. Or, Lucy wondered, a little startled—more than a little startled—was the glare meant for *her* instead of Judd?

She looked away uncomfortably, let her eyes linger briefly on the wall where a faint outline was all that remained of the forged Jefferson portrait, made a mental note to mention the spot to the head housekeeper for cleaning, and realized that she was just that—*uncomfortable* with the new Henry. She wasn't sure she knew him.

Henry finished his coffee and put the cup down on the large coffee table between them, on top of which Judd Sims had spread his inevitable notes and papers. "With a crisis of this sort," he said, "opposition is automatic. There are bound to be differing points of view, some strongly felt—"

"And expressed," Sims broke in. He pressed his point. "That's what we have to counteract before it starts. There are plenty of hotheads in Congress who'll be jumping to demagogue this one, once the smoke has cleared, once it's obvious you can't bring it to a quick conclusion. We're in the honeymoon phase now, everyone standing firm behind the President, but it's been four days; it won't last much longer. We can't allow this situation to become too volatile, and what we do now, Mr. President, could make all the difference later. Uxmal could be your making or breaking."

Lucy made a show of finding and lighting a cigarette, remembering her own words to Henry when the first call came through about Uxmal. His *chance*, now his making or breaking. He had been horrified then, but now he only looked a little more weary.

"That may be," he said. "I don't underestimate hotheads in Congress, but I think *more* members will be on my side. I'm concerned about other things. I don't want anger, demonstrations, violence here at home—or in Mexico, for that matter. I don't want people getting *hurt* by this."

"Then all the more reason for you to go straight to the people. You can give vent to *their* anger." Sims leaned forward, his eyes earnest on Henry's face. "We'll write you an opening statement," he said, "a strong statesmanlike posture. We'll show you calm under fire. You'll call for restraint, and you'll set a good example. If it works, they'll love you for it."

"If it works," Henry muttered. "Why can't the same thing be accomplished with a speech? I don't want to hold a press conference now. There are too many questions I simply can't answer."

"Because," Sims replied, "to make this work, we've got to have the press on our side, and they're snapping to get at you. Their sympathies are with us so far. They know this is tough. But we can't keep putting them off, or we'll lose them."

Henry nodded vaguely.

"And you don't have to worry about the questions you can't answer publicly. We'll give you answers ahead of time. We'll alert the networks for tomorrow night, which will leave us a full day to rehearse. Meantime, I've got someone working on your opening statement. We can have a draft for you by this time tomorrow."

"No." Henry's face changed; his eyes turned hard, like his voice. "If I must do it, then I want the draft before I go to bed tonight, in time to order changes if I want them."

Sims shrugged agreeably. "Certainly, if that's the way you want it."

"Is there anything else?"

Sims glanced through his papers and picked out a memo, which he scanned quickly and then looked up. "Your Florida trip."

"For the space shuttle launch?" Henry frowned. "I thought the damn thing was broken."

"NASA called this morning. Whatever their problem was, they've fixed it. The launch is on, and we need to decide if you're going to go—or if, under the circumstances, the trip ought to be canceled."

Henry sighed. "I suppose I should be glad they've solved the problem—the director seemed pretty gloomy the last time we talked—but, hell, do we have to make a decision this afternoon? Can't this, at least, wait?"

"It can't wait long. The launch is next week."

"Then let's use Uxmal as an excuse and cancel."

"I don't think you should." Sims paused, glanced at the memo in his hand, and then dropped it on the table.

"Let me give you a straight opinion. You may have some tough opposition in the Florida primary next year, and it's an important one to win. The campaign committee down there is all primed for your visit. A lot of key people have been invited to sit in the VIP stands; even more are coming to a reception after the launch. It could be an extremely valuable trip. I hate to see you pass it up."

Lucy, watching him thoughtfully, wondered how much Judd Sims really wanted Henry to win the election. There was talk he was thinking of going back home and running for Congress himself, that Conklin Pierce was encouraging him to do it. She leaned forward and asked, "But how would it *look*?"

Sims turned to face her. "That's the problem, of course. People may think the President ought to be in the White House, and they don't understand after all these years that where the President goes, the White House goes with him. On the other hand, I think we can get away with it, and possibly score a few extra points, if we stick with the image of calm under fire. The President won't be pushed around by terrorists. He's on the job, in control, but he's also going to continue business as usual."

Lucy flinched inwardly. They might have been talking about a piece of cardboard. She put out her cigarette, glancing at Henry as she did, resentment rising once more inside. Sometimes she wondered how much *he* wanted to win the election.

No, Lucy knew Henry better than that. He did want to win. For all his protesting, for all his doubts, for all his discomfort with the pressures of power, he liked being President. It was something that ran very deep in him. He wanted the job. He just didn't want to say so.

And that ran deep too—back to a father whose accomplishments and success, whose very manner so overwhelmed the son that they became self-defeating. Even now that his father was dead, as a matter of proof and perhaps striking back, Henry *needed* to succeed in a way that was undeniable. As President he surpassed his

80

father—in the public view if not his own—in politics, the most fiercely competitive national arena. But the job had come to him almost for the asking, quite literally by accident. The title was his, but not the victory; he knew he hadn't earned it. The proof he was looking for—proof of his own worth, his own mettle—was still lacking.

Now, facing the chance to run and win on his own, he wanted the prize but feared the fight. The very public nature of the job, which he needed for reinforcement, also raised the spectre of public failure. To compete for the prize Henry had to declare his intentions, and he was reluctant to do that. Because he might lose, a simple fact of political life. He did not want the world to know that it mattered.

All of this, Lucy realized now, though she hadn't quite seen it then, was what she had meant when she spoke to Henry of the *chance* offered by Uxmal. But the election was almost irrelevant, she thought, because Henry, whether he knew it or not, needed a different kind of success, something solid to lay at his own door, unmistakably, something that wasn't affected by national mood or whim or the shifting trends of public opinion. He needed to give real leadership in a matter of lasting importance. He needed to *win* at Uxmal. He needed to know *he* had done it.

And wasn't that what the new Henry was trying to do?

Lucy pressed back conflicting thoughts. Perhaps she could make the election trip for him.

A short buzz sounded from the phone before she could suggest it—one buzz, a signal for the President. Henry picked it up, listened a moment, and something in his face tightened. "We'll meet in the Cabinet Room in ten minutes," he said and put the phone back into place. He stood up. Lucy looked at him, waiting.

"I have to go now," he said. "We've had news." He turned to Sims. "The Florida trip will have to wait."

"News?" Lucy asked, but Henry was on his way to the door. Sims gathered his papers, shoved them into an attaché case, and moved quickly to follow. Lucy watched them go, her eyes puzzled, her lips slightly parted. There was a firmness in Henry's step that she didn't like without knowing why.

Then, at the door, he turned back, and the mask suddenly fell away. A side of Lucy rose up ferociously, overpowering doubt and resentment. There was *nothing* she wouldn't do for him when he needed her, when she saw in his eyes that he did—and she saw it now. More than that, she saw that he was frightened.

"News," he said. "We've had contact from the terrorists."

¤¤ 11 ¤¤

After Henry had gone, Lucy phoned down to her secretary to bring her mail and appointment book here, to the West Sitting Room. She didn't feel like working in her office, nor like working at all, for that matter. But mail, busy work, she supposed, would keep her mind occupied and away from larger problems. As she waited, she crossed the room to the stereo cabinet and started to thumb through the records.

Then the telephone rang again. She picked it up, reaching for her cigarettes.

"Yes?"

She found her lighter, flicked it on and off. Her attention focused.

"Yes, Mr. Bingham," she said. "Have you learned anything about the portrait?"

Conklin Pierce arrived in the Cabinet Room later than the others; Nichols was glad to see him. If his presence helped stiffen Henry's spine, then his presence was welcome, because stiffening Henry was going to need if he hoped to grab a shred of control over Uxmal. The news was not only bad, but impossible.

Impossible, and the Speaker knew it as soon as he entered the room. Futility hung in the air above the long mahogany table and was mirrored in the eyes of the cast already assembled. Eight players in leather armchairs, with White House paper and sharpened pencils lined up at each place, as if a few finely honed notes might help them avoid the showdown that was coming.

Pierce made nine. He lowered his slight frame into a chair across from the President. "I came as soon as I could," he said. "What is it?"

"Tell him," Henry said, with a nod to the Secretary of State.

Daniel Callahan picked up the cable from the folder that lay open before him, then shifted in his chair to look at the Speaker. "The Mexican government has made contact on our behalf with the terrorists," he began, his voice cool and precise, professionally void of emotion. "These are their stated conditions. It seems they have three separate demands and are going to reveal them one at a time. When we fulfill the first one, they will release the nonofficial hostages. With the second, they'll release the staff members. With the third, all but one of the congressmen. That one will be held as insurance until they've abandoned the site, and then released in a manner to be determined later."

"That's a little vague," the Speaker observed, and Callahan nodded.

"That's the only point where they are vague," he said. "The rest is quite clear. If at any time we fail to meet their conditions, they say they'll set off enough explosives to blow Uxmal to the stars and all remaining hostages along with it."

Pierce winced. "Do they mean it?"

"We certainly can't assume they don't." Callahan paused briefly, then consulted the cable once again. "Their first concern, they say, is 'economic redress for years of oppression caused by Yankee imperialism in Latin America.' Their words, of course—not mine, not the Mexicans'. What they want is legislation—"

"*Legislation?*" Pierce frowned, startled.

"—to change the status of all Mexicans currently in the United States without legal sanction, and to open the border to others who want to work here. In fact, to throw the border wide open. Essentially what they want is unrestricted passage for any Mexican citizen who can

84

find a job, permanent or temporary, anywhere in this country."

"Dear God, is that all?"

Callahan dropped the cable back into the folder. "That's it, and it's only the first demand. I don't like to think what they'll ask for next."

There wasn't much point in worrying about the next one, Nichols thought to himself. If the terrorists meant what they said, he couldn't reasonably see a way around this one. The American people, sons and daughters of refugee stock, were in no mood to make room for anyone's huddled masses yearning to be free—or at least employed—and with some cause. Jobs were scarce as it was. The golden streets of the Land of Opportunity had been rolled up, the welcome mat yanked in, the porch light extinguished. In the face of that and the first demand from Uxmal, Henry's hopes for a peaceful settlement looked pretty well shattered.

Pierce looked suddenly older, old and bent, and more than a little worried. "They can't be serious," he said. "What they're asking for is preposterous!"

"But where does that leave us?" asked General Marks, running a hand through his iron gray hair, resuming the discussion where it had been interrupted when Pierce arrived. "We can't hope to reason with them."

"We can try," Henry said. He turned back to Pierce. "What do you think you *might* get through Congress?"

The lines in Pierce's forehead deepened. "I don't think I understand—"

"As a point of negotiation we might, for example, offer to raise our immigration quotas for Mexico and agree to apply the increases against the same number of illegals as their presence here is discovered."

The Speaker was openly astonished, like everyone else at the table, including Nichols, who, leaning back in his chair, sat up sharply. Daniel Callahan gasped. George Dent cleared his throat. Judd Sims's eyebrows shot up and his mouth fell open. Pierce's mouth opened too, but nothing came out. It was Bert Engel who expressed the dismay they were all feeling.

"Mr. President," he said coldly, "we *can't* negotiate a demand of this kind. We can't even give them a *piece* of what they're asking for."

Henry turned to him slowly and said, "I'll do what I have to."

"But it's blackmail, as you well know. A dangerous, *dangerous* precedent—to consider changing the law of the land in response to terrorists' threats. Congress will go berserk! Christ, we just can't do it!"

Henry stuck to his ground. "Congress has gone berserk before. Any new law we pass can be repealed later."

Nichols, not normally one to quibble over expedience, agreed completely with the National Security Advisor. Henry's spine had stiffened all right—but he was wrong, way out of his depth. On his own, of course, he couldn't change any law, since he couldn't force Congress to act, and he couldn't hope even to influence Congress without the cooperation of the Speaker. And Pierce, who was studying Henry's face with a mixture of shock and disappointment, would never permit such a thing. Henry couldn't have his own way, thank God, but the line of his thinking was frightening. Nichols leaned back again, blessing the Founding Fathers for making the branches of government separate but equal. He also swore a silent curse on the mountain that killed Ben Riker.

Then a new thought struck him and he sat up again. "Wait a minute," he said. "There's something interesting in what you just said, Mr. President. Any new law we pass could be repealed later. The terrorists surely *know* that. And if they do, what kind of game are they playing? Why are they asking for something that could be so easily undone once the hostages are released—if they really plan to release them?"

"Perhaps they're willing to take what they can in the time they have," Henry suggested. "Or maybe they're using this first demand as a test, to find out how far we're willing to go with them."

"In which case it's time to let them know how far we *won't* go," Engel insisted.

86

"Not necessarily." Henry turned to Nichols. "You've made a good point, Ed. Maybe we can give them exactly what they really want—a clearly specified time, say two weeks, a month perhaps, of unrestricted border passage that wouldn't count against existing quotas." He looked back at Pierce. "What do you think, Connie? Could you get a temporary suspension of quotas through Congress? Bear with me for now. Is it even remotely possible?"

Pierce continued to study the President's face, but his gaze had turned thoughtful. "It certainly wouldn't be easy," he said. "There would be a lot more to it than we even see here. I wonder, for instance, how we'd prevent the Communists, or even smugglers, from exploiting the situation. Problems like those would have to be considered and dealt with before I could give you any real appraisal. I don't know." He shook his head. "I've collected a good many chits through the years. I suppose I might get something through if I called them all in at once. But Henry, we could be talking about *huge* numbers of people. Even if I can get Congress to act, the American people are going to be hell-bent to hang us."

"That's a risk I'm willing to take," Henry said. "I don't think it will happen. What I want to do is buy time."

"Toward what end?"

"If the terrorists think we're serious about cooperating with them, that we'll even attempt to change the law, then they'll have to give Congress time to act—for legislation to be considered and written, passed through committee, reported onto the floor, debated, amended and voted on—and all of that in both houses. That could take a couple of months, don't you think?"

"It could take a couple of *years*," Pierce said.

"Months is enough. By the end of March, we'll have succeeded or failed. We'll either have the hostages home, or Uxmal will have been reduced to ashes." Henry turned to Hayfield and said, "Tell them about the Delta plan."

Hayfield, smug as ever, opened his attaché case and

removed a thick file bound in blue, which he opened on the table. He looked up, turning his head for a brief, direct contact with each pair of eyes looking back at him. Then he began. "Most of you will remember Major MacKendrick. . . ."

Nichols's breath caught in his throat. Yes, they would all remember MacKendrick, except perhaps Judd Sims, who was probably no more than twelve when the fighting broke out in Korea. No first name was needed. There was only one MacKendrick, and he belonged to the Pentagon. He was one among thousands of soldiers sent to Korea, but he proved his ability countless times, leading raiding parties into the north to rescue American POWs. His name surely would have been set in bronze if he hadn't violated every law ever conceived in the name of justice. MacKendrick was effective because he was ruthless. But he *was* effective.

And now, Nichols knew as he listened to Hayfield with a cold anger growing inside, now DIA, which had taken MacKendrick for its own after Korea, had made him a gift of Delta Squad, the Army's tough antiterrorist strike force. DIA had given him carte blanche for resources and expenses. And MacKendrick had come up with a plan. Nichols loosened his tie. Hayfield deserved to be smug. He'd done it again, been there first with what the President wanted. Well, Henry might be impressed, but Nichols, sniffing the air, smelled disaster.

"MacKendrick claims he can bring the hostages out with a high probability of minimal casualties on our side," Hayfield was saying, "using sixty men, four lightweight glider planes, a dark night, and two dozen cannisters of incapacitating gas. We've been through it with him step-by-step, and we think he can do it too. There's only one problem. The plan requires maneuvers Delta currently isn't trained to perform, primarily landing gliders in that jungle, and MacKendrick won't take his men in there—he won't risk their lives—until they're fully prepared. He needs time."

"How much time?" someone asked.

"Two months."

Henry Brendan's strategy came clear on two fronts. With his willingness to negotiate an unthinkable price for the hostages—a position that would, as the Speaker said, stir harsh public opinion against him—he was only stalling for time until he could *seize* the hostages back from the terrorists. And Henry had just given a fine performance. He knew he wasn't held in high esteem by some of the men at this table—his own advisors, his own crisis team. He knew and had set them up, had played on their easy assumption that he simply couldn't make tough decisions. Nichols had to admire the man, even though he had been trapped with the rest. Damned if Henry hadn't been downright cunning!

But if he were laughing up his sleeve, it didn't show on his face. "Two months," he said. "Two months at the most, and during that time we have to give every appearance of trying to negotiate in good faith. The terrorists must be made to believe that we mean it, that the lives of the hostages are our paramount concern, that we're willing to pay very nearly any price they ask, or at least that we're serious about trying. If they think we're weak, all the better; they'll only hold out longer. In the meantime, Delta will be in training, under conditions of absolute secrecy, and it goes without saying that I won't tolerate a whisper of any of this from anyone at this table."

He turned to Callahan. "You, Dan, will leave for Mexico City tonight. I want you to supervise the negotiations directly. If the terrorists won't agree to a counter-proposal, then tell them we'll try for the whole thing, a complete lifting of quotas. Just make sure they understand we can't do it overnight. Make sure you keep them hanging."

Next, he looked at Pierce. "As soon as we know what they will accept, I want you to start moving legislation through Congress. Do your damnedest to hang it up in committee and, if you can, keep it from being associated publicly with the terrorists."

"I'll do my best," Pierce said, "but I can't give you any guarantees about keeping it quiet."

"Your best is good enough. If someone blows the lid off, I'm willing to take the heat for it." Henry paused, then added, "Are you?"

Pierce smiled. "I've taken a lot of heat in my time."

Henry returned the smile briefly. Then his eyes shifted to Hayfield. "Tell MacKendrick he's got three weeks."

"Three *weeks*! But Mr. President . . . !"

"As a matter of fact, I'll give him a month, but tell him three weeks to give us a margin of safety."

"He may object."

"If he does, he's fired. And I'll cut off his pension."

"Yes, sir, I'll tell him."

"I want to move sooner with this," Henry said. "I don't know how long we can maintain the pretense. But from now until this is finished, all of us, in our public and private behavior, will conform absolutely to the deception I've outlined here. We're firm in our conciliatory posture. We intend to negotiate this through, whatever the cost. Is that understood?"

There were nods of agreement around the table. Chairs were pushed back, and the cast rose as Henry got up to go. A few minutes later, the Cabinet Room was empty.

Among the men who emerged from the West Wing door into the brisk winter air and a sea of waiting press, there might have been others like Nichols who doubted the wisdom of Henry's plan, but even they could no longer deny the existence of a living President.

◈ 12 ◈

Back in his office, Henry collapsed into his chair, his face pale, his hands sweating, his knees so weak he wasn't sure he could stand up again if he had to. "My God," he said, "I need a drink!"

"No, you don't," Conklin Pierce replied and sat down in a chair by the desk.

Henry glanced at him, scowling. "Don't tell me what I need!" he snapped, but then his face blanched at the sound of his voice and he reached across to clasp Pierce's arm. "I'm sorry. I'm just tense from the strain of the meeting. I couldn't have gotten through it without you."

"Nonsense."

"I mean it. You or a drink."

Pierce chuckled at the company he was keeping. "Well, you don't need a drink," he said, "and you're underestimating yourself, as usual. You were brilliant in there, in absolute control from the beginning. You're doing fine. I'm proud of you, Henry."

"Whatever you say." Henry leaned back and closed his eyes, trying to ease the tension out of his body. He didn't want to argue about his own feelings.

"What's more," Pierce said, "your father would have been proud."

Henry grunted without looking up. "It's never too late, I suppose."

"He was always proud of you."

"Maybe so. Maybe so." Henry still didn't want to argue, but he opened his eyes to look at the face of his

91

old friend. He sometimes forgot that Connie had known his father, that they were friends first, years ago, when Henry was still a boy. He sometimes forgot that there were more than twenty years between them. Now, in the soft light of the Oval Office, seeing the lines etched into Connie's skin, the soft look of age in his eyes, the frailty of his body, Henry was suddenly gripped with a new fear.

But Pierce, who knew him so well, seemed to know what was on his mind. "Don't worry," he said gently. "I'll be here as long as you need me."

Nichols never understood winter street conditions in Washington, where the threat of mere flurries was enough to activate snow emergency routes, make government offices send thousands of workers home on staggered hours, and still cause a late traffic snarl that would do credit to Cairo in a blizzard. He leaned back in the seat as his driver came to yet another full stop by the Lincoln Memorial, where lights brightened the great pillars and square-cut stone in spite of reconstruction work in progress. Nichols glanced at the monument absently, his mind on the meeting just finished.

He did not share the President's confidence in Mac-Kendrick, if only because MacKendrick's record was fashioned so long ago. He'd been an advisor to DIA since Korea, but he had retired from the field twenty years ago, and twenty years was ample time to get rusty. The rescue mission might work if MacKendrick were lucky, but Nichols had no intention of leaving Owen to a whim of fate, nor to the statistical chance of "probable minimal casualties." He had no intention of calling back Emma Thatcher.

On the other hand, he was willing to admit that the President didn't have much choice. Negotiating the law was out of the question. MacKendrick's plan was probably as good as any, at least until Owen was reached and rescued and came up with something better.

Nichols sighed as the car moved ahead once again, into a position where he could see the figure of Lincoln between two pillars. Workmen were carrying supplies inside, past barricades and Parks Service guards, no doubt collecting overtime pay as they worked through the night to shore up the shrine, to make it safe for tourists again. Then he turned away, switched on a small light, and opened his attaché case.

There was nothing he could do now but wait until he heard from Thatcher.

Colonel Boris Kreuzer, unaware of the proximity of the CIA director, was supervising the arrival of crates, meant to look like construction supplies, in the foam-enclosed caverns under the Lincoln Memorial. One room was full now, its door tightly sealed. Another room was filling.

If Kreuzer had known Nichols was nearby, caught in a jam of slow-moving traffic, he might have been given a moment's pause, grounds for worry. But then he probably would have smiled as a show of faith in his own security system—and because accidental proximity brought with it a certain touch of irony.

The Lincoln Memorial would reopen sometime in the future, when each of its newly built underground rooms had been filled and sealed for storage. But the caverns beneath the monument would be declared officially unsafe and off limits—the construction company would insist—and Nichols, among others, was not to know why.

Until the time when it no longer mattered.

⊠ 13 ⊠

To the ancient Maya caves were places of dread—gates of Hell, the home of the dead, the unearthly—and at the moment Emma wasn't inclined to argue. It didn't help much that the mouth of this cave, however hidden by jungle scrub, came complete with jagged teeth. She ducked past them, shining her flashlight ahead, expecting to find the throat and belly of a slumbering beast who was mean when aroused and probably ticklish. But the throat was merely a tunnel, long and low, and the belly the first of several vault-ceilinged chambers. Emma moved ahead quickly, wondering if Jonah himself had performed with such valor.

She carried the flashlight in one hand, her automatic in the other, but the light was only a pinpoint ray, so deep and vast was the night here. The darkness had a presence of its own, almost tangible. Emma shook off a chill, though the cave was warm, and memories of monsters who lurked beyond the edges of light, under the bed, and in yawning closet caverns. She glanced over her shoulder, then stopped, looking back. Her light played across limestone walls that towered above her. There was nothing here, only silence and gloom. No spirits. No glyphs or paintings. No pottery shards. No sign that the people of Uxmal ever left high ground to explore their own cellar.

And that, Emma thought, was a point for their good judgment.

She hurried on, breathing harder now. The air was no

94

longer warm, but hot and heavy. There was moisture somewhere, and heat locked in, like a New York subway in summer. Heavy air, vile smelling. She might have known there were bats here.

And snakes. Dear God! Two of them slithered across the beam of her flashlight, bright green with grinning yellow mouths. Emma raised her gun and fired two shots, spats of thunder in silence and gloom; two flashes of blue lightning pierced the darkness. She stayed where she was, scarcely breathing. Then slowly she moved the flashlight again. One snake was dead. The other one was missing.

Emma saw no advantage in staying to find out where it went. She moved ahead, almost running now, past leering serpents and devil bats with their teeth bared, past spiders and lizards, past monsters far worse for their unknown shape, the ones that crept out of dark closets. Then the ground suddenly dropped away, and she found herself sliding—down and down on fanny and feet, over bruising rocks and something wet she hoped was just mud. She was really beginning to wonder if Owen was worth it.

She came to a stop with a bone-jarring jolt in yet another cave chamber, and her flashlight caught the glint of something shining. She raised the beam into the darkness ahead. Precious water, right here! An underground river, so clear, so long undisturbed, Emma had to look twice to be sure it was there. She couldn't tell how deep it was—not more than a foot or two, she thought—but still it was water. How like the gods not to tell the Maya.

Emma knelt by the river, looking more like bedraggled Odysseus than Amphitrite. She wasn't dressed for this steamy underground climate, in a veil of gauze for a water sprite, but for the night air, for camouflage, in khaki-colored combat fatigues to blend with stone walls and terrorist guards. With them she wore a full dark beard, a wig to cover her own smooth hair, heavy eyebrows to counter the feminine lines of her eyes and thick lashes—all of that and a backpack full of equipment that came on the four o'clock plane, special order from Nichols. She leaned forward, dipped a hand into the water, splashed it onto her neck and face, leaned forward again.

But this time her hand halted above the river. Something moved beneath its glass-smooth surface; it moved unseen, more sensory than certain. Emma stared at the place where her hand had been, wondering if her mind had given way to the heat or the darkness—or her own loathing of the cave. She looked closer.

Fish, of all things! Even here in this dark cavern river. They had tiny black eyes and skeleton bones; their skin and flesh, deprived of light, were transparent. *Ghost* fish! Emma's skin crawled. A mistake, surely. Not even nature would have thought to create them.

Her palms and forehead felt clammy. Ghost fish in the river, bat stench in the air, and monsters in the darkness. Enough of this! She pulled herself up and switched off the flashlight. A moonbeam shot down to replace it.

Frank's hole in the ground, fifteen feet overhead. Her exit.

Emma switched on the light and studied the wall beneath the overhead opening, seeking notches and crevices in the stone, hand and toeholds for climbing. She touched the wall and, as quickly, drew back, a reflex against sense of movement. Then she reached out again. A tingling met her fingertips—and, yes, it was there in her feet as well. She had been too absorbed to notice.

Vibration, somewhere. From where? What *was* it?

Oh, lord! The cave was about to come down in a thundering of rubble, entombing the monsters and ghost fish and Emma right along with them. Hand and toeholds appeared on command. She was up and out of the cave in the flash of a second.

Out into the open air of the night, out into the bramble and trees. The Governor's Palace, though blocked from view, was only yards away. No city ever looked so good. Beautiful, civilized jungle!

She slipped off her backpack, breathing in cool air, and laughed at herself in the darkness. The ground, of course, did not cave in. The vibration she felt, for that much was real, was probably caused by a rock slide in the distance. Frank said these caves were everywhere, that some of them interconnected. Still, she was glad to be out in the open. She checked the time. A quarter to one. Fifteen minutes to wait. She didn't mind. No cave, no monsters, no ghost fish. The jungle was lovely!

She leaned back and looked up into the trees, where a snarl of branches and heavy vines made a patchwork of the moonlight. Last night's overcast sky had opened up to a quarter moon and a million stars. Nature, as usual, didn't want to help make things happen. And yet the sky was spectacular, as big a sky as she'd ever seen, huge above the hedge-clipped trees. Deep. Vast and eternal. No wonder the Maya had studied the stars. They lived on the very threshold of *space*—and they always had, according to their own ancient epics, for in the beginning before there was man, never mind his rib; before animals, birds, and insects; before stones and caves, forest and jungle; even before the great dust puff of creation, there was only the sky. It had always been with them, an invitation to seek and to know. Nothing had really changed very much in the meantime.

Except something pricked Emma's spine, a warning. Then a hiss of sound sent a chill through every nerve cell in her body. A vine arched its back, swung its head around, and found her.

The snake was black, a silhouette. Emma couldn't see the pattern of its skin and didn't have to. One shake of its tail was revealing enough. She had seen its design carved into the temples of Uxmal. *Crotalus Durissus*. Ahau-Tzab-Can. The rattlesnake of the Yucatan, long sacred to the Maya.

The snake stiffened and hissed, its nasty tongue darting past poison fangs, its castanet tail speaking in cold vibrato. They were face to face, a few feet apart, Emma and the evilest of gods.

Ahau-Tzab-Can meant to make her worship.

⧳ 14 ⧳

Frank, dressed in black, his face smudged with dirt, crouched in the bush less than a mile from Emma, in back of the concrete building where tourists bought their tickets to see Uxmal. He knelt in the dark, which was deep against the contrast of spotlights at the front of the building, where a paved stone walk led into the ruins near the Pyramid of the Magician. The smell of coffee and a murmur of voices came to him through the night. Voices and occasional laughter. The ticket office was the terrorists' cantina.

But Frank was behind it, away from the door, away from the ticket window, facing a small wooden shed that backed onto the concrete building. At 1:00 A.M. he slipped out of the bush and moved toward it.

The lock on the door was a simple one, so Emma said, designed to discourage vandals and not professionals. Frank was a professional, in a manner of speaking. He removed a slim metal wand from his pocket and slipped it into the keyhole, as deftly as a surgical probe, then bent an ear close to listen for the click of moving tumblers. The latch opened and he stepped inside, closing the door behind him.

A control console sat on a table before him, lengthwise across the back, filling half the room, leaving space for no more than one or two people. A confusion of switches and levers and keys. A small data terminal. Computron's model XR450 computer. Frank touched the lever under one edge and opened the computer cabi-

98

net, where he checked to make sure the wiring was just as Emma left it, that her plan hadn't been discovered. Then he closed the cabinet with a soft snap of metal against metal and stood still a moment, listening. Voices beyond the adjoining walls of the shed and the building continued to murmur.

No one appeared. No one heard him. Frank let out a deep sigh and stooped beside the computer. With one hand, feeling his way, he reached up behind it. The black box was there, seeming harmless enough—two inches long and a half an inch deep—attached to the main power line that ran hidden along the rear wall of the shed. The box was a computer itself, a miracle of micromini chips and transistorized electronics. Its switch was turned off and Frank left it that way. None of Emma's advance work had been discovered.

Then he lined up the position of the box with a smudge of grease on the floor, for quick access later, and turned his attention to the wire Emma had shown him. An insulated screwdriver loosened it from its moorings, loosened but didn't detach it. Frank stepped back outside, pulled the door softly shut, hurried into the bush where he had been hiding.

Lights blinked off and on across the ruins and inside the ticket office—off and on, off again. They caught and held briefly, then flickered once more, and finally the office door burst open. Feet sounded against the pavement in front of the building, running into the ruins, and one man came around the outside. Frank watched as the man fit a key in the lock and let himself in. A moment later the lights stopped blinking.

The man emerged into the night again and returned to the ticket office. "Just a loose wire," Frank heard him report.

"To hell with that," a comrade replied. "This coffee-pot isn't working now. Take a look at it, will you?"

Frank relaxed as someone slammed the door and the voices returned to a murmur. Stage one complete, a warning. He looked at his watch and waited.

Then, once again, he moved out of the bush, crept up

to the shed, picked the lock, and entered. This time he left the door standing open. Moonlight was enough to give shape to his work, and when it was done he would have to move very quickly. He found the circuit box on the wall above the computer, let his hand come to rest on the main switch, took a deep breath, and glanced down, finding the smudge of grease on the floor, lining up the position of the black box, anticipating precisely the swiftness of his own action. Then he moved—one, two, three—without pausing to breathe or think about what would happen if the terrorists caught him. He pulled the switch, plunged the ruins outside into darkness. He dropped to one knee and turned on the black box. Then he pushed himself up and made his escape, once more letting the door lock behind him.

He ran as fast as his silent feet would take him, compelled to hurry by instinct and by cries of alarm now spreading across the ruins. He ran through the bush toward the Pyramid of the Old Woman, from which, according to Emma's plan, he would open the past and unleash his people.

Stage two was underway. Stage three was waiting.

Emma, motionless, barely breathing, stared at the snake with cool eyes, assessing distance and line of fire, its natural instincts versus her own cold-blooded intentions. No, not it, but he—Ahau-Tzab-Can, his devil fangs showing in silhouette, his head erect and swaying across her gaze, revealing the strength and whiplash speed of his long, lean body. He was utterly loathsome, and something more—with the threat to her life, less threatening. Not a monster to be feared, but an enemy to be dispatched. Ahau-Tzab-Can stood in the way of what Emma came here to do. She shot him.

She moved as he rose to strike, her hand at her hip, and fired her Taser gun, which was loaded with electric darts, not bullets. Then she retrieved the dart, still attached to the gun by a tether, and tossed the snake into the underworld with the rest of the unearthly.

The Taser was designed for use by police on hazardous duty, to immobilize suspects fleeing scenes of crime without doing permanent damage. It was small and light-weight, like a flashlight, a metal cylinder with a sliding trigger and a gauge for adjusting the level of voltage that charged the darts and passed into the body of the victim. At its lesser strength, it could knock a man out at fifty yards. Turned up, as Ahau-Tzab-Can briefly knew, the Taser could be lethal.

Emma reloaded the dart and pushed the Taser into her belt along with her automatic, briefly scrutinized the vines overhead for any suggestion of movement, and then made her way to the edge of the trees, where the Governor's Palace lay directly before her.

She was standing about forty yards from the south end of the building, where light was peripheral at most, coming from spotlights aimed across the front and back of the structure. The dark side of the moon, so to speak, but still too bright to suit Emma's purpose. She waited there several minutes, watching the guards as they filed by at the second terrace level, thirty feet overhead, and counting in seconds the intervals between them. Not much, but enough. As one guard turned the corner at the front, he left the end of the building briefly un-guarded, until a new man appeared from behind. Emma watched until the pattern was sure. Then, crouching in scrub, she started to scramble forward. It was 1:00 A.M. by her watch, which was synchronized with Frank's, when she reached the base of the lower terrace. Two minutes later the lights began to flicker.

Stage one: blinking lights, the source of their trouble easily found and fixed, designed only to explain what happened next, to make plausible a natural sequence of developing problems. Frank was doing what Emma had taught him to do, and doing it right on schedule. She slipped off her backpack and began to assemble her equipment.

Nichols had responded promptly to her specifications: one automatic rifle that was more than a prop; it was loaded. Ropes attached to grappling hooks, rubber coated for silence. Wire clippers with rounded blades and insulated sleeves on both handles. A pair of gloves, rubber lined and made of spun copper; like surgeon's gloves, they were tight-fitting but supple. From the sleeves of her shirt Emma produced the bare ends of two rubber-sheathed wires that ran down under her fatigues to the thick soles of her boots, where they were grounded. She attached the gloves to the ends of wire, one on each side, but let them hang loose for now, since the rope might burn them on the way up and she didn't need them until later. And then there was a set of fatigues, a beard, and a wig for Owen. Emma wondered, briefly, how many people had worked through the night at Langley to supply her.

She stored the things she didn't need yet in the large pouch pockets of her trousers and slung the rifle by its strap over her shoulder. Then, again, she looked at her watch. It was almost time. She wiped her palms against her shirt, picked up a rope, and stood ready.

Frank was still on the job. At ten after one, the lights went out at Uxmal.

Shouts erupted from above as guards rushed toward the front of the building, toward the hostages and the failed electric door screens. Emma stepped back for better aim, caught the hook on the roof with her second try. She drew the rope tight and scaled up fast, like a spider—up over the massive terraces and onto the flat roof of the building, where she pulled the rope up, leaving no trace of her presence. Stage two, ascent in darkness. The electrical system at Uxmal was, step-by-step, going crazy.

The Governor's Palace, for all its fine lines and costly restoration, was plainly in need of a haircut. Scrub that once smothered the entire building still sprouted across the roof, hard to kill, and Emma was grateful for it. Sudden dousing of lights was good for creating moments of contrast blindness; only moments, no more. Her own eyes were starting to focus in the moonlight, picking out broad outlines of the great white city, then smaller dark shapes, the invaders who held it hostage. And if she could see, then so could they. She crouched low on the roof, catching her breath, which was heavy from the strain of the climb.

The first startled shouting settled into commands: "The power's out! Cover the doors!"

"You men stay here. The rest of you spread out to the perimeters!"

"Keep an eye out for planes. Get that missile launcher into position!"

Emma didn't look up. She held her head low, crawling flat on her stomach in the scrub, until she thought she was somewhere over Owen's door. Then she crawled to the edge of the roof and looked over.

Nichols was right, an army! The terrorists were aiming their flame throwers into the dry bush, holding them ready, while others crouched behind submachine guns and manned the missile launcher. Helicopters were taking off. A hundred men, most roused from sleep, spread across the ruins and dropped flat, drawing their rifles up, forming a defensive ring against an invasion from the jungle. They swarmed like bees, and Emma had climbed right into their hive, knowing that if someone saw her he would sting first and wonder what she was doing here later.

Still, it was no more than she expected. No more and no less. They reacted as she had known they would, by the book, as Emma herself had learned it. They took up a defensive position—facing out, alert for attack. A counter invasion, if that were what the power failure had signaled, wasn't likely to come from the heart of the hive, from the roof of the building that had been the most heavily guarded.

Had been and was now. Thirteen guards remained in place at the Governor's Palace, and what they relinquished in numbers they made up with attention. This was not the time to expect less caution on their part. The screens were unlocked now; current no longer passed through them.

Emma ducked at the roaring of engines above; she buried her head as a helicopter made a pass at the building and disappeared over the jungle. Then, once again, she peered over the edge, discovered she had overshot Owen's door, and carefully moved back to it.

Owen's fire had nearly died out below, like the others that warmed and lit the hostage chambers. She could tell by the glow of red embers that burnished the stone in the path of his door and the back of the terrorist guard standing before it. This wasn't the time to make her move. Emma drew the Taser and set it for a knockout dose. Then she eased back from the edge of the roof and turned over, looking up at the sky.

There wasn't a prayer of getting to Owen as long as the lights were out, as long as the door screens weren't working. She was in position, ready to go. She could only wait now. For the lights to come *on*. For Frank. For stage three.

Priests and warriors.

Frank was at the Pyramid of the Old Woman, across from the Governor's Palace, when the lights came on again across the ruins. They came on full for ten seconds or more, until Emma's black box, activated by the return of power, began to draw power back out of the system. The lights flickered twice and then settled in at a low-level emission. Stage three had begun. The blackout was over; a brownout commenced. And unless the terrorists found the black box, this one would last much longer.

Frank gripped the remote switch in his hand as the ancient temples faded in partial darkness. He looked at his watch and waited five more minutes. Then he pressed the button that was keyed into Uxmal's computer.

Several seconds passed before anything happened. Then a hum of sound rose up in the distance. It grew as it came, swelling to an earsplitting pitch. A drumbeat came right behind it, rumbling over stone and hard earth, over terrorist guards. And above the drum, the cry of a flute, sharp and eerie. It was all up to Emma now. Frank's job was done.

He had summoned his ancestors.

≋ 15 ≋

The electrician named Santinas spun around in the computer shed as the door behind him was yanked open. "Ramon!" he gasped, more startled than frightened as the terrorist leader's frame filled the doorway. Their flashlight beams crossed, brightening the darkness inside the shed, revealing both faces.

"What are you *doing*?" Ramon hissed, his eyes black with venom.

The electrician turned away.

"Look at me when I talk to you!" Ramon's voice was a whisper of malice. "I want to know what's going on here, and when we'll have full power again, and how you're going to explain yourself. First I hear it was a loose wire. Then a blown fuse. What are you going to do next, trip on a cord and rip out a socket? Are you trying to *sabotage* us?"

Santinas bristled inwardly. It wasn't his fault if they'd chosen this spot in the middle of rocky nowhere, where electric power was so unreliable that hotels stocked candles as a staple supply. But he kept his feelings to himself. Ramon's moods were erratic, his temper harsh, his vengeance often painful, and Santinas was no fool. He wasn't going to volunteer for a demonstration.

"I don't think you should worry," he said. "The electrical circuits are overloaded, and that's no surprise around here. We've got a drain on the system."

"What does that mean?"

"Something is drawing power out—"

"From the outside?"

"Possibly. I don't think so. Look, it could be anywhere on the lines from here to Merida, or it could be at the generator. But I think the problem is right here."

"Why?"

"Because of the way it happened." Santinas bent down to point the beam of his flashlight under the computer and began to explain the sequence of events as he saw them. "I figure we were already pushing the circuits close to overload with the power we were draining off for the door screens," he said. "We'd have been okay, except this wire came loose, causing the lights to flicker and the circuits to overheat. The main switch blew and shut everything off. We had a temporary blackout." He got up and turned the light onto the circuit box on the wall. "Then, when I switched the circuits back on, our power returned to normal, but only briefly, because the loose wire was just the trigger. It takes more power to turn lights on and off, and on again, than it does to keep them burning; the blinking lights started it all. But the real source of the overload still exists, and the system has rearranged itself. It's accommodating the demand of the door screens by dimming the lights—and the screens themselves, for that matter. It's all automatic, designed to prevent a fire."

"That's comforting," Ramon observed. "Where does that leave us?"

"With partial power."

"For how long?"

"Until I've had time to rewire the screens. It's enough. You'd still get a hell of a shock if you touched one."

"But could these things have been caused from the outside?" Ramon pressed.

"Not likely." Santinas shook his head. "If we'd had a sudden blackout, or even a sudden dimming of power, I'd be more concerned that someone was purposely manipulating the system. But this wire came loose behind a locked door."

"You're sure it was locked?"

"I've been back here twice in the last twenty minutes. The door was locked *both* times."

Ramon's eyes narrowed suspiciously, with his compulsive need to fix blame. Santinas knew he was handy, the obvious target, but he was also on firm ground. What had happened, under the circumstances, was neither unusual nor surprising.

"Why don't you put a guard on the door, if you don't trust me," he suggested.

Ramon opened his mouth to reply, then abruptly turned his head, listening.

Santinas heard it too, a sound coming from the ruins. A hum—growing, *piercing*. Drums and a flute. He swung around to the computer, knowing at least that he couldn't be blamed this time, and Ramon himself was his witness. He began to push buttons, pull switches, but the music only grew louder. Then it gave way to a thundering chant—*"Chaaaac! Chaaaac! Chaaaac!"*—that might have shaken the rain from the sky if it didn't actually rouse the recalcitrant rain god.

"The whole system's gone mad," he shouted above the din.

Ramon's voice was strangely clear even over the swelling sound. "Shut it off!"

"Hell, I'm trying!"

Santinas opened the computer and shone his flashlight on the intricate wiring inside. Spotlights were changing color across the ruins, the source of their pattern emanating from here. The drumbeat rose again, even louder now, resounding off stone and jungle and sky. Ramon covered his ears with the flat of his palms. "What's the matter, you fool! Can't you *find* the off switch?"

"It doesn't work. Neither does the volume control."

"Then pull the wires!"

"And risk losing power altogether?"

"I don't care what you do. Just stop that noise!"

Santinas knew that Ramon would care once the sound was gone; that if he knocked out the power for good, shutting off lights and disarming the door screens, Ramon would take a pound of flesh and then some. But he didn't know how to shut the sound off. He was an electrician; he'd had no experience with the complexities of a computer.

"I can figure it out," he said at last, reluctantly, "but it will take time. . . ."

Madness flared in Ramon's eyes. His jaw dropped open, revealing teeth and tongue. Muscles rippled, inching him forward. Santinas raised a hand to defend himself, but Ramon didn't strike. The sound drew him off. He came close, but then he swung around and hurried out into the ruins.

Santinas expelled a sharp breath of air. Ramon would be back, but not right away. There was only one way to shut the sound off without risking power completely. Someone had to go out there and yank out the speakers.

"Father of Light! Be kind this day to your children . . . !"

The voice of the priest boomed across the big night sky, pleading for relief from the sun. Emma felt the force of the sound against her eardrums as she fixed the hook on the edge of the roof and watched the pattern of light moving from one temple to another. Now it was the great Pyramid of the Magician, lit blue against the dark sky. It faded to green, then flamed up red as the priest's voice gathered momentum.

"Do not turn to cinder the rocks that would burn our feet, Lord. Wilt no more the plants in our fields. Protect Uxmal, which lives beneath your light and your heat. . . ."

Colored spotlights moved to another part of the ruins. The pyramid vanished in darkness, then emerged again dimly lit in the night. Emma smiled to herself. Frank had activated the sound and light show exactly to her instructions, after she had rewired the computer, increasing the volume to a din and leaving the surface switches useless against it. Stage three.

She watched the guards on the terrace below, saw confusion grow into chaos. Their attention shifted from the hostage cells as the priest's voice battered their senses. Then the word was passed—find the speakers and rip them out!—the signal Emma was waiting for. Every nonessential guard was enlisted to help—and none too many, she thought. There were forty-two separate speakers out there, scattered the length of the site, and most were hidden by scrub or rock lest tourists should stumble across them.

Only one guard stayed on duty below. Not worried about escape, but attack, he made his way down the wide steps to the plaza, where he took up a stance with his rifle, facing the path of approach to the building from the jungle. Emma waited until the sound and light show shifted its focus and the dim light of the Governor's Palace turned to fire, like the eye of the sun, Lord Istin. New sounds erupted out of the speakers: bird calls and the croaking of frogs. The people of Uxmal chanting for rain. *"Water! Give us water!"*

With the power half gone, red light was almost no light at all; the Governor's Palace was suddenly lit like a darkroom. Emma moved fast. She pushed herself up, grabbed the rope with both hands, and scaled down the face of the building, landing lightly on the floor of the upper terrace. She threw the rope back up onto the roof, out of sight, out of reach. No matter; she had two others with her. Then she looked around. The guard's back was still turned. Drumbeats pounded like tom-toms, reverberating against the night. He hadn't seen or heard her.

Behind Owen's door screen, embers of fire faded against red light, barely visible. Emma called to him softly, but got no reply. She called again. No answer. Was it possible that through all of this he was *sleeping*?

Of course not. No one could exert such control. Did she have the wrong door then? Not unless they'd moved him, and she had seen him here earlier this evening. Probably, like the guard below, he simply couldn't hear her.

Emma pulled on her spun copper gloves and produced the wire clippers, whose blades curved and met like a buzzard's beak to cut toward, not away from, the hands that held them. The terrorists might wonder later what

Owen had used to sever the wires, but it would be clear that the cutting had come from inside his cell. As she opened the blades to move them into position, the people of Uxmal continued their plea: *"Come rain! Dance wind! Lord of good rain, give us water!"*

Then abruptly she stopped, sensing movement far off to her right. A new guard appeared from the corner at the north end of the terrace. Emma turned away from the door, let the rifle slip off of her shoulder. One hand moved to the belt at her waist as she took up a guardlike stance of her own. And then the terrorist saw her.

But he saw her in beard and fatigues, with a rifle, in shadowed red light: he obviously thought she was one of them and kept walking. Emma waited. Her hands were damp, but her throat was dry. More than anything now, like the Maya, she wanted a drink of water.

The guard stopped, and a match flared in the cup of his hands. His face was lit briefly as he dipped a cigarette into the flame. He shook the match out and looked up, startled by a sudden earsplitting cry. Uxmal had welcomed Kukulkan, the great plumed serpent. The guard paused a moment, looking around, as if Kukulkan might show himself in full-feathered regalia. Then he shrugged and started walking again, heading straight for Emma.

Emma drew the Taser and fired fast from the folds of her sleeve. The man didn't have time to react, nor even to know what had happened. He stiffened, went limp, and collapsed, unconscious. Emma shook her head slowly as she drew on the tether to retrieve the dart. He really should have watched where he was going; his own fault if, in the dark, he had brushed a door screen.

But there was no time to waste now. Emma started to turn, and her hand closed on the clippers once more. Then suddenly, so suddenly that she barely had time to catch her breath, an arm seized her from behind and a hand came down firmly across her mouth. The arm held her tight as lips brushed her ear. A man whispered.

"What took you so long?"

Emma glared at him as he pulled her past the door screen, which offered no resistance at all, into a dank room with a dying fire, into the Governor's Palace. Then, slowly, the hand released her mouth.

"You son of a bitch," she whispered back. "I should have let you rot here!"

16

"Did you bring the Marines along?" Owen asked once he'd released her inside his cell. "Or is this a social call?"

Emma, he thought, as he watched her gaze rise to a thin band of silver that ran across the top of his door, did not look amused, and he hadn't really expected her to. But he had been expecting her, or at least he'd known there was a good chance Nichols would put her in charge of a rescue mission if there was one, and there surely would be. He had known and left the latch off for her.

His own gaze rose in the same direction, to the silver chain he'd taken from his straw hat and spliced into the wiring around his door the day he was locked in here, while the terrorists were hanging other screens, before they turned the current on. He had run the chain up over the door and down to a corner of the room, where he grounded it in a large pile of dirt and debris. The screen was made of iron mesh. Silver, much lighter as metals went, was the dominant conductor.

Owen looked at the chain, then back to Emma, and chuckled. He'd practically left the porch light burning for her.

And now she knew it too. Her dark eyes were flecked with red, reflecting back firelight, such as it was, dying embers. "Put these on," she said and thrust a bundle into his hands. Fatigues, beard, and wig. "You're going to escape from this place and, like it or not, you're going to do it my way."

Owen started to pull the fatigues on. "It's all right with me," he said. "What about the rest of the hostages?"

"They're not going anywhere tonight. DIA has the option on them, on orders from the President, and the Pentagon's making a flap over risks and casualties."

Owen paused, but Emma's red-flecked dark eyes looked back at him without blinking, and he knew the rest without being told. Outside the sound and light show went on, with the wedding of the lord of the Xiu, the ruling family of Uxmal, but the red spotlights were fading. And there were no Marines awaiting a signal from Emma. She wasn't here to *lead* a mission—she *was* the mission, and he was its sole object—for the President had aligned himself with the Pentagon, not the CIA, and the Pentagon had cold feet over Uxmal. Owen hurried to finish dressing. He could guess how that would sit with Nichols.

And how the rest would sit, Michelangelo's secret. Things were going to get worse for Ed before this night of "escape" was over.

"I'm ready," he said. "Let's get going."

Emma looked him over and approved his disguise. "You take the rifle. I've got a Taser and my automatic."

"Which way?"

"To the right, to the end of the building. I'll go first and have the rope ready."

With that and a last look outside, Emma stepped past the screen and fell into patrol step along the upper terrace. Owen covered her from the door with a rifle. Then he, too, stepped into the light, out onto the territory of his captors. Night air felt fresh on his face as he left the clammy cell behind, but they weren't free yet. He spotted two guards. One had his back turned at the base of the steps; the other was on the terrace floor, unconscious.

The sound of wind howled in Owen's ears as he moved to the right, a harsh crack of thunder, a drumbeat of rain. Chac had awakened, too late. Lord Xiu's bride had been stolen by a prince of Chichen, and the people of Uxmal were thirsty for blood, not water.

A conch shell called the soldiers to arms—"War! War! War! War!"—for the Toltecs had come and superimposed their ways on the peaceful Maya. The Toltecs carved skulls into their temple walls, and leopards or eagles, their claws dripping blood as they dined on sacrificed human hearts. A pleasant lot. The new invaders, Owen thought, especially Ramon, should feel right at home with the old ones.

He turned the corner.

Emma was there, rope waiting. They both scaled down, one terrace at a time, wrenching the rope free behind them. They hit hard earth, and Emma retrieved her backpack, leaving no evidence of outside help. Then, with darkness for cover, they made a run for the jungle, Emma in front, leading the way to the realm of the unearthly.

As they dropped into the cave, horns sounded shrill against the sky. War came to an end with no victors, only death and famine and drought. Soon the great white city would be abandoned.

⊠ 17 ⊠

Frank was waiting in the clearing at the mouth of the cave when Owen and Emma emerged together. Relief broke across his face. "Are you all right?" he asked, looking from one to the other.

"We're fine," Owen said. "When this is over we'll have a few drinks and a long talk, but there's no time for that now."

Frank nodded and turned to Emma. "The radio's ready. I'll go back to the pyramid to keep an eye on the ruins. Signal if you need me." He glanced at Owen and then walked away on his silent feet, leaving them alone in the clearing.

Owen couldn't help smiling as he looked Emma over by the light of the moon—a vision with a hairy face, like a victim of Puck's mischief; in heavy boots with their extra-thick soles, as attractive as corrective shoes; in mud-streaked fatigues that were lumpy at best and succeeded in hiding any hint of gender. His confinement aside, he felt sure he looked no worse than she did.

"Nice outfit," he said. "Who's your couturier?"

Emma pulled off the beard and wig, as Owen did. "Nichols, of course. I'd like to arrange a meeting for him with a new friend of mine. Ahau-Tzab-Can."

"They're a pair of snakes in the grass, all right. What, for sending you here?"

"For wasting my time."

"Nothing's wasted. I was counting on you."

"Next time don't."

115

Owen studied her face, waiting. Then, Emma conceding—Owen won this round—they both burst into laughter. Owen caught her up in an embrace that said he was grateful for her trouble, an embrace which, returned, said that she was relieved to find him well. But neither of them would say so, because real feelings between friends, between adversaries who were on the same side, were sometimes better unspoken. Anyway, one more victory scored, the game would continue between them.

"Poor Ed, so worried about his budget," Emma said, bringing them back to the same side again as she knelt on the ground by the radio. "If only he knew, you could have left whenever you were ready."

"If it makes him feel better," Owen said, "it's true I could have left my cell, but without your help I probably wouldn't have got past the first terrace."

"You're admitting that?"

"You can tell Ed I am."

Emma smiled. "All he wants to know is that you're free. We have a secure frequency here. Anything you want me to tell him?"

"Not yet. We need to talk."

Owen found a patch of hard earth and sat down, watching Emma, who was looking herself again, skin fair, eyes dark in the moonlight. He admired the cool look of her face, the deep, soft tone of her voice as she raised Nichols at Langley.

"Firefly to Scorpion. Firefly to Scorpion."

"Yes, Firefly, this is Scorpion. Go ahead."

"Chameleon is free and with me now. . . ."

Owen lit a cigarette as he listened. The deep voice, Emma claimed, wasn't a gift of nature as much as experience, the result of some number of years lived in Washington. ("The only way to be heard," she said, "in a town where so much talking goes on, is to pitch your voice at a level that's barely audible.") But she never explained what she was doing in Washington. Nor did she ever dignify rumor with comment.

The rumor was that Emma had been married once. To

116

a congressman. And more, that she had killed him, on assignment for the CIA.

"You always did put your work first," Owen told her, chuckling, the first time he heard the story.

Emma had only shrugged and said, "I spoke to him twice, but he was engrossed in his Whip Memoranda. If he'd only looked up, I might not have done it." Then she had smiled, teasing. The good widow Thatcher.

Mrs. Who? That secret had died with the late Mr. Who, if he ever existed. The story was no doubt apocryphal, a part of the myth of Emma, which she cultivated every chance she got. *Probably* it was apocryphal. It didn't matter. Emma might have done it. Owen was glad to see her.

Spotlights still colored the sky over the ruins, shifting across the night, but the sound that rose from the last of the speakers was no more than background noise now. Soon even that would be gone. And by morning, if not before, his absence would be discovered. He started to pull his thoughts together.

"Ed wants to know why you didn't go to Jakarta," Emma said. She looked up and smiled. "And what the hell 'moving islands' means."

Owen smiled back in the darkness. "Tell him to stick around, you'll call him back. Then shut that thing off. We don't have time for interruptions."

Emma sent the last of the message and switched the radio off before Nichols could demand something more. She closed the radio into its case, swung her legs around, clasped her knees in her arms, and looked at Owen with steady eyes. "Now," she asked, "are you going to tell *me*? Or did I come all this way for nothing?"

"Of course I'm going to tell you," he said. "I'm looking for moving islands. I don't know what that means, but I do know what I'll find there. And I want to tell you how I found out, because it's all part of the story."

Owen drew on his cigarette. "It was nearly a month ago," he said, "in Marrakesh. . . ."

* * *

In fact, his last night in Marrakesh. He'd been ready to leave for Jakarta when he received the package.

It arrived unremarkably at the front desk of his hotel, delivered there by messenger, a small man in *fuuta* and turban, as the concierge described him later. No one Owen knew or was meant to know, the last man of a relay team, not from Langley but from Waterford. The mark was there, a black *W*, smudged like a streak of dirt, in the lower left-hand corner of the package.

Owen went to his room and locked the door behind him. He knew what was in the package, a paperback book, one of two current titles—*The Orestian Trilogy* of Aeschylus or Stendhal's *Le Rouge et le Noir*—both slender volumes, easy to mail, both commonly published and available anywhere in the literate world. Inside, there would be a message in book code. Waterford was a farmhouse in the countryside of Virginia staffed by CIA clerical help who had proven their discretion beyond any doubt; a farmhouse and a clearinghouse through which field agents on far-flung assignments could bypass desk-bound superiors and make contact directly with each other.

Owen wondered idly, as he tore the package open, which old friend he was hearing from, for what purpose. Someone making a date or breaking one, however much rules forbade frivolous use of the system, setting up a lunch in Paris or a weekend in Rome. Or, possibly, something even more appealing.

He tore off the wrapper and stared at the book, frowning. Not Aeschylus or Stendhal, but Conrad. Joseph Conrad. A mistake? Had they changed books and failed to tell him? No, if there was anything they excelled at out at Waterford, beyond their much vaunted discretion, it was stainless steel efficiency. And obedience to their instructions. They passed along anything that found its way into their post office box, even this, *The Secret Sharer*, which wasn't and never had been on the Waterford list.

And yet the inscription was there, inside the back cover, a penciled notation, a series of numbers which, when rearranged by a memorized formula, would reveal a pattern of pages and words to be lifted from them. The inscription was there, and so was a piece of the original wrapping. A name and a return address. The package didn't come from Paris or Rome. It came from a state prison in Pendleton, Indiana, from an inmate who called himself Miller.

"What was the message?" Emma asked, leaning forward.

Book code was usually stilted because it used preexisting words, not necessarily words of choice, and this one was no different. Owen recited from memory: *"Intolerable murder! Desperately need your help. My own life in danger as well. Be quick! If we fail to meet, I will hide the name for you to find at the ruins. Look beneath the moving islands of the sea. And remember."*

"Cryptic," Emma said.

"Meant to be," he replied. "Meant to set me on a trail, no more than that."

"Do you know who it came from?"

"Oh, yes." He dropped the name without warning.

Emma's face froze.

Owen flicked an ash from his cigarette. Who indeed! Emma was stunned, as he had been, but not for the same reasons.

He had known who sent the message, though there was no signature in the book; none was needed. He saw the name signed in the story itself, indelibly, unmistakably, as clearly as Conrad's captain saw his own face in the pale oval that looked up at him from a darkling sea. His *double*. And old friend, all right. An old friend and once trusted partner, a fellow agent turned assassin-for-hire. A man who had seized on the old Waterford system, without knowing which titles they were using now, as a means of finding Owen. Owen recognized the feint of a hand so like his own. A mind that worked alone in the dark. A shadow, intangible and illusive. His own gray ghost.

His double.

Michelangelo.

Owen hadn't heard from him in years, hadn't wanted to, didn't want to now. He leaned back in his chair, staring absently at the book in his hand, briefly lost in a mixture of feelings. Anger. Betrayal. A sadness he thought he had long since forgot. Profound loneliness he could not suppress. Then, slowly, softly, he began to chuckle.

The Secret Sharer was Michelangelo's gauntlet, an irresistible dare. Joseph Conrad's dark tale of a young sea captain brought face to face with a killer and a looking glass, drawn to help his double. Inevitably. As Owen was drawn . . .

A gauntlet, not just irresistible but cunning. Owen couldn't refuse the challenge. He had to find Michelangelo, to help him, perhaps to save him. He had to face the dark side of himself.

Owen flicked off an ash and looked at Emma. "I found it all rather intriguing," he said.

"I should think so! He was setting you up, of course."

"And wouldn't deny it. But in an odd way, I trust him. If he said his own life was in danger *as well*, then the target for murder was someone else. And a murder that's intolerable by Michelangelo's standards is intriguing indeed, worth preventing at least."

Emma didn't argue the point. "So you went to Pendleton instead of Jakarta."

"And found out that Miller had been released before I got there. Before the book was sent or received. He was gone, but he'd left me a letter."

A letter addressed to Joseph Conrad, the only name Owen could have used when he arrived at Pendleton, since the captain of the story, his own assigned role, was as nameless as the ship he mastered.

Dear Joe, it began, friend to friend, and rambled on through several pages, mostly meaningless words about needing a job, of no interest until the last lines: *I'll be staying with Hiatt. There's room for you there too.*

Before he left the prison, Owen went back to the visitor's desk and asked one last question. "What was Miller in for?"

The man glanced at Miller's file, which still lay open before him. "Auto theft."

Owen almost laughed, but the answer confirmed the seriousness of Michelangelo's purpose. He had gone to prison for a crime he could have committed with his left hand and not been caught, and there could be only one reason for that. He was hiding.

From what? From whom?

What threat could have been so large that he chose prison, with its fingerprints and photographs, nemesis to an assassin? What could have scared him enough that he chose to leave a record behind, however disguised, as a lesser risk? What was he afraid of?

Intolerable murder. A hidden name.

The answers, Owen knew, had to be close by. The nearest Hyatt-Regency was in Indianapolis. He took State Road 67 out of Pendleton and was at the hotel in an hour. A reservation was waiting for him.

"Mr. Conrad," the desk clerk said as Owen was checking in, "your friend Mr. Leggatt had to leave last week, but he left an envelope for you. He asked us to hold it for your arrival."

So, Leggatt had come and gone—Leggatt, the sea captain's double. Owen wasn't surprised. He paid for one night in advance and went up to his room, but Michelangelo didn't show up there either.

Inside the envelope, Owen found a small locker key, engraved with the number 28, but no clues to the whereabouts of the locker. Besides the key, there was only a three-by-five card, and on it these words: *Look up Billie. She's a friend of Grant Martin.* The note was written in Michelangelo's hand, and he'd added a telephone number.

Seven digits without an area code, but that was all Owen needed. He left the hotel, went to a pay phone, and rang information.

"May I help you?" a woman asked.

"I hope so," Owen replied. "I've got a phone number

121

here, but I don't know the town or the area code. The prefix is seven-four-seven."

"That's Muncie," the woman said. "Area code three-one-seven, the same area you're calling from. Just dial one and then the number."

"Thanks."

Owen hung up and consulted a map. Billie wasn't far away. Muncie was northeast, on the other side of Pendleton.

The main branch of the Muncie Public Library was a jewel of a building in need of repair, a remnant of Carnegie money and probably not much appreciated in the great rush to plastic and chrome and grassy lawns in the suburbs. The librarian pointed Owen to the reference section and a book called the *City Directory*, where, among other things, telephone numbers were listed consecutively. Billie's number was followed by a man's name: Charles Stanford. Owen turned to a different part of the book and found Stanford listed again, as president of a local bank, with a home address on Berwyn Road. Billie might be his wife, or daughter, or maid. Whoever she was, she hadn't been worth a mention.

Daughter, he decided when she came to the door in her skinny jeans and knee boots, with her dark-lashed green eyes and flawless face. She said nothing, only looked him over appraisingly, part seductress, part imp, a cross between Lolita and Tom Sawyer.

"I'm a friend of Grant Martin," Owen began, and the sultry gaze altered sharply. Billie's face went pale, her eyes flat with fear, and she started to close the door between them. Owen raised a hand to stop her. "Grant *sent* me," he said.

She hesitated. "What's your name?"

"Joseph Conrad."

"Like the writer. Yes, he said you'd come. But I don't want to talk. Go away, please! Leave me alone!"

Owen pushed forward. "What's the matter?"

Billie only shook her head.

122

"Look, I need to see Grant, and it's important. Do you know where I can find him?"

The answer showed painfully in her eyes before she even spoke the words. "He's *dead*!"

Dead! Owen pulled back, his thoughts cold. He wasn't sure what it was he felt—not surprise, certainly. Something more like anger. He took a deep breath and let it out very slowly, all the time studying Billie's ashen face. And he made a guess. "If you won't talk to me," he said, "I'll have to talk to your parents."

The heavy eyelashes flickered. Billie was no longer frightened; she was stricken. Owen knew his guess had hit home. Sudden death had put fear into her heart, the fear of Grant Martin's enemies—but more than that, he thought, fear of an affair known to parents and peers here on Berwyn Road. He'd discovered the way to put pressure on Billie.

She swallowed hard and stepped back. Owen followed her into a living room full of Louis Quinze expensively recreated. She sat down in a straight-backed chair, her resistance gone, her eyes vulnerable, her face fragile.

Owen sat down beside her, changing his tone. "When did it happen?" he asked gently.

"A week ago today."

"How?"

"Someone put a bomb in his car."

Billie got up and left the room. She was back in a moment with a newspaper clipping. Owen read through it quickly.

A professional job. Explosives set on a timer. The victim was traced through car rental forms (to yet another *G.M.*, George Mason), traced to a nonexistent address, and not very much beyond that. Reading between the lines, Owen knew the local police—or the sheriff's office, since it happened on a rural road in an adjacent county—suspected a mob connection. And that would be that. No one wanted to take on the mob over the pieces of a broken, unidentified body.

"How do you know it was Grant?" he asked.

"Because I saw him." Billie's voice was calm as the

123

story poured out; she was relieved to be talking to someone. "Grant asked me to meet him for lunch that day, at a diner near the intersection where it happened. I was waiting for him outside in my car, and I saw him coming, saw him stop for the light. And then, just as I got out of my car, there was a terrible blast. I could feel it where I was standing—an explosion, fire. His car was *engulfed* in flames. *He* was!"

Owen gave her a moment to compose herself, then asked, "You saw *him*? You're sure it was Grant who was in the car?"

"I saw him as clearly as I see you now, or nearly so. I knew him pretty well, you know."

Owen looked at her face and knew she wasn't lying. "What did you do?"

"I panicked. I got back in my car and drove off as fast as I could. I don't think anyone saw me."

"Then no one but you knows it was Grant."

"No one even knows I knew him." She paused, then added, "I know he worked for the government, but . . . my God, if Mom and Dad ever find out . . ."

"They won't," Owen assured her.

For the government. So she didn't know who "Grant" really was. No, Billie wasn't lying.

"You're like him, I guess," she said. "Do you work for the CIA?"

Owen smiled at her candor. "If I did, I wouldn't tell you."

"Just like him." Billie smiled thinly. "He never answered questions directly either."

"How long was he here?"

"Three weeks on and off. He made some trips. Once, I think, he may have left the country. I didn't ask him why he was here, and he didn't say, but I had the feeling he thought he was *safe* here. Do you know what I mean? Safe with me. Safe in Muncie. Safe *from* something." She lowered her lovely green eyes. "I guess he was wrong."

"I don't think so."

Billie looked up, startled.

"I think he knew exactly what he was doing. He knew his life was in danger. That's why he made contact with me. I have to know everything you know, from the moment he arrived. If you tell me now, I won't have to come back. No one else will ever bother you."

Billie didn't need convincing. She began with Grant's postcard and the meeting at the country club in Pendleton. She didn't know where he came from that day, didn't make a connection with the prison. "We drove to Indianapolis, to a bookstore," she said. "There was something he wanted to buy."

The Secret Sharer. Owen nodded. "Go on."

"Then we went to a toy shop. He bought me a present."

"Do you still have it?"

Billie left the room again. This time she returned with a doll, which she handed to Owen. It was an ordinary doll, dressed in tulle and lace, with painted cheeks and plastic eyes; and it cried mama, more or less, when he tipped its head over.

"Grant insisted on naming the doll," Billie said and shrugged. "He called her Dayton. I can't think why."

Owen could.

"May I borrow this?" he asked.

"You can have it," Billie said. "I'm too old for dolls. I was too young for Grant Martin."

The Trailways bus station in Dayton, Ohio, just over the Indiana state line, looked like every other bus station Owen had ever passed through and was glad to be out of. The lockers were lined up against one wall. He found number 28 and opened the door with the key Michelangelo left in the envelope at the hotel. Inside was a pair of ski boots.

Owen took them and left. He drove out into the country.

"Ski boots?" Emma asked, frowning thoughtfully.

"Ski boots," Owen said. "And stuffed down in them, I found three things: a hand-held radio transmitter, a year-old copy of *Time* magazine, and another copy of *The Secret Sharer*.

Emma's frown deepened.

And Owen went on: "The boots were equipped with electric foot warmers that operated on battery packs fit into the soles. And the batteries were still there. They looked harmless enough, but they tested at six thousand volts apiece. Two in each boot. That's nearly twenty-five thousand volts, enough to cause a hell of a shock." He paused and added, "Or a hell of a fall."

Emma's lips parted. She stared at him.

Owen nodded. "The magazine dispelled any doubt. There was a piece in it about President Riker's last trip to Aspen."

Emma gasped. "Then you weren't supposed to *prevent* a murder—"

"—but to know that one had already occurred. Michelangelo put the proof into my hands. Benjamin Riker was assassinated."

⊠ 18 ⊠

Owen watched Emma in the darkness, as moonlight moved patterns across her face and threw her eyes into shadow. Like the rest of the world, she was no doubt stunned by the death of a President who had been so alive, who took life and politics alike, often skiing too close to danger.

As he had that day at Aspen, challenging fate, skirting the edge of a precipice once too often. An accident, so the world thought, more clever for leaving no trace of an assassin—because, of course, the accident wasn't an accident. President Riker was *made* to fall as he neared that edge, by electric shock, transmitted by radio signal to receivers built into his ski boots. The assassin could have been close by, or might have been miles away, even on another mountain. All he needed was knowledge of the slope, an unobstructed view, and a good grip on the hand-held transmitter.

Emma shook her head slowly. "It's a masterpiece! No one but Michelangelo *could* have done it."

"Michelangelo didn't do it."

Emma stared at him with her moon-darkened eyes, more startled by this than by revelation of murder.

"He told me he didn't," Owen explained. "It was there again in *The Secret Sharer*, in the copy I found with the ski boots. The book was unmarked from front to back, except for one line underscored in red: *Am I a murdering brute? Do I look it? By Jove!*"

"He looks it."

"Perhaps."

"Then why do you believe him?"

"Because I know him."

"As simple as that?"

"As I know myself," Owen said. "Michelangelo would kill me if he got the chance, but he wouldn't lie, not about this, because it wouldn't prove anything. Anyway, he liked Riker, and he never took contracts on anyone he cared about—people he liked *or* disliked—because he knew feelings, good or bad, could throw off his timing and cause him to fail." Owen stubbed out his cigarette angrily. "Of course he's a killer, as cold-blooded as any I've known, but this time he didn't do it."

"All right," Emma said. She believed him. "But then why did he put you through all of this?"

"For the best of motives from his point of view. *Revenge.* He wants the truth to come out even now. He wants me to reveal the plot. And the real assassin."

A name hidden at the ruins. *What* ruins?

Owen sat behind the wheel of his car on a country road near Dayton, Ohio, looking over the trail markers Michelangelo had left him. Two copies of the Conrad story, each with a message in it. A pair of ski boots that were an assassin's weapon. A radio transmitter, an old magazine, a key to a bus station locker. And a mama doll with a tinny voice that might have sufficed for the real thing if you were six or seven.

Owen had taken the doll apart twice and put it back together. There was nothing inside but the mechanism that activated its whimpering cry. He was starting to think it was nothing more than Billie believed, a present. And yet there had to be more.

He held the doll in his hands and bent it forward, setting off the mechanism inside. "Mama," it whimpered unconvincingly. No, not quite "Mama," but "sssssh-ma." Ooosh-ma . . .

Ooosh-ma!

Owen smiled and started the car. He caught a plane for Miami that night. The next day he arrived at Uxmal.

128

* * *

"And the same day you arrived," Emma said, "Uxmal was taken hostage, along with four members of Congress. Did Michelangelo know what was going to happen?"

"What do you think?"

"Of course he did."

"He had to. You were right about something else too. The assassination was a masterpiece, because the master *planned* it."

"Michelangelo."

"Or his double."

Emma raised an eyebrow.

Owen went on: "I think Michelangelo agreed to kill someone else; then his own plan was used to kill Riker."

"Someone else?" Emma asked. "On the same ski slope?" The words were barely past her lips when she realized their significance. "Oh, my God! Abdul Passan!"

Owen nodded. The Saudi crown prince, who was skiing that day with Riker. "It fits a pattern I've seen before. Michelangelo was hired to kill Prince Abdul, to create an accident so convincing that the royal bodyguards would be taken in by it. But he was the one who was taken in. Whoever hired him set him up, used him, deceived him into planning the death of a man he would not have killed."

"Then imagine his shock," Emma said, "when he heard that *Riker* was dead . . ."

"Ah, yes, *he* would have known and been furious. Grounds for revenge without any doubt, and grounds for going into deep hiding."

"In a prison."

"The last place anyone would look." Owen leaned forward. "When he was released last month, he had to know he was dead if the contractor found him, because he alone could prove who did kill Riker."

"Prove it how?" Emma asked. "Contractors don't usually sign an assassination order."

"If they wanted Michelangelo, they did. Besides a high fee, he always extracted insurance—something to bind the people who paid him into a pact of silence, so

129

that if he were caught and tried for his crimes they could be held accountable with him." Owen shrugged. "He got away with it because he never had real competition."

"So that's it," Emma said. "Moving islands. He hid his 'insurance' at Uxmal—and then, in case something happened to him, put you on the trail of it."

"Something like that." Owen turned to look toward the ruins. "I don't know how any of this relates to the terrorists, but I don't think the hostages are in immediate danger. The terrorists have provided too well for a long-term stay. On the other hand, their leader's strung out like a wire. He's volatile. Probably dangerous."

"What's his name?" Emma asked.

"He calls himself Ramon. Garcia Ramon."

Emma made a note of it.

"You'll need to send someone for the ski boots," Owen went on and smiled as he produced a key. "I left them at the Trailways station in Miami, in locker number twenty-eight." He handed the key to Emma. "One more thing Nichols needs to know. The terrorists aren't Mexican. They're Cuban."

"Cuban! Are you sure?"

"I've had plenty of time to listen to them talking."

"My God, do you suppose Havana's behind this?"

"Could be," Owen said. "Or it could be Moscow."

Silence fell over the clearing at the mouth of the cave, with the ruins still dimly lit behind them—dimly lit by shifting spotlights and Emma's power outage, which was still in effect, though the sound had been shut off while they were talking. Owen looked at his watch. "Well," he said, "it's time for me to go back now."

Emma sat where she was, not moving, her face composed, her eyes still lost in shadow.

"You'd better tell Ed what I've told you," he added then. "I assume you'll be seeing him before I will."

Emma found her voice, which was as calm as the dark of her eyes. Calm and deep, and soft with malice. "I really should have let you rot here."

Owen laughed gently. "I never asked to be rescued."

"And I never asked to know you at all."

130

"Don't worry, we'll stay in touch. I'm going to need your help."

"Stay in touch with someone else. I'm not going to sneak back in there to pick up your messages."

"You won't have to sneak. You can walk in. I'll send you an invitation."

"By carrier vulture? Here, you'd better take these." She started to assemble supplies—weapons and ropes; binoculars; insulated gloves and instruments; a makeup case filled with things he would need if he wanted to become a passable terrorist, and she felt sure he would before the seige was over. "And this," she added, producing a bottle from a bag. She gave it to him as he got up, as she stood up beside him. "Touches of home tend to make confinement more pleasant."

Owen looked at the bottle and smiled, much as he didn't want to. A fifth of *Glenfiddich*, his favorite malt Scotch! His intentions had been no surprise at all! He looked back at Emma, caught her smiling too. She'd known *all along* that he would go back. She'd known and prepared ahead of time. Heaven knew how far she'd had to look to find this little announcement!

This point was hers.

"No ice?" he asked, but he knew she knew he drank it straight, like brandy. He owed her one now.

He lifted her chin and kissed her cheek. Then he took his Glenfiddich and supplies and vanished into the darkness.

131

⊠ 19 ⊠

The smile disappeared from Emma's face as she watched Owen go. She wasn't worried that he might be caught slipping back into the ruins, since if he were he could probably bluff his way through it. A reluctant hostage, perhaps failing in an escape attempt.

No, she was worried about something larger—that Owen would be identified for what he was, that his presence would be revealed as an active threat to the terrorists. But, of course, she couldn't have stopped him.

Emma had known that he would go back from the moment Frank told her that Owen said he was *sent* here. She had seen another hand at work and assumed Owen saw it too. Whose hand she didn't know then, but what had been merely predictable became an inevitability with the mention of a name. Michelangelo. Owen had to go back for the challenge of it if nothing more. He'd been drawn in by a plea for help from a professional killer, his old partner. And, clearly, because of something personal.

Emma knew all that and more, that it wasn't smart to make friends in this business. But she didn't like rules any more than Owen did.

She switched on the radio and called Nichols. "Firefly to Scorpion. Chameleon has returned to the nest . . . ."

Crawly things! If Nichols had chosen the code names, then maybe he did have a sense of humor.

* * *

Nichols, sitting at his desk, staring at Ardry on the other side, looked as if he might explode. He bellowed across the room: "What does she *mean*, he went back!"

Ardry, at the radio, repeated the question for Emma.

"No need to shout," Emma replied. "Just that. He went back. He didn't want to be rescued. Are you so surprised?"

Nichols sighed. "Yes, but I don't know why."

Ardry transmitted the question and added another. "Reasons?"

"Both compelling and urgent," Emma said. "We have to talk, face to face if possible. Any chance of a quick meeting in Miami?"

Ardry glanced at Nichols, who nodded. "How fast can you get there?" he asked Emma.

"There's a plane out of here at eight o'clock in the morning."

"Hold on, please."

Ardry opened a panel in Nichols's desk and punched a question into the computer. An address showed on the terminal screen. And a name: Kritch. He turned back to the radio and gave Emma the address.

"Go to suite four-oh-eight," he said. "We'll make an appointment for you at noon."

"An appointment?"

"You'll see."

"I can't wait. Firefly out."

Ardry signed off for Scorpion.

Owen didn't go straight back to his cell. He reentered the ruins as Frank had escaped, by way of the Great Pyramid, which stood behind the Governor's Palace at the south edge of Uxmal, its base at the rear hardly separate from the jungle. Owen climbed up the back, a solid mass of encroaching bush, and made his way around the top shelf to the front, where wide stone steps had been cleared and restored and ran down to what had once been another paved plaza. He paused there, crouching in scrub and taking stock of the terrorists' mood after a night of unrest. No one seemed overly nervous for the experience; security had eased up again. They were, if anything, more relaxed for surviving the night without an attack. False alarm, an electrical problem. Emma's show had succeeded. Or maybe they were only worn out. Most of them seemed to be sleeping.

There were no guards at all near the Great Pyramid, which was as misnamed, in a way, as the buildings that never housed nuns or a governor. By comparison to its cousin down the way, the towering Pyramid of the Magician, this one was short and squat, a jewel of a different kind, its lines less graceful, more square cut, like the *Castillo* at Chichen-Itza. Nor was it as important as its cousin to the creators of the *son et lumière*. No spotlights shone directly here, only the wash of light from the neighboring Governor's Palace. From where he was, Owen could see without likely being seen; he had a clear view of the ruins.

It was his first view, in fact, of the plaza behind the Governor's Palace, which rose up on its terraces to the right, forming a right angle with the pyramid. Across the plaza sat a small temple that was, at a glance, more Greek than Mayan. Beyond that lay the Ball Court, a pair of solid stone structures facing each other across more paving stones, where Mayan athletes once competed for high stakes; death was the punishment for losing. In the distance, he could see the Nunnery, where he had started to search the ruins, and the huge cousin pyramid with its everpresent sentry.

The sky was still dark, the spotlights still dimmed, and dawn was still an hour away. Enough time, but none to spare. Owen moved across the steps, his khaki fatigues blending with stone in the darkness, to a door leading into a room at the top of the pyramid. Inside, it was darker still. Owen paused, letting his eyes adjust, and slowly the room began to take shape. Patterns of light and shadow emerged in the darkness. Wooden crates lay stacked and waiting, some pulled forward and already open. The crates, Owen knew, were filled with food, both canned and dried, and bottles of purified water. He knew because a guard, politely asked one day how food could be stored in such heat, had told him about this room. Whatever purpose it served once, it was now the pantry, as cool a spot as Uxmal had to offer.

Cool and dank, like his own cell. Owen began to feel his way around and through the crates, not daring to use a flashlight since even the narrowest beam would be as obvious here as a beacon. He was looking for a container, something fairly sizable, and found one among the cleaning supplies, which were also stored in the pantry. Then he left the way he had come, taking a three-gallon plastic bucket with him.

He was back in ten minutes and had the job finished in half an hour. He stood back, surveying the room carefully, making sure everything was in its place, as he had found it. Then, once more, he left the room, moving fast to the right and into the cover of scrub, where he stopped to study the pattern of guards patrolling the Governor's Palace.

There were fewer now, marching with wider intervals between them. Owen charted his course in his mind: down the pyramid to the south end of the building; up the side using Emma's ropes; waiting, as she had, for red spotlights to diminish his own visibility—not to the roof this time, but to the upper terrace, where he would fill an interval between guards and return to his cell at the first opportunity. Return to his cell and remove the rocks he had left in his bed in the form of a sleeping man. He would pick up the book that had fallen when he dozed off, maybe read a few pages, but probably not. He started to make his way down the slope of the pyramid.

Suddenly he stopped, spinning around in a crouch, his attention yanked back to something his eyes had passed over—to the small "Greek" temple on the other side of the plaza. No, not to the building itself; it was the frieze crowning its walls that riveted Owen's attention. He produced his binoculars and focused them on the relief carving, which was almost three-dimensional, almost lifelike—realistic, not stylized like typically pre-Columbian

Mayan sculpture. A small smile appeared on his face. The Galapagos. Michelangelo.

He *remembered*.

But there was no time to explore the small temple. Dawn would be breaking soon. Owen had to go back to his cell while he could; he could wait no longer. He dropped the binoculars into a pocket and made his way down the pyramid. Tomorrow would be soon enough, because he knew where to look now.

Because he had found the moving islands.

⊠ 20 ⊠

The sign on the door said FARLEY KRITCH, D.D.S., *Practice Limited to Oral Surgery*. Emma stepped into the reception room, picturing Nichols with scalpel in hand, her own mouth pried open, her expense account at last to be reckoned with. But bravely, reminding herself that she had been given a dispensation from torture class at training school because she'd survived natural childbirth, and that dispensations were not given lightly, she crossed the room to the woman sitting behind the desk.

"I have an appointment at twelve o'clock," she said without mentioning her name.

The woman looked her over, as a loan officer in a bank might look over a shabby applicant. "The doctor is waiting for you," she said. Then she got up and led Emma down a carpeted corridor, where piped-in music was playing softly, suggesting the existence of an electronic sound-shield system. Emma knew where she was. This wasn't just a CIA front—the woman was much too real for that—but an agency dentist set up to facilitate treatment and insurance forms for patients who were on a federal group plan but weren't allowed to admit they qualified for it. In Miami, there must be hundreds of them.

The woman opened a door at the end of the corridor, silently gestured Emma inside, and turned back the way she had come. A treatment room, sparsely furnished, with little more than the large reclining chair and the dental equipment that surrounded it. The fluorescent overhead fixture was off, but the room was half lit by sunshine that filtered past angled slatted blinds and a layer of sheer curtains. The air smelled medicinal, thoroughly clean, and not very pleasant.

But Emma smiled as she closed the door, because Nichols was already there, and the tools he had laid out on the floor didn't, thank God, include one drill or scalpel. He was sitting on the dentist's stool, perspiring in blue coveralls with *Dental Instruments, Inc.* written in script across the breast pocket. The room was comfortably air-conditioned, but Nichols wasn't used to working undercover. The KGB already knew about him. He was in disguise to prevent his appearance from drawing attention to Emma and exposing this location to foreign agents who routinely monitored his movements.

Emma took the only available chair, pushing the instruments tray aside as Nichols pulled his stool over beside her. On her other side, water dripped into a paper cup, keeping time with the background music.

"The room is secure," Nichols said. "We can talk openly here."

"That's good. I'm afraid I have a bombshell for you."

"I assumed you did. Go ahead. Let me have it."

"President Riker was assassinated."

Nichols looked confused, unable to absorb a piece of news that seemed to have no relevance here, let alone start to deal with the probability or implications of it.

"That's not all," Emma said. "The plot to kill him involved Michelangelo, though Owen doesn't think he did it, and it's all related somehow to the seizure of Uxmal."

The mention of Michelangelo's name had its effect on Nichols, as it had on Emma and Owen. Anger flared in his eyes, and Emma knew why. A trusted agent turned master assassin had proven to be too elusive. And he was something more than that—an extremely dangerous, potential source of embarrassment for the agency, for the country. What he had been, his identity and his training, were firmly guarded state secrets. Few people anywhere knew that the man called Michelangelo ever

138

was a CIA agent. That the truth should come out now was unthinkable. And yet, if he had actually killed a President, it wasn't the sort of thing you could hide.

"Owen is *convinced* he didn't do it," Emma added by way of assurance. "But Riker was murdered. And that's still not all. The terrorists who are holding Uxmal are Cuban."

Nichols stared back at her blankly for several seconds, his eyes hidden by the glint of sunlight on his glasses. He removed the glasses, produced a handkerchief, and wiped his face, all in silence. Then he looked up.

"No wonder Owen went back," he said softly.

"I told you he had compelling reasons."

"All right, let's take them one at a time. *Why* does he think Riker was murdered? There hasn't been a hint of that. Not a whisper! The whole goddamned world believes it was an accident, including me all this time. Including the best security men of two nations. He was skiing with Prince Abdul, you know, when it happened."

"And that only makes the way it was done more clever." Emma told Nichols what Owen told her, how he happened to be at Uxmal, how he had followed Michelangelo's trail from Marrakesh to Pendleton, Indiana, and then on to the Yucatan. She gave Nichols just the gist of it, the necessary outlines, because too many details would only rile his ulcers, and he had grounds for three new ones already. She told him about the car bomb, that Billie had seen the car burst into flames with the driver, "Grant Martin," behind the wheel, and she thought Nichols looked disappointed to hear it. Was it because he wished he had planted the explosives himself? Or was he only sorry he hadn't been there to see it happen?

It didn't matter. He was also relieved, but the look on his face wasn't to last. Emma told him what Owen believed, that Michelangelo had been deceived—hired to kill the Saudi prince, his plan twisted and used on Riker—that he wanted justice, or revenge, and was counting on Owen to carry on for him. She told him where the ski

139

boots were and gave him the locker key, along with the name of the terrorists' leader. And then she returned to the big question. Who had sent Cuban terrorists to Uxmal? The same people who had hired and then double-crossed Michelangelo?

"Christ," Nichols said, "could the Soviets have killed Ben Riker?"

The thought had occurred to Emma too, inevitably, though she didn't much want to face it or the thoughts beyond it. "Why would they?" she asked.

Nichols shrugged. "Henry Brendan is an old hawk, but he isn't very effective."

"And Riker was a peacemaker. Is it possible Michelangelo had become a Soviet agent?"

Nichols shook his head. "Not unless they were willing to pay him from the crown jewels or the treasures of the Hermitage. He left us for money—no more than that—and the KGB wouldn't have paid him significantly more than we did."

Emma conceded the point. At least they wouldn't have done it on a long-term basis, and Michelangelo was much too smart to be taken in by a promise.

Nichols stood up. "There's nothing to be gained from conjecture. I've got to see the President, and you've got to get yourself back to Uxmal. If Owen's so bloody insistent on staying there, then we're going to need a means of access to him, a way for him to pass us information—including an emergency signal if he gets into trouble."

Emma smiled. "Don't worry, he has something in mind. He said he would send me an invitation."

"And you're going to leave it at that?"

"For the time being, yes. I assume he knows what he's doing."

"Well, I don't!"

"You still lack faith."

"Among other things. Right now, I could use a few things explained. All right, I'll leave that for you to work out, with the understanding that some form of contact must be established. How are Pious, Pompous, and Gooch? And What's His Name?"

"Owen doesn't think they're in immediate danger, but that could change at any time."

"I suppose that's as much as we can hope for. Well, you go first. I'll take the service elevator."

Emma started to get up, but Nichols suddenly gripped her arm. "Wait a minute," he said. "Is Owen *sure* the terrorists are Cuban?"

"He says they speak Spanish like people born to it."

"He wouldn't be wrong about that."

"No."

"Damn funny, then. If they're Cuban, why are they so fired up about *Mexican* aliens?"

Nichols told her about the contact made with the terrorists and the first of their demands.

When he was finished Emma was also puzzled. "Obviously, they don't want us to *know* they're Cuban."

"And the whole issue of the demands is a hoax," Nichols said. "At least the first one."

"But *why*?"

"Maybe Uxmal itself is a hoax."

"My God, Ed, they've got four members of Congress! That's some joke!"

"I said hoax, not joke."

Silence fell over the room again, as the water dripped and the music played. They were back to the same question again. Who was it?

Havana or Moscow?

⊠ 21 ⊠

Owen leaned back on his elbows on the lower steps of the Great Pyramid, straight down from the pantry door, feeling the sun on his face and arms and listening idly to pieces of conversation between two congressmen higher up the steps behind him. The regular exercise period had been extended today, while some of the terrorists worked on rewiring the door screens, trying to prevent a repeat of last night's events. The shifting spotlights had finally shut themselves off in response to an automatic light sensor. With them went lingering doubt on the part of the terrorists—and, for the hostages, lingering hope, if there had been even that. The two congressmen Owen was listening to hadn't put much stock in Emma's show, at least not after the first startling moments.

"I was nervous, I'll tell you," Shackford was saying when they first sat down. "I thought Mexican troops were about to come charging in here."

Jack Renaud laughed edgily. "I had a bad moment too," he said. "Scared the hell out of me! But I guess it was a simple electrical failure."

Not so simple, Owen thought—Emma might have had grounds for being put out to hear her work so blithely dismissed—but he knew the congressmen were demonstrating typical hostage reactions. The prospect of rescue often produced oddly mixed feelings, setting the urge to escape in conflict with the instinct for survival. A lot of people had been killed during rescue missions.

But the terrorists, it seemed, had come to the same

conclusion. The incident had been self-contained, a simple electrical failure. Their manner was less defensive today, less abrupt, more tolerant. They were more inclined to grant liberties, within limits, than they had been—not out of anything as noble as kindness, but probably the sheer need to rest. Tension had left them tired and drained, a reminder to Owen of yet another behavioral truth. The seizure of Uxmal would take its toll on the captors as well as the captives. Terrorism wasn't a stress-free career; it wasn't easy, regardless of motivation, to sustain will under these conditions.

Which meant, perhaps, they were wearing down under pressure. Or they might be relieved because Ramon wasn't around; Owen hadn't seen him all day. Or maybe they were just hot and thirsty. Owen smiled. It was noon now. The air was heavy with the heat of the day, the sun at its high point, bleaching the sky to a pale glare and drawing the burnished glow from the stone structures. No one moved too fast across the plaza behind the Governor's Palace, in front of the Great Pyramid. Hostages milled or sat around, talking or thinking their own thoughts, while around them, perspiring, with no shade for cover and nothing but bottled water to drink, reluctant guards stood their ground. The moment seemed more caught in time than hostile, with two sets of people stranded together and waiting, as if a weary truce existed between them.

And yet there was also an undercurrent of tension, something undefined but clearly felt. Vaguely ominous.

Owen, on his side, intended to make good use of his liberties. He was waiting for the right time; he did not want to show too much interest in the small temple.

The congressmen behind him were two old friends having a talk that might have occurred on the Capitol steps if they ever took the time to sit down there. Renaud, the civil rights activist, was telling Reuben Shackford about his boyhood in Washington, D.C., where his father taught physics at Howard before moving the family west for a job at the University of Chicago. A solid middle-class background, but still urban. Shackford, who'd apparently always lived in Maine, and who, it turned out, was the son of a lighthouse engineer, injected a question now and then. Urban problems never had been his specialty.

"In those days, of course," Renaud said, "Congress cleared out of town for the summer. It was too damned hot to fight. They headed out of town the first of July and didn't come back till September."

"People think we still do that," Shackford replied, with a trace of exasperation. "They think we come back for a week or two and take off again in October."

They both laughed, with the kind of warmth that suggested common experience with a common public misconception. Owen glanced at them over his shoulder. Shackford, he noticed, was looking a little peaked.

"I was thinking of that," said Renaud as his gaze swept the ruins. "I was thinking how much time the job takes, and how much my wife would like this."

"This?" Shackford looked a little startled.

"Under other conditions, of course." Renaud smiled briefly. "She's been complaining for years about our 'vacations'—that we only get one every two years, and then, when we do get away, all it takes is one news report and my head is back in my work again. There goes the vacation."

"Ah, yes." Shackford, who had heard the same story at home, it seemed, chuckled. "She's got a point. And this is a nice place. There's a kind of peace in the isolation. No newspapers. No television. Radios that speak nothing but Spanish. Hell, the world could be at war out there, and we wouldn't know it."

"Or we might be the first to know," Renaud observed pointedly.

There was a brief, heavy silence between them. Then Shackford asked, "Do you think we'll ever get out of here?"

"I wonder sometimes, especially at night, locked into that stinking cell. I suppose Henry's moving as fast as he can. It's a big undertaking for him."

"Henry will be okay. I'm not so sure about us, though.

And to think Andy didn't have to be here at all. If he hadn't gotten his nose out of joint he wouldn't have been at the conference. He wouldn't be *here* now. He'd be back in Washington, probably clearing snow out of his driveway."

Congressman Cass, Owen had learned, was chairman of the House Committee on Merchant Marine and Fisheries, but he wasn't among the original names selected for the delegation to the Cozumel conference. Apparently he'd insisted on coming along and then doubled his own pure bad luck by opting for the day trip to Uxmal.

"We should have thought to include him," Renaud said. "Andy's always sensitive about jurisdiction, and fishing rights were on the agenda from the beginning."

"Can't matter much now."

"No." Renaud paused thoughtfully, then raised his hand in a wave as he noticed a tall, gray-haired man climbing the steps toward them. "Hello, Tom. Come join us."

Thomas MacGregor, the congressman from Minnesota, lean and elegant even in this sweltering heat, nodded to Owen as he passed by and sat down with his colleagues. A frown crossed his face as he looked at Shackford. "Say, Reuben, are you feeling all right? You don't look so good."

"It's the heat," Shackford said.

MacGregor nodded. "I know, it's been bothering me more today. I'd give anything for a nice cool bed with sheets, and a couple of aspirin."

Owen wasn't feeling so well himself. He turned back to the plaza, scanning the milling people for the missing fourth congressman, for Andrew Cass, who wouldn't have been here at all except for getting his nose out of joint.

Owen found him, a short heavy man, with a hand shielding his eyes from the sun as he gazed at the back of the Governor's Palace, one terrace up, more than twenty feet above them. As Owen watched, Cass waved to attract the attention of a guard, who called down in passable English: "What do you want?" Cass explained

145

that he wanted to come up for a closer look at the rear of the building. The guard glanced both ways along the terrace, where there were six terrorists in all—plenty to deal with one aging fool who had nothing better to do in this heat—and shrugged his approval.

Cass started to climb. Since there were no steps on this side of the Governor's Palace, he had to go up the side of the terrace at a sharp angle, half walking, half crawling, clinging to scrub with both hands and growing visibly short of breath from the effort. It was obvious that he wasn't in peak condition. Nonetheless, Owen thought, if the congressman could go sightseeing, so could he. He pushed himself up off the pyramid steps and started to amble across the wide plaza. Midway he stopped, studying the small temple from a distance. Then, with a little more purpose, but keeping his expression no more than idly curious, he walked the rest of the way across and stopped once again within ten feet of the temple.

In Spanish, it was called the *Casa de las Tortugas*. In Mayan, *Akilne*. Either way, the House of the Turtles— and it must have been the only building at Uxmal with a name that was undeniably appropriate. A band of sculpture ran around the cornice of the temple, a row of perfectly carved stone turtles. There were six of them at the end where Owen was standing and three times as many along the side, he noticed as he walked slowly to and around the corner. Turtles, a symbol of water perhaps in this waterless land, in this arid climate, but to Owen a symbol of something else. He remembered the Galapagos. He remembered being there with Michelangelo.

It had been ten years or more, but one night came back in clear detail, because he and Michelangelo had been trapped on a beach together, with gunmen firing at them from the road and nowhere to go but into the water. Into the water as swimming targets, easy to pick off in bright moonlight—dead now, odds were, if it hadn't been for the timely appearance of a herd, or a flock, whatever it was, of giant sea turtles.

Michelangelo spotted them first and thought they were an outcrop of rock, an island, until he realized that the island was moving. Away from the beach, downshore. Owen grabbed one of the huge shells, Michelangelo another. They hitched a ride and nearly drowned, but they eluded the gunmen and had a good laugh later.

Moving islands. And now here he was, at the House of the Turtles at Uxmal.

Two guards on the plaza shifted position as Owen moved slowly around the temple, one behind him, the other ahead—and a third one, he noticed, had turned to watch from the terrace of the Governor's Palace—but none of them interfered with him. Sightseeing today, it seemed, was acceptable.

Once around revealed pillared openings at each end of the temple, which was composed of three rooms, lying end to end and connected only by shared walls; there were no interior openings. Access to the center room, where part of the roof had caved in, was by way of exterior doors on both sides of the building. From outside, the end rooms were lost to Owen in darkness; without going in, he couldn't see much past the pillars. But the center room, open to the sky where the roof was gone, was as brightly lit as the plaza. And that, Owen knew, was where he had to look for the secret Michelangelo had hidden.

He also knew there would be something there to point to it, something large enough to be seen from where he stood, near the doorway—because if Michelangelo knew that Owen might be taken hostage, and he surely did, then he wouldn't have chosen a place too obscure. He would have known that timing was vital. It had to be as obvious, to Owen if no one else, as the stone turtles marching around the cornice.

The floor of the room was entirely overgrown with scrub, and the walls were perfectly plain blocks of stone, surprisingly unscarred by time. But here and there, at shoulder level, and at intervals suggesting a plan, holes had been cut into the walls in positions directly across from other holes like them. They were each the size of a large man's fist, big enough to support a series of low-hanging beams or rafters. The House of the Turtles, Owen supposed, might have been a large closet once. Or maybe the Toltecs hung their sacrificed human hearts out to dry here, with the turtles to act as a lure for the rain god's attention.

Owen smiled, because either way the sign was there and unmistakable. A hole in the far wall had been filled with a piece of rock, and on the rock was a carved initial. The letter *M*. Michelangelo's secret.

Owen took quick stock of the three guards, one of whom had turned away. The others were still watching him—not intently, but not without interest. The one on the terrace was too far above, harmless as long as Owen did nothing to inspire the use of his rifle. The other one, swarthy and sweating, with shoulders as broad as a dining room table, was the one in position to stop him. He was on the plaza, not more than ten yards away.

Owen, of course, would have the advantage of making the first move, and making it unexpectedly. He took his hands from his pockets, keeping them in plain view—no surprises here, no gunfire please—and stepped into the center room.

Inside, moving fast, he reached the far wall in two long strides, grabbed the rock and yanked it free, then reached into the hole and withdrew a small cardboard tube wrapped in plastic. He shoved the tube into his belt, let his shirt fall back to cover it, and had his hands free, on his hips, in plain view and unoccupied, by the time the terrorist guard appeared in the doorway.

It was Broad Shoulders, his eyes black with anger. "What are you doing in here?" he roared.

Owen turned, visibly startled. "Oh, sorry, I was only exploring. I didn't mean to cause trouble."

The guard made a gesture with the barrel of his rifle, a mixture of threat and obscenity.

"No problem. Whatever you say."

Owen started to move, when suddenly loud voices erupted from the plaza outside. Angry words, spoken coldly in Spanish. Someone shot back in English, "Don't push me!''—unleashing another torrent of angry Spanish. Owen recognized one voice and knew that Ramon was back. Worse, one of the hostages was challenging his authority.

Broad Shoulders growled and grabbed Owen's arm with a huge hand, yanking him through the door and onto the plaza. Owen's gaze rose to the terrace overhead. It was Congressman Cass. He had one arm raised toward, not touching, Ramon; he was glaring at the terrorist leader. "Don't push me!" he said again, angrily. "I'll go. I'll do whatever you say. *Just don't push me!*"

But the congressman, overweight and unfit, was no match for the lean, muscular Cuban—not in stature, nor strength, nor potential for fury. Owen pulled away and took off for the terrace wall, sensing what was going to happen. Broad Shoulders reached out to stop him, but Owen was just beyond his grasp. He ran on, his gaze intent on the scene above, until a massive weight struck him low in the back and brought him down. The odors of dust and sweat filled his nostrils. Broad Shoulders was on top of him, pinning him down. Owen couldn't move. He could only watch with a growing sense of foreboding.

He saw Ramon grab a rifle from a guard, saw him swing it back like a club, the muscles of his arms and shoulders rippling in the sun, tendons standing out in his neck. He swung the gun back and then let go with all the force that was in him. Heavy metal struck Cass at the base of his skull, and he started to pitch forward. But Ramon didn't let it go at that. He planted a foot in Cass's back and gave him a shove over the edge. For a moment, the congressman was flying.

No cry emerged from his mouth. There was no sound at all but the thud when he hit the ground flat, on his chest and face, and bounced over onto his back. Even the jungle fell silent.

But Ramon wasn't finished. Driven by fury, he leaped off the edge of the terrace himself, landing lightly on flexed legs, springing back up on the balls of his feet. He grasped the rifle in both hands, holding it by the barrel, brought it up in an arc and then down sharply on Cass's head. He did it again and again. From above, from the side. Blood spattered his clothes. His lips were drawn back, baring sharp teeth, his eyes frenzied.

Later Owen remembered seeing other hostages' faces. They were horrified, or terrified. Some were sick, including Shackford, who lay on the ground retching. Two people fainted. But no one moved to stop Ramon. The terrorists were still in control, and none of them, for whatever reasons—whether loyalty, fear, or futility—made any attempt to reason with their leader.

But Owen remembered these things later. At the time, pinned down, unable to move, he only saw Ramon and the insanity of his murderous temper. All Cass had said was "Don't push me."

Finally, with a great heaving sigh, Ramon stopped. He stood back to study his work, his face now entirely void of emotion, which was somehow even more insane than the violence that had gripped him. Owen felt his own stomach churn. He felt the weight of the man on his back and the sun baking into his skin, even as his blood turned cold. Ramon snapped his fingers, and calmly ordered two guards to dispose of Cass. Then he tucked the bloody rifle under his arm and walked away from the evidence of his madness.

The evidence spoke for itself, fair warning. Broad Shoulders got up, but Owen stayed where he was, trying to get a grip on his own raging anger. And when that was past, he was left with a new sense of urgency. He thought of the cardboard tube in his belt and wanted to get back to his cell. He thought of Emma and his invitation. He needed her back here now more than ever.

The terrorists weren't likely to make a public announcement about the fate of Andrew Cass. There could be no doubt about his condition. His head and shoulders were thick with blood, his skull shattered, his brain exposed and whipped up like eggs. The unthinkable had happened.

And witnessing a purely violent act made certain aspects of it no less practical. Ramon had killed a congressman in a fit of temper. One way or another, there was going to be hell to pay for it.

22

22

Henry Brendan, sitting at his desk, his eyes fixed on Nichols, was visibly shaken. His face was as pale as the ghost of Benjamin Riker—and if he didn't need a drink now, Nichols thought, he would never need one again, because Riker had come to life in the Oval Office. He had come to life with the fact of the ski boots between them on the desk the late President never really relinquished.

Except for the ghost, they were alone. Nichols had requested a private meeting.

"Assassination," Henry said quietly, as if repeating the word might make him believe it. "It's hard to shake my mind loose. All this time we *assumed* it was an accident!"

Nichols went back through it again, because Henry's disbelief was understandable. He'd had trouble accepting the truth himself, but there was no place for doubt. They *were* Riker's boots, the ones he was wearing that day at Aspen. After his death, they had been released by the Secret Service and returned to the President's widow, along with his skis and clothing. She, in turn, had given them to the Smithsonian, where they were catalogued and sentenced to gather dust in the attic, with Herbert Hoover's collar stays and Chester Alan Arthur's mustache combs. No one there knew, of course, that they were a murder weapon, or that they were later stolen out of the attic. When the theft happened, or how, no one knew either. Before Nichols's inquiries, no one had noticed the boots were missing.

All of this Nichols learned in a flurry of phone calls and interviews after he'd met with Emma. The small transmitter, which Henry now held in his hands, absently turning it over and over, was in the locker with the boots, and it too had been examined. It was, as Owen thought, the trigger, tuned by radio signal to high-voltage batteries in the boots. Case closed, on one point at least. Benjamin Riker had been murdered.

A few questions remained.

"Where did you *get* these things?" Henry asked, his expression bewildered.

"In a sense, at Uxmal."

"In a sense?" Henry sat forward. "What on earth are you *saying*?"

"That there's a connection between these"—Nichols gestured to the ski boots—"between the assassination and the Uxmal crisis."

"*What* connection?"

"I don't know."

Henry was truly astonished. More than that, deeply alarmed. "What even makes you *think* such a thing?"

"The fact that the boots came to me through an agent of mine who's one of the hostages."

"At *Uxmal*?" Henry raised himself up out of the chair, leaning hard against his desk and staring at Nichols with sudden horror in his eyes. "Are you telling me there's *a CIA agent at Uxmal*?"

"I'm afraid so." Nichols raised a hand before Henry could have his head. "I didn't know he was there myself when the takeover occurred. He was trailing Ben Riker's killer and got caught there."

"But why at Uxmal? And why *now*?"

"That's the point," Nichols said. "He was sent there by the man we call Michelangelo."

"Good Lord!"

"It's worse than you know." Nichols paused a moment and then plunged ahead. "Michelangelo was once a CIA agent. For the obvious reasons, we've tried to bury that piece of information, but I don't know if we can keep it quiet now.''

"Christ!" Henry sank back into his chair, his shock fading to horrified silence.

Nichols told him briefly how Owen had come to be at Uxmal. "It could be a blessing," he said in the end, moving to take the offensive. "Owen is the best man I have, and he's there on the inside. He's already managed to get a message out."

Henry looked startled. "How, if he's a hostage?"

Nichols had no intention of telling Henry about his other "best man," Emma Thatcher, or about his own plan to rescue Owen. He told a half-truth. "Through a friend of his who lives down there, one of the Mayan Indians. But that's not what matters. Owen's information is vital to us. There may be a foreign power involved. He says the terrorists are Cuban.''

Henry stared back at him for a moment in silence. Then his eyes turned skeptical. "What makes him think that?''

"They speak Cuban Spanish. And you should take his word for that. Owen's ear for language is damn near infallible.''

"But it doesn't make sense," Henry said. "If the terrorists are Cuban, why would they try to negotiate new rights for illegal Mexican aliens?''

"I wondered myself. I don't know.''

Nichols did know that Henry's mind was still partly numb from the shock of his disclosures, and he would have expected no more from a man twice Henry's measure, not even from Riker. He had expected disbelief. But not skepticism. He'd hoped for something different from the President. These were things, after all, that Hayfield and the DIA failed to notice.

"Well, there it is," Nichols said. "Now what do we do with it?''

"I don't know." Henry was, at least, quick with an honest answer. "This twists everything, doesn't it?''

"Twists! This screws the hell out of everything, as far as I can see. That's why I'm here. You had to know.''

Henry got up and started to pace the room—to the fireplace with its carved antique mantel and back again to the globe that sat beside his desk. He gave the globe a sudden, sharp spin and stopped it with a practiced hand. His eyes lingered a moment on the southern tip end of Mexico. "I still don't see the connection," he said. "If your man Owen was onto something related to Ben Riker's death and happened to choose a bad day to go to Uxmal, it doesn't have to mean the two things are related."

"That's Owen's judgment," Nichols replied. "He doesn't believe in coincidence."

"He doesn't *believe* . . . ?" Henry spun around. "How very nice! I can't make life-and-death decisions based on what one man does or doesn't believe in."

"Two men," Nichols said. "I agree with him. I don't believe in coincidence, either."

"Well, I don't much myself, but you're not giving me a hell of a lot to go on." Henry sat down. "And now you want to throw in a foreign government! *Why* would the Cubans—or the Russians, if that's what you're getting at—take four congressmen hostage and then play around with our immigration quotas?"

"Maybe they want to stir up trouble for us."

"I don't believe it!"

Nichols didn't either.

"Anyway," Henry went on, "are you suggesting the Cubans, or the Russians, might have killed Ben?"

Nichols shrugged. "I'm not suggesting anything, but it has to be considered."

"Maybe so, but if I'm going to do anything beyond what I'm doing now, I need something more than your agent's instincts and ear for language. Look, Ed, my goal is to save the hostages, and to do it honorably. We've got a plan and it may work, but now you're throwing in a whole new set of problems. I've already told you how I feel about the CIA, that I want you to stay out of this, for reasons that aren't your fault—or maybe they are, because you've been so damned effective—but the Third World doesn't look on you people

155

kindly. They think you're everywhere, and it seems they're right. You've even got an agent inside the ruins!"

Henry paused and shook his head. "It's touchy. More touchy if we have to consider a foreign government. There's no evidence, *no* indication, these terrorists are Cuban except your agent's report, and I can't take his word against everything else. It's not enough that you think he's probably right. In this case, he *can't be wrong*, and you can't possibly guarantee his infallibility."

Damn near, Nichols thought, but he knew it was pointless to carry the argument further. Henry didn't want to be convinced.

The President pushed back his chair and stood up, a signal that the meeting was over. "As for your agent," he said, "for God's sake, if he makes contact with you again tell him to lie low. Have you considered what could happen if the terrorists find out who he is?"

"Of course," Nichols said. "I don't want to lose him."

"And I don't want to lose the rest of the hostages, including the three best friends I've got!"

"The terrorists won't find out who he is. Owen is a professional."

"What do you think *they* are, a bunch of half-assed amateurs? No, Ed, I'm serious. There's not much I can do about this man of yours being there, but if he makes contact, or if you have any way of reaching him, I want you to call him off. I don't want him lifting a finger unless it's to eat or to blow his nose."

"Okay," Nichols said. "But how are we going to find out who killed Ben Riker?"

"We'll find out later if we're meant to know. Right now, I have one priority. Saving lives. I'm sorry if Ben was murdered, and I want to know who killed him too, but the hostages are still alive. I don't care how many questions go unanswered. I don't intend to let anything happen to them."

Nichols was scowling as he left the Oval Office and the West Wing, heading for his car. Henry Brendan, he believed, though no man's fool, was wrong. Dead wrong.

And it was up to the CIA, to Owen and Thatcher, to prove it.

Because obviously no one else was going to.

Henry saw things the other way around. Though he had his moments of doubt, he believed that what he was doing was right, in the best interests of the country, because Uxmal couldn't become more complicated than it already was. And he thought Nichols would agree with him if Nichols knew what he knew. But Nichols didn't and couldn't be told.

Yet Henry wasn't convinced that he was up to handling what he was doing. And now, here was *Riker* back. Would that man's ghost *never* leave him alone?

He pushed a button in the panel on his desk.

"Yes, Mr. President?"

"Get me Conklin Pierce on the phone," he said. "And while I'm talking to him, call my wife and tell her I have to see her."

23

Emma and Frank had taken up their regular position on the slope of the Pyramid of the Old Woman, whose legend was now a familiar story to Emma. There had been little else to talk about, because nothing new had happened.

It was night again, with a clear sky and the wind blowing up in a way that might have been ominous if there were any chance of rain at this time of year. Night again, more than twenty-four hours since she had gone to Miami, since she had promised Nichols that Owen was going to arrange a way for her to walk into the ruins. She couldn't outguess Owen this time. She had no idea what he had in mind, but she did believe he would do it.

Only *when*? There was nothing to do but wait for his invitation.

The ruins seemed strangely subdued tonight, though she wasn't sure why she thought so. The hostages were locked in their cells; the terrorist guards were standing watch on the terrace. That was one thing—they were standing and not marching, as they had been before. There weren't as many of them either, only four across the front, and two of them looked so listless they might have been dozing. Something was sapping their energy, or their will.

That couldn't be a bad thing, she thought, and focused her binoculars on Owen's door. He was there, inside, stretched out on his cot, one hand resting on his forehead, obscuring his face. He wasn't reading tonight, but maybe he had nothing left to read. Emma made a mental note to bring him some Zola or Balzac. But somehow, tonight, the idea didn't amuse her.

There was something *wrong*.

She glanced at Frank in the darkness, remembering one of the later legends of Uxmal, that it was an unhealthy place. In the days long after the ancient Maya abandoned the city, as the jungle reached out to suffocate what they had left behind, the Indians who remained, their descendants, knew that Uxmal was there. But for years they avoided the ruins, believing them to be a place of sickness and death. Emma assumed the legend had some basis in fact, that they'd stumbled onto something akin to malaria. But now she wondered. Now she felt it too. She shook off a chill against wind and night air and brought her thoughts back to the present.

To something moving in her mind—no, under the ground—the vibration she'd felt once before, in the cave, on her way to rescue Owen. She felt it again now—subtle, but there.

Good lord, the earth was moving!

"Frank," she said, leaning close to his ear to be heard without shouting above the wind, "do you ever have earthquakes here?"

He flattened his palms against the scrub of the pyramid. "I feel it too," he said. "It's not an earthquake. It's too regular, too steady."

But even as he spoke the vibrating stopped, only to begin again moments later.

"Are you sure?" Emma asked.

"No."

Emma sat up in the scrub. "If you don't mind, I'll find someone who knows. I'd just as soon be warned before it happens."

Emma posed the question to Ardry by radio, and he was back with an answer within the hour. Seismographs positioned to cover the Yucatan had registered no activity beneath the earth's surface in six months and nothing of significance in the last year.

159

She went back to the pyramid to tell Frank. "Whatever it is, it's not an earthquake."

"It's not normal, either," he said.

"No, it's not. If we haven't heard from Owen tomorrow, or maybe even if we have, I think I'll go back to your cave and do some exploring."

Alone in his cell, Owen felt the vibration too, but he thought it was coming from somewhere inside his own body. He wasn't feeling good at all, but neither were most of the terrorists. That was only more proof that they didn't come from around here because if they were Mexican they wouldn't be suffering from dysentery.

If he were Mexican, neither would Owen. He'd have built an immunity to the indigenous parasites years ago, as he had when he lived in Cairo and New Delhi. Since those days, he hadn't put down in one place long enough to get used to anyone's local water. And so his knees felt weak and his stomach cramped as he sat up on the cot, seeking comfort from a different body position. It didn't work—his head spun—but he sat there anyway, reminding himself that dysentery didn't last forever.

And thinking that Michelangelo would be amused if he could only see what was happening.

Owen reached into his shirt pocket and removed the single piece of paper that had been in the cardboard tube in the House of the Turtles. It was only that, a glossy page torn out of a book and labeled with a plate number in Roman numerals. A photograph of a Mayan stela, intricately carved, with hieroglyphics surrounding three male figures. Frank might be able to read the glyphs, though as Owen recalled, the ancient writing that remained to be read ran more to months and years than to concepts, to pieces of history pulled out of the Mayan long-count calendar. Or there might be symbolism in the figures: two were full-sized, one a dwarf. None of it meant anything to Owen.

Nor did the pencil drawing in the margin—an inverted box with its flaps open, a three-sided rectangle with lines drawn out from the open side at the bottom. In the rectangle, near the top, was a letter *w*. A direction? West? And a large backward *L* into which were drawn two bisecting lines and two numbers: 45 on the left, 55 on the right. The numbers were probably angles, with the lines of the *L*, a right angle itself, to give them a base, an anchor. And beside the drawing, written by hand, was the name of the rain god, Chac, who might have been any one of the three male figures, all fierce-looking souls, including the dwarf. The sort who would happily turn a deaf ear on the needs of a thirsty people.

The drawing was a chart or a map, of course, and the bisecting lines no doubt pinpointed target zero. There was only one problem: no reference points. A map of what? Where was Owen supposed to *go* to figure these angles?

He folded the page, put it into his pocket, and lay back on his cot, hands behind his head. Michelangelo's secret was here somewhere, plain to see, hidden but perfectly obvious. It had to be, for the gauntlet meant nothing unless it was fair, and the challenge was false without a worthy opponent.

Then suddenly he pulled the blanket up to stave off a new round of chills, so violent they made his teeth and bones shake. His fire, untended, was dying now, and the cell was turning clammy. The blanket helped, but sleep would help more. Then, just before he closed his eyes, he noticed something in the darkness of the corbeled ceiling. A soft light flickered on and off, barely visible. Owen smiled as he drifted to sleep.

A firefly. Good company.

Emma would be here with him tomorrow.

Frank was awakened in the night by someone pounding on the door of his clinic. He roused himself and got out of bed, pulled on his jeans and shirt, and made his way to the reception room. A patient, he assumed. A familiar face. A farmer. A mother.

He opened the door, still half asleep, his mind vaguely thinking of chicken pox and due babies, and then he froze. *Not* a familiar face. He had never seen the man

161

before, at least not at close range. The man growled and gestured with his rifle.

It was too late to slam the door, too late and probably futile. Frank stepped back to let the terrorist enter.

24

Dawn was starting to break over Muna when Frank's sister, Nicte, shook Emma awake in her sleeping hammock. "Frank is here," she whispered softly, not to awaken the children or her husband. "He said to tell you the invitation has come at last."

Emma climbed out of the hammock. "Where is he?"

"In front. In the van. One of the terrorists is with him." Nicte raised a finger to her lips before Emma could react. "Put this on," she said and held out one of her dresses, an embroidered *huipil* with a white petticoat and flowers encircling the hem and neckline.

Emma raised an eyebrow, observing the appreciable difference in her height and Nicte's.

"It will fit well enough," Nicte said. "You'll just have a little more of the petticoat showing."

She was right. Emma slipped the dress on over her head and stepped into her sandals. Then she pulled her hair back from a center part and pinned it into a knot at her neck. While she was dressing, Nicte told her what had happened.

"Frank came to the door and spoke to me briefly in Mayan. The terrorist was annoyed by that and insisted he speak only Spanish, but Frank had time to say enough—that the invitation had come, that you should dress as one of us."

"Why?" Emma asked.

"They need a doctor at the ruins. I don't know why,

163

but they know about Frank and seem to think his sister is a nurse. You are to be me."

"Who does the terrorist think Frank was talking to?"

"He didn't call me by name," Nicte said. "I could be anyone, another sister, a cousin. We often have more than one family living together." She held out a bright red flower. "For your hair. We always wear them."

Emma pinned the flower into her hair as she went out the door, admiring Nicte's calm, knowing she must be terrified for her brother. Frank, no less calm on the surface at least, started the van as soon as he saw her coming. The terrorist got out and motioned her in with his gun. She sat between them.

Frank said something in Mayan as he made a U-turn and headed back to the highway. Then he glanced at the terrorist and went on in Spanish. "They need us at the ruins," he said. "They have fifty-two people sick out there."

Emma turned to him, worried. "What is it?"

"Nothing serious. They're probably pretty uncomfortable, but they'll live. They've had a bad outbreak of dysentery."

Dysentery! Emma nearly laughed, but the Nicte in her would not be startled, and so she nodded.

"Apparently they got a bad lot of water." Frank gestured to the back of the van. "We're taking them a fresh supply."

Emma glanced over her shoulder and saw cartons of bottled water stacked in the back, as Frank began to discuss treatment in terms that would give her a clear picture of what she had to do once they got there. Fortunately, dysentery was not as complicated to treat, a matter of knowing medication and dosage, as some things Owen might have concocted.

For she had no doubt that Owen had created this epidemic. They weren't pushing through the jungle this time, but driving right up to the ruins. And then walking in, albeit with an armed escort. They had been invited to come, just as Owen promised.

She smiled to herself while keeping her eyes averted

164

from the terrorist beside her, on her hands in her lap. She could guess what Owen had done. He had managed somehow to invade the supplies, to contaminate the purified water. He was an archaeologist, as far as the terrorists knew. He might well have been here before, might know about the doctor in the village, might even have mentioned his sister the nurse. The setup bore Owen's mark as clearly as if he'd handwritten the invitation.

And if she had to guess more, she thought she knew how he had done it. There was only one natural source of water within walking distance of Uxmal. Emma knew because she'd seen it herself—she remembered the transparent ghost fish—and because she knew Owen. He had been back to the cave. He had siphoned off some of the underground river and put it into the bottled water.

But her smile, unseen, faded quickly. She also remembered the feeling she'd had observing the ruins only hours before, through wind and darkness from the Pyramid of the Old Woman. Uxmal was *not* a healthy place.

And dysentery was not enough to explain it.

"Did you have to make *yourself* sick?" Emma asked softly once she got to Owen.

She had been keeping her voice low, in the manner of the Maya, with each of the patients she had seen, terrorists and hostages, questioning them about the severity of their symptoms. And now she switched to Portuguese, knowing it sounded enough like Spanish to keep from alarming the guard assigned to her as she made her rounds. The guard wasn't feeling well himself. He stood in the doorway of Owen's cell, watching her more than he was listening.

"I had to make sure they let you see me," Owen replied from his cot.

"You succeeded. You look terrible."

"Thanks." He smiled.

But Emma knew Owen meant what he said, that the symptoms had to be authentic in him, because he never did things halfway. She also knew that some corner of his mind had insisted he not exclude himself as a matter of fairness.

He slipped something into her hand. A piece of paper, folded.

Emma glanced at it and then reached into the bag Frank had given her, producing a bottle she had saved after treating someone else. The bottle was empty.

She turned to the terrorist and said, "I've run out of medication. Please bring me more."

He hesitated.

"Anda lé pronto!"

She was soft but tough, like the Maya. The man took the bottle and left, and Emma unfolded the piece of paper.

"Listen quickly," Owen said. "Things have changed. They've killed a congressman."

"Oh, Christ! Which one?"

"Cass."

Emma felt coldly angry as Owen told her what had happened. "Ramon is vicious," he said in the end, "and probably psychotic. We have to move fast now. I've found the moving islands." He pointed to the paper in her hand. "Try to get Frank alone and show him that picture. Then get back to me before—"

"You don't need Frank," Emma said as she studied the three male figures. "It's the dwarf. Mayan legend." She looked up. "Your problem is you don't know your pyramids."

Once, so the story went, there was nothing at Uxmal but the peasants' thatched houses, the great white palace of the king, and a ramshackle hut where the witch lived, ostracized, because no one liked her. The witch went to the wise men who lived in the caves where the Moan birds cried, to beg for a son to share her isolation. The wise men, laughing—because they shunned the witch as much as everyone else did—gave her a giant egg and told her to keep it warm on her hearth. One day, they claimed, a fine son would hatch from it.

A son did emerge from the egg on the hearth in the

witch's shanty. He was full-grown, though just seven hands high, a dwarf, and his face was even more hideous than the face of the old witch mother.

But the witch was not to be outmaneuvered. She invested her son with her magic powers and sent him to call on the king, who suspected a threat to his throne and, with foul play in mind, invited him to spend the night. The dwarf demurred, claiming he preferred to sleep in his own palace.

His own palace? He had none! The king went to sleep unworried.

But come the dawn, when the peasants awoke and emerged from their thatched *chozas*, a great city that had sprung up in the night surrounded the king's palace. And from the heart of it rose a shining white pyramid, with a house far more splendid than anything they had ever seen. The peasants fell to their knees. Then they seized the king's crown and placed it on the head of the dwarf, who was thereafter known as the Magician.

Owen lay back on his cot. "So, it's the Pyramid of the Magician."

Emma nodded. "In legend the lofty house at the top is the home of the dwarf. It's also a temple to Chac," she added, noting the rain god's name written beside Michelangelo's drawing.

She had seen the small *w* in the drawing too, and like Owen assumed it was a direction. The inverted box was no doubt the west door of the lofty house, looking in or out. Either way, it was perfectly clear: Michelangelo's secret was hidden at the top of the huge pyramid, under the nose of the sentry there, at the highest point in the ruins.

Owen looked toward the door, then at her again. "The guard will be back soon," he said.

Emma bent her head close to his and they whispered.

Sam Ardry was a determined man, not inclined to give up when his instincts told him he was on the trail of something. He had run the name Garcia Ramon through the computer under every possible spelling and turned up nothing. Now a new variation occurred to him, the simplest of all; once he saw it, the most obvious. He placed his fingers on the keys once again and inverted the name.

Ramon Garcia.

The computer printed the name back, paused, and then came to life before Ardry's eyes, which grew calmer as he read what the machine had stored in its memory bank. Ramon Garcia was Cuban, all right.

When the machine had spelled out everything it knew, Ardry looked very calm indeed. He picked up the print-out and hurried off to find Nichols.

25

Nichols arrived at the diplomatic entrance of the White House a few minutes before ten and was shown upstairs to the Blue Room, where he waited, pacing restlessly, among waiters filling demitasse cups and small brandy snifters, among portraits of the Presidents and First Ladies. He could hear the official toasts being raised in the State Dining Room down the hall—by the visiting Dutch Prime Minister and then by the President—and he wondered what Henry was toasting with. Black coffee, he hoped, strong and straight, because Henry was going to need it.

Thatcher had reported in, and the crisis had deepened in the worst way. A congressman had been murdered.

Nichols paused briefly by a tall window as applause greeted the end of the toasts and eased into subdued conversation. The state dinner was winding down. Soon the guests would be moved from the dining room to the Blue Room for coffee and cognac, and from there to the East Room, where they would be joined by other guests for a concert by a string quartet Nichols had never heard of. Nichols wasn't included in either group and didn't mind. He resumed his pacing.

Finally Henry Brendan appeared, elegant in his dinner clothes and polished patent leather shoes. "Come with me," he said softly.

Nichols, who was wearing the same suit he had put on at seven o'clock in the morning, followed him to an anteroom that wasn't on the public tour. They stepped into a small elevator, and Henry pressed a button. The doors closed, but the elevator didn't move. It merely ensured their privacy.

"Talk fast," Henry said. "This place is crawling with press, and these days they watch every blink of my eyes."

"I've got news for you," Nichols replied. If Henry wanted to hear it fast, then he wasn't going to mince words. "Andrew Cass is dead."

"What?" Henry staggered backward, and his face went as pale as the white of his silk shirt front.

"Killed," Nichols said.

"No! My God! I don't want to believe it!"

"You don't have a choice, I'm afraid. I have an eye-witness. Cass was brutally beaten, his brains literally smashed to a pulp, by the leader of the terrorists."

Henry grabbed hold of the brass railing beside him. "When?" he asked almost inaudibly.

"The day before yesterday."

"Two *days* ago?"

Henry closed his eyes, and Nichols wondered if he was going to be sick right here in the elevator. Henry was obviously stunned by the spectre of violent death, by the menace of Uxmal grown larger—and by the fact that he hadn't been told for more than forty-eight hours. Well, Hayfield was in charge. Let him explain it!

Nichols told Henry what he knew, and as he spoke, Henry's eyes grew numb, a defense against reality. It was probably just as well, since he had to go back to his guests as if nothing had happened.

"That's not all," Nichols said. "We've identified the terrorist leader. He's a Cuban refugee by the name of Ramon Garcia."

Henry's eyes darted back. "A refugee?"

"He was one of the boat people who arrived here in droves a few years ago."

Nichols shifted his weight uncomfortably, feeling confined by close air and small space. The truth was the CIA had welcomed the flood of refugees from Cuba, because they offered a fertile field for recruitment. And the Cuban government knew it.

"Castro knew," he said, "and used it to play a fine joke on us. His secret police cleaned out their jails, got rid of their dirty wash, so to speak, by handing it over to us. Among hundreds of genuine refugees, they packed the boats with thieves, rapists, murderers. They knew we'd have the devil's own time trying to figure out which was which, never mind what we should do about them." Nichols shook his head. "A *fine* joke! It caused us no end of trouble."

"And this man," the President asked, "this Ramon Garcia—he was one of those?"

"One of the worst, I'm afraid. Far more than just dirty wash. He was once a lieutenant in the secret police, an interrogator, but he was fired. Seems he broke his prisoners down too effectively before he found out what they might know. By all the intelligence we were able to pick up, this man's nothing less than insane. He enjoys hurting people. He's violent beyond control. The secret police didn't even want him. He might have been executed, except they thought of a better way to dispose of him. They sent him to us."

Henry's eyes blazed. "For Christ's sake, why wasn't he deported? If you people knew all of this, why didn't you *tell* someone?"

"We *did*," Nichols said. "Of course we did! We reported him to Immigration as soon as we knew who he was. We thought he'd been sent back, in fact, because he disappeared from the refugee camp he was assigned to, and that was the last we heard of him. Now, I believe we'd better find out where he did go."

"Now it's a little late," the President replied sharply. Then his anger vanished, and a look of pain crossed his face. He turned away, seeking refuge from his own anguish. "Andy Cass," he said. "I suppose we'd better notify his family."

"There's something else to think about first. It's possible that our dossier on Ramon Garcia is planned misinformation. It's possible we were meant to believe that he'd been expelled from Cuba in disfavor, that he actually entered the country as an agent of Havana or even Moscow."

Nichols paused, knowing Henry couldn't duck the issue any longer. "Frankly," he said, "I've got a hunch it isn't that simple, if only because his behavior at Uxmal so strongly bears out what the dossier says about him. On the other hand, foreign involvement has to be considered now. We can't rule out a conspiracy—"

"No."

"—involving, perhaps, the assassination of a President and certainly the murder of a congressman. And it could have been planned in Cuba or in the Soviet Union."

"Dear God!" Henry exclaimed. "This is getting out of hand."

Nichols very nearly laughed, but the words struck a cold nerve in his spine. It had been out of hand from the start. Was it possible that Henry was too naïve, or too blind, or too frightened to know it?

"Perhaps we should make diplomatic contact with Havana," Nichols said.

"Why? If they are involved, they would only deny it."

"Of course they would, just as they would deny sending us Ramon Garcia. But if they are behind this, or involved in any way, and if they know we suspect it, they might be scared off. We might be able to avert a confrontation."

"Too late to help Andy."

"In time, perhaps, to save the others."

Henry nodded. "I need time to think about it."

"There isn't much time."

"Hell, I know it!" Henry looked at his watch and pulled himself up. "I have to go. I can't stay away any longer. I'll have the National Security Council briefed on everything you've told me, but I'm not sure when we'll actually meet. I'm going to Florida tomorrow."

"Still?" Nichols stared at him, astonished.

"I told you, I need time to think."

To think or avoid, Nichols wondered.

"And I want to get some questions answered. Among other things, I want to find out if MacKendrick might have Delta ready sooner."

MacKendrick! Christ! Would Henry never learn whom he ought to trust within his own intelligence community?

Nichols waited until Henry left and then slipped out of the White House unseen, without causing a ripple of curiosity. He was deeply worried. He had done his best to convince Henry that Uxmal was even more dangerous than it seemed, but Henry didn't want to listen. And he wondered how much worse it would get before Henry was willing to pay attention.

◫ 26 ◫

Early in the evening, while sunlight still shone through the screen over his door, Owen studied his face in the mirror of the makeup case Emma had given him. The face that stared back was not his own. It was bearded, dark-haired, and solemn. A face not quickly disguised, designed to deceive as long as no one came too close, but painstakingly transformed into the face of a terrorist.

Owen felt sure he would pass muster even on close inspection—and he'd better, because tonight there would be no red safelight for cover. Once he left his cell he would be in the open, lit by the full glare of spotlights, alone with his own bravado and a hundred-odd men who were not inclined to be gracious. At least, he thought, he didn't look remotely like a hostage, and there were only two kinds of people here. Expectations were on his side. The terrorists weren't likely to guess that one of their captives might join them for dinner.

Owen stored the makeup case with his other supplies in the dark rear room of his cell. He pulled on the khaki fatigues, completing the transformation, and poured himself a drink. Then he crossed the room to the door of his cell and looked out, taking care not to let himself be seen prematurely.

The sky above Uxmal was clear, with no hint of clouds as far as Owen could see, but great dry gusts of wind were blowing across the ruins, raising dust and diffusing the last golden light of the day as the sun descended into the jungle. The terrorist guards were

174

shielding their eyes with their hands; some had tied bandanas across their noses and mouths; some were wearing dark glasses—and in this wind they might well leave them on even after the sun was gone. Owen raised a cup of Scotch to his lips, felt its warmth in his throat as he downed it in a swallow. Daylight was fading fast now. He turned back into the room and lay down on his cot, pulling the blankets up to prevent discovery. He lay still, a man like so many others here, trying to throw off the effects of a nasty illness. His stomach was still a little queasy, but the cramps had passed with the fever and chills, victims of medication and rest and a fresh supply of water. He was feeling better, good enough. Now he could only wait.

And sleep. He let himself doze lightly, his mind tuned for a sound that would come and rouse him as surely as an alarm. When it came—the clank of his screen being raised a few inches off the floor—he waited a moment, then slowly sat up and looked around. Except for the light in the path of his door, his cell was entirely dark, his fire purposely unlit, his tray on the floor this side of the screen, which had been dropped into place. The terrorist who brought the tray had moved on to another cell; it wasn't his concern, it seemed, if the fourth door from the left slept through dinner.

Owen was hungry. He hadn't had much to eat in two days, but there was no time now. He moved quickly, replacing the bulk of his body on the cot with piles of rocks, pulling the blanket up, arranging a book once more in a dropped position. Then he picked up his rifle, hung it over his shoulder, and moved to the door.

It was quiet outside except for the wind, which was still blowing up clouds of dust. A skeleton crew, thinned by lingering fever and chills, was on duty outside. Four men. Two had moved the food cart toward the center of the building and were occupied delivering trays. Another had his back to Owen's door. The fourth, turned this way, was reaching for cigarettes in a shirt pocket.

Owen put on his dark glasses, leaving practically none of his face exposed, and waited a moment, until the fourth guard produced a lighter and lowered his cigarette to it. Then, stepping over the tray, he slipped past the screen unobserved.

Where there had been four terrorists, now there were five. Owen moved along the terrace floor with an easy stride, not acknowledging with furtive or faltering step, nor with an urge to hurry, that his presence here was unexpected. Sheer bluff, requiring more gall than courage. He reached the food cart and stopped. The guard with his back turned spun around, startled.

"I need a tray," Owen said in Spanish, stepping into the silence before the terrorist had a chance to voice surprise or objection. "Ramon's dinner wasn't delivered tonight, and he's hungry enough to eat the first thing that catches his eye."

The words had their intended effect. The guard didn't move to stop him but, squinting against the dust, studied Owen carefully, wondering perhaps if he'd seen him before. Or if he hadn't. It would be hard to tell with so much of his face covered.

"Where did you come from?" the man asked.

Owen looked a little startled himself. "From Ramon. I just told you."

"No, how did you get here?"

"I walked up the steps. What's the matter with you?"

"*I* didn't see you."

Owen frowned. "Is something wrong?"

"I didn't see anyone on the steps."

"Well, I didn't fly up," Owen replied sharply. "Maybe you're still a little light-headed. Or maybe you should be paying more attention."

The terrorist looked suddenly defensive. "Wait a minute—"

"Don't worry," Owen added quickly as he reached for a tray. "I won't tell Ramon you weren't watching. But if you can't stay alert, maybe you'd better report in for a replacement. Ramon's a little testy tonight, and you'd make a fine dinner for him."

The guard laughed uneasily, not quite sure if this

compatriot was joking. Owen seized his advantage, took the tray, and made his way down the steps, right down the center of them, aware of the guard's eyes on his back. He reached the plaza of the two-headed jaguar and turned left, glancing over his shoulder. The guard, apparently satisfied or possibly only disinterested now, was no longer paying attention. Owen kept going. He'd had to leave his cell early to take advantage of the dinner cart, to create a reason for the appearance of an extra man, and now he had two hours to kill. Two hours to fit in. Two hours in which he had to *be* a terrorist.

Uxmal lay before him in contrasting patches of spotlight and shadow. Ahead of him, in the distance, the huge pyramid was brightly lit, and below it so were the Nunnery buildings. From the Ball Court, where off-duty guards were eating their dinner or sleeping, came the snap and glow of a fire, but the rest of the ruins lay in darkness. A narrow flight of stone steps angled down the side of the terrace from the plaza and out of the circle of lights that shone on the Governor's Palace. Owen made his way down and turned toward the Ball Court, where the fire crackled and leaped in the air, sharply drawn against the blackness of sky and jungle. There he sat down—not by himself, but with a small group of terrorists—and quietly ate his dinner.

"You on duty tonight?" the man beside him asked after a while.

Owen, leaning over his tray like the rest of them, trying to protect his food from the dust, grunted and went on chewing. The man was so close he could hear him breathe, smell the odor of his body. "Not tonight, I'm not," he said, looking up. "Thank God. This dust is about to get me."

"Yeah, they ought to increase our pay for hazardous duty."

The man laughed, and so did the others in the circle. Owen busied himself eating.

A new voice spoke up. "Anyone have a guess how long we're going to have to be here?"

"It won't be over soon," said the man beside Owen.

"Another month," someone else confirmed. "A month at least, maybe longer."

The fire rose, blown up by the wind, in spite of sandbags piled up to protect it; it rose and sank, spitting sparks that dropped to the dry earth and died there. Owen finished his dinner having learned two things: that these were *paid* terrorists who didn't especially want to be here, and that in their view the seige would not be over soon.

He turned to the man beside him. "I don't know about you," he said, "but I'm going to get some sleep."

The man didn't bother to look at Owen as he stood up and ambled away from the fire, found an empty sleeping bag, and crawled into it, putting his rifle on the ground beside him. He lay in semidarkness, his face turned from the firelight, feigning sleep whenever anyone passed by. In between, he studied the view ahead, the great elliptical Pyramid of the Magician.

On the west slope, which faced into the ruins, a grand staircase rose on two levels, first to a point about ninety feet up where a door opened to a small temple, and then, dividing around the door, to the lofty house at the top of the pyramid. There was no dwarf in residence now, though the sentry on the roof did look something like a toy soldier.

Owen also kept an eye on the time. At nine o'clock guards changed shifts across the ruins, and at the top of the pyramid one sentry replaced another. Owen watched with particular interest as the new guard made the steep ascent, up the west slope on hands and feet, grasping a heavy iron chain that had been bolted into the steps, which were well lit but apparently treacherous. The wind was strong, and once the tiny figure slipped, catching and hanging onto the chain, lying low on the steps until the wind passed, and then climbing on. The new sentry cleared the top and the old one came down, scrambling backward.

Owen smiled to himself, because he had the same

178

climb ahead—no, a worse climb, up the steeper steps on the east side of the pyramid, and he would have to do it in total darkness.

Michelangelo never did like to make things easy.

22

⊠ 27 ⊠

Frank was once again in position behind the ticket office, his hands protected by rubber-lined gloves, his feet encased in thick-soled shoes, more of Emma's special equipment. On the ground beside him lay a tool that looked like an ordinary set of pliers; it lay there waiting to be grabbed up, but Frank's hands were occupied now. He held his binoculars to his eyes and focused them on a rear corner of the building where the main power line came in from the road. There was nothing subtle about this operation.

He was here to cut the line, and to do it in a way that the terrorists just might think looked like the result of natural obsolescence. But to do it, no matter what. To shut the lights off. And if the terrorists recognized that sabotage had occurred, Emma said the prize would be worth it.

"These clippers won't cut sharply," she said. "They'll *fray* the line first, and you may get a jolt. Be ready for it. As long as you're wearing the gloves and shoes, it can't hurt you. But it will take a good ten seconds of steady pressure before the line breaks. Stick with it. Don't let up until it goes. Then get yourself out of there pronto."

Frank smiled at the ease with which she dismissed a mere "jolt," a sensation of shock to be ignored. And one thing he didn't have to be told was to move out fast once the job was accomplished. The rest he wasn't so sure of. But he focused in on his target, the place where the power line actually entered the building, where it might most likely fray of natural causes. It was clear to see, or clear enough, in the wash of light that fell this way from the spotlights mounted in the trees at the entrance to the ruins.

Frank looked at his watch—five minutes to ten—and let the binoculars fall loose on their strap as his hand closed around the clippers. He forced himself to breathe evenly, suppressing the fear that within a few minutes he might not be breathing at all. In a moment, he checked the time again. Four minutes to go.

He waited.

Owen took the long way around, behind the Nunnery buildings, avoiding spotlights but encountering guards, to whom he raised a hand in silent greeting. And as he emerged on the far side, the Pyramid of the Magician rose before him, its lines gently curving from east to west, its steps rising sharply to the sky. He continued to make a wide circle around it, to the back or east face, which looked across the jungle. And there he stopped, studying the angle of climb, very nearly straight up, over a hundred feet in the air. If the Maya had strived for height, they achieved it here without any doubt. The pyramid was magnificent.

Looking up, Owen felt his head spin, and he closed his eyes, impatient with the interference of his own body. Then he looked up again. A chain like the one on the other side ran up these steps too. Made of iron and bolted fast, it lay flush against the stone a few feet from the edge of the steps, which were built out from the pyramid and dropped off sharply on each side. Except for the chain, there was no railing or bannister. Owen cursed himself for drinking his own bad water. Then he looked at his watch, saw the second hand sweep up to ten o'clock. There was no time to think about vertigo now. A moment later, the lights blacked out all around him.

He pulled off his dark glasses and shoved them into a pocket, running forward as confusion broke loose across the ruins. He grabbed the chain to start his ascent, keeping low against the steps, moving swiftly but cautiously, making time while he could since the wind was strong and going to get worse. The steps were worn smooth by nature, and by years and years of use. They were smooth and incredibly shallow, carved for feet less than half the length of his own, less than the length of his hand—quite possibly for the feet of a dwarf. He slipped twice as he scrambled for height, but caught himself with his grip on the chain. The Maya, of course, climbed their pyramids at an angle, in grand ceremonial processions, but ceremony wasn't in order tonight. The wind gusted fiercely as he reached the level of the trees and the open air above them. To release the chain now would be suicidal.

Still, he was halfway up the steps before he felt dizzy again, and he stopped, sprawling flat, shaking his head, pressing the bridge of his nose between two fingers. The feeling faded, then returned again, and he felt himself floating, with pinpoints of light popping open behind his eyelids. The pinpoints grew into starbursts, and would not go away. He wondered if the Mayan sky lords were trying to scare him away from their sacred precinct.

The starbursts faded, but Owen knew his senses were dulled, his vision dimmed, his reflexes not what they should be. He moved on, feeling his way, keeping low against the wind. Then his feet slipped against the smooth stone and he started to slide. The steps seemed to flatten beneath him. He could not get a grip with his rubber soles. He bore down on the chain with both hands, pulled himself to a stop with a wrenching force he felt in his shoulders and his spine and all the way to his fingertips.

He lay still a moment, catching his breath, his head floating, wafting away from him on a fine breeze, then returning with no sense of haste and reattaching itself to his body. One hand, caught under the chain—made heavier by his own weight—was scraped and bleeding, not seriously, but blood mixed with sweat on his palm, making the hand wet and slippery. He wiped it against his shirt, getting ready to climb, to recover the height he'd lost. And then the gods turned vicious.

They unleashed a harsh blast of wind that caught him under the chest and, with incredible power, flung him over onto his back, toward the edge of the steps. He couldn't see where they dropped off or if he had a margin of safety. He clung to the chain with one hand and tried to get a grip on the steps with the other. And suddenly there was nothing to get a grip on.

The wind pushed at him relentlessly; he was already at the edge, his arm hanging free, his margin of safety, if ever it was, exhausted. He held to the chain with fingertips and then, with enormous force of will, heaved himself over onto his chest. The gods withdrew, perhaps to retire, perhaps to regroup, perhaps to return more fiercely.

Owen's arms and back ached, but the chain was under him now, secure for the time in his two hands, and he raised his head to look down. A mistake. Nausea rose in his throat. Soft moonlight turned to a gray haze, and he felt himself slipping again, a nightmare sensation—headlong over the edge into an ancient crevasse that was filled with the bones of sacrifice, broken bodies flung from the lofty house . . . by the Toltecs, Frank would insist! The Maya never engaged in such brutality. Owen saw Frank's face intent on preserving the purity of his heritage, and against it all he had to smile. This wasn't real; he wasn't falling. He grabbed hold of his mind as he'd grabbed the chain, and for a moment heard nothing but his own breathing.

Then voices emerged from below, vague and distant, and when he looked again the haze was gone. He saw Uxmal by moonlight; there was no one nearby. The terrorists, predictably, were focusing on the Governor's Palace and the outer edge of the ruins. Flat against the steps at this level, Owen felt safe from ground observation. And when he looked up—a safer move than looking down—he couldn't see the House of the Dwarf, which was set too far back on the flat terrace top of the pyramid. He couldn't see the sentry, either. He took a deep breath, set his teeth against the wind, gripped the chain, and continued climbing.

And when at last he reached the top, pulling himself up over the edge, he lay there, breathing hard, forcing back lingering nausea. He did not look down the way he had come, nor did he look into the black cavern doorway beside him. He did not see the figure emerge from the door.

But then he did see the rifle.

"What took you so long?" the sentry asked.

Owen looked at her and smiled. The sentry was Emma.

⊠ 28 ⊠

"The next time you climb a pyramid in high wind at night," Emma said once they were inside the House of the Dwarf, "try not to make yourself sick before you do it. It's a beastly climb when you're in the best of condition."

"I noticed." Owen looked at Emma, who was standing in the path of the moon, dimly lit—her face, like his, once more hidden behind the beard of a terrorist. "Did you have any problems getting here?"

"No, I headed the regular sentry off and claimed a mistake in assignments—two of us on the same shift—and when I volunteered to take the shift he was glad to let me."

"Good." Owen looked around, saw three rooms lying end to end, with interior walls now in ruins. It was pitch black away from the doors, which stood across from each other, open to the night and the steps that ran down from them. Then he glanced back at Emma, who had been here for more than an hour, time enough to know each hidden corner.

"Come with me," she said.

Owen followed her, staying close to the wall, until they reached the west door, which was wider than it was tall, like the three-sided rectangle of Michelangelo's drawing. It was wide and open to a broad view of Uxmal under a black sky, thrown into reverse perspective. The great white city was nestled against the land like children's blocks on a patchwork rug, with moonlight shining in through the nursery window. A few toy soldiers left out for the night remained in place at the Ball Court, near a fire no bigger than the flame of a match. The rest were scattered across the site; feet and yards were reduced from this view to inches.

One match-flame fire, and the rest was dark. A great black void. Emma raised an arm, pointing out and down at an angle. Owen's eyes followed the direction of her gesture, and he laughed, though he wasn't much amused. Michelangelo *wouldn't* want to make things easy!

The legend of the dwarf aside, archaeologists believed the Pyramid of the Magician was built in five stages, over a period of three hundred years, each time with a new lofty house placed higher than the last one. The first three houses were either destroyed or buried inside the pyramid as it grew taller, but the fourth house was left in place when the fifth one, the "current" House of the Dwarf, was built above and behind it. From where he stood, Owen looked out on the flat roof of the lower temple and the stone walkway that connected it with the floor of this one. Looking down past the walkway, he could also see the rear wall of the lower temple, its intricate carving thrown into relief by the moonlight.

And it was there that Emma's hand was pointing, to the left side of the rear wall, to a square block of stone that was four or five feet down from the edge of the flat roof. The face of the stone was part of the wall's design; it was edged and trimmed, with a hole cut into its center.

"That's it," Emma said. "I've checked the views through both doors, in both directions, from inside and out, and it has to be there."

Owen knew she was right. He crouched on his knees, positioning with his mind's eye the backward *L* of Michelangelo's drawing and the bisecting lines running from it. At the point where the lines would intersect was the hole carved in stone: target zero. Michelangelo's hiding place, as safe as Fort Knox. A gymnast would be reluctant to try to reach it—for the walls of the lower temple blended into the mass of the pyramid and the flat roof was a towering perch, with no sides; it dropped off sharply into the void of darkness.

Emma produced a rope and began to unwind it, tossing one end to Owen. He secured it around his waist, tightening the knot with a sharp twist. They worked in silence and careful haste, each knowing what had to be done. Emma fastened the other end of the rope around her own waist, and then dropped to her knees, to her stomach. Since she might have been seen from below if she stood, seen abandoning her rooftop post, she crawled out onto the walkway and vanished over the edge. Owen waited for her signal, which would mean she had secured the rope inside the lower temple room. The signal came, two sharp pulls of the rope, which lay flat across the roof now. Emma pulled in the slack as Owen crawled forward.

Forward and to his left past the walkway, to the edge of the roof, where he took a breath and looked over. Sense of height was sharpened here, with no walls to enclose the mind's pitch and sway, with ground far below and sky all around. Owen returned the signal, letting Emma know he was in position. The rope went taut. He slipped over the edge feet first, over and down, as Emma gave him additional length, and suddenly he felt his head spinning.

But it wasn't a trick of the mind this time. He *was* spinning, at the end of the rope. He reached out a hand to touch the wall and slowed the spin. Two more times, and he stopped it.

The hole was to his left at shoulder level. He changed hands on the rope and reached across. His fingers touched plastic, a cardboard tube. He twisted his hand, pulled it forward.

And a moment later, he had it.

Another cardboard tube wrapped in plastic.

They descended from the pyramid fast and didn't look inside the tube until they were deep in the jungle, surrounded by heavy bush, a safe distance from the ruins.

Emma switched on a flashlight, while Owen pulled off the plastic wrapping.

This tube was much larger than the first one, and even without benefit of the light Owen would have known what his fingers touched—a painting done in oils, an old one judging from the softness of the canvas. He unrolled it, extending his upper arm to keep the canvas taut, and turned it toward the beam of Emma's flashlight. The light revealed a ruffled white shirt above a dark waistcoat, a high collar around a banded neckline; a firm chin, a straight mouth, a patrician nose, and brown eyes that were slightly aloof but still piercingly human.

Emma gasped. Owen stared. Then they turned to each other and said, both at once, *"Thomas Jefferson?"*

"I can't think he killed Riker," Owen said and looked deeper into the tube, where he found something else: a photograph. He retrieved the picture and unrolled it under Emma's light.

Owen had thought after all these years that he was beyond shock, but now he discovered he wasn't. Nor was Emma, who let out a small cry beside him. Owen picked up the painting again and turned it over. On the back was a small piece of paper; the portrait was painted by Rembrandt Peale in 1800, it said, and belonged to the White House collection. Beneath that came a scrawl of writing, across the back of the canvas itself, a signature. Owen turned cold inside, and once again looked at Emma. She was shocked too—it was clear in her eyes—because the painting also appeared in the photograph, rolled with the face inside, but with the small paper and the signature showing. It appeared in the hand of one man, who was giving it to another.

The photograph was, in its way, as priceless as the portrait. It was also one-of-a-kind, probably the only picture extant (not counting subsequent mug shots done in Pendleton, Indiana) of the man who called himself Michelangelo. He was reaching for the painting here. Reaching for his payment, due in advance, for murder.

This was Michelangelo's proof, his insurance. The man handing the canvas to him was the same man whose name was signed across the back of the portrait, and it wasn't Rembrandt Peale. It was a man who stood where Thomas Jefferson stood once, where Benjamin Riker stood two centuries later. The signature was the President's, and so was the face in the photograph.

Henry Brendan. Michelangelo had named Riker's killer.

◼ 29 ◼

Henry stood alone, his mind paralyzed to inaction, at the great fan-shaped window in the West Sitting Room where the Jefferson portrait once hung, with the West Wing and the Oval Office lying at his feet beyond the glass, almost in touching distance. He knew he didn't belong here, didn't now, and he never had. He *was* an imposter.

Christ in heaven, what had he done!

He gave a small laugh as he raised a glass of Scotch to his lips. He knew what he'd done, and he hated himself for it.

It was after midnight now. Downstairs the concert was over and the guests had gone home. The crystal and china had been washed and polished and put away. Tables and chairs were folded and stored, linen sent to the laundry, lights dimmed or put out for the night. The staff had retired. The White House was sleeping.

But in the West Wing, a single light was still burning. Henry wondered who was working late—Sims, no doubt, a young man out to get ahead—but he didn't really care. He was alone with his thoughts and his guilt, with the consequences of his own actions.

He was a *killer*.

Oh, yes, he had blood on his hands, whether or not he had done it himself. He was responsible for murder.

But he had wanted this job, and no one else could make the decisions for him. There was only one thing to do. He put down his Scotch and picked up the phone.

Behind him, unseen, Lucy Brendan was watching.

Vanessa Nichols, who had noticed that her husband was preoccupied, to say the least, with the Uxmal crisis, but who dealt with his inattention by ignoring it, on the grounds that she didn't want to know why, roused herself to answer the phone when it rang at two o'clock in the morning. She acknowledged the familiar voice, tapped Ed on the arm, and handed him the receiver.

"Sam Ardry," she said.

Vanessa went back to sleep as Nichols sat up in bed, rubbing his eyes. "Yes, Sam, what is it?" He listened a moment, groping in the dark for his glasses, as if they might help him hear. "All right," he said, "I'll be there in twenty minutes."

The Nicholses lived on Langley Hill Drive, five minutes from the CIA. Ed took his own car, not wanting to waste the time calling for his driver—because Thatcher had tried to reach him with something so urgent that she wouldn't leave a message even with his trusted right arm. Ardry wasn't offended; he understood the significance of her refusal and summoned Nichols out of bed on a cold night. Snow was piled on both sides of the agency's gate as he drove through. The air was biting, the sky heavy with clouds and moisture. There would be more snow before the day was over.

If the day ever got started. Two A.M.—or two-nineteen, as the clock read when Nichols walked into his office—didn't count. It was still last night.

He nodded to Ardry and said, "Get her back on radio, will you?" Then, because he had hurried to dress without taking time to shave, he dropped his coat into a chair, loosened his collar, pulled off his tie, and disappeared into his private bathroom.

Ardry had the radio set up on Nichols's desk and Emma back in a matter of minutes. He called to Nichols, who returned with a towel draped over one shoulder. Ardry left the office, closing the door behind him.

Nichols sat down. "Are you there, Firefly?"

"Here and in a hurry," she said. "Are you sure this line is secure?"

"Secure and scrambled. Go ahead."

Emma got straight to the point. "Michelangelo has named names. One name. Henry Brendan."

Nichols's hand, in the act of raising the towel to wipe a trace of shaving cream from his cheek, froze where it was. "Henry Brendan," he exclaimed when he had caught his breath. "What the hell does that mean?"

"Michelangelo is making an accusation."

"You're kidding, of course."

"No, I'm not."

Somewhere inside, Nichols had suspected it. He leaned back in his chair, and when he spoke his voice was much calmer than his stomach, where new ulcers were forming with alarming speed. "I don't believe it," he said. "Henry may be a lot of things, and most of them I don't like, but he doesn't—*wouldn't*—have the stomach for murder."

"Maybe that's why he hires it out."

"No, never! Hell, he wouldn't know what to say to a man like Michelangelo."

"You might be surprised," Emma said. "We've got a picture of the two of them together."

"You've got *what*?"

"A photograph."

"Of the President and an assassin?" Nichols suspended his disbelief and listened.

"In the picture," Emma explained, "Brendan is giving Michelangelo a painting. It's rolled up; we can't be sure it's the same one, but we've got a painting here too, both courtesy of our former colleague, and it's not a painting you'd expect to find at Uxmal. It's a portrait of Thomas Jefferson, property of the White House. And across the back is Henry Brendan's signature."

"Christ, his *signature*?"

"You'll want to verify it, of course, but it looks authentic to me. The painting is real; I'm sure of that. The photograph too. I've examined it carefully; neither figure is superimposed. Brendan and Michelangelo met, once at least, and we have a record of it."

"Jesus!"

"I need a courier as fast as you can get one here. I want these things out of my hands as soon as possible."

"I'll send someone on the first plane." Nichols seized the first name that came to mind. "Code name Hermes."

"Good. Tell him to look for Frank Luc-Can at the airport. I've got something else to do, and Owen is sleeping off a bad night."

"Where is he?"

"You know where. He went back."

Nichols wondered why he'd bothered to ask. Then he sat forward, worried. "You haven't told Luc-Can what you found . . . ?"

"When I wouldn't even tell Sam? Of course not. Don't worry, Frank can be trusted as much as your courier. I've really got to get going now. Do you have any questions?"

Nichols sighed. "Do you have any answers?"

"I may have one soon. What they're doing here."

"They? Who?"

"The terrorists."

"I should think it's rather obvious!"

"Maybe not. We'll see. I'll get back to you later."

"Wait a minute!" Nichols paused. *"Thatcher?"*

Emma was gone, the radio dead. Nichols disconnected and pushed his chair back from the desk. Two of a kind, he thought, and wondered why his best agents were always such self-starters. He got up and strode across the room to the door, yanked it open, and bellowed for Ardry, who was sitting less than three feet away.

"Yes?"

"Come in here!"

Ardry did, and Nichols closed the door. "I want you to order a courier," he said. "No, make that two couriers, the most reliable men we have, and a plane to fly them immediately to Miami. I want them on the next commercial flight to Merida. Give them maximum security—weapons, federal marshal IDs, permits, chains

193

and locks, and a large bag, one of those portfolios artists carry. And give them a copy of our file photo of the Mayan doctor. He'll be at the airport in Merida with something for them. The one who makes contact should call himself Hermes and report back to me. To me, personally. Do you understand?''

Ardry nodded. It was as good as done. "Is there anything else?" he asked.

"Not unless you've got the judgment of Solomon.''

"Is there something you want to talk about?''

"A hell of a problem," Nichols said, but he shook his head. "One I have to think through myself. Stick around, though. I may need you later. In the meantime, I don't want to be disturbed for anything.''

Ardry turned and left the room, and Nichols crossed to the windows overlooking the Potomac. Washington, a sensible city, not as exciting as some, was sleeping through the predawn hours on the other side of the river. Or so it seemed. Nothing stayed open late here, except Congress and the back rooms where decisions were made in private. Nichols liked working in back rooms; he preferred to move through the back doors, inauspiciously, and he wondered which ones, in this administration, were still open to him.

Where *did* you go when you thought the President of the United States might be guilty of murder?

To the FBI director? To the U.S. Attorney? Over both of them to the Attorney General? With what? Some circumstantial evidence and Owen's instincts about the fundamental honesty of an international assassin? They would never believe him. He almost didn't believe it himself. He was actually giving credence to the possibility that the President was a murderer!

And yet he felt sure Owen and Thatcher were on to the truth. He was thinking about how Henry had changed, how *much* Henry had surprised him. There was something there. As Owen had said: more to Uxmal than met the eye. More to Henry.

But what? An assassination?

Was it possible?

Then another thought struck him with jolting force. What if he went to the FBI chief, or to the U.S. Attorney, or to the Attorney General, and *was* believed? What if Henry was indicted, tried, and found guilty? Dear God, it turned his heart and mind cold! If the people went into collective shock once when a President committed obstruction of justice, setting off a constitutional crisis unparalleled in modern American history, what would they do if they knew their President hired an assassin to kill his predecessor? Would the truth, if that were the truth, destroy every shred of faith they had left in their own political system?

Where *should* he go?

Where, indeed, he had to admit—because it nudged the back of his mind—to guarantee fairness to Henry himself? Such an accusation would ruin him if it became known, even if an investigation revealed that the charges were groundless. He could never *prove* that he didn't beat his wife when no one was looking. His integrity, once brought into enormous doubt, would be utterly blackened by association with a scandal of such magnitude, assigned to judgmental purgatory forever. Such was the price of public life. Yes, fairness to Henry—that mattered too. Nichols didn't believe in human sacrifice, no more than the ancient Maya did. But where should he go? To whom?

The answer came in a flash of inspiration as he stood by the window, looking out over the skyline of Washington, where by federal law no building rose to block or diminish the great dome of the Capitol. He would go to the man who was second in line to succeed the President, on the unlikely chance it came to that. To a man who controlled Congress with a quiet voice and a sure instinct about people. To a man who had lived eighty-odd years and was unquestionably devoted to his country. To Henry's friend, as close to Solomon as anyone the government had to offer.

As soon as the couriers were back, as soon as he had seen the evidence and had it verified as authentic—

because Nichols knew in his bones it would be—then he would go to see Conklin Pierce, the Speaker. And maybe between them they could figure out what they ought to do about Henry.

⊠ 30 ⊠

Emma gave Frank the wrapped cardboard tube and with it directions for meeting the courier Hermes. "Don't tell anyone what you're doing," she warned, "and for God's sake, don't look inside the package. Do you have your gun?"

Frank had his service revolver. "What's in here?" he asked. "The specifications for your newest big bomb? Or is it a plan for a U.S. attack on London?"

"Moving islands," Emma replied. "Beyond that, you don't want to know. When Hermes makes contact with you, just give him the tube and forget you ever saw it."

"And shoot anyone who asks for a light or the time before I find him?"

Emma smiled. "Use your own judgment. And don't worry, he'll find you. Take care, Frank. I mean it."

Frank left in his van, and Emma turned to make her way into the night. Into the jungle.

The sky was still dark over Uxmal as Owen, who was back in his cell but restless, lay on his cot smoking. Michelangelo was on his mind—Michelangelo and Henry Brendan; he had his own thoughts about both of them. He stared absently at the red glow of his ash and then flicked it off on the stone floor beside him, aware somewhere in the back of his mind that something outside was changing.

Had changed. The thought came forward, and Owen froze, alert, listening. The wind had died, or at least eased up, revealing sound—no, less than that, *sense* of movement. People moving in the night, too quietly. A shifting of air, a feeling of stealth, like awareness of an unseen intruder. And then footsteps on the pavement of the terrace. Just as Owen was starting to rise, a beam of light split the night through his door, a flashlight. It hit his face, and he didn't move, except to raise the cigarette to his lips; to inhale, exhale; to stare back at the dark shape of a man in the doorway.

A voice spoke to him in terse, Spanish-accented English. "Go to sleep."

"That's one thing you can't make me do."

The terrorist pulled the flashlight back enough to give shape to the lines of his face—eyes dark, nostrils flaring in exaggerated elongation—and to reveal the automatic rifle he was holding. "Try," he said, and in his tone there was warning.

Owen put his cigarette out and rolled over on the cot, his back to the door, waiting. When the flashlight moved on, he got up and crossed the room in silence.

Moonlight shone through the silence of night on the steps of the Governor's Palace, on the plaza of the two-headed jaguar, on the faces of terrorist guards on alert. Owen frowned and looked at his watch, turning it toward the pale light that seeped past the iron mesh of his door screen. It was just past 1:00 A.M., but the terrorists were assembling as if for parade. Twenty at least, and there had to be more beyond his own field of vision. *Why? Why now?* As he watched, his questions were answered.

Ramon appeared on the terrace, from the edge of Owen's view, from the center of the building, and started down the steps to the plaza. Behind him came more terrorist guards, forming a phalanx around the captive congressmen. They followed Ramon down the steps and across the plaza. At gunpoint they moved—Shackford, MacGregor, and Renaud—across the plaza and into the jungle.

Something new moved in Owen's mind, darkly ominous, and the pieces came down in different places. *He knew.*

He knew and returned to his cot, to shut it all out. He was sure of two things—that he was tired, very tired, and that the Uxmal crisis would soon be over.

He lay down and in a moment was sleeping.

Emma stepped past the teeth of the cave, out of the moonlight and into the underworld of the Maya. Utter darkness closed in around her, and she shook off a chill as she flicked her flashlight, then followed its beam through the throat and belly of the slumbering beast and into the hind quarters. This time she was ready for the drop in the floor and took the down slide at her own pace. At the bottom she found the underground river.

But if the ghost fish were still there, their presence was less easily detected. The surface of the river was no longer glass smooth, but a mass of moving ripples. Getting warmer, she thought. Vibration. It existed where it hadn't before, which had to mean the source of it was moving—either that, or growing stronger—and Emma intended to find its source before she breathed open air again.

Warmer, yes. The cave was still hot, a tomb for underground moisture, but Emma was better dressed for the heat than she had been before. She had shed her terrorist disguise—fatigues, boots, and layers of hair—in favor of basic black in one piece. Even inches behind the light in her hand she was as good as invisible.

Now she threw the beam up into the ceiling, to the hole in the ground that had been her previous route out of the cave, and back down again, seeking the remains of Ahau-Tzab-Can. The snake was there, more or less, a skeleton now, having been finished off by his own kind, the unearthly. Emma smiled to herself. There were times when she approved of the ways of nature.

She swung the light back across the river, looking for a different escape, a route to another part of the cave, but she didn't find it. Yet Frank said it was there. She shut the light off and stood still in total darkness.

Or near total darkness. What appeared after a moment or two was too insubstantial to be called light, but it couldn't be anything else—unless the ghost fish had taken new form, floating through the air and drawing the intensity out of the darkness. The light seemed to exist in two places: over the riverbed, as if rippling movement had carried it here, and from a seemingly unbroken wall on the other side of the river. No footbridge. No stepping-stones. Emma waded into the water, which rose to her ankles and then to her knees, and came out again on the other side. Behind a deep cleft in the wall, she found another opening.

It was what she was looking for, a tunnel.

What Emma didn't know was that someone else had entered the cave behind her, someone who spotted and followed her through the jungle. He did not use a flashlight, but followed hers, as he followed her scent, his muscles propelling him inch by inch. He didn't know who Emma was, but he knew she had no business here, and that was all the excuse he needed.

Ramon was there now, in the darkness behind her.

⊠ 31 ⊠

The tunnel was barely wider than Emma, and so low she had to crawl on her hands and knees to get through it. She crawled at least seventy yards, winding down and around, to the left and the right, and under ledges with inches to spare—but mostly down—before the tunnel began to expand. When at last she could stand erect, she stopped to check her progress. Flashlight off. The other light source, still dim, barely seen, was nonetheless growing brighter.

Emma listened and knew she was getting closer to something. The deep silence of the cave was less heavy here. A faint murmur was coming from the distance ahead. It was steady, low-pitched, hardly audible. A baritone ghost humming softly. Emma touched the wall at her side, felt it moving beneath her fingertips, responding to the baritone's deep timbre. Then she glanced around, listening again, staring into the darkness at her back, alerted to something by instinct.

There was nothing now—no ghosts behind and only the baritone ahead. She moved on, stopping to rest now and then, to wipe perspiration from her hands and face. The light remained little changed, but the sound continued to grow steadily louder. It had reached the level of a soft roar, suggesting that the baritone was something a bit more substantial than a ghost. A waterfall, maybe. More likely a piece of equipment with a powerful engine. Finally the tunnel opened up into another vast cavern, the belly of a twin beast with a huge vaulting rib cage. An *angry* beast. This one was hungry and rumbling.

Emma looked at her watch. She had been in the cave for more than an hour, but she'd lost her sense of time in the winding darkness. With it went sense of direction. She only knew she was deep in the ground and a long way from the mouth of the cave. She turned back, cocked her head, listening.

Suddenly, the beast reared up on its haunches, bellowing. The cave floor rose and fell, with a roaring and a rush of hot air that knocked the flashlight out of her hand and sent her sprawling. Pieces of rock loosened overhead and came crashing down around her. She lay still, stunned as much by surprise as by the blast. This wasn't the work of nature at all. Emma knew the sound of man-made explosives.

It was over in a moment. She pulled herself up to look around. Her flashlight was gone, but she didn't need it now. There was light, real light, coming into the cave from a fissure high in the far wall, perhaps thirty feet above the floor. Light as bright as the sun, too bright for the moon. It had to be electric.

Now Emma knew where the sound she had followed was coming from. There was another cave beyond the wall of this one. She got up, moving carefully across the stone floor, past fallen rocks, until she was standing directly beneath the fissure.

More rocks were piled against the wall at an angle, an accumulation of years. Emma started to climb, then abruptly she stopped, as the beast came to life again. Sound erupted once more in the cave—not an explosion, but a harsh, grating roar. The wall started to crack in a running tear that shot off in branches before her eyes. Limestone trembled and bulged. A huge piece of it was buckling, shattering, bursting its bounds. The wall was coming down. Falling *toward* her!

Emma clung to the insecure mound of rock, which was starting to shift beneath her. Then she pushed down hard with her feet, forcing her body to slide away fast at an angle. The word escape hadn't formed in her mind.

There hadn't been time. This was raw, automatic. Survival. Then one foot caught in the moving rocks and was quickly buried. Emma struggled to get free, in vain. The foot was firmly wedged. She was trapped here.

Trapped! And as she looked up a black metal drum broke through the collapsing wall, spitting up dust of pulverized stone and baring heavy, jagged teeth, each one at least a foot long; they made the teeth at the mouth of the cave look inviting. Rows of sharp points clawed the air at the top of the mound, seeking a morsel of stone—or, barring that, flesh—to satiate the pounding roar of their appetite. Then from each side of the rotating drum came two long arms, scooping up air. Burning eyes glared at her through the dust. Emma stared at them in disbelief. It *was* a monster, more vicious than anything ever created by nature.

Her hands flew at the mound, throwing up broken rock like pebbles. She buried herself as well as she could and lay there, breathing the dust of the deep earth and feeling the crush of sound bearing down, coming nearer.

Let the vile thing blow a fuse, she prayed to the ghost gods of the Maya, whose deaf ears would be no handicap here. Let it run out of gas, or reverse itself and go back to the evil world it came from. She didn't expect the ghost gods to answer.

But they did in a hairsbreadth of time. The monster died. Suddenly, there was nothing but great roaring silence.

🖾 32 🖾

Emma stayed where she was, listening, and heard the monster's motor start up, its treads spinning. She realized it was backing away from the collapsed wall and raised her head to get a look at the driver, but all she saw was the back of an olive drab shirt and a yellow hard hat.

The dust was starting to settle, and with light pouring through from the next cave she could see what the monster was—a continuous miner, standard heavy equipment in the coal country of West Virginia, Silesia, the Ruhr Valley. But there was no coal in Yucatan, nor much of anything else in the way of resources. And even if there were, why would it have to be mined in secret?

Who were the miners?

She leaned forward to pull away the rocks that had trapped her foot in the mound, lifting them off one at a time. She freed the foot and tested it with her full weight—nothing seemed to be broken or sprained—and then climbed on up to the gaping place where the wall had been, peering over the edge of broken rock. What she saw there was utterly startling.

The adjacent cave, lit by strings and strings of electric bulbs, was nothing less than enormous, and much bigger now than nature had made it. The side walls had been carved away to a height of thirty or forty feet, and twice that depth; it was like a brimmed hat on a giant scale, with roof bolts in place to support overhanging layers of rock and keep them from crashing down on the miners.

It was a mine. It couldn't be anything else. The cave was full of men, identically dressed in green work shirts and pants, in yellow hard hats with headlamps, in plastic safety glasses. Their faces and clothes were smudged with white dust; they looked like coal miners laundered. Men and heavy equipment: shuttle cars full of broken ore and others standing by empty, all attached to a conveyor belt on a track that ran once around the cave floor, then rose at a steep angle and disappeared somewhere beyond the ceiling.

There were two more of the hulking continuous miners, the monster machines, each one as big as a large room, efficient beasts that mechanized several stages of work once done with pickax and shovel. The teeth on the drum, or rotating head, that rose up from the front of each beast were made to tear rock with a gnashing force, breaking the ore into pieces. Then the giant arms, one on each side, gathered the pieces into their grasp and dumped them into the shuttle cars for transportation out of the mine. One continuous miner, alone, was capable of processing twenty tons of ore in the space of a minute. Three, operating continuously, could only be incredibly productive.

Now the monsters—all three of them, including the one backed away from this wall, or what was left of it—were at rest as one set of workers departed the mine, making way for fresh hands in what appeared to be an around-the-clock operation. Emma knew she had to move now or else wait for the next shift change, and she didn't know when that might be. She pushed herself up through the cave wall, making straight for the conveyor belt, and slid under one of the shuttle cars with no more than two inches to spare above her head and shoulders. The car was long enough to enable her to lie flat on her stomach, on the belt itself, with nothing protruding, but she folded her arms in front of her face, hid her bare hands, and kept her chin down. Black hair, black clothes, all covered with dust in deep shadow. Nothing but eyes and forehead showed, and those only if someone were bending over and looking.

Soon the conveyor belt started moving, following a slow path around the circumference of the cave. Emma saw boots and clean olive drab legs. Few words were exchanged, none to discern, and she wondered if the miners wore earplugs for protection. Before she had gone halfway around, the monsters roared to life again, and their sound at close range obliterated all other noise, great and small. Grating. Pounding. Crushing. Iron teeth assaulted the rock face, chewing up ore and spitting out dust. Arms began their steady job of scooping, lifting, dumping. Pieces of ore came down into the car ahead, and then into the one where Emma was hiding. A shower of broken rock spilled over the edge, lodging in the conveyor belt and hitting the floor beside her. The air was full of limestone ash. Emma's throat caught, and she tried to suppress a sharp urge to cough. Then she realized it hardly mattered if she coughed or not. She could have screamed bloody murder, and someone standing three feet away would not have been able to hear her.

And then the conveyor belt started climbing.

It rose sharply on steel supports, at least sixty feet into the air, to the ceiling of the vast cavern. Emma tried to look ahead, but beyond the bright lights she could see nothing. Her hand darted out, seized a piece of ore before gravity pushed it off, and shoved it into a pocket. Then she looked down. The cave floor was dropping away. The yellow hats and monster machines were growing smaller and smaller.

They were gone. The conveyor belt and shuttle cars continued to rise through an angled shaft that was too straight, too sure, too direct, to have been the work of nature. Emma reached out in fading light, touched the rock face on both sides of the car. There was no extra space, just enough to pass through. This tunnel was clearly blasted out with explosives.

Sound diminished with the lights, and the grating roar faded behind her. The conveyor belt moved on through darkness and eventually heavy silence. Emma wasn't sure how long she was climbing, but finally the tunnel leveled off, and a dim glow of light showed again in the distance. The end was in sight. Emma backed out from under the car and stood on the conveyor belt, bending under the ceiling of the tunnel. As the light grew brighter, she stepped off to one side. Her feet found the steel support and she turned, her back to the tunnel wall, leaning against it. The conveyor belt moved on by her, the shuttle cars with their heavy load passing within inches of her stomach. There was room, enough. She edged her way along the support until she reached the mouth of the tunnel. And there she stopped.

There was yet another large cave, this one much closer to the surface of the earth above. More men in olive drab and yellow hats. More electric lights strung across the ceiling and around the walls. But what was going on here was quite different. Emma knew she had found some sort of loading facility.

About ten feet out of the tunnel the conveyor belt started to climb again, supported underneath by a steel trestle. Thirty yards more, and it swung to the right, moving along overhead to a point in the middle of the cave, where the shuttle cars, each one in turn, tipped and dumped their contents into a chute. As Emma watched, a black van appeared; it was old-looking, battered, and bruised, but from under its hood came the sound of a finely tuned engine. The van backed into position at the lower end of the chute, and one man opened a hatch in its roof while another released a gate, allowing the ore to pass through. Then hatch and gate were closed off and the van drove away, passing out under the trestle.

It was followed by a pickup truck in the same kind of condition. When the truck was full, a tarpaulin was thrown over its load and tied down. The truck, too, exited under the trestle.

Next came an old schoolbus, but Emma had seen enough of the loading process. The miners were moving ore out of the cave, under cover of darkness, in vehicles that would not be out of place on rural Yucatan roads. But she wondered how so many of them had managed to avoid aerial surveillance. Did they drive without head-lights? How far? How often? How many?

Where were they going? And what was their load? What had been found in the limestone ash of the Yucatan? Who had found it? And why did it have to be mined *in secret*?

Two men appeared not far away. Emma drew back fast to avoid being seen. She took several deep breaths of air, though she doubted if her throat and lungs would ever be free of the clinging dust, and tuned her ears to listen.

"From here," one man said, "we take the ore over-land one-point-seven miles, always traveling at night to avoid risk of observation. There the ore is dumped into another cave, where we have a small retort set up to do some refining. The refined ore is then mixed with water and moved on through a slurry pipeline. For the most part, the pipeline passes through existing caves, though we did have to blast through in three places. And of course we'll blast it all out when we're finished."

"Without detection?" the other man asked.

"Without detection," the first confirmed. "They're deep caves. And we'll do it all with remote timers to make sure we're out of here first. If the blast is detected by some means we don't anticipate, all evidence of our presence will have been destroyed. There will be no way to connect this with us."

"That's vital."

"I know that, sir."

"How fast can you dismantle if you have to?"

"In an emergency, two hours. We won't try to take the equipment out with us. We'll blow it up with the mines. That way we only have to move ore and people."

"And how much ore have you processed so far?"

"This cave, of course, is only one of three operations. We've moved sixty-five thousand tons, and there's more in the pipeline. Since we only need it in trace amounts for production, that's enough to last a good fifty years by my figures."

"We want more," the second man said.

"Yes, sir, and we'll give you more, as long as we can keep working. But if we should have to stop sooner than planned we've got a good supply. In fifty years we may have an entirely different technology."

"We'd rather not chance it," the second man said, "and we don't want to have to come back here after we're finished." Then he lowered his voice and went on so softly that Emma had to strain hard to hear him. "In the meantime, with what you've accomplished here, you've guaranteed our survival and our dominance in the world for another fifty years. You should be proud of what you've done, you and your men."

"It's our job, sir."

Emma, perspiring, felt cold inside as shock raised the hair along her neck and forehead. Now, slowly, she leaned around to look at the men, to confirm what her ears had told her.

And when she had seen, she went limp inside. Uxmal *was* a hoax. An incredible lie. It was only a mask, a *falseface*! The men spoke English, excellent English, and for a very good reason. They were American.

Everything suddenly fell into place—why the ore was being mined, or stolen, in secret. Why President Riker was killed and how it related to Uxmal. Who the terrorists were. Cuban, yes, they were refugees. *Exiles!*

Not Havana. *Not* Moscow.

Emma knew because she had seen the two men and recognized both of them. One was MacKendrick of the DIA. The other one was Congressman Reuben Shackford.

209

As Shackford and MacKendrick went on talking another man approached them, handed MacKendrick a note, and turned away. The major read it, frowning, and looked up. "The Pentagon's trying to reach me," he said, "and that can't be good news. My orders are to maintain the strictest radio silence, no exceptions."

"Better find out what it is," Shackford said. "I think I'll come with you."

The two men walked away, out of Emma's view. She knew she had to act quickly, to get back to her own radio and report to Nichols what she'd seen, and then tell Owen. But there was only one way out. The miners working the loading facility were blocking the vehicle exit. She had to go back the way she had come, down through the shaft, through the mine, the caves, and the jungle. She started to edge along the trestle bar, her back to the wall, as the shuttle cars continued to move past her, sidestepping in long strides, her feet sure, her mind on the implications of her discovery.

She didn't know what the ore sample in her pocket was, but she thought she knew what it represented: a major advance in weapons technology, highly secret. Something that would secure the future of the United States and its dominance over the rest of the world for at least fifty years. Something Benjamin Riker opposed.

Emma moved on, making good time as light faded from the mouth of the shaft, lost in the distance above. She was on the downward slope now and the air around her was heavy and dark, oppressive, almost breathing. And then, beside her, the shuttle cars stopped moving: the conveyor belt came to a halt on the steel trestle. Emma stopped too, her back to the wall, her palms pressed flat against it. She held her breath, straining to hear what she thought she'd heard just before the belt stopped moving. But now there was nothing. The air seemed to be holding its breath. There was only the silence, deep and dark, pressing into her mind and touching off secret senses.

Holding its breath . . .

She knew all at once that she wasn't alone. Something, or someone, was there in the dark. Something softly, almost imperceptibly, *hissing*.

More than that, it knew she was there. A flashlight flared on not five feet away, catching her in the reach of its beam, giving vague shape to the creature who held it. Emma recognized him. His smooth-shaven head swayed back and forth at the end of a long, muscular neck; his eyes were black pinpoints in the dark; his lipless mouth was drawn back and leering. Ahau-Tzab-Can, the evilest of gods, had come back to life in human form. Emma stared at him with real loathing. But in the instant it took for the light to flash on, she had also reached for her automatic.

It was gone.

She'd *lost* it somewhere in the cave, probably when she lost her own flashlight. And now it was too late. Her automatic emerged from the dark.

Ramon had it.

It was still dark when Nichols arrived at the Broadmoor, but morning lights were coming on across the city and early risers were out in their cars along Connecticut Avenue. Nichols left his own car with the doorman for parking and took the elevator up. His couriers had returned in the night, and experts he had standing by had confirmed the worst from the evidence Thatcher sent him. The Jefferson portrait was real, the photograph untampered with, the signature on the back of the portrait Henry's. So, now what? He hoped the Speaker would have a wise answer.

Pierce opened the door fully dressed in suit and tie, as well turned out as he would have been for a royal address before a joint session. He was a bachelor and lived alone. The apartment, a piece of another time, like the Speaker himself, was attractive, roomy, and comfortable.

"I appreciate your seeing me so early," Nichols said as he strode through the door. "I wouldn't have called if it weren't urgent."

"I assumed as much," Pierce replied. "Don't worry about it. I've already had one visitor this morning."

"Oh?"

Pierce sat down and signaled for Nichols to take the chair beside him. "Bert Engel," he said. "He left twenty minutes ago."

And what was the President's National Security Advisor doing here before dawn? Nichols wondered, and then grunted to himself. If someone had known *he* was here, it would have been just as startling.

And with good reason.

"I have the feeling your visits might be related," Pierce went on, "but I want to hear why you've come first. Then, if it's germane, I'll tell you what Bert wanted."

"Fair enough." Nichols cleared his throat and leaned back in the chair. There was no hope of softening the blow. "I have reason to think Henry Brendan murdered Ben Riker."

The shock that showed on the Speaker's face was so cold, so harsh, so complete, that Nichols suddenly feared it might kill him. "Can I get you something?" he asked, leaning forward.

Pierce raised a frail hand. "No. Thank you. Just give me a moment—my God, *why*? Whoever said Ben *was* murdered?"

Nichols told him. Everything. As he spoke, dawn broke across the sky. There was no real sunrise this morning, no clear light to put things into a brighter perspective. There were only more clouds and more threatening snow. Another bleak winter day in Washington.

But the Speaker heard him out without interrupting, and by the time Nichols was done Pierce looked shattered. He had pulled into himself, looking old and shriveled and drawn, his eyes clouded, his skin almost transparent. He said nothing for several minutes but, watching him, Nichols saw something new in his face. The wise old man of the government was badly shaken.

The look passed. Behind it came a tight edge of anger barely under control. He shook his head. "How could Henry throw everything away like this? How could he do it?" Pierce was shaken, angry, and deeply disappointed.

But he didn't seem to doubt that Henry was guilty, and that surprised Nichols, who had thought he would have to be convincing even beyond the evidence in his possession. Now he wondered if Pierce had known something all along, something that made him ready to accept news about an old friend that could not have failed to be profoundly shocking.

Of course, he knew *Henry*.

Pierce looked frail, but his voice was strong. "Well," he said, "you certainly have grounds for an investigation."

"An official investigation? Is that what we want?"

"We may not have a choice, but I'd like some time to think about it."

"What do we do in the meantime?"

"I don't know." Pierce paused. "I think I ought to speak to Henry. I'd like to hear what he has to say for himself. Perhaps he'll offer his resignation."

"Do you think that's wise—now, in the middle of a crisis?" Nichols shook his head, uncertain. "It could be very bad timing. A shock for the people and the government. And if the Soviets are involved, what kind of signal would we be sending?"

Pierce sighed. "That's one thing we don't have to worry about."

"Why not?"

"Look," Pierce said, "you know my position regarding the Soviet Union—I've never thought we could trust them or any agreement we make with them—but I think I can assure you that the Soviets had nothing to do with Uxmal."

Nichols said nothing, but he was listening carefully, his eyes intent on the Speaker's face.

"It has to do with what Bert told me," Pierce explained. "I seem to have become everyone's father confessor. Last night the National Security Agency intercepted a message on a radio frequency they'd been ordered to leave alone." He shrugged. "Bert, it seems, wondered why and put a special team on it. And he found out. The message originated in the Situations Room of the White House, which DIA is manning on Henry's orders. It was received at Uxmal."

"What?" Nichols frowned. "What was it? Did they decode it?"

Pierce nodded. "Two words. *Abort now*."

Nichols stared at him in silence, momentarily confused. Then his mouth dropped open.

It was morning when Owen awoke, and sunlight shone brightly into his cell. He sat up, instantly alert, staring through the doorway. Staring and listening. The morning was utterly silent.

No, *not* silent; that was the point. He heard a bird cry out to its mate, heard crickets chirping softly. But that was all he heard. He got up and crossed the room to look out—to breathe deeply, because the air seemed sweeter and fresher with darkness purged from it. The two-headed jaguar was still there, staring sightlessly over the ruins in two directions. Owen followed its gaze; he looked left and then right. He stepped through the door and walked to the end of the terrace.

The House of the Dwarf was still there too, at the top of the Pyramid of the Magician. The Nunnery and the Ball Court were there. Ruins—quiet, timeless and brooding. Scrub and brush and piles of rock; Chac masks by the hundreds. All there under the morning sun. Only the terrorists were missing.

Owen smiled. Nine days after it began, it was over. Uxmal was, once again, abandoned.

≋ 34 ≋

The terrorists had gone in the night, as suddenly as they came, and they took everything but the hostages with them. The door screens were gone, the electric cable. Their weapons and equipment. They hadn't left as much as a scrap of paper. Owen wasn't surprised. And he knew that the crisis wasn't, by any means, over.

Other faces began to emerge from the doors along the face of the building. Young staff aides peered out in astonished bewilderment, reluctant to believe what their eyes told them. Then one of them burst free of his cell and leaped into the air with a triumphant cry that might have been heard all the way to Muna. The others quickly followed. Men normally rather staid, Owen guessed, were hugging each other and whirling for joy amid shouts of delight for their unexpected freedom. Owen smiled to himself, because that much was real. But the congressmen were there too, surprised and happy like the rest, *play acting*—as they were play acting last night at gunpoint, marching off with Ramon and a phalanx of "guards" to an undisclosed fate beyond the edge of the jungle, as they were play acting from the first day of their capture.

Owen had seen what wasn't in their faces last night—neither fear, nor shock, nor even resigned acceptance. Physically, they had played their parts—they allowed themselves to be pushed along—but they looked like men going to work, not to their own executions.

He felt it then and knew it now. The good congressmen Pious, Pompous, and Gooch were no more hostages than Ramon, who worked for them. They were the masterminds of Uxmal, whatever it meant, with an assist no doubt from Henry Brendan. For what purpose they'd staged this small affair, he still didn't know, but he did know they were behind it from the beginning. And Cass? Was he in on it too? Or was he really only there because he got his nose out of joint and insisted on coming along? Was he a mastermind? Or was he their unknowing victim?

Owen saw Frank coming out of the edge of the jungle, approaching the steps to the Governor's Palace at a run, and he hurried down to meet him.

"My God, you're *free*!" Frank exclaimed and clasped Owen's shoulders in both hands. "For Christ's sake, what happened?"

"They left."

"I can see that! *Why?*"

Owen shrugged. "They didn't tell us. Where's Emma?"

Frank's face changed. "She isn't here?"

"I haven't seen her since I came back last night."

"Uh-oh . . ."

"What's wrong?"

"She didn't get back to Nicte's last night, either. I assumed she'd come here, and—"

"If she did, where is she?"

Frank looked at him grimly. "She was going into the caves last night. She wanted to know what was causing the earth to tremble."

Owen's face turned cold. His instincts were all standing on end and shouting. Then, suddenly, he pushed Frank down as a whining sound pierced the air and something struck the building above and behind them. He looked up and saw Reuben Shackford's face, wide-eyed and puzzled. Owen wasn't sure if he knew it or not, but a bullet had narrowly missed him. The air whined again, and this time the bullet almost struck MacGregor. Someone was firing at them from the jungle.

If the first shot caused surprise, the second one was enough to send the freed hostages scrambling for cover.

But not before a third shot was fired. This one, as Owen guessed in the fraction of time before the bullet came spinning through the air, buzzed Renaud, missing him by inches.

There was a pause, a moment's truce, and then a fourth shot went further afield. Owen was ready and saw it hit the Pyramid of the Magician, raising a burst of stone dust as a point of reference.

"What the hell's going on?" Frank asked and started to rise when it seemed the shooting was over.

"Nothing to worry about," Owen said, but his gaze swept the edge of the jungle. "It's an old friend of mine, and if he wanted to kill someone here he'd have done it."

Michelangelo, back from the dead. Owen had wondered who'd really been driving the car that exploded in flames before Billie's eyes. A hired stand-in, no doubt. An unfortunate look-alike for an assassin. Certainly it wasn't the man Billie knew as Grant Martin. Owen knew him too well; he would never have been caught by a clumsy thing like a car bomb.

No, Michelangelo was alive, at work again—or still—doing what he did so well: plotting murder. Owen had known he would have to appear, and now he had, unmistakably, for the last shot struck the pyramid near the top, where bisecting lines intersected and pinpointed target zero.

Another gauntlet. Michelangelo was not only alive, but naming his next target—the man on whom he had sworn revenge. Henry Brendan. He was going to kill the President. The assassin was announcing himself and, more than that, *daring* Owen to stop him.

Owen smiled at the thought of confrontation. It was inevitable and had been for a long time.

"Where's the radio?" he asked.

At the moment, he was more concerned about Emma.

35

Emma didn't think he would shoot, not mad Ramon. He had to have something better in mind—maybe rape, maybe torture. Certainly a colorful death, something to excite his psychotic fancies. But she had no doubt that to kill her was what he intended. From what she'd heard, death was as natural to Ramon as it was to the evil rattlesnake god he resembled.

Let him try, she thought and stood her ground, licking her lips in hopes of expressing both fear and invitation. Let him come just one foot closer. . . .

He did, and Emma was ready. Her leg shot up into the air and her body twisted; her heel struck him across the chin, producing a cry of pain or indignation. Then she pulled up and hit him again with a swinging blow of her arm from the side, knocking the flashlight from his hand and upsetting his balance. He was toppling toward the conveyor belt when the flashlight, careening down through the shaft, struck the wall with particular force, extinguished itself, and plunged them back into darkness.

But Ramon still had his automatic.

He fired twice, flashing thunderbolts in the confinement of the shaft. Bullets ricocheted off stone, unseen and threatening for it. Emma ducked beside one of the shuttle cars, knowing that Ramon was as vulnerable as she was, that he wouldn't fire again yet. Then she heard him grunting as he started to rise, and knew she had to move faster than he did. She pulled off her shoes and flung them at him. In stocking feet, keeping low, she balanced herself on the steel sidebar, tucked in her head, hugged her knees, and let herself slide. She hit Ramon hard, knocked him back, and kept going.

It was not a secure feeling, hurtling down through the void of cave night, picking up speed, having no sense at all how far she was from the bottom, but she knew the mine would send up sound and light as a warning. From above, Ramon started shooting again. One bullet gouged the wall to her left, and the next one passed so close to her head that it raised the hair at the back of her neck. Stone walls curved in around her. She might as well have positioned herself inside the gun barrel.

She had to get out of his line of fire and reached out blindly with both arms, grabbing the edge of a shuttle car and hanging on against her own forward momentum. Her arms felt as if they were being torn loose from her shoulders, but she stopped the slide and rolled onto the conveyor belt, found shelter. In the darkness Ramon continued to fire. He emptied the automatic.

When Emma reached out again, the walls of the shaft had vanished. She had traveled much further than she knew and was on open trestle in the mine, near the roof of the cave. But where were the lights? The roaring machines?

Where were the miners?

A sense of foreboding rose up in her breast and at the back of her mind, but she didn't have time to set it in context. Her automatic came flying past her and hit the floor somewhere below. Right behind it came a large chunk of ore, then another. Ramon was trying a new tack, more primitive but, with his advantage of height, as lethal.

Emma, however, had the advantage of space in which to maneuver. She dropped over the edge of the trestle and climbed down fast, wishing she hadn't flung her shoes at Ramon so blithely. Sharp pieces of rock pressed painfully into the soles of her feet as she reached the cave floor. Ramon was still heaving rocks from the shaft, but she heard his heavy footsteps too, pounding down the trestle bar, abandoning caution for speed, coming for her.

She stopped, looked around. There was no light at all, only the darkness pressing in with a force of its own, deep and silent. She fixed her position in her mind—the trestle behind, the circle of the conveyor belt all around, the opening to the adjacent cave ahead and to the left. She did not think about the long, winding tunnel leading from the other cave, of traveling its length without comfort of light, or even of trying to find it in the darkness; there were other things to accomplish before she got there. Cautiously, like Columbus defying the edge of the earth, she crept forward.

The noise Ramon made gave her an anchor for bearings, something to move away from, but then that stopped too, leaving her without light or sound, with nothing from which to make use of her senses. And then she realized why Ramon had continued heaving rocks down the shaft even after he must have known he wouldn't hit her. He had used them to judge his own position. Any hope Emma had that he might come pounding out of the shaft, lose his balance, and crash to the floor vanished from her mind. Wishful thinking.

She stood still, listening. The hissing emerged again, from behind—no, off to one side. Utter darkness, like fog, absorbed sound, picked it up and reflected it elsewhere. She didn't know where he was, only that he had reached the cave floor, here so far beneath the earth. The sun must be shining above ground by now.

She moved on, found the conveyor belt, and climbed over; stopped to picture the layout in her mind, her position relative to it. She turned slightly left and hurried on, hands extended before her, feeling the way. The cave wall came out to meet her. Ramon's soft hissing continued—in the distance, close by, over here, over there. Then she heard something else, a sharp click—a safety being released—and she knew Ramon had his rifle.

Her pace quickened.

She kept one hand against the stone wall while the

221

other one swept the darkness, feeling for the monster machine that had been backed away after crashing into the adjacent cave. It couldn't be too hard, even here, to find something as large as a continuous miner. Then she stopped again, ears straining, listening to *silence*. The hissing had stopped. Where was Ramon?

And then she knew. She heard his breath, saw his face in her mind, felt his touch in the dark, cold and snakelike. But she had surprised him too, and wrenched free of his grasp in the instant before he knew he had her. She turned and ran, crashed into one of the shuttle cars, leaped over the conveyor belt to the relative safety beyond it—and just in time, since a spray of gunfire came right behind her. Then a motor roared to life and headlights shot through the darkness. She stood exposed in the glare of twin beams, of burning eyes. Ramon got there first. *He* was behind the wheel of the monster.

And starting to move toward her.

The conveyor belt and the shuttle cars were all that stood between her and the great black rotating drum with its fierce iron teeth, which was up and going, leading the charge for the other side. But the headlights also brightened the mine. She moved, looked around, found the monster's mates and ran for the nearest one. She leaped up into the open cab and took quick stock of the controls, a dismaying assortment. Then she sat down and turned on the ignition. It couldn't be too much different from a Ferrari.

She stepped down on the gas as she let the clutch up and turned on her own headlights, which shone on the wall a few feet away. The beast's engine gave a roar and lunged forward. Emma gripped the wheel hard and spun it sharply to the left, missing the wall by inches. As she came around, her headlights met Ramon's, who was crashing through the conveyor belt, splintering the shuttle cars where she had stood moments before, twisting steel and crushing spilled ore under the weight of massive caterpillar treads. Their headlights touched and crossed, and then Emma's veered on past him. She was caught in a difficult turn before she had the feel of the

222

beast, and it lurched heavily out of control beneath her. No, not a Ferrari. The monster was perhaps a little less agile.

But the principle was the same. Good driving required a firm grip, a cool head, and unflinching concentration. She depressed the clutch, swung the wheel back to come around, but her treads failed to get traction. They spun against the rock-strewn floor, whining above the roar of two leviathan engines. Worse, she was sideways to Ramon, who was coming forward relentlessly, and in the roofless cab, more defenseless than she would have been on her feet in the open. She took a deep breath. Calmly, disregarding the glare of the oncoming head-lights, she tested a series of levers across the dashboard, taking advantage of the stall to get to know her equipment. Then she shifted down and let up on the gas. The treads caught, spitting up rock. The beast swung around to the right, bent on confrontation.

Headlights glared eye to eye across several hundred feet of cave floor that still lay between them, outlining the teeth of Ramon's raised rotating drum. Emma saw his face beyond the teeth—grinning, leering, evil—and looked back at him coolly as she stepped on the gas to close the gap. At the same time, she reached for a lever on the dash and dropped her own drum head into its lowest position.

Then, above all the noise, she heard a separate sound that pierced the primeval core of her spine and turned her skin to gooseflesh. It was the sound of yet another leviathan engine. The last time she looked, there were two human beings in the mine, if you counted Ramon. Then *what* had come out of the dark and turned on the third monster?

Her eyes swung away and then back to Ramon, who was bearing down, coming nearer and nearer. Whatever it was would have to wait until she had dealt with him. His great black drum was almost upon her.

Emma let him come as close as she dared, then threw the beast into reverse and backed off sharply. Ramon's eyes glistened with triumph. Emma let him force her back several yards. Then, without warning, she braked and shifted gears once again. She shot ahead in forward.

She was braced for a head-on crash. Ramon wasn't. His hands broke loose from the steering wheel on impact, and he fell back, but the look on his face gave her even more satisfaction. No more gloating triumph; he was afraid. He hadn't expected her to strike back. Emma pressed her advantage.

She gripped a lever on the dash and her own drum head started to rotate. With steady pressure she brought it up. Then a sharp thrust locked it in place under his. Teeth clashed and sparks flew, and the air screamed with a terrible grinding. Emma's hand fell back to the gearshift. She shifted down, gave the engine more gas, pushed harder. Ramon's monster jolted up at the front, and Emma edged her drum head in under it. She had him beached, nose in the air, treads spinning. Ramon tried to reverse, to back away, but Emma stayed right with him. Fear flared in his eyes. She smiled. She knew she had him.

And then Ramon changed the rules again. Gripping the wheel with one hand, he reached down and grabbed his rifle. He held it firmly under one arm, its barrel steadied against the dash, his hand on the trigger. Emma maneuvered the gearshift quickly. She braked and then gave the gas a fast shot, bumping him hard from below, and succeeded in throwing his aim off. A burst of gunfire caught the windshield on her far right, missing her by at least two feet, but Ramon was realigning his aim. There was no time to waste now.

Emma hit another lever on the dash, and a great mechanical arm swung away from the monster's side. Ramon fired. As he did, she grabbed the gearshift and bumped him. This time the gunfire passed over her head, within inches. Her hand moved back to the dashboard, and the arm swung wide, away from Ramon, then came back around him, caught him by the chest in a scissor grip. Emma pulled back hard, resisting the urge to crush, and lifted him up out of his seat. He rose in the

224

air, kicking and struggling. All trace of triumph was gone. He glared down at her in a rage of venomous fury.

Ramon struggled against the grip of the arm and managed to get his own arms free above it; he still had the rifle. He took careful aim. Emma's hand closed on the lever; she was poised to shove it to the right, then sharply left, and to do it again and again until he had exhausted his ammunition. But suddenly Ramon's arms flew wide and he dropped the rifle to the ground. His legs jerked and fell back, limp and dangling. His black eyes went flat, his leering mouth froze, and blood poured out of a neat bullethole in his forehead. Emma, watching, was very nearly as astonished as he was.

Then she saw the third monster moving up on her left and knew who was behind the wheel, a driver who was indeed questionably human. Owen, come to save her! To step in at the end and walk off with the victory.

She fell back against the seat, laughing, torn by old frustration and new relief, and by the numbness of spreading exhaustion. Damned if he hadn't done it *again*! She considered swinging the monster around to take him on here and now, but instead she shut off the ignition. She was too tired, simply too tired.

Too tired even to notice that Owen had shut his engine off too, and yet the cave wasn't silent. The roaring went on—rumbling, building, distant. Then the ground beneath her heaved, and Emma sat up, sharply focused. No lights! No miners! The mine was closed down when it should have been going around the clock; MacKendrick himself had forewarned her. He had said they would dynamite these caves if they had to evacuate fast, to obliterate any trace of American presence. And then he'd had a summons from the Pentagon, breaking the strictest radio silence. Emma knew this was it. They *had* called it off. The start of obliteration!

She leaped down from the cab and, ignoring the stabs of pain in her feet, tore across the cave floor to warn Owen. He jumped down too, and they both ran.

Hard on their heels came another explosion.

36

When Nichols returned to his office, Ardry was waiting for him. "We've had an urgent message from Owen," he said. "Direct this time. He called in himself. You're not going to believe this, Ed, but the terrorists are gone. They packed up and—"

"I believe it."

Ardry stared at him in open surprise, a reversal of roles. It was Nichols whose face showed a deadly calm.

"You're not going to believe *this*, Sam, but they were called off by the same people who sent them there—by DIA, acting on orders of the President."

Ardry's mouth dropped open.

"You heard me, and it's as bad as it sounds. I've got some thinking to do. I'll tell you about it later."

"Not so fast," Ardry said. "Owen had more to say. Michelangelo is alive."

"But he can't be! We have—" Nichols stopped as the truth dawned. "He *planned* it that way! Owen *knew* he planned it that way!"

"Apparently. And now Owen says Michelangelo's going to kill the President."

Nichols stood there for several seconds. Then he turned and sank into his chair. "Maybe we ought to let him."

Ardry's face turned catatonic.

"Take it easy, Sam. It hasn't come to that yet. Why does Owen think so?"

Ardry repeated what Owen had told him.

And when he was finished, Nichols grunted. "You'd better alert the Secret Service."

"I've already done it, though I haven't told them who the assassin is. Owen wants to see the President first, before he knows. Owen wants to tell him his own way. He says you'll know what he's talking about."

"Yes, I do, and I think it's time I told you. But first I want you to get back to Owen. Tell him we're sending a plane for him and Thatcher, and order one for me too. We'll meet them at the Cape. I want you to go with me."

"I may not be able to reach him just now," Ardry said. "Thatcher is missing. Owen has gone to find her."

Nichols turned away as Ardry explained, steeling himself against a new source of worry. Now, finally, Owen was free, and Thatcher had turned up missing. Then something clicked in his mind and he looked up sharply. "Get me Michelangelo's file," he said.

"Now?"

"Now."

Twenty minutes later, with the file open across his desk, Nichols leaned back, frowning deeply. It was all there. Christ! No wonder Owen wanted to see this thing through. It was *Owen* who planned Ben Riker's death!

And, yes, Henry Brendan needed protection.

Owen knew a shortcut out, a tough climb through a natural shaft that rose sharply from the cave floor, but it kept them above the dynamite charges that ripped through the deep earth, blowing heavy equipment to shrapnel and collapsing telltale mines forever. Dust shot through the air, propelled by hot wind from below, stinging their eyes, coating nostrils and throat, making the beam of Owen's flashlight useless. But they climbed on—Emma in front, Owen close behind—and burst through an opening at the top, into daylight and open air, blessed jungle!

Emma dropped to the ground on hands and knees, coughing up dust, as blinded by the morning sun as she was by absence of light in the caves, her hearing numbed by the great belching roar of man's own monsters.

Vaguely she heard Owen on the ground beside her, gasping and coughing ash from his lungs, and she knew that he was all right, or would be. A moment later he pressed something into her hand. Emma seized it, a flask. Precious water.

Then, as she unscrewed the cap, she laughed at herself, even as she went on struggling for air. There was nothing wrong with her sense of smell. Owen knew what a flask was for—not water, but Glenfiddich!

The flow of malt Scotch in her throat was like alcohol on an abrasion, but it also washed the dust away, enough to make breathing easier. Emma sat up. Glenfiddich, straight, was a drink to be sipped under any circumstances. As the first drink of day it was, indeed, bracing.

And probably just what Frank in his professional role would have ordered. Emma looked around, rubbing dust from her eyes as her vision began to function again. Shapes emerged from the glaring light—the bramble of trees and, yes, the peak of the *pyramid* rising above them. She realized that for all her traveling during the night, sharply down and then up, she had never been more than a mile horizontally from the ruins. The blasting wasn't audible here—it was too deep and too confined—but she felt the earth shuddering below. The caves, the cellar of Uxmal, were being destroyed. No one would ever know they had existed.

Owen's face emerged too, pale and ghostlike. He was covered with limestone ash, as she was, a veneer of stone dust broken only by rivers of sweat and a pair of eyes looking back at her undaunted. Cool. Pragmatic. Invulnerable.

"Good thing I arrived when I did," he said.

"Oh my, yes," she replied. "If you'd come any later I might have had things wrapped up without you."

"Or you might be dead."

"I doubt it."

"That's the thanks I get?"

"Thanks! You want *thanks*? The worst moment I had down there was when you came roaring in unannounced. I thought the closet monsters were coming."

"Closet *monsters*?" Owen frowned, smearing dust and sweat, causing creases to cake across his forehead, but new lines showed around his eyes and mouth. Emma gathered that he was smiling.

"They lurk in the dark," she explained, "and they pounce if you turn away, or if you dare to close your eyes."

Owen continued to look at her, and then he burst out laughing. "Closet monsters, indeed!" he exclaimed. "You're only afraid of the things that aren't real. You do have the most perverse sense of danger."

"Ah, yes—the *worst* fears. The ones you can't see. Fears of the past. Fears of the imagination."

"When there's a perfectly real rifle aimed down your throat in the present?"

Emma shrugged.

"Perverse," he said. "And if I may say so, you're also distinctly ungrateful."

"If there's gratitude to be given out, it seems to me we both owe it to Frank. I assume he's the one who showed you that handy shortcut."

"You're right. Without Frank, I might not have reached you in time."

"You're not going to drop it, are you?"

"Not while I can make it stick. You'll get back at me someday."

"I intend to!" Emma smiled. "In the meantime, at least I don't have to explain why Ramon is dead and not on his way to interrogation."

"*Touché.*" Owen smiled back, but then as quickly his eyes turned cold. "We've got better people than Ramon to interrogate. To start with, a trio of congressmen who have only been pretending to be hostages."

So, he knew that.

"But do you know why?" she asked.

"Cover, it seems, for a deep mine."

"Three mines. You only saw part of the operation." Emma produced the ore sample from her pocket and handed it to him.

Owen turned it over in his hands. "What is it?"

"Something to do with weapons research, I think. Whatever it is, Uncle Sam has just stolen sixty-five thousand tons of it from the Mexican people." Emma told him what she'd seen in the mine, what she heard, and who she saw there. "Imagine, *MacKendrick*," she said in the end. "He's supposed to be training Delta Squad for a rescue mission."

"That won't be necessary now," Owen said dryly and told her about the terrorists' departure. Emma wasn't surprised. The dynamite was announcement enough of a total—and thorough—evacuation.

"Well, you have filled in a few gaps," he added and got up, extending his hand. "Can you walk on those feet?"

"I wouldn't if I had a choice, but I don't suppose we'll find a cab."

"The next best thing. Frank's waiting with his van to take us to the airport, and Nichols is sending a plane. Our mission isn't finished."

Emma studied his face as they set off through the jungle. "So," she said, "Michelangelo finally showed up."

Owen glanced at her, smiling. "You knew he was alive?"

"Of course I knew. He wouldn't have started that car without checking it for explosives."

Owen nodded appreciatively and told her what had happened at the ruins. "Three shots," he said in the end. "Three fired, three missed, and an extra one as a signature. It's Brendan he's after."

"*Only* Brendan?"

Owen didn't say anything.

"It strikes me that he has another target as well," Emma went on, "and that he has had all along. You, of course. Oh, he's not going to kill you—no, worse, he's going to *defeat* you. He intends to set you up, give you every chance to stop him, and then kill the President in spite of your best efforts." She paused to let Owen reply, but his silence was confirmation enough. "What

230

is it between you two?'' she asked. ''Don't you think
it's time you told me?''

Owen still remained silent, his face reflective, his eyes
briefly haunted by something Emma hadn't seen there
before. Then, abruptly, he turned to her.

''What's between us is simple enough,'' he said. ''Michelangelo killed my father.''

... ...
... ...
... ...
... ...
... ... he said ...
... ...

⧓ 37 ⧓

Emma stopped and spun around, staring at him in the sunlight that filtered through jungle vines. Staring, weighing, measuring. Once, only once in all the time she had known him, and in a setting far different from this one, had Owen talked about himself. It was two years ago, but if it had been two hundred years Emma could not have failed to remember.

They had been fogged in at Robin Hood's Bay on the rugged North Sea coast of Yorkshire, fogged in and alone in the lounge of a small seafront hotel, hearthbound, with the warmth and scent of burning peat to repel the invading dampness. Owen had seemed reflective then too, reflective but not haunted. Shadows of firelight moved gently across his face as he sat back in one of the chintz-covered chairs, gazing into the hearth, saying nothing.

Emma, likewise settled down for the nonce—she remembered how comfortable those deep chairs were—had said nothing either for a long time. Then, on an impulse, she asked him, "Where do you come from?"

Owen continued to gaze at the fire. "Everywhere. Nowhere. I'm not sure I know."

Emma sighed. It was what she expected: no answer.

"I mean that," he said then, glancing up. "For what it's worth, I was born in Egypt."

She raised an eyebrow, surprised, for he'd never revealed even that much before. "Where, in Cairo?"

He laughed. "In the back of a Daimler on the road between Kadesh-barnea and Thebes."

"You're joking!"

Owen shook his head. "My parents were on an official outing and, it seems, lost track of the time."

Not to say the midwife. Emma knew the road, which ran through desert even today. "Well?" she asked.

"Well what?"

"*Are* you Egyptian?"

"Yes and no. I breathed my first air there, and that counts for something. But my father was English, a career diplomat."

"Then you're British."

"By half. My mother, bless her heart, was American. Boston-born. An heiress, the only career she ever knew or wanted." Owen chuckled softly as his gaze shifted back to the fire. "A love match," he said. "Mother married Father for his title, and he married her for her wealth. I was the obligatory heir, conceived for the sake of appearances and custom. I was, I might add, so good in the role that they never considered producing a sibling." He shrugged. "It was just as well. I always did work better alone."

Emma held her breath. Truth, she thought. "Even then?"

"Oh, yes, though I don't suppose I had much choice. By any practical measure I was always an orphan. I was brought up by nannies two years at a time, in a series of houses that had two things in common, splendid rooms and long marble corridors. But I was an explorer too, more intrigued by back streets than palaces, and by the time I grew out of my knee pants, I'd learned how to fend for myself. How to minimize my own presence. How to find out what I wasn't meant to know without anyone being the wiser. I couldn't have been better trained, I should think, if I'd been left in a basket on the doorstep at Langley."

Emma laughed lightly, but she also took a stiff drink. The fire seemed to be losing ground; the fog, unseen, to be creeping in from the darkness behind, wet and cold, deeply chilling. "Where was your family posted after Egypt?"

"Madrid. Then Istanbul. New Delhi. Paris. Those were all home, more or less, by the time I was ten years old. At twelve I was sent back to England, to Eton and Oxford. Balliol College. Father's schools."

"And got highest marks, I suppose."

Owen laughed. "Not always. The street languages I'd picked up didn't much impress my Latin masters." He reached for his cigarettes and lit one. "But then Latin was *there*, and so I learned it, among other things—history, philosophy, literature. I discovered challenge as a distraction from boredom. I did well enough academically, but I wasn't very keen on the regimentation."

"No, you wouldn't be."

A flicker of something passed across Owen's face, and he lowered his eyes to the fire once more. It passed by and was gone. His face suddenly became entirely passive. "I was seventeen," he said, "in my first year at Oxford—in fact, reading Dostoevsky that night—when a solicitor came around to tell me that my parents were dead."

Emma's eyes widened slightly. "*Both* of them?"

"Not only that," he said, looking up, "but for lack of imagination, I suppose, they'd left everything to me. Property on two continents. Their investments. A numbered account in Zurich. I had no use for property and gave it away as soon as the deeds were legally transferred to my name. Nor was I interested in managing a portfolio; I gave the investments to charity. I tried to unload Father's title too, on the grounds that it might bring some needy cause a good price at Sotheby's, but a peerage isn't that easily discarded."

"A peerage? Good God!"

"Indeed," Owen said. "Still mine. If I ever tire of this life, I can always go back and take up a seat in the House of Lords."

Emma stared at him for a moment, utterly speechless, and then she started to giggle. To giggle! She couldn't help it. Owen robed and wigged, bowing before the woolsack, was a picture her mind refused to produce! But above all else she was curious.

"Lord *Who*?" she asked, leaning forward.

But Owen had drawn the line there. "*Mrs.* Who?" he returned, and they both laughed, because they knew the conversation was finished.

Almost. Emma asked one more question. "How did your parents die?"

"It was a plane crash in Tibet. The propellers iced up and they went down in the mountains. . . .''

Now, years later, in the Yucatan bush—a long way from Tibet, from Balliol College and Robin Hood's Bay— *Michelangelo* was Owen's father's killer. Had he also killed Mother, bless her heart? Presumably they were in the same plane. Or were they?

It didn't matter, not even if there had been a plane, because ·Emma knew Owen was telling the truth that night by the hearth. Oh, the story itself might have been fabrication, embellishment, a part of the game. The Daimler, the nannies, the peerage, and iced-up propellers—they might have been real, or they might have been nothing but ghosts by the fire, created for an idle space in time, for his own and for her amusement. Emma knew she might never know. But she also knew there was truth at the *core* of the story, because Owen would deceive, but he wouldn't lie without saying so. And because, in a chill at her back, she had sensed the truth so strongly.

Yes, Owen—whoever he was—had closet monsters of his own. He might well have been an orphan. But if he did have a father, and if Michelangelo killed him, Emma felt sure of one thing: Owen would *not* have resented him for it.

And so he was lying now, plain to see, and inviting her to catch him. The reason for the lie was equally clear. She had asked him a question: *What is it between you two?* Apparently he didn't intend to tell her. He might simply have said so, of course, but that wasn't Owen's way.

Nor Emma's. "Remarkable," she said. "What did he

235

do, disguise himself as the Dalai Llama and shoot the plane down with an ice gun?''

Owen smiled. ''Something like that.'' Then the smile disappeared. ''I'll tell you as soon as we're out of here. Nichols is expecting us at Cape Canaveral.''

''At the Cape! Why?''

''That's where the President is.''

''And we've got to save him from your friend.''

''From him,'' Owen said, ''and from someone else who doesn't seem to like him much—because I've got a hunch that before we found out, Henry Brendan knew nothing about Riker's murder.''

Owen, belted into a window seat in the forward section of the plane, watched as the runway dropped away and they circled, banking sharply, over the jungle. There were no pyramids to be seen below, no last view of the great white cities. There was only the bush, spreading thickly across the peninsula, and the big sky into which they were climbing. Nothing had changed. The land had been pillaged before. The Yucatan still wore its cloak of enduring silence.

But Owen wondered how much they had seen, the Indians who lived with the land and understood its moods, its whims, its every deviation. He wondered how much Frank knew.

Frank had been good-natured enough when they said good-bye at the airport, even to the extent of pointing out, with fully intentional malice, that Owen had a week to go before he could be sure his brush with chicken pox had not left him afflicted.

"Watch for spots," he had warned. "As a rule they appear first on the stomach. And they itch. No, in children they itch. At your age, they burn like fire." He had smiled then.

No questions, no answers passed between them.

But when Owen ran up the steps to board the plane, and then turned back for a final wave, he had caught Frank with his guard briefly down, with sadness showing in his dark eyes—and parting with him, Owen felt sure, wasn't enough to explain it. There were years of history in Frank's face, years of patience, of quiet waiting. And an edge perhaps of something Frank had taken from the land. Tenacity. Even defiance.

Owen smiled to himself as the plane leveled off and soared out over the Gulf, leaving Yucatan behind. He wasn't really interested in the whys of Washington policy, nor in determining guilt or fault. But if Frank did suspect what had gone on, and if he demanded redress in some form—well then, more power to him.

"Look at this," Emma said, touching his arm.

Owen turned to her in the next seat, and to the newspaper she held out, with a banner headline trumpeting the end of the siege: TERRORISTS ABANDON UXMAL. And then in smaller print below, a subhead: CONGRESSMAN CASS MURDERED.

Owen took the paper and scanned the story. It seemed no one knew why the terrorists left so abruptly. There were rumors of threats from a dozen quarters, and of secret negotiations, but no one knew that Uxmal was only a subterfuge, a falseface, designed to hide a deeper, highly secret operation.

"I suppose the White House will release the straight story," Emma said dryly. "Prepared months ago in variations to cover any contingency. I wonder what will happen."

Owen wondered too. He glanced out the window as they cleared the clouds and burst into the brilliant sunshine above them. Somewhere ahead Air Force One was making its way north to Washington—or to Andrews Air Force Base, where a team of military professionals would be standing by to conclude the charade with a sham debriefing. The President had sent his own plane to bring the hostages home—the least he could do, Owen thought, to recompense inconvenience on the part of those who were in on the plan, fear among those who were not, and grief among Andrew Cass's wife and children. But Owen and Emma were alone on this plane, except for the crew on the other side of the cockpit door, and a steward retired to the rear to stay there, on orders, unless he was called for. It was something more than a two-hour flight with a strong tailwind behind them. Owen loosened his seat belt and turned to Emma.

"There's only one way to stop Michelangelo," he said. "Conventional methods won't do it. We have to anticipate him, to predict what he's going to do. To think the way he thinks and be there first. To understand what he believes is at stake here. And you're right that he's drawn me into this for a reason. He's *daring* me to stop him, which means it will be much harder to do. He's going to be at his best for this one."

"And he's always been the best."

"Not always." Owen gave her a small smile. "It's not widely known, and surely not something he'd like to have known, but the master assassin's first target is still living."

Emma was slightly astonished. "You mean he *failed* once?"

"He did, indeed, and it was my fault. It was also the last time we worked together."

The smile faded from Owen's face, and old feelings rose cold in his breast, where they had lain—now dormant, now active, but never exorcised—through the years that had intervened. What happened to Michelangelo had happened before and would happen again. He had burned out. Then he sold out. He wanted more money.

And Owen could have dealt with that. He was never surprised when a colleague burned out—a risk they all faced, an occupational hazard. And, generally speaking, he had no quarrel with a colleague who wanted to better himself financially. He even might have accepted the notion that an old friend had become a paid killer, since acceptance in his mind had nothing to do with approval. If Michelangelo had gone his way and stayed away, Owen might have put an old friend out of mind without praise or condemnation. But that was not the way it happened.

Owen reached for his cigarettes and lit one. Then he settled back in his seat. "We were in Algeciras," he said, "and needed to make a side trip to Tangier. I left our hotel to make arrangements for a boat and was gone

239

for several hours. When I returned, my partner—he wasn't called Michelangelo yet—told me we'd had an urgent message from Langley in my absence. It was blue code, top secret, so secret that Langley didn't trust it to writing, but had it delivered orally by a political officer from the embassy in Madrid. So secret, in fact, that once we had done what we were to do, we were never to speak of it again unless further contact was initiated from Langley.

"It seemed that a certain African dictator was preparing to invade a neighboring country, a French client state that had no army to speak of. Washington had a strong interest and was weighing several options for discouraging him. One was to kill the bastard before he could launch the attack. Effective, but risky—and according to the man from Madrid an if-all-else-fails contingency. *We* were to develop a plan in case it had to be done, and then go back to business as usual, the Algeciras assignment, and forget it. Until and unless further contact was made."

Owen raised his cigarette to his lips, inhaled, exhaled, balanced it in the ashtray. "There was only one specification," he said. "The operation had to be carried out in such a way that obvious political murder would look like an accident, an accident so convincing that it would fool the man's own bodyguards. No one was ever to know an assassination had occurred."

Emma's eyebrows shot up and she started to speak, but Owen raised a hand for silence. "You'll recognize more than that," he said. "The operation we planned—no, *I* planned, because my partner didn't contribute much to it—was based on high-voltage batteries implanted not in ski boots, but bedroom slippers. The dictator was going to die, if it came to that, in a fall from his own balcony, with nothing to show later but natural injuries."

Emma gasped.

"That's right," Owen said. "*I* devised the plan that killed Ben Riker."

"Did you *know*?"

"Not when it happened. Too many years had passed

240

and there was no reason for me to connect one fall with the other. But I should have known, because Michelangelo told me himself, a year after the incident with the dictator, the last time I ever saw him. He said he wanted to be there, laughing, to enjoy my dismay when I discovered what my plan accomplished. Obviously, he never forgot."

And he wouldn't have, because when he sold out, he had tried to take Owen out with him, for Owen was the one man who might have stopped him—who did stop him once, as it turned out—and might again. Neither had Owen ever forgot. The score still remained to be settled.

"The dictator didn't fall," Owen said, "though he did die soon after that. Langley never got back to us, so I made contact myself, and I learned there was no invasion planned, that the dictator was already dying of cancer. I found out there was no man from Madrid. That my partner had taken a contract to kill. That he'd already turned, for pay, and was lying to me."

Emma stared at him. "I don't understand. You said his first target was still—" The truth dawned in her eyes. "Oh, my God, *all* of it happened before. The dictator never was his target!"

"All of it," Owen confirmed, and stubbed out his cigarette angrily. "My own partner had set me up. He got *me* to plan his first job. He tried to use me to help him kill a man I would not have killed, and he did it by naming a different target. Now you'll see why I recognized the same plot all these years later."

"Someone else did too," Emma said. "Someone turned the same deception on Michelangelo."

Owen nodded. "Of course he didn't know that at the time. He was only given an order for an assassination by accident, and he pulled out my old plan. When I didn't recognize it, he had to tell me."

"And set you on the trail to Uxmal."

"Ah, yes. And he's out there now, a man of his word, laughing."

"Who knew?" Emma asked. "Who knew what happened back then?"

"I don't know. Nichols. We'll have to ask him who else has had access to the records."

"And who was his target?"

"A head of state from the Middle East who'd declared war on drug traffic in his own country and run afoul of organized crime."

"You mean Michelangelo took a contract from *a drug syndicate*?"

"I don't know who the contractor was, but you're in the ballpark," Owen said and shrugged. "He wanted out, and he wanted money. He took what he could get. But he failed because I put him under surveillance and found out who he was really after. I alerted Langley, and Langley alerted the target. The existence of a plot was revealed and died in a glare of publicity. The contractor could not have been pleased. Michelangelo vanished as a matter of survival, and under his own name he never resurfaced.

Emma would know the rest. He went underground and created a new identity, a man with no name and no history. Within the next year, three political assassinations occurred in three different countries, and the killer escaped without leaving a trace or a trail behind. Police agencies began to realize they were looking for one man, but as time went on and more killings occurred, he left them in a whirlwind, utterly baffled. The press started to call him an artist among his kind. Yet another assassination occurred, in Florence, at the Academy. The target fell at the feet of Michelangelo's *David*. The assassin had chosen his own *nom de guerre*, and the press had a heyday with it.

"I knew," Owen said. "I could never prove it, but I *knew* who the assassin was. I saw the hand of an old friend at work. But he wanted to make sure I knew, and one night he paid me a visit. It wasn't a warm reunion."

"I wouldn't think so."

"Among other things, he said he wondered why I cared. Weren't we, after all, *doubles*?"

"The Secret Sharer."

"My own gray ghost."

"Nonsense, you're nothing like him."

"You're wrong there," Owen said. "We're not doubles, no—that's his view, not mine—but we are alike in so many ways. We work alike. We think alike. The truth is I *want* to kill him."

"Then why haven't you done it before?"

"Because it was personal. My anger would have been in my way; I wouldn't have succeeded." Owen paused as old feelings rose up with fresh force. "Anyway, anger alone isn't good reason for killing a man. Anger suffocates choice. But now he's daring me to kill him before he kills the President."

"And will you?"

"No." Owen felt the anger draining away. "I'll stop him from getting to Brendan, but I won't get to him; he won't let me. When that confrontation comes, one way or another he has to win."

"Richard."

Owen chuckled. "Don't worry, I'll win too. I'm not as generous as he is with my options."

Sir Edward Nevins, the British ambassador to Washington, spun around in his chair, his face gray with shock, and said to the man sitting on the other side of his desk, "You mean my wife's having her International Club *here* tomorrow?"

"That's right, sir," the man replied. "Forty ladies for luncheon and a film. She hoped you might join them, at least for sherry beforehand."

"You're not serious! *Sherry?*"

The man cleared his throat. "Sherry or fruit juice. Lady Jane is no happier about it than you are."

She wouldn't be. Lady Jane liked her martinis. But to serve them to the International Club, he supposed, would be in violation of the bylaws, if not the Magna Carta and the Constitution.

Sir Edward looked very glum indeed, but then a twinkle appeared in his eyes and he smiled benignly across the desk. "Isn't that space shuttle launch tomorrow?"

"I believe it is, sir."

"Well, then, we're in the clear! Ring up the Secretary of State, will you? Tell him I'm accepting his kind invitation."

⚎ 39 ⚎

Kennedy Space Center, Cape Canaveral, was every inch as flat and scrubby as the Yucatan Peninsula some seven hundred miles to the south—not especially attractive terrain, but it had certain features Yucatan lacked. Primarily water. Aside from the Atlantic Ocean, which formed its long eastern shore, two wide rivers breached the Cape vertically, breaking it into a series of miscut jigsaw pieces that were interconnected by causeways. This was marshland, not bush, and the climate was sultry. Owen pulled his jacket off as he climbed into the back of the car at the edge of the shuttle landing strip, which looked wide enough to land three jumbo jets flying wingtip-to-wingtip and long enough to land an airborne freight train. Emma got in from the other side and Sam Ardry, in the driver's seat, sped off down the flat two-lane road toward a white monolith that was standing straight, shoulders square, in the distance.

"Where are we going?" Emma asked.

"To the KSC Headquarters Building," Ardry replied. "We've taken over the main conference room. Ed's waiting there to see you." He glanced over the seat at Owen. "Your meeting with the President is set for this afternoon. We've got a chopper to fly you on over to Patrick."

Owen nodded. The President was staying in one of the VIP guest cottages at Patrick Air Force Base nearby. "How long is the flight?" he asked.

"Three minutes." Ardry looked at Emma. "We've

arranged for you to see the launch director—guy named Les Finn, the top man around here until *Pilgrim* clears the launchpad—and Harry Nesbitt, who's the head of the Secret Service detail traveling with the President. It's good to see you, by the way. Good to see both of you, in fact. This one has been a little dicey.''

"It's going to get dicier," Owen said and turned to his window. There was water wherever he looked, on both sides of the car; excavations along the Cape had turned up a good many Indian relics, but he felt sure there would be no Chac masks among them. And perhaps that explained Chac's ill-mannered disposition. Taken for granted in damper climes, a petulant god of rain could hardly fail to make up for it in the dry ones.

Emma was talking to Ardry now, but Owen wasn't listening. Somewhere nearby cars would be lining up, filled with people willing to wait through the night for a good view of tomorrow's launch. But there was no traffic on this road, which cut through the heart of the Cape. No traffic and no sign of people. They might have been on the road to Uxmal, except for the fact that the trees were well scattered across an open landscape here, with pelicans and gulls—Owen even spotted an eagle's nest—to stand in for the circling vultures. There were towering structures here too—more beyond the white monolith, which was growing larger as they approached it—and they rose straight up from the flat land at wide intervals, much higher than the pyramids of the Maya. Isolation. Towering structures. And on launch days, from all reports, a *son et lumière* that was nothing less than spectacular. But there was no brooding silence here, and certainly no sense of patience—for with the launch and then return of the first reusable orbiter, Kennedy Space Center had become the world's first spaceport. It looked forward, not back in time, and the only mysteries that remained were out there in the big sky the Maya once sought to understand, little dreaming that mortal man might one day go there.

The white monolith turned out to be the Vehicle Assembly Building, a structural wonder where internal par-

246

titions could be drawn back to accommodate the height and bulk of a space shuttle, its huge tank and booster rockets. The United Nations Building would fit through the doors of the VAB; it was nearly five times as tall as the Pyramid of the Magician. A few small buildings were clustered at its base, like fallen rocks at Uxmal—including the Launch Control Center and temporary stands set up for the press—but otherwise it stood alone, stark against the flat land, looking across open terrain to other giants of a different kind, the fixed service gantries that marked the launchpads along the ocean.

The space shuttle *Pilgrim II* was there, in place and waiting.

And if this site were abandoned someday, this civilization absorbed by time, its achievements lost and forgotten, Owen wondered what distant generations would think if they found these structures in ruins. Huge steel skeletons rising into the air along a vast seacoast. Surely virgins must have been flung from their heights to appease yet another petulant god, of sky or sea, moon or planets. And he smiled, wondering too at man's incapacity to accept the void left by things that were unknown. A void and a need to fill it. There always had been an urge to explain the mysteries of the universe. On the one hand, it led people to create whole pantheons of irascible gods and to enrich literature far more than knowledge. On the other hand, it led people to *explore*— inevitably, irresistibly—and eventually to banish false gods in the brighter light of discovery.

Two cultures, so far apart, both strove for airy heights and achieved them. The Maya were as remarkable once as the pioneers of the space age. But where Uxmal was a triumph of art, earthbound and sufficient unto itself, the Kennedy Space Center was a triumph of science. People came here for something else, for a flash of fire and a roaring of sound, for an affirmation of their own driving force, for a glimpse of infinity.

Owen's mind shifted back to something more immediately pressing: *Pilgrim II*. Launchpad 39. It was now 3:00 P.M., and the countdown, begun two days ago, was at T-minus-eighteen hours. Not much time to find and stop a killer.

Because Owen was sure of one thing. Like the tourists lining up in their cars, Michelangelo had a rendezvous with a flash of fire and a roaring of sound. Owen didn't know how he would strike, but he did know when. Day and hour. Tomorrow, at 9:00 A.M.

At the moment of lift-off.

40

Owen had never met Henry Brendan until the President walked into the sitting room of the cottage where he was staying, along the Atlantic shore, and extended his hand in a manner that was reserved and vaguely hostile.

"I understand you were a hostage at Uxmal," he said.

"That's right, Mr. President."

"Bad luck."

"I'm not so sure."

The President's jaw tightened slightly. "Well," he said, "Ed Nichols insists that what you have to tell me is vital to the national security. I told him I would hear you out. Sit down."

They sat in chairs facing each other across a low table. Coffee had been served before Owen arrived, in a silver pot etched with the President's seal, on a silver tray with gold-embossed china cups. But the Air Force steward had gone, and they were alone.

"Do you mind if I smoke?" Owen asked.

The President gestured to an ashtray on the table. It was crystal, etched like the coffeepot, and a packet of White House matches lay inside it. Owen wondered, as he struck a match and held it to his cigarette, if the cottage were always kept this way, or if the trappings were brought along to make the President feel at home here. If so, it didn't seem to work. Henry Brendan looked anything but comfortable. His jaw remained tight, his face rather cold, his eyes hostile.

"What's this about?" he asked.

Owen kept his face purposely void of expression. "Mr. President," he began, "we know Uxmal was a hoax. We know who the terrorists were, who trained them, and who sent them there. We also know why; we have a sample of the ore."

A look passed across Brendan's face. Wariness, Owen thought. Maybe weariness, maybe both—but he didn't contest what Owen had said. If he weren't likely to confirm the truth here, at least he wasn't quick to deny it either.

"Perhaps you should be more specific," he said.

But Owen shook his head. "That's not why I'm here. There are people you may have to answer to for what went on down there, but I'm not one of them."

"Then why are you here?" Brendan asked crossly.

"Because the job I set out to do when I went to Uxmal isn't finished. I'm here because President Riker was assassinated."

Brendan's face didn't change; he already knew this much.

"And because," Owen went on, with no change of his own expression or tone, "we have evidence that suggests it was *you* who hired the assassin."

Wariness vanished from the President's face, along with reserve, hostility, and color. His skin went pale, his eyes blank with shock, and he sat forward abruptly.

"*What did you say?*"

"I said we've got evidence."

"But you *can't* have! I didn't *do* it!"

Brendan looked stunned and dismayed, like a child told something beyond its ken. Stunned and a little frightened. But no cry of outrage emerged from his mouth, no righteous indignation. None of the masks he might have had ready to march out, like the presidential trappings, if he'd known this moment might come. He was caught unprepared, and Owen was strongly inclined to believe him.

Still, he wanted to know more.

He opened a manila envelope he had brought along

250

and placed a photograph on the table in front of the President. Brendan picked it up and studied it briefly.

Then he looked back at Owen. "Is *this* your evidence?"

"Part of it."

"Then I don't understand. What does this photograph have to do with Ben Riker?"

"Do you remember when it was taken?"

"Very well. I do a lot of these things, ceremonial meetings for one cause or another, but this one had special impact on me." Brendan looked at the photograph again. "This painting, though you can't see it here—there were other pictures taken that day, better ones I would think—was a portrait of me when I was Vice President. It was done by a child with leukemia. She sent it to me and asked me to autograph it. Someone on the White House staff called it to my attention and thought it would make a good human-interest story. We invited the child to come to Washington, so that I could personally give the painting back to her, but she wasn't able to come. This man is her father."

"Her father." Owen drew on his cigarette.

"He came in her place."

"No, Mr. President. That man is Michelangelo. The assassin."

Brendan's eyes widened, and his mouth dropped open. He looked from Owen to the photograph, and back again. "It can't be! Are you sure?"

Owen nodded. "I know him very well. When he worked for the agency, Michelangelo was my partner."

The President sat quite still, but real fear started to show in his eyes. On his face was the look of a man who knew he was at the edge of defeat but didn't have the heart to fight it.

"There's more," Owen said. "The painting you signed that day wasn't a portrait of you, but another portrait, much older. I can only guess that one painting was mounted very skillfully behind the other, because we have the painting too, with your signature on the back. It's a portrait of—"

"Thomas Jefferson," Brendan said before Owen could.

He fell back in his chair, his eyes closed, his face numb. "Oh, Lord, it all fits!"

"So it would seem," Owen replied. "Someone has gone to a great deal of trouble to make you look guilty."

Brendan didn't move. Then, suddenly, he opened his eyes, more startled in a way than he had been before. "You *believe* me?"

"Yes."

"But why?"

Owen shrugged. "Instinct, reinforced by your own reaction. I doubted you did it when I came here, and now you've convinced me."

Brendan sighed heavily. "Thank God!"

"But you're not off the hook," Owen went on, "because the assassin is still free, and *he* believes you hired him. Not only that, he believes you double-crossed him. He intends to kill you for it."

The President's face went whiter still. "Are you *serious*?"

"As serious as he is. He's going to do it while you're here, when you go to the launch tomorrow."

"How do you know?"

"Because I know him, and because, in a way, he told me," Owen explained. "Your normal protection won't be enough to prevent him from getting to you. He knows how the Secret Service works. I daresay he's already planned a way around them."

"But they're trained agents—"

Owen raised a hand to cut him off. "Whatever else you do," he said, "don't underestimate him. Michelangelo is a master. He can get past any security, and he's never been more intent on a job than he is on this one—because it will be his last job, and a matter of personal revenge. The Secret Service won't be able to stop him."

The President looked more baffled than frightened. "Then what do I do?"

"You could go back to Washington right now."

"But if he's bent on killing me, wouldn't he only follow me there?"

"Probably. But that's still the wise course."

Brendan shook his head. "I don't want to do that. I don't want to run."

Owen knew he meant it. "We could send a substitute to the launch in your place."

Brendan shook his head again sharply.

"Then you're going to have to trust me," Owen said. "I know Michelangelo better than anyone, and I can stop him, but I've got less than eighteen hours to do it. I'll need extraordinary authority, full command over the Secret Service and everyone who works for NASA. They'll have to take their orders from me, no matter what I ask them to do, without argument. You can talk to Nichols first, if you like—he'll confirm what I've said—but do it fast. There's no time for delay."

"What do *you* plan to do?" Brendan asked.

"I plan to outthink him. I plan to be there before him."

"Where?"

"Here." Owen picked up the coffeepot. "Because he's already here. Close by. Here and waiting."

Henry Brendan's face froze. He needed to hear, to see, no more. Four words were scrawled across the bottom of the coffeepot. A message.

Four words: *Come and get me.*

Michelangelo pulled the white jacket off and tossed it into a corner. Owen would find it, of course, as he would find the message under the coffeepot. Michelangelo wanted them found—for two could play Owen's game of disguise, and a certain Air Force steward assigned to the President's cottage was about to vanish forever.

In the meantime, he had been *that* close to the President, and Owen would know it. Owen was here and on his trail, and he would soon know where to start looking.

But there were some things he would not find, until it was too late. Confrontation had begun, and it would be over soon. Michelangelo, dressed differently now, let himself out through a back door and vanished.

253

⊠ 41 ⊠

"The *audacity* of it!" Nichols exclaimed. "Walking into the President's cottage as a steward! It sounds like something you would have done."

"It *is* something I would have done." Owen smiled, reached across the table, and pulled a sheet of paper toward him. It was the steward's Air Force personnel record. His name was Harold Overmeyer and he had been transferred from an American base in West Germany, where he'd worked for the base commander, less than two weeks ago. "That's my point," Owen went on, "and that's how we're going to stop him. When it's all over, you'll look back and say it was just the way *I* would have done it."

Nichols's gaze, no brighter, shifted from Owen to Emma on the other side of the table, to Sam Ardry beside him, and then back to Owen. "If you don't mind, I'd just as soon notice before it happens. Do you have a crystal ball up your sleeve?"

"No crystal ball. Just some good hard thinking."

Owen leaned back in his chair at the end of the table. They were in the main conference room on the top floor of the KSC Headquarters Building. Three stacks of paper as thick as urban telephone books—the latest KSC personnel lists—were lined up before them. Thousands of names. Scientists and administrators, clerical help, test pilots and astronauts, maintenance workers, mechanics. An up-to-date list as of 5:00 P.M., when the

254

names were spit out of a computer. And Michelangelo could be any one of them.

"He's here," Owen said. "We know he's here. And I'm convinced the attempt will occur at lift-off, when everyone's watching the launch. I can't conceive of a better diversion."

"I won't argue with that," Nichols said.

"I'm also convinced his weapon is already out there, within striking range of the VIP stands, in place and set to work with or without him. If it weren't he would never have risked revealing himself."

"But if that's so"—Nichols paused—"Hell, that means we can't stop him even if we catch him!"

Owen smiled. "We have to do both."

"And we will," Emma said. "If the weapon is there, we're going to find it. The Secret Service has called in reinforcements from Washington and a dozen regional offices. We're going over everything, including the ground itself. Inch by inch, we're going over it. We're taking the stands apart. Everything. Don't worry, Ed. We'll find it."

"We'd better," Nichols grumbled and sat back to worry. "I wonder, could *Pilgrim* itself be his weapon?"

"You mean he might crash it into the stands?"

"Or blow it up. Something."

Owen shook his head. "That's the first thing I thought of, and rejected. Michelangelo isn't a mass killer. He's out to kill one man, not a crowd, and he prides himself on precision. We won't take chances—security at the launchpad can be reinforced—but he's not going to kill the President with the shuttle."

"Then what?"

"I don't know." Owen glanced at Ardry. "What did you find out from the White House photographer?"

"The President told you the truth," Ardry said. "The photographer shot a whole roll of film that day in Brendan's office, but none of the pictures were released. The negatives disappeared from his darkroom and were never recovered."

"Stolen?"

Ardry shrugged.

"Quite a thief we have in the White House."

"And I may know who it is," Nichols said. He reached into his jacket, withdrew a piece of paper folded lengthwise, and handed it to Owen. "That's a list of people who've asked to see our files on Michelangelo."

Owen's gaze caught his. "You remembered."

"Michelangelo's debut as an assassin." Nichols nodded. "I finally remembered what happened then, and of course I saw the parallels. I went to the files myself. As you see, my name is the last one."

Yes, Nichols was the last person to request access to a set of files the CIA had buried almost beyond reach, the records of an agent-turned-assassin—including a final report filed by his partner. Buried almost, but not quite. A good many people had made the request over the years, asking for Michelangelo by name—or, more often, for anything the CIA had on assassins in general or unsolved political murders—but only six requests had been approved. Five names on the list, including Nichols, were high-ranking CIA officials. The sixth was, at the time, chief counsel to a congressional subcommittee investigating a specific assassination. A young lawyer who went on to work at the White House.

Judd Sims.

Owen handed the list to Emma. "Is Sims here yet?"

"Not yet," Ardry said. "He's arriving early tomorrow morning with the congressional delegation—which, by the way, will include our friends Shackford, Renaud, and MacGregor. They're heroes now. They're going to watch the launch from the President's platform."

"Right in the line of fire." Owen chuckled. "I can't think of anyone who deserves to be there more."

Ardry blinked twice, very calmly. "I assume you'll want to question Sims as soon as he gets here."

"You question him," Owen said. "Better yet, get someone in Washington to pay him a visit tonight. All I want for now is his résumé."

"What are you going to do, hire him?"

256

"I want to know where he comes from. Can you get it fast?"

Ardry got up to go. "I wish everything were as easy."

"I have to go too," Nichols said. "I've got an appointment of my own with the President." He pushed his chair back, but sat there a moment longer, looking at Owen. "I'm nervous about this," he said at last.

Owen looked at him calmly. Nichols was on the sidelines, and that was enough to make anyone nervous. "Don't worry," he said.

"That's easy to say."

"I know." Owen wasn't worried, but neither was he as calm as he looked. Confrontation, finally. The showdown. A pair of killers come face to face. Only one of them could outthink the other.

Nichols rose and followed Ardry out, leaving Owen alone with Emma. Daylight was fading outside, the sky growing dark now. The countdown was at T-minus-fifteen. Michelangelo was still missing.

"Are you sure he's there?" Emma asked with a nod for the three stacks of paper on the table.

"He's here, all right," Owen replied. "He's abandoned the steward role, and he has to have another one. Without it he'd be picked up through routine security."

"Well?" Emma asked, "what *do* you know? What did he *make sure* you would know?"

Owen's thoughts were running the same way. "That he was the steward."

Emma pointed to the steward's personnel record. "Harold Overmeyer. He's dropped the initials *G.M.* Maybe there's something in that."

"Maybe." Owen picked up a notepad and started writing.

"I'll leave it to you for now," Emma said. "I have to get back to the VIP stands and see how the search for the weapon is going. I'll check back with you later."

Owen nodded vaguely, so absorbed in his own thoughts he was hardly aware she was leaving. He was thinking about book code, hidden signatures, *word games*, and he'd written out the alphabet on the notepad. Now he

257

gave each letter a number assignment, one through twenty-six, and found *G* and *M* in positions seven and thirteen. He reversed the system, numbering *Z* as one, but reversal didn't produce the results he wanted. He was looking for *H* and *O*. Harold Overmeyer, the steward. He scratched out what he had done and tried a different system, numbering *A* as one, *Z* as two, *B* as three, and so on, but the meaning of the steward's initials still eluded him.

He worked on for an hour or more, trying every combination of numbers and alphabet he had ever known to be used as code, but none of them gave him what he was looking for. Finally, he pushed the notepad away and himself up out of the chair, stretching, easing the ache of tension out of his muscles.

It was there. He could feel it taunting him, just beyond reach, because Emma was right—the steward's name was the one thing he knew, and Michelangelo would not have made an appearance without a purpose. There had to be a clue in the name, a place to start, the first in a new series of trailblazers. Owen started to pace the room, turning it over in his mind, over and back, over again, seeking a new direction.

And then he stopped. It *was* there, plain to see, in Emma's own words. Michelangelo had dropped his old signature, the initials *G* and *M*. He had *dropped* them.

Owen picked up the notepad and wrote out the alphabet once again, in conventional form, *A* to *Z*. Then he marked out *G* and *M* and renumbered the letters from the beginning. A smile spread across his face. The new positions seven and thirteen were occupied by *H* and *O*. Harold Overmeyer's *raison d'être* lay before him.

But there was someone else to be found.

Owen reversed the letters again, numbering *Z* as one, eliminating *G* and *M*, and found two new letters in the old positions. He thumbed through the personnel lists, which were alphabetically arranged, until he found the right combination. There was only one, a man, and he'd worked here for years, but three weeks ago he'd requested a change in his regular hours. He worked the night shift. Harold Overmeyer was a nine-to-five man; they could have coexisted.

The *night* shift. He was working *now*.

Owen turned and left the room in a hurry.

⊠ 42 ⊠

Emma stood on the President's platform, watching the work going on under spotlights. Secret Service agents and NASA security guards had divided the grounds into grids and were covering them one at a time, using trained dogs and metal detectors to search for buried weapons or explosives. Others were tearing up floorboards from the wooden bleachers set up for ordinary VIPs and from the platform where the President and his special guests would watch the launch from plastic chairs, from behind a bulletproof plexiglass shield that was being erected. Sound speakers were being dismantled and rewired by electricians. Even the spotlights, though they wouldn't be on for a daytime launch, were being checked for heat-sensitive explosives, toxic gas packets, or missile-firing devices.

If this search didn't turn up a weapon, Emma thought, then there was no weapon to be found. She had never seen anything more thorough. But there was a weapon, and it had to be found before the President came here tomorrow morning.

Behind the bleachers, more agents were taking apart the souvenir and refreshments stands and the restrooms. Carpenters, working in pairs under Secret Service supervision, came along behind to rebuild them for the people who would be queuing up here. And straight ahead, three miles away at the edge of the ocean, *Pilgrim II* sat on her launchpad, lit by moon from above and floodlights from below. The countdown was at T-minus-fourteen hours and twenty-eight minutes.

The shuttle was as invulnerable to sabotage as a thing sitting on an open launchpad could be. Security around the ship included surveillance of land, sea, and sky, and was tightly drawn even without the proximity of the President and an assassin. But *Pilgrim*'s systems had been given an extra check, and the astronauts scheduled to take her up had been assigned extra bodyguards. Emma agreed with Owen. Michelangelo wouldn't use *Pilgrim* as a weapon. They were looking for something much closer at hand. But, like Owen, she believed the shuttle would play a role in his plan, if only because it was there, dominating the land even at three miles with the focus and force of its presence. Michelangelo could hardly overlook it.

"Emma?"

She turned and smiled at a red-haired man in a suit with no tie coming toward her up the steps at the rear of the platform. "Hello, Harry. How's it going?"

Harry Nesbitt, who headed the Secret Service detail traveling with the President, was broadly built and square-jawed, with sharp eyes under a wide forehead. "Nothing," he said. "Not a damn thing! I'm beginning to wonder if there is a weapon."

"Don't. There is. I've got it on the best authority."

"Who have you been talking to, the assassin?"

"Next thing to him. His double."

The Secret Service man frowned.

"Never mind," Emma said. "There's time yet."

"Not much. Christ, these things make me edgy!"

"You don't look it."

Nesbitt smiled. "I'm trained not to. But I've never gotten used to the pressure of knowing the world is full of potential killers."

"When you do, you'll be out of a job."

"No, they'll just put me behind a desk." Nesbitt shook his head. "I don't know which is worse, a lunatic or a professional. You can't predict either one. But we've got our eyes open; you can be sure of that. No one's going to get to the man if we can help it."

Emma didn't doubt it, nor that Nesbitt would gladly throw himself between "the man" and an assailant. But Michelangelo would know that too. He wasn't going to do anything as obvious as charging the President.

Nesbitt turned around as two men in coveralls—one about sixty, the other half that—came up the steps and presented their NASA ID cards. They were working men, carpenters.

"We're supposed to make sure the flooring is sound," the older man said, "and that the chair bolts are securely tightened."

Nesbitt handed back their cards and nodded. Then he positioned himself to watch what they were doing.

So did Emma. "How much longer will this take?" she asked.

"I don't know. An hour maybe. If we haven't found anything then—"

"We'll start again," Emma said.

Nesbitt nodded. "And we'll seal the area off so tight that no one can get in or out of here."

"Until tomorrow."

"Yeah, the crowds. Washington is sending us portable gates with electronic weapon sensors and x-ray equipment for purses and bags. Cameras won't be allowed this time, except for the working press; people who want snapshots will have to buy postcards. We're making special provisions for handicapped guests; anyone in wheelchairs or on crutches will have to check them at the gates and use ours, which we're getting straight from a reliable supply house. This place is going to be more sanitary than a surgeon's hands."

Emma nodded appreciatively; she believed him. She was impressed, and she might have been feeling confident if the killer were anyone else. These things had to be done. But Michelangelo wouldn't risk having to pass a personal inspection. He would be on the inside before the gates were set up, or else he would have a way around them. And his weapon was already here.

But they hadn't found it.

Owen drove to the VIP stands, parked the car he'd been given at the side of the road, and hurried to find Emma. She was talking to Nesbitt at the foot of the steps that led to the President's platform.

"What's wrong?" she asked as he approached.

"I know who he is," Owen said, "and I'm betting he's here tonight, helping to tear this place apart and put it back together."

Nesbitt looked worried. "Here *now*?"

"Right now. He's a carpenter by the name of Thomas Newman."

"Christ!" Nesbitt's face went pale. "He just left! He was working on the platform—"

"Try to stop him before he gets out of here," Emma interrupted.

Nesbitt took off at a run, gesturing as he went for other agents to join him, and Emma turned to run up the steps with Owen right behind her.

"He claimed to be checking the floor and tightening the bolts in the chairs," she said. "And that's all he did. Harry and I were both standing right here."

Owen bent down to look under the chairs. There were three rows of them, ten seats across. They were solid plastic, body and legs, molded as a unit with no chrome parts for hiding a bomb. The padding that made them comfortable had been removed and would not be replaced for this launch. They were perfectly plain, but the end of each leg turned up and out at the bottom, with a hole drilled through for bolting the chair to the floor.

"We'll have all the bolts changed," Owen said. "And we'll have these floorboards pried up again. He might have slipped something down between them." He glanced at Emma. "Which one is the President's chair?"

It was in the front row, at the center. They converged on it together.

After a while, Nesbitt returned empty-handed. "Gone," he said. "He claimed he was sick and going home, but he hasn't checked out. We've got the gates covered. Maybe he'll check out yet." He shrugged; it was obvious he didn't think so. "Have you found anything?"

"Yes." Owen was bending over the President's chair, running his hands slowly and carefully under the edges of it.

"What is it?" Emma asked urgently.

"Step back. Nesbitt, get a demolitions expert over here now." Owen looked up. "That's right, it's the chair. The *chair* is a bomb. It's molded of plastic explosives."

⊠ 43 ⊠

Nichols nodded routinely to the agents outside the President's door, twice the usual number, and started to move past them, but one of them placed an arm in his way.

"Sorry, sir, no one gets past us tonight without an identity check. Not even Mrs. Brendan."

Nichols turned back, startled. It had been a long time since anyone asked to see his official identification, but the agent's face was perfectly serious.

"Not even Mrs. Brendan, eh?"

"No, sir, she's not expected."

Nichols got out his wallet and rummaged through it, hoping he still had the card. He found it and gave it to the agent, who pushed it into an ultraviolet scanning device designed to reveal the flaws of a forgery. A small beep sounded, and Nichols was cleared. The agent handed the card back.

"Go ahead, sir."

"Was this Owen's idea?" Nichols asked.

"Not the scanner—we use it from time to time—but he did suggest the assassin might try to pass himself off as you."

"Oh, he did, did he? When you see him, tell him I said *he* should have thought of the scanner."

"I will, sir."

Nichols turned around, scowling. Sons of bitches had no sense of humor. He knocked at the door of the cottage and was admitted.

Henry Brendan—alone, in his shirt sleeves—had just finished eating his dinner.

"I hope someone tasted that food before you did," Nichols said.

"Are you kidding?" The President rose, a white linen napkin in his hand. "I don't breathe around here without someone testing the air first." He wiped his mouth, tossed the napkin down beside his plate, crossed the room, and sat down, signaling Nichols to join him.

"I've just come from Owen," Nichols said as he lowered himself into a chair. "Is there no way I can talk you out of going to the launch tomorrow?"

"You want me to stay here and hide?" Henry smiled thinly. "If this killer's as good as you people say, he'd only go into hiding himself and come after me later."

Nichols didn't try to deny it. "You'd be giving us time, though."

"For what?"

"To catch him."

Henry glanced at his watch. "You've got fourteen hours. Do it, by all means. God knows, you've got my blessing."

Nichols was surprised to find no sign of fear in Henry's face. He seemed cool, self-assured, *presidential*. "Is that your last word?"

"It is."

"All right then."

There was silence in the room, soft lamplight, shadowed corners. Nichols's face was calm, but tension showed in a pulse at his jaw and in the slight flaring of his nostrils. He was angry.

Angry—because the agency had been left out of the biggest, most daring covert operation the United States had ever undertaken. Left out and badly undercut in the great pecking order of Washington, where observers were keenly tuned to status and appearances, and quick to detect vibrations of change. Washington played its own guessing game, like Kremlin watching turned inward, and the way things looked, Hayfield had been in

266

the front row for the May Day parade in Red Square, while Nichols wasn't even on the platform.

"What do you want from me?" Henry asked, breaking into the silence quietly but forcefully.

Nichols studied his face, surprised, because Henry never liked confrontations. No small talk this time. No mincing of words. "The truth," Nichols told him.

"The truth." Henry smiled regretfully. "I suppose I should have told you a long time ago and saved us both a lot of trouble."

"It would have been better," Nichols said. "Among other things, we could have steered you away from Ramon."

"You think that hasn't occurred to me?" Anguish flared in the President's eyes, and he turned away. "You don't have to spell it out. If I'd told you sooner, Andy Cass might be alive. I don't think I'll ever forget it."

"Cass might be alive," Nichols agreed, "and the mines under Uxmal might still be producing."

Henry looked up, and their eyes met in silent understanding. Nichols knew Henry had made a tough decision when he closed down the mining operation, that he wanted to be sure no one else died, because he felt responsible for Cass's murder. But Nichols also knew that the real issue was the ore. Without it, the rest didn't matter.

"Why *didn't* you tell me?" he asked.

"Security. We included people on the strictest need-to-know basis. You should understand that."

"I don't understand! For Christ's sake, you trusted the *Pentagon*!"

"You've got it wrong. The Pentagon discovered the ore. It was Hayfield who told *me* about it."

Nichols's jaw pulsed as he thought of Hayfield in the Oval Office the day Uxmal was taken hostage. Hayfield, with his maps and photographs, his reconnaissance planes in the air almost before the takeover was finished. Johnny-on-the-spot—oh, yes—and now Nichols knew why. Colonel Smug, Colonel Slick—Colonel Dueling Scar—had *known* what time the terrorists were expected! He'd probably made up their schedule!

"I'm reluctant to tell anyone," Henry went on. "Even you. Even now. But Owen says you have a piece of the ore, and I gather I ought to believe him."

That was one lesson Henry had learned, Nichols thought, and he nodded.

"Then you have to know what you're dealing with." Henry paused, his eyes intent on Nichols's face. "What you have," he said, "is as potentially dangerous in the wrong hands as anything since the plans for the Manhattan Project. Indeed, far *more* dangerous. If I asked you to give me that piece of ore, would you?"

Nichols shook his head. "I have to know what Uxmal was. I intend to have the ore tested."

"And involve still more people. I can't let you do that."

"I don't see how you can stop me."

"I can stop you by giving you what you want. The truth. The reason for Uxmal."

Henry got up from his chair and started to pace the room, his hands in his pockets, his face thoughtful. "It's all true," he began. "Uxmal was our own operation, planned and carried out with my approval. The hostage crisis was an elaborate ruse, designed to seal the area off for a period of time so that we could go in and take what was there without anyone knowing we'd done it. It was ours from the start. Even the Cozumel conference was a part of our planning."

Cozumel, the meeting that took the hostages to Mexico in the first place. Nichols wondered if anyone bothered to tell the Mexican delegation.

"The terrorists were Cuban exiles," Henry went on, "as you were much too quick to find out. DIA recruited and trained them, though the Cubans don't know that. They can't reveal the truth because they never knew it."

"What about the miners?"

"Handpicked from the Army Corps of Engineers. Reliable men. But most of them don't know where they

268

were. They were moved in at night and lived underground, and they had no contact with the terrorists or the hostages."

"Except Shackford," Nichols said. "We know he went to the mine, and that some of the miners saw him."

"A few. But the rest will never know they were part of Uxmal."

"And of course Shackford was in on the plan. He knew before he went down there that they would be captured."

"Not just the plan, but the planning," Henry said. "Reuben and Jack and Tom. All three of them."

"Not Cass?"

The regretful smile crossed Henry's face again, and he shook his head. "The other hostages didn't know either. Only the three congressmen. They volunteered to go, to keep an eye on things, and because with high officials there, in the hands of terrorists who were formidably armed and positioned to defend from attack, I had clear justification for rejecting any kind of immediate action."

To stall for time. In retrospect, what Henry had done, everything he had said, seemed so obvious.

"Who else knew?" Nichols asked.

"No one. Only the congressmen and the top people at the Pentagon."

"Not Callahan?"

"No."

Nichols actually smiled, though he was shocked, for it seemed he was in good company on the outside. Henry excluded *everyone*, even his own Secretary of State! And once his pals Pious, Pompous, and Gooch were locked away behind iron mesh screens, he'd been left pretty much on his own, with no one to talk to but Colonel Dueling Scar. Or was it Hayfield who had done the excluding?

That much no longer mattered. Nichols was shocked but also impressed, because Uxmal, right or wrong, had been an audacious plan, a stalemate in which Big Brother was brought to his knees by a band of terrorists. It wouldn't occur to anyone that Big Brother himself trained and deployed the captives and the captors. As a falseface. To hide the truth and focus attention at the wrong level of action. Audacious. Gutsy. Effective.

A falseface, a mask, everything—from the flame throwers and minefields to the first of the terrorists' demands. From the President's indecisive way to MacKendrick's rescue plan. Delay. More ore flowing through the pipelines. And all of it done by prewritten script, with parts assigned even to some who hadn't been told they were in the cast. It was Daniel Callahan, after all, the patient professional diplomat—the traditionalist Secretary of State, so predictable—who handed Henry his first cue by articulating the need for caution.

An incredible plan. And Henry had done a hell of a job of managing it from the White House. Maybe Conklin Pierce was right, Nichols thought, remembering their talk outside the Oval Office. Maybe the crisis, however different it was from what it had seemed to be, had shocked Henry into becoming the kind of leader he could have been all along, if only he'd known it. Nichols sensed the beginnings of a new alliance. His anger vanished.

"What is the ore?" he asked.

Henry stood over him, looking down. "It's called halycite."

"Never heard of it."

"Few people have. It didn't exist until we found it."

"But what *is* it?"

"The future of everything we know. Human life itself. Possibly the continued existence of the planet."

Nichols didn't know what to say. Whatever he'd been expecting, it wasn't this, not the whole goddamned planet! But Henry's face was serious, void of doubt, and Nichols knew he wasn't equivocating, that he was telling the truth as simply as he knew how to.

Henry returned to his chair and picked up a NASA press kit that was lying on the table in front of him. "Ironically," he said, "it started where it ends, right here, with *Pilgrim II*. On a previous mission, nearly two years ago, sensors attached to the shuttle picked up an unexpected piece of information: evidence of mineral deposits in the Yucatan peninsula. Apparently it was a startling find, because Yucatan was supposed to be barren of natural resources. It was startling enough, anyway, for NASA to turn the information over to the Pentagon, where it was classified pending further study.''

Henry dropped the press kit back onto the table. ''In the meantime, the Army Corps of Engineers had a unit in Yucatan, working on a joint government water project, some such thing, and they were ordered to take some rock samples.''

''Johnny-on-the-spot again,'' Nichols grumbled.

But Henry went on: ''The samples were turned over to a top-secret Defense Department R and D section. And they proved to be startling, all right—a brand *new* mineral had been discovered. They called it halycite and, after some preliminary tests, sent it on to weapons research.''

Thatcher was right, Nichols thought. It was the arms race. ''Why?'' he asked.

''Because they discovered that when halycite is added to existing metals—steel or chrome, even aluminum or tin—it creates an alloy that's virtually invulnerable to heat and light. The process only requires trace amounts of halycite, and it works with metals we already have in abundant supply, or metals we can easily manufacture.''

Nichols frowned. ''Light and heat?''

''Invulnerable to both. A test satellite was built and launched to prove the point. Its outer shell was made of steel, its inner parts aluminum, both treated with small amounts of halycite. It withstood every test designed to destroy it. Not only that, it performed with more efficiency than anything ever built in its class. Long-standing problems of aim-point time were corrected to the smallest fraction of a second. Visibility had no effect on its range. Its aim and trajectory functioned with stunning accuracy, and it—''

''Christ almighty!'' Nichols broke in. ''You're talking about *laser beam weapons*!''

271

A small smile appeared on the President's face, and he nodded slowly. "We've perfected them, and made them invulnerable to their own kind. We've produced the invincible weapon."

Nichols sank back in his chair, his mind reeling against the implications, caught between exhilaration and worry. Thatcher had called it, all right. The arms race, raised to a dramatic new level—for there were rarely times when a major technological breakthrough occurred that set one superpower way ahead of another, and if everything Henry said was true, then this was clearly one of those times. It opened a new frontier. *Infinity*. Full of promise. Fraught with terror.

Space war, no longer the realm of science fiction, not related to UFOs or extraterrestrial invaders. This was more of what had begun with the atomic bomb, a race between two great nations for strategic control of the planet. War fought *from* space, to be more exact, by unmanned sentinals, high-energy laser beam satellites—orbiting cannons of light with lethal power against surface targets or missiles in flight, able to knock out a single tank or a massive ICBM attack; to strike across vast distances at the speed of light, nearly 200,000 miles a second; to destroy matter at the flick of a hand, like God going back on creation.

Not the realm of science fiction, no, and it hadn't been for a long time. Laser beam weapons were in the development stage on both sides of a bipolar world, with major flaws to be worked out. Some armaments experts predicted deployment by one side or the other—and more likely by the Soviets, since they reportedly had an edge—before the end of the twentieth century. More experts thought those predictions were premature, but they all agreed on one thing: the side that won the race in the end, the side that dominated space, could render all preexisting forms of warfare as obsolete as gunpowder muskets. Could, with wise use of superior force, avert a nuclear war. Or win it. Disarm the world on command. Or destroy it.

Killer satellites, the wave of an uncertain future. But

272

they were in the *future*, until now, because one side had taken a mighty leap forward; and whatever safety came with the threat of two mutually destructive powers, poised on the brink and facing each other down, had vanished in the instant that it happened.

"I know what you're thinking," Henry said. "Halycite is a substance we might have wished no one ever discovered. But we have, and with it a challenge we have to face. We'll soon be prepared to deploy a highly effective space arsenal, years ahead of anyone else. Even if the Soviets move ahead fast—if they solve the old problems and match us weapon for weapon; if they *double* our production—we will still control the skies, and thus the earth. Because they don't have halycite. They don't even know it exists. Against anything they can build, our arsenal will be invincible."

"And so war comes to an end," Nichols said. "Or is this the beginning of the last one?"

"The power to end it will be in our hands," Henry replied. "Better there than elsewhere, I think. No, I firmly believe it."

Nichols did too, but he'd been around too long to believe that democracy insured against a President lacking wisdom. In the end, it wouldn't help much to know that the person who destroyed the world was freely elected.

"That's it," Henry said. "Now, maybe you'll understand why we did what we did, and why we went to such lengths to protect the secret of Uxmal."

"I understand, all right," Nichols said. "I also understand why we have to continue to protect it. This isn't a matter of keeping a secret that's known to exist out of the hands of an enemy who wants to steal it. In this case, if the enemy knew there *were* a secret, he wouldn't stop till he found it himself. No, I'm with you on this. I don't know if I would have been if I'd been asked ahead of time, but done is done—and what was done at Uxmal *must* stay buried forever."

"And the sample you have?" Henry asked.

"I'll destroy it. You have my word on it."

273

"That's good enough. I believe you."

"One question," Nichols said. "Where have you hidden sixty-five thousand tons of classified secret?"

Henry smiled. "Under the Lincoln Memorial."

"Under the *what*?"

"You heard me. We had the caves underneath remodeled for long-term storage."

"Then all that construction work, that business of keeping people out—"

"Part of the plan. We tried to be very thorough."

"And so you were!" Nichols laughed out loud, because he'd fallen for the cover story—that the monument was closed for repairs—along with everyone else. It hadn't occurred to him to doubt it. And now the ore was hidden under Abraham Lincoln's feet, where millions of visitors would walk on it without ever knowing it was there. Honest Abe! It was probably as safe a place as any.

But then Nichols's mind shifted to a different President, also the victim of an assassin. "There's one thing we can't bury with the rest of the truth about Uxmal," he said. "We have to find out who killed Ben Riker."

"And why he was killed," Henry added.

Watching him, Nichols thought Henry knew, that he had put the pieces together—as Nichols himself had, as Thatcher and Owen had—and come to the same conclusion. Ben Riker died so that Henry would be President, so that Uxmal could go forward as its planners intended, because Riker was as predictable as Daniel Callahan. He was a fierce arms control proponent—stubborn, strong-willed, independent—and he would have opposed stealing anything from a neighbor's land on principle. Henry, on the other hand, was as easy to manipulate as anyone who had ever occupied the Oval Office. Or he had been. And the person who planned Riker's death, who hired Michelangelo and then double-crossed him, had to be someone close enough to manipulate Henry.

"The person we're looking for," Nichols said, "is someone who had access to the Jefferson portrait. Someone who brought a child's painting to your attention and suggested inviting her to Washington for a photo session. Someone who got you to sign the painting—"

"Judd Sims," Henry said. "It was *Judd* who made those suggestions! Christ, I never liked him much, but I can't believe he's a killer!"

"Does he know about Uxmal?"

"No, as a matter of fact, he doesn't."

Nichols frowned. "Are you sure?"

"If he does, *I* didn't tell him. But wait—" Henry stopped and looked up, surprised, as the door burst open and Lucy Brendan flew into the room, her blue eyes wide, her face distraught with worry.

Nichols was surprised too. He remembered the agent at the door—Mrs. Brendan wasn't expected tonight—and a new thought struck him, cold and harsh.

There was no one in a better position to manipulate Henry than Lucy.

"Darling," she cried as Henry got up to greet her. "They told me someone is trying to *kill* you!"

Henry put his arms around her. "There's nothing to worry about," he said. "No one's going to kill me. They've got me guarded six ways to Sunday, not to say the rest of the week. I'm surprised they let you in here."

"But they told me it was *a professional assassin*!" Lucy was actually trembling.

"Yes, well . . ."

Given what she already knew, Henry told her the truth, softening it only by tone of voice and his own assurance of confidence. Nichols had gotten to his feet and was watching. Watching both of them, but mostly Lucy.

No, it didn't make sense, he thought, dismissing suspicion, only to let it rise again as he continued to look at her. He didn't know Lucy Brendan well, certainly not as a confidante, but he had been observing her from a distance for a good many years, and he thought it was perfectly obvious that she was a woman of strongly conflicting emotions. That she was at least as devoted to Henry's success as she was to the personal needs of the man she married. That she sometimes confused one with the other. That she confused her own role. That she *must* have resented Ben Riker—because Riker occupied the office she wanted for Henry, and perhaps for herself—and because Henry was diminished beside him. But did she resent Riker enough to kill him?

Nichols studied her face, her movements, her manner. She was a lovely woman, no doubt of that—even now, distraught—small and elegant, superficially the model First Lady. But on the inside he knew she was strong. Even tough. Bitter perhaps. And certainly capable of manipulation.

She could have stolen the painting more easily than anyone, and she might have masterminded a plot to get Henry to sign it. She even might have had an affair with Judd Sims and learned what she needed to know about Michelangelo, though that didn't seem terribly likely. But if she could have done all those things, there was one thing she would not have done under any circumstances. She would not have framed her husband for a murder he didn't commit, if for no other reason than what it would have done to her when he was "caught."

It was also just possible that she loved him.

She turned around, seeing him for the first time. "Ed!"

"The President's right, Mrs. Brendan," he said. "If a man can be protected at all, I assure you he is."

She nodded and lowered her eyes, taking little comfort from his words. For whatever reasons, she was clearly worried.

The telephone rang, and Nichols picked it up. It was Owen, for him. He listened for several minutes. Then he put the receiver back, shaking his head, his jaw tight.

"Progress," he said.

New hope showed in Lucy's face. "Have they found him?"

"I'm afraid not. The assassin is still out there somewhere. But they found his weapon, a plastic chair."

"A chair!" Henry stared at him, while Lucy looked on bewildered.

"*Your* chair," Nichols said. "It was made of plastic explosives."

"My *God*!"

Nichols thought the reality of the threat had finally pierced Henry's calm. He looked frightened.

"It would have given you quite a jolt," Nichols said. "It's been removed and replaced now, but . . ."

"But what?" Lucy asked when he hesitated. Fear showed cold in her eyes too. "I don't understand what's happening."

"Owen says he was *meant* to find the chair," Nichols explained. "And that means there's another weapon."

Another weapon, and yet another identity to be assumed by Michelangelo. Owen got up from the table in the conference room at the headquarters building. There were papers strewn over the tabletop and others discarded on the floor. He'd been at it again for more than an hour, playing around with the alphabet, with his sevens and his thirteens, but nothing worked. Nothing fit. Michelangelo was still missing.

He crossed the room to the coffeepot and refilled his cup. "Want some?" he asked.

Emma handed him her cup and looked at her watch. "Eight hours to go. We're not getting anywhere, are we?"

"Not yet." Owen brought the coffee back and sat down. "But we will. The trail ended here, and this is where we'll pick it up."

Emma sighed and lifted the coffee to her lips, blowing on it gently. Then she looked up as Sam Ardry appeared in the doorway.

"Good, you're taking a break," he said and sat down. "I've got some things you wanted. Langley sent someone to talk to Sims and just phoned me a report. He refused to answer questions. He's scared within an inch of his life and insists on having a lawyer." Ardry blinked. "Of course, he is one."

"If he's scared," Owen said, "then he's showing good sense. He should be scared. Is he still coming down in the morning?"

"I don't know. I doubt if he knows. Here, by the way, is the résumé you wanted. It's his dossier from Langley, but it includes his full employment record."

Owen took it, read it, and handed it over to Emma. They exchanged a glance. Then he looked back at Ardry. "What else have you got?"

"The names of the people who are going to be sitting with the President tomorrow."

Owen looked the list over and handed it to Emma too. "Tell Nesbitt to keep an eye on the British ambassador," he said and got up, heading for the door.

"Where are you going?" she asked.

"To pick up some clothes. Then I'm going back to the VIP stands. And Sam—Judd Sims is only a dupe, or at most an accomplice."

Owen crossed back to the table and pulled Sims's dossier around so that Ardry could see it. His finger came to rest on the page.

"There's your killer," he said. "You'd better call Nichols."

An hour had passed, and Owen leaned back in the President's chair, the new one, his feet propped against the railing that ran along the front of the platform, his gaze sweeping the view that was open, save for a shrub or two, a stand of trees, a plexiglass shield, and an army of security guards, all the way from the VIP stands to the launchpad. It was just after 2:00 A.M. Countdown was at T-minus-six hours and fifty minutes. The ground crew had finished filling the shuttle's sound suppression water tank and loading the launch cameras. A clear sky was holding; wind and weather looked good. *Pilgrim II* would be blasting off in less than seven hours.

Owen was still convinced the assassination attempt would happen then, at the moment of lift-off, and now for a new point of view he had put himself in the position of the target. In his mind he pictured how this scene would look tomorrow morning. There would be people milling below, including a press pool here to cover not the launch itself but the President watching the launch, since the regular press viewing stands were set up near the VAB. Press photographers would be admitted with cameras, but they had been warned not to load them ahead of time, unless they wanted their film exposed during a rigid inspection. There would not be a gun hidden inside a camera.

But there was another weapon here. Not only a weapon, but a way to fire or detonate it—to set it off, whatever it was, from a distance, possibly with a remote-control switch. But if a remote switch were used, then there had to be a receiver. Owen's eyes scanned the grounds before him, where people would turn to stare at the sky, behind barriers already in place, among light poles and loudspeakers set up off the ground, among hundreds of security guards in uniforms and plainclothes. He pictured the scene as it would be, running minute by minute through the final countdown procedures. He put himself in the place of the target. Then he turned it around. He became the assassin he knew so well, who was so like himself.

Twenty minutes later he stood up. He knew now. He knew how it had to be done, how he would have set it up, and it was almost foolproof. Impossible to circumvent, unless the plan itself were revealed. He knew where the weapon was and how it would be activated, and where the assassin would be tomorrow morning. But he still didn't know what role the assassin would assume, or what he would look like.

He hurried down the steps, returned to his car, put it in gear, and took off for Launch Control, where he saw Les Finn, the launch director. Finn roused the public affairs director out of bed for him, and they all had a meeting at 3:00 A.M. Then Owen returned to the conference room, where he stayed in his chair through the night, not talking to Emma on the other side of the table. Both of them worked in silence. Finally he looked up and smiled.

"I've got it."

Emma looked at the pieces of paper all around him, saw the Cyrillic alphabet written out and rearranged countless times. "Russian?" she asked.

"No, Greek."

Owen pushed forward his notepad. On it were the letters of the Greek alphabet: *alpha*, *beta*, *gamma*, *delta* . . .

"It's *eta nu*," he said.

Emma picked up the personnel lists and ran her finger down the *N* pages. "No one here with those initials," she said.

Owen nodded. "It figures."

☒ 45 ☒

The plane carrying the congressional delegation, having left Andrews in the dark of night, touched down on the Shuttle Landing Strip at 7:00 A.M., two hours ahead of the launch, and Nichols was there to meet it. He watched as the passengers disembarked and made their way to the buses that would take them to a breakfast reception. He spotted Pious, Pompous, and Gooch, with their wives along, but he made no move to stop them. Other Washington officials were on the plane too—Rhoda Dickman of the Arts Caucus and her husband Dan, with a sunflower stuck to his lapel; Reverend Wright, the House chaplain, who prayed better than anyone in or near Congress; Daniel Callahan of State; George Dent of Defense; and Sir Edward Nevins, the British ambassador. Finally, Nichols spotted Conklin Pierce and hurried forward to meet him.

"Mr. Speaker!" he called.

Pierce stopped, looked around, and then, leaning on his walking stick, waited. "I didn't know you were coming down," he said as Nichols approached him.

"I didn't either when I saw you last, and I didn't have time to call you once I did know. A lot has happened, and it changes things. I've got a car."

Pierce told the people he was with that he'd join them later and went with Nichols. "You know I haven't seen Henry yet," he said when they were in the car and pulling away from the strip.

"That's one of the reasons I wanted to head you off,"

Nichols replied. "There's something you need to know before you see him. Henry, it turns out, is innocent."

"*What?*"

Nichols turned onto the road. "It would take too long to explain it now, but basically it comes down to this. Henry was in on the planning of Uxmal, and he did, as you and Bert Engel guessed, terminate the operation from the Situations Room that night, but he didn't hire the assassin to kill Ben Riker."

"Thank God! Oh, thank *God!*" Pierce let out a deep sigh of relief. "But what about the painting and the photograph?"

"Manufactured evidence. Someone set him up to take the blame and very nearly succeeded. We think we know who it is too, but that's all on hold for now. Michelangelo is here and intends to kill Henry."

"Dear God!" Pierce took a handkerchief from his pocket and wiped the sheen of sweat from his face. "This is very serious."

"Indeed it is." Nichols glanced across the seat, then switched on the air-conditioning. "We've got Henry wrapped in wool right now, but he's scheduled to leave for the launch in an hour, and I'm convinced he must not go. I don't want to take risks with the assassin still at large. I've tried to convince Henry and failed. Do you think you could do it?"

"I'll try," Pierce said, "but good heavens, *Henry?* What's gotten into him?"

"I don't know, but he's toughing it out like a soldier. I think we can catch him with time to talk before he goes. It's our last chance. We'd better."

"I'll do my best," Pierce said and turned to the window. "Does he know we thought he hired the assassin?"

"I didn't tell him I talked to you, if that's what you mean."

Remembering that meeting now, before dawn in the Speaker's rooms at the Broadmoor, Nichols thought how wrong he had been. Thank God they'd decided that morning to take no rash action.

"Then I'll have to tell him," Pierce said. "If I'm

going to prevail on him, I don't want to start with a lie. I'll tell him and hope he understands how damning the evidence seemed then."

"You'd know about that better than I would. But try not to upset him."

"Where is he?" Pierce asked.

"He's staying at Patrick. It's just a few minutes from here."

"Then why don't you tell me what you can before we get there?"

Nichols told him.

Sir Edward Nevins glanced at the Secretary of State and said, "I'm enjoying this, Dan. I'm glad you asked me to come."

"You haven't seen anything yet," Callahan replied, and clasped him on the shoulder. "This is our biggest show."

"Fourth of July fireworks, eh?"

"Bigger than all of them, with your Guy Fawkes bonfires thrown in for good measure. Brighter anyway. You'll see."

Sir Edward nodded affably.

He was a large, loose-jointed man with a distinctly patrician face and a shock of gray hair that continually fell loose over his forehead; with a great roaring laugh that belied a dry wit and charm that was famous on five continents. Now he looked up as a young woman in Air Force blue approached the table where they were sitting.

"There's a call for you, Mr. Ambassador. It's the embassy calling from Washington."

Sir Edward turned to Callahan with a look more pained than anything else. "I won't be a minute, I hope. See if you can order a Scotch for me, will you?"

Callahan smiled, and Sir Edward stood up.

"Now then, young lady, if you'll just show me where the phone is . . ."

"Come with me. It's right this way, sir."

*   *   *

The President was waiting when Nichols arrived with the Speaker. He was dressed and ready to go, bandbox fresh in lightweight pinstripes, groomed to his fingertips, but his face was drawn and tight with tension.

"Henry," Pierce said, "I understand you're being obstinate."

"How's that?" Henry asked.

"Ed tells me you insist on going to the launch."

"Of course I'm going. That's why I came here."

"But *why?* Why *risk* it?" Henry didn't say anything, and Pierce turned to Nichols. "Perhaps you'd better leave us alone."

"No," Henry said. "I want Ed to stay. I have some things I'd like to discuss with both of you."

The Speaker nodded a little vaguely and lowered himself into a chair, propping his walking stick against it. Then he rested a hand on Henry's arm. "You've got to listen to me," he said. "This is dangerous. Ed says this man is a world-class assassin. If you don't care about yourself, then remember your position. You owe it to the country to avoid putting yourself in obvious danger."

"So did Ben Riker."

"That may be," Pierce replied, "but I'm talking to you. You're the President now."

"I'm aware of that."

"Then don't go."

Henry leaned back in the chair, drawing his arm away. "Connie, we've been friends for years, or I thought we were. Why did you do it?"

Pierce didn't flinch, but his eyes turned cold. "What are you talking about?"

"We know it was you who hired the assassin."

"Nonsense! Good God, have you been drinking?"

"It's too late for that. We *know.*"

Pierce rose up out of the chair.

And Henry's gaze rose with him. "You," he said, undeterred. "But how could you do it? How *could* you kill Ben? And why—*why*—did you try to set me up for it?"

285

46

"He's right, Mr. Speaker," Nichols said, placing a hand on the old man's shoulder and slowly lowering him back to his chair. "We know you did it."

Nichols sighed. It had been a long night. Ardry had caught up with him and passed on a message from Owen: It wasn't Sims, but Pierce who had hired the assassin. Then the President remembered what he'd been about to say when his wife burst in on them. He hadn't told Sims about Uxmal, but he had told someone else—his old friend and mentor Conklin Pierce, because he trusted Pierce and needed someone to talk to through the crisis. Armed with that, Langley went back to Sims, and Sims talked. A lot of people had trusted Pierce. Nichols himself had.

"Two days ago," Nichols said, "when I came to see you at your place, you claimed to be shocked at the possibility of White House involvement in Uxmal, but now I know you knew about it already. You knew because Henry told you."

Pierce sat stiffly in the chair, listening but saying nothing.

"We know about Sims too," Nichols said. "That he was a page in the House years ago, appointed by you, and that you began to manipulate him even then. We suspect he made a mistake of some sort, that you covered for him and never let him forget it. We know you've been using him for a long time, as you've used Henry and so many others.

286

"We know Sims stole the Jefferson portrait and replaced it with a forgery. We know he got Henry to sign the painting and arranged for him to be photographed handing it to the assassin. We know he stole the photographer's negatives and gave them to you. We know he had access for a time to the CIA's secret files on Michelangelo and that he told you what he saw there. We don't know yet if Sims understood what he was involved with, or if he was only acting as your errand boy, but we do know that what he did, he did on your instructions."

Pierce looked terribly old. His eyes were sunken in his face, darkened, dull, and lifeless; his skin had turned doughy and pale. He didn't move. He seemed to be hardly breathing. And now Nichols also knew how the Speaker had managed to maintain his quiet control over so many people all these years. He was a master of certain forms of persuasion. He knew how to find a person's weak spot, and then, knowing, how to cast himself in the role of trusted friend. Counselor. Confessor. The one who would never reveal your secrets but who did remind you from time to time that he knew what they were. He knew how to create hidden need, an insidious sort of dependence. It was blackmail in an unspoken form, and yet worse—less coarse, but more evil.

"Why did you do it?" Nichols asked.

There was a long moment of silence. And then something stirred behind Pierce's face, something arrogant, chilling. His eyes were no longer gentle.

"For the good of the country," he said.

"Perhaps. But why?"

Pierce pulled himself up, and his voice was as cold as the look on his face, cold and yet matter-of-fact. "We had to have halycite," he said. "We *couldn't* let this chance go by. The Soviets were ahead of us in laser beam weapons development, and I knew the time would come when we'd find ourselves unprepared against them. Ben didn't see it that way, of course."

"*Ben* didn't!" Henry looked surprised.

287

Pierce's eyes shifted to him. "Oh, yes, Ben knew about Uxmal. Hayfield told him, just as he later told you. But Ben was actually going to *reveal* the discovery, to use halycite as a lever to force an immediate arms control agreement. That was when Hayfield came to me, hoping I might influence him. I saw Ben myself. And afterwards, I knew I had to stop him."

"But why?" Henry asked, leaning forward now, his anger entirely gone, his face lined and hollowed by sorrow. "Why did you have to involve *me*?"

Pierce looked at him, almost smiling. "Because, Henry, getting you to cooperate was so easy. So *easy*. It always was! You've always done what I wanted you to."

"Was it so easy," Henry asked, "to overlook years of friendship? Did I really mean so little to you?"

"Don't be a fool," Pierce said irritably. "I never really cared much for you. I admired your father a great deal, but you're not the man he was."

That remained to be seen, Nichols thought. Henry leaned back in his chair, and if the words stung, as they surely must, it didn't show. Nothing showed in his face but deep sadness.

"How much of this does Judd Sims know?" Nichols asked.

"Very little," Pierce replied. "And nothing about the assassination. Judd's sin, like Henry's, is weakness. He's pliable, cooptable. He doesn't know where he stands."

"What about Hayfield?"

"I certainly didn't confide in him!"

Nichols felt oddly relieved. "Then who made contact with the assassin?"

"I did. I didn't trust anyone else to do it. I told him I represented you, Henry, and that he would be paid with a valuable White House painting. He wanted more—your signature on the painting, and a photograph of you handing it to him. Well"—Pierce raised his hands in a gesture—"you know the rest. I arranged the meeting through Judd Sims. Of course I warned Michelangelo that nothing could be said to you directly while he was in the

White House. He didn't care. All he wanted was the painting and the photograph. It was all very easy."

Nichols listened with a mixture of feelings. He acknowledged a certain selflessness in Pierce's motive for murder, since he wasn't likely to live long enough to experience the Soviet dominance he hoped to prevent, rightly or wrongly, and thus had no personal gain at stake. But none of that made up for the rest. What he'd done was not only illegal, but reprehensible. Michelangelo, used himself, had no way of knowing that Henry had been used too, in a way that was far more malicious. The assassin misperceived Pierce's lies and had sworn his revenge on the wrong man.

"Who actually killed Riker?" Nichols asked. "You weren't there that day at Aspen. Who held the remote switch that caused him to fall?"

Pierce spoke the name with a clear distaste. "Ramon Garcia."

Nichols nodded. Ramon got what he gave.

"What are you going to do with me?" Pierce asked dully.

"I don't know," Nichols said and meant it. The Speaker wasn't likely to charge Thatcher on a monster machine in a deep cave; he wasn't likely to meet the same fate Ramon did. Yet the normal channels to justice were out of the question in this case. Pierce would have to resign, but was that enough? Nichols didn't know. The frailty of the old man stood in contrast to his crimes. A hard one to call.

"For the moment," he said, standing up, "I'm going to take you with us. I can't spare anyone to stay with you, and so you'll have to come along and act as if nothing's wrong. It's time for us to be leaving."

Pierce turned slowly to Henry, and an odd look passed through his eyes. Regret perhaps. Or was it disdain? Was it arrogance?

Henry looked back at him. Sadness still showed on his face, but his jaw was firm, his gaze steady. "I don't like this much, either," he said. "Just looking at you makes me realize how vulnerable the human race is. How very, very fragile."

Pierce said nothing. He reached for his walking stick and got up to go with them.

⊠ 47 ⊠

The sun was bright in the blue sky, the countdown at T-minus-thirty-five minutes. The flight crew was suited up and onboard, preparing to set the ship's computers to launch configuration. All systems were go. *Pilgrim II* was holding for lift-off.

Three miles from the launchpad, Emma was circling the President's platform, where guests had assembled around Henry Brendan's empty chair—among them two cabinet officers and the three congressmen from Uxmal, all wearing their NASA guest nametags with gold dots to show they belonged with the President's party. There, too, was Sir Edward Nevins. Emma watched him with special interest, even as she gave every appearance of not looking his way, but he had done nothing untoward. He was behaving himself like the gentleman he was supposed to be, even to the extent of casting a charming, but clearly lascivious glance at her when she passed by him. Oh, yes, he was in character. Countdown moved on to T-minus-thirty-four minutes.

Then the people in the stands broke into applause and got to their feet. The President arrived with Mrs. Brendan, Conklin Pierce, and Ed Nichols, with a wedge of security agents clearing his path and keeping the crowd back from him. He waved as he reached the level of the platform. On the other side of the plexiglass shield photographers began clicking off their pictures. Emma moved in a little closer. The President shook hands with Callahan and Dent. With Shackford, Renaud, and MacGregor.

With Sir Edward, who gave him a firm grip and a cheery smile.

Then suddenly Harry Nesbitt was at her side, his voice a harsh whisper in her ear. "Where the hell is Owen?"

Emma's eyes widened slightly. "You haven't seen him?"

"No."

She glanced around, then turned back to Nesbitt. "Look," she said, taking his arm and drawing him away, "now that you're here I have to go. But before I do, I'd better tell you something."

The sight of the applauding crowd stirred Henry to shed private feelings and assume his public posture. He stopped at the base of the platform while a nametag, gold-dotted to prove he belonged here, was pinned to his lapel. Others were given to Lucy and Pierce, even to Nichols, who nodded his approval, since Owen himself had checked and cleared this procedure. Then *The President* and *Mrs. Brendan*, since that's what the nametags said, climbed the steps. Henry turned to smile and wave at the crowd, to shake hands with his guests. And with no more than a glance at the chair that had been replaced, he took his seat on the platform.

Conklin Pierce, beside Nichols, behind Henry in the second row, turned as a hand came to rest on his shoulder. A man with a Secret Service lapel pin was standing above him.

"I'm sorry, Mr. Speaker," the agent said, "but for security reasons you'll have to give me your walking stick. We'll replace it with a cane that's been cleared and give it back to you later."

Pierce moved like a man in a daze, but he gave up the walking stick without objection.

Sir Edward, his smile fixed in place, kept his eyes moving continuously. There were security guards lined up all around the platform and more in the crowds below

292

and behind. But he saw no face from the past, no sign of the one man he had come here to have it out with.

Countdown reached T-minus-twenty minutes.

He turned to laugh at a joke made by Daniel Callahan. Then suddenly his gaze shifted to a man standing thirty feet away, on the ground in front of the platform. Square-jawed, red-haired. He didn't look the same, but his stance gave him away. An old friend. No disguise could hide him. Their eyes met, and they recognized each other.

Sir Edward jumped up and leaped off the edge of the platform.

At the Launch Control Center near the VAB, NASA's director of security kept his eye on the computer consoles that were registering final checks of *Pilgrim*'s systems. Then the red phone buzzed beside him, and he picked it up.

"Christ Almighty!" a voice roared in his ear, "there's someone *out* there! Someone running, a man! No, *two* men—"

The director's eyes shifted immediately to a small closed-circuit TV set. "It's all right," he said quickly. "The second one is the British ambassador."

"*What?*" came the astonished voice.

"Leave them alone," the director said. "Those are orders from Finn himself. The British ambassador is Owen."

Secret Service Agent Jeff Riggs knocked at the door of a cottage near the President's at Patrick AFB, though with the President at the Cape no one should be inside now. When he got no answer, he produced a key and went in. Then he grabbed his radio, flicked it on, and barked out an urgent warning.

Owen was right! *Eta nu*—translated from Greek to English: *H.N.* Harry Nesbitt was here all right—on the floor, alive but unconscious, his mouth taped, his arms and legs trussed up like a turkey. And that meant one thing. The Nesbitt who reported for work on time, to protect the President from a man who intended to kill him today, wasn't Nesbitt at all.

He was the assassin.

Owen ran with the wind at his back and the fury of years of pent-up anger behind him, throwing off extra clothes and padding for speed as he'd thrown off the layered rubber face, the gray hair, and the eyebrows. Ahead of him, raising dust in his wake, Michelangelo shed his disguise too, but maintained the distance he had held since Owen leaped off the platform and went for him. Owen knew the killer was drawing him off, away from the President before the moment of lift-off. He knew and didn't care. He *wanted* this confrontation.

The crowd noise had vanished behind them, and now there was only open space all the way to the ocean. Open space and scrub and *Pilgrim II* growing larger ahead. Somewhere, the final countdown had started.

But Michelangelo ran on, with Owen keeping pace behind, until they had passed the last warning signs and were inside the launch perimeter, within two hundred yards of the shuttle. Michelangelo stopped and spun around, one arm extended into the spin, knees flexed, feet apart. The other arm moved in to his waist and came smoothly forward again. In his hand was a .45 caliber pistol.

Owen, unarmed, stopped ten yards back and rested his hands on his hips, breathing hard. "You've lost none of your old grace," he said. "That was a good move."

Michelangelo was short of air too. "I can't think I surprised you."

Owen shrugged. "You had to stop somewhere, or go for a swim."

"And maybe catch a ride on a giant sea turtle?"

They both smiled, but not with any show of warmth. He hadn't changed, Owen thought. His blue eyes were like ice in a suntanned face, and his hair was as black as it ever had been. He looked lean, strong and fit—well-oiled, finely tuned—like the sleek space shuttle behind him. But *Pilgrim II* sat silently on her launchpad, mated to a huge external tank and the world's largest solid rocket boosters. Her windows were black unseeing eyes pointed skyward. She seemed oblivious to the fanfare and fuss, as well as to the presence of intruders.

Two solitary figures perilously close by. No one was allowed this near a launch, not even the red emergency crew, which they had passed at the one-mile mark. The grass around them still showed signs of having been singed in the last launch. But Owen had worked all this out with Finn, the launch director, and his orders were clear—give us free rein, and don't stop the launch no matter what happens.

Two narrow streams of white smoke emerged from the aft end of *Pilgrim*'s rockets, and static flared from the loudspeaker systems set up across the cape. A voice came clear: *"We're at T-minus-one minute, twenty seconds, and counting. . . . We can see the purges of the main engines as we prepare for ignition."*

Owen's gaze shifted to the gun in Michelangelo's hand, then rose to meet the ice blue eyes, and he started walking slowly forward. "You can kill me if you want to," he said.

Michelangelo was still smiling. "You seem awfully sure I won't."

"If you do, I'll miss your great moment of glory."

"Liquid hydrogen tank is at flight pressure," the voice of the countdown announced. *"T-minus-one minute, marked and counting."*

Pilgrim continued to purge steam from her engines, but she remained mute and motionless on her launchpad. None of the flurry going on inside as the flight crew set her systems for launch caused a ripple in the aloof calm of her surface.

"I'm not sure you need to be here as an eyewitness," Michelangelo said. "Brendan is as good as dead."

"You'd better hope not," Owen said and kept walking.

"T-minus-forty seconds and counting."

Michelangelo raised the gun. He aimed the barrel between Owen's eyes.

"The flight instrumentation recorders are on. T-minus-thirty-five seconds . . ."

Owen walked on.

Michelangelo squeezed the trigger.

≋ 48 ≋

Kneeling low in the scrub not far away, Emma saw them coming. She saw Michelangelo stop and turn, saw a gun in his hand. And she saw Owen stop as abruptly without one.

But Emma had a .45 too, a replacement for her lost automatic. It was not as comfortable as the old gun, but it was more effective at this range. She raised it to firing position.

"You can kill me if you want to," she heard Owen say as he walked forward fearlessly—or perhaps foolishly—though this close to the launch, Emma supposed, it probably didn't matter.

"You seem awfully sure I won't."

"If you do, I'll miss . . ."

She heard the countdown hit one minute, marked and counting. Michelangelo took aim on Owen, and Emma took aim on the assassin, on the gun in his hand. She was smiling.

Now she was going to *get* him, Owen, for the times he had saved her life without asking. He didn't know she was nearby, but she was going to let him know before he could get himself out of this one. Her hand tightened on the trigger.

But then she looked back at Owen's face and something happened. The years rose up in her mind—growing trust, growing affection. Their game was a front for all of that, because they were a good match, because they both enjoyed the competition. Owen's life mattered to her for more than professional reasons, but something else mattered more—the implicit understanding that lay between them. Owen wouldn't have come here unarmed except by choice, unless he *wanted* to settle this score with something more satisfying than a gunfight. And he no doubt knew what he was doing.

Or thought he did.

Emma looked at him, and from him to Michelangelo, to the finger that was starting to squeeze the trigger, and the game vanished from her mind. There was *more* at stake here—real danger, conflicting emotions. Her instincts all cried out in alarm, and her brain sent up an urgent message to save him—not for the game, but for his sake, and hers. Yet another part of her mind told her she mustn't. *Because* she cared. That this time she couldn't interfere. That she had to let Owen stand his own ground, this time if never again. That she had to let him make his own choices.

She lowered the gun and with it her eyes. This moment was his, whatever it meant. She had to let him have it.

Owen stopped midstride as the gun clicked harmlessly in Michelangelo's hands. The assassin laughed and tossed it aside. It never had been loaded.

"So damn sure of yourself," he said. "It's not one of the things I like about you."

"Then don't be so obvious," Owen replied. "If you were going to kill me here, it wouldn't be with a bullet. Anyway, you don't want to kill me. You want to defeat me."

"And I have."

"T-minus-twenty seconds and counting."

"Are *you* so sure of yourself?" Owen stopped smiling. "Brendan isn't going to die. And if he did, you'd have killed the wrong man."

Something moved in the ice blue eyes as the countdown seemed to gather speed: *"T-minus-fifteen, fourteen, thirteen . . . T-minus-ten, nine, eight . . ."*

"I don't believe you," Michelangelo cried.

"You *know* I'm not lying. But it doesn't matter now. *Listen!*"

There was a pause, a brief but most significant pause, and Owen didn't move or blink from the gaze of his old partner. They looked at each other in a quiet truce, through the last stark moment of silence. Then the silence exploded in a great roaring blast, in a rolling of thunder and a flashing of fire, and *Pilgrim II* set the earth shaking.

Henry Brendan was listening to the same countdown as conversation went on all around him. People shifted restlessly in their seats and chatted among themselves as relief from the boredom of waiting—because, until the launch occurred, there was nothing to see but scrub and sky and *Pilgrim* sitting in the distant view; there was nothing else to do here.

But Henry wasn't in a mood to talk as the countdown entered its final phase, and he spent the time looking nervously around him. Owen had said it would happen now, if it were going to happen at all, and though Henry was still firm that he wanted to be here, to face the assassin down, he found it damned hard to stay cool with the moment approaching.

Approaching fast. *"Seven, six, five, four . . . !"*

All at once conversation stopped as engines ignited in the distance, sending thunder rumbling across the land with a force that could be physically felt. *Pilgrim* sat there for several seconds, and then started to rise. The crowd roared to its feet as she broke free of her moorings. There were great whooping cheers, cries of awe and delight. Glowing eyes. Gaping mouths. Tears and laughter. And a swelling applause that was one with *Pilgrim's* soaring momentum.

Henry's breath caught in his throat, and he jumped to his feet with the rest of the crowd. He watched as she vanished into a cloud and emerged again, climbing sure and strong. Tears welled in his eyes too, and he forgot there was an assassin.

The gleaming white ship remained in view for several

minutes, and then was gone, absorbed by the vast black reach of the universe. Henry, his eyes on an empty sky, felt briefly lost, as if purpose were gone, so intense had been his concentration. But then, lowering his gaze to the ground—to himself, his own arms, hands, and face, pinstriped sleeves—he remembered he was *alive*. Fear swept through him with a mind-numbing force, as only it could when the threat was past and courage collapsed, permitting a free range of feelings.

He *was* alive!

Fear passed, and relief took its place. He turned, smiling. He reached out a hand and found Lucy's.

"Seven, six, five, four. . ."

Pause.

In that moment of pause, and in the next when *Pilgrim*'s engines ignited behind him, Michelangelo looked around urgently, as if he might find the voice of the countdown and force it to do his bidding. At the same time his mind formed a question: Where was *three*? There had been time to hear the three-second count before *Pilgrim* came to life and drowned out everything else, but he hadn't heard it. Now, with the numbing roar all around, his mind threw up the rest of his doubts. If three wasn't spoken aloud, was two? Was *one*? Self-assurance fell away, and his eyes shifted back, glaring, shooting ice and fire, loathing and fear, at Owen.

This *was* the moment of confrontation.

Michelangelo knew coldly in his breast that Owen had won, had perceived his plan and undone it, that he'd silenced the countdown from three seconds on. Three and two didn't matter—but one did, because one was the trigger. A weapon for murder was well within range of the President, no matter how many plexiglass shields they put up, no matter how firm his bodyguards' intention to throw themselves between him and the thing that would kill. It was there, in range, but rendered harmless by silence.

Or by silence of one kind, for *Pilgrim* had come to life and was making it known as she roared against her restraints. She needed no voice commands, which were only there for human ears; she took her cue from computers. And now it was too late to go back, to find out if Owen meant what he said. *Was* Brendan the wrong man? Of course, because Owen *wouldn't* lie! Michelangelo knew he had failed. And he saw in the face looking back at him, without loathing or fear, with a steady-eyed calm that spoke of a challenge successfully faced that Owen knew it too. It was over.

These thoughts passed through his mind in the span of a second, no more, before *Pilgrim* broke free, and as he turned she was still straining against the huge gantry beside her. He started to walk, then to hurry, to run; he ran *toward* her. Then her engines reached their full thrust and she rose. Gases poured out with her exhaust, which shot out to the right and left. Noxious fumes filled his nose, dried his mouth, stung his eyes, but he ran on without looking back, aiming himself irrevocably at the fire and fury that flared from her twin rockets.

Death was escape now. He could not, would not, let Owen take him.

Emma stayed where she was as the countdown went into its final seconds. She saw *Pilgrim*'s ignition flare and felt the earth shake with the pounding thrust of her rockets. Still, Owen stood his ground. Then Michelangelo turned to flee. He was gone. Owen's moment was past—they could go now—but the shuttle was already starting to rise from the launchpad.

Emma jumped up and ran, with the ground rumbling under her feet, her mind fierce on the task of maintaining balance. And when she was close enough, she called out his name.

"Richard!"

A moment later, she felt herself falling.

Michelangelo faded against a sunburst of light as *Pilgrim*'s engines ignited, but not before Owen saw his expression change, saw truth dawn in the ice blue eyes and hatred flare on the face of an assassin. Owen had won, and in him hate vanished. He felt something closer to regret as Michelangelo turned to flee, to follow the only course he could, but he made no attempt to stop him. Instead, his gaze rose to the shuttle.

He had the best seat in the house. No one had seen a launch from this view, except through cameras positioned behind extraordinary protection, and he thought it was probably worth the price he was going to have to pay for it. Cameras couldn't possibly capture the full fury nor the sudden drama of *Pilgrim*'s departure. The silence that preceded the launch didn't fade against steadily building sound; it was vanquished in an instant of time, by a flash of fire and a thundering roar that erupted full force.

When her ignition flared, *Pilgrim* began to breathe on her own, and to strain against the bolts that held her down, raising great white clouds of exhaust that melted the lines between earth and sky, mushrooming out on each side, growing, spreading, smothering. Then explosions, unheard against her own roar, blew the bolts away and she was free, climbing straight up on a pillar of fire and pounding the earth with the massive thrust of her rockets. The ground heaved. Owen felt his shirt beating hard on his chest, and the audio shock was deafening. This was the center of the storm, the heart of the thundercloud, the volcano's crater, the epicenter of the earthquake. But it was the work of man, not nature.

Owen's eyes rose with her, irresistibly, for *Pilgrim* evoked nothing less than total focus. He forgot about Michelangelo and ignored the white death cloud rolling toward him, from the right, from the left. He stared, mesmerized by the spectacle. Apollo himself, driving his chargers across the sky, his golden hair streaming behind as he pulled the sun into orbit with Earth, could not have been more startling, nor more impressive.

Only one sound could have broken through that, and he heard it. *"Richard!"*

He turned and felt his heart sink. *"Emma, go back!"* he called, but he knew as he said it that there wasn't time, that she was as trapped here as he was.

"Good thing I got here when I did," she cried and tossed something across the space between them.

Owen caught it and held it up in his hands, and then started to laugh. It was a portable gas mask. Triumph showed on Emma's face as she produced another one. She had him. She finally had him! She had saved his life—not before he could, but when he could *not* have done it himself. Then the white cloud rolled over them, and a blast of heat knocked them to the ground. He caught Emma as they fell and tried his damnedest to keep her covered.

But even then his gaze rose to the sky, to a tail of fire so bright that it penetrated the cloud, and he watched *Pilgrim* climb with mind-stopping, godlike power. His breath caught, and he felt himself soaring with her, on a great last glowing wave of exhilaration.

⊠ 50 ⊠

The President got out of the car near the VAB and stepped up to a microphone to talk to the assembled NASA staff and, by television, to the American public. He was flanked on one side by his wife and on the other by Conklin Pierce, and surrounded by assorted guests who had been with him on the viewing platform. All but Pierce were beaming, and even he seemed moved by the launch they had just witnessed.

Nichols stood back to watch and listen.

"We're all proud to be here today," Henry said, and though Nichols was close enough to hear, no words came through the public address system. A technician appeared to look over the microphone. He made an adjustment and stepped back.

"Try it again, Mr. President."

Henry bent his head toward the microphone. "Testing," he said. "Three, two, one—I believe we have lift-off."

Everyone else was caught up in the same spirit and laughed with him. Even Nichols had to chuckle. But then, suddenly, he was running forward.

Conklin Pierce had clutched his chest, and his knees were giving way as he started to pitch forward. His eyes bulged and his skin turned blue.

"My God!" someone cried. "*Help* him!"

Henry grabbed him before he fell, and by that time Nichols was there.

"Put him down," Nichols said.

A Secret Service agent shouted orders. "Get back! Give him air! Get the President's doctor."

Nichols knelt beside Pierce on the ground and felt for a pulse, but there was none. He looked at Henry, on his knees too, and shook his head.

"Oh, Lord," Henry said, and genuine sadness filled his eyes. "I guess his heart couldn't take it."

"I suspect that's what the doctor will say," Nichols replied and lowered his voice, "but I have the feeling Michelangelo got him."

⊠ 51 ⊠

Emma finally got her hot bath, a long soak with scented oils and a snifter of brandy, VSOP, on the edge of the tub in handy reaching distance. Her next stop was going to be Qum. She'd be lucky to breathe there, let alone have a bath or a drink. She closed her eyes and put everything out of her mind, concentrating on the luxury of the moment.

Or tried to put everything out of her mind. She still had a phone call to make, and she didn't want to do it.

She shook off a chill, for the water seemed suddenly cold, and decided she might as well do it now. She got out of the tub, wrapped herself in a robe, and made her way into the bedroom. She sat on the bed and picked up the phone, studying the dialing instructions. On the table beside the phone lay her passport, French, neatly stamped, and a wallet full of francs and her French identification. She put the receiver back.

"Damn!" she said to herself, aloud, though no one was there to hear—or perhaps because no one could hear. "How I hate this!"

But it was her turn. She picked up the phone and dialed the operator.

"One more thing," Nichols said as he stood beside Owen's hospital bed, looking down. "I want to know how you did it."

"Did what?" Owen asked blankly.

307

"Conklin Pierce's heart attack was just a little too handy."

"An act of fate," Owen said. "I had no way of knowing what would happen."

"But you did give fate a hand."

"I switched the nametags, if that's what you mean."

"I don't understand."

"Michelangelo's weapon *was* the President's nametag. A toxic gas was mixed with the ink used to write his name. It was harmless when it dried, but activated it gave off a short, sharp burst of lethal air that kills on intake, instantly, and dissipates before it can spread. The gold dot was a miniature receiver, set to pick up a certain soundwave—in this case, the word *one* amplified—and then to radiate enough heat to melt the ink and—"

"Jesus Christ!" Nichols broke in, "how did you figure that out?"

"It's what I would have done."

"But what made you *think* of the nametags?"

"Process of elimination. The only person who didn't have to pass muster with the Secret Service was the President himself. The weapon had to be on him, but it couldn't have been a tie tack, or a cuff link, or a shirt button, because Michelangelo couldn't have known what he would wear that day. Brendan even owns more than one wristwatch. There was nothing else left. I checked and found out the nametags were being held in NASA's public affairs office; I asked to see them and made the switch, put an overlay on each one, had new names written on top of the old ones. Conklin Pierce was wearing the President's nametag."

"But why did you switch them?" Nichols asked. "What if you'd been wrong?"

"I wasn't wrong. I switched them precisely to leave it to fate."

Nichols shook his head slowly. "Sometimes I'm glad you don't tell me what you're doing. Well, I have news for you too."

"The lab reports?"

Nichols nodded.

308

Owen knew they had never found Michelangelo's body, and that they'd swept up the residue of the launch for analysis, but he hadn't heard what the laboratory had found in the ash.

"No sign of human remains," Nichols said. "Of course we have no precedent, no record of anyone running into the tailwind of a launch before, and it's probable given the level of heat that nothing would be left of him, but . . ."

Owen didn't have to hear the rest. He smiled to himself as he thought about Michelangelo's last exit. Or had he somehow escaped? Was his last scene just another falseface?

Owen didn't think so. "I saw the look on his face, Ed. He had two choices, *Pilgrim* or me. For him that was no choice at all."

Nichols sighed. "I hope you're right. I don't want to hear that man's name again."

"If I should hear from him, then, I won't bother to tell you."

Nichols cleared his throat pointedly and opened his attaché case. "A couple of things came in the mail that might interest you. I got a letter from your friend at Muna."

"Frank? What's he writing to you about?"

"He's holding me up, that's what!"

Owen took the letter and scanned it quickly, his eyes brightening as he went along. It was carefully written, nothing quite spelled out, but the point was clear. Owen got to the last line, *. . . and so I trust you will see the proper appropriations officials in regard to a foreign aid package for the people of Yucatan,* and laughed. "Good for Frank!" he said.

Nichols said nothing.

"Fair is fair, Ed."

"To tell you the truth, there's a generous aid package already in the works. It was Henry's idea. And a good thing. If I had to tell him about this letter, he'd have a fit or something worse."

"Don't tell him then. The secret's as safe with Frank as it is with anyone. What else came in the mail?"

Nichols produced a paper-wrapped package. "This, for you. It came by way of Waterford. And I don't want to know what it is, so I'm leaving."

Owen grinned. "So long."

"I'll be back to see you later."

Owen left the package lying on his bed, because he knew who it came from, and got himself a drink of water. An awkward maneuver with his hands encased in white cotton gloves, the kind they used on children to keep them from scratching. Frank was right. Chicken pox burned like fire, and Owen should know, since he had them.

It was Ardry who insisted on putting him up at Georgetown Hospital, because (so Sam said) everyone thought sick spies were stashed away at Bethesda or Walter Reed. He was better off here, so the theory went. Obviously Sam hadn't met Nurse Bradshaw, who ruled this floor as though she'd done her training with Himmler.

The phone rang. Owen picked it up. It was Emma.

"Did you get my package?" she asked.

"Nichols just dropped it off. It's still wrapped."

"Then *open* it."

"All right, but you'll have to give me a minute." He put the phone down and addressed his gloved hands to the wrapping paper, tape, and string. Books, eight of them. Proust's *Remembrance of Things Past* and St. Augustine's *Confessions*. Waterford must have thought they had hit the jackpot.

He picked up the phone again and said, "Thanks. They're just what I wanted."

"I knew you'd like them," Emma said. "No one ever gets time to read all seven volumes of the Proust, and St. Augustine should always be kept handy. How are you feeling?"

"Bored. When are you coming by?"

"I don't know. Maybe this afternoon."

Owen nodded. It was a lie, a permitted lie. Emma was probably already back in Paris, but if she weren't it wouldn't make any difference. She wouldn't be here this afternoon. He knew it, and she did too. The lie was permitted because they both hated saying good-bye. And so they didn't do it.

"Where are you going next?" he asked.

"To *Q*, I think."

Owen took in a sharp breath of air and said nothing for several seconds. *Q* was current code for Qum. Iran. The Ayatollah's holy city.

"Damn it, Emma," he said at last. *"Why you?"*

She was silent for a moment too. Then she said, "You're not supposed to ask that sort of question."

"I know." He paused. "Take care of yourself."

"I always do. You too. I'll see you."

Owen hung up and closed his eyes, feeling suddenly alone. A permitted lie, an evasion. He didn't know when he would see her again, or if he would. He never did know.

And then, from nowhere, a voice asked cheerily, "Are we sleeping?"

Owen opened his eyes and saw a face floating above his bed, and it radiated more good cheer than he'd ever seen in one place before. It was, he noticed, once he looked, attached to a woman who was done up in gray and black, in skirt and jacket and flat-heeled shoes, with blond hair pulled back from her face and no makeup. Around her neck she was wearing a wooden crucifix.

"I'm Sister Olivia from the pastoral service. Is there anything I can do for you?"

Owen could not have refused to smile if he wanted to. He wasn't sure what a nun could do for him, but she was a clear improvement on Nurse Bradshaw. "No thank you, Sister. It's nice of you to ask, though."

"Ah, I see you're reading St. Augustine."

He shifted uncomfortably in the bed as she picked up the book and glanced through it. Then, suddenly, she looked perplexed.

"My goodness! This isn't the same St. Augustine I read in convent! But I suppose it might suit your purposes better." She smiled as she put the book back on his bed and gave it a pat.

Now it was Owen who looked perplexed. As far as he knew there was only one St. Augustine. He opened the book to see for himself. And then he laughed—he roared—for Emma had sent him a farewell gift that was just what he needed here, especially when Bradshaw came around to see if he had his gloves on. At the same time she was reminding him that the last round was hers, indisputably, by unanimous consent of both judges. He really did owe her one now!

He looked the nun over carefully as he picked up his water cup and emptied it into his water pitcher. Then, from the pages of St. Augustine, he took Emma's gift and unscrewed the cap. It was, of course, a bottle of Glenfiddich.

"Care to join me, Sister?"

"Oh, I couldn't do that. I have work to do."

"Come now, I happen to know you have nothing to do till you get to Qum."

Emma started to laugh and dropped down on the bed beside him. "When did you know?" she asked.

"The minute you came through the door."

"You weren't even looking when I came through the door."

"Then when I opened my eyes."

"Sorry, I don't believe it. I had you going with St. Augustine."

"For a minute maybe." Owen took her hand. "You weren't supposed to come."

"I know. And I started to call you from my hotel, but I changed my mind. I used the pay phone down the hall. I cheated."

"I'm delighted you did."

"So am I."

"I've got something for you too," Owen said and opened the drawer in his bedside table. He found a box and handed it to her. "I didn't have a chance to get it wrapped, but here it is."

Emma took the box and opened it, and her face lit up with surprise and delight. "It's my automatic!"

"I stumbled over it in the cave and brought it back. And I had it fixed."

"It's a good surprise." She bent over to kiss him.

Owen held her there for a moment, his lips next to her ear. "Are we even now?"

"Even!" Emma pulled back. "My gun for your life? Not a chance! You're going to be working a long, long time before we're ever even again."

Owen smiled. His turn would come.

Emma smiled back.

They would figure out how to avoid their good-byes tomorrow.

ABOUT THE AUTHOR

Marilyn Sharp is the author of two previous novels, *Sunflower* and *Masterstroke*. She lives with her husband Philip and two sons, Jeremy and Justin, in Washington, D.C.